NEW POMPEII

DANIEL GODFREY

TITAN BOOKS

New Pompeii
Mass-market edition ISBN: 9781785656033
E-book edition ISBN: 9781783298129

Published by Titan Books
A division of Titan Publishing Group Ltd
144 Southwark Street, London SE1 0UP

First mass-market edition: October 2017
10 9 8 7 6 5 4 3 2 1

A CIP catalogue record for this title is available from the British Library.

Printed in the USA.

FOR MY MUM AND DAD

NEW POMPEII

AD 79, POMPEII

Manius Calpurnius Barbatus looked down at his daughter, but didn't smile. She was kneeling in front of their household shrine, her prayers no longer being whispered with any sense of hope. Instead, she recited the same words over and over until they were nothing more than an incantation. Perhaps, eventually, she'd be heard. But not today. Because the gods' ears would already be full of unanswered prayers, and the fate of her husband would likely be low on their list of priorities.

Still, he continued to watch Calpurnia – just long enough to detect some of her coldness towards him – and then cast his eyes over the other members of his household. None of his slaves or freedmen had deserted him. That, at least, gave him a grim feeling of satisfaction. He'd chosen them all personally, and now it seemed they would remain with him until the end. Two of the slaves had even started a new fresco to cover a recently damaged wall. They dabbed quickly with their brushes, applying paint to the wet plaster despite surely knowing they might never get the chance to see their work finished. He admired them for it. Perhaps it would be enough to earn them their freedom.

From above, the timbers supporting the roof gave another groan. Barbatus glanced upwards. At first, the ash had been light. He'd seen children playing ankle-deep in it as if it had been nothing more than a freak fall of snow. Calpurnia herself had been quite taken with it – perhaps thinking it would signal the end to all the tremors that had been shaking the town. Perhaps thinking it would be something new for her to record and study. But as the flakes became heavier, and the cloud from the mountain had all but blocked out the sun, she'd soon come inside.

Barbatus felt his shoulders tighten. He'd been wrong. It wasn't like when the earth shook twenty years ago. Outside, people were dying. Cut down by the pumice stones falling from the sky, before being buried in the dark. His own roof would only support so much more weight before it finally buckled. And then there'd be no more need for shrines.

Calpurnia slowly got to her feet, perhaps coming to the same realisation. She gave a bitter grimace as she rose. But at least there was some resistance in her eyes. She hadn't given up, and whoever met her at the gates of Elysium would surely regret it.

Barbatus smiled inwardly at the thought, and again looked at the members of his household. He saw them shaking. Saw their terror. But he also knew many had faced death before. And maybe they believed that, even at the last second, the gods might swoop down and carry them away to safety. So it wasn't over. Not yet. The dice were still rolling. He could almost hear them scattering, alongside the final complaints of the roof above them.

"There's no point living in fear," he whispered, "when we're already dead."

1

KIRSTEN CHAPMAN WOKE, and screamed.

She gagged on a mouthful of water. Saw bubbles stream away from her face. Felt the pressure tighten around her lungs as if someone was using her torso as a stress ball. As if she was going to die.

She kicked out. Let her mouth find the surface just before her lungs exploded. Only the tail end of her cry echoed in the bathroom, however. And she didn't have time to suck in any more air. Her head was going under again – the water once more lapping across her nose and lips. She reached out with her legs. Made her thighs tighten and twist as she searched for the end of the bath. But her body just slid against the porcelain. And the water surged higher. Deeper. Her vision started to go black…

Tap – tap – tap.

I'm going to kill you, bitch!

Kirsten's arms found the side of the bath. She levered herself forward – upwards – until she could pull her body on to her elbows. Until her head once more found frigid air.

Around her, water sloshed on to the floor. Inside the tub, it continued to ripple back and forth for a few more seconds. Kirsten didn't move. She was quite alone. Finally, she opened her mouth. This time though, her scream was no more than a whimpered cry, interspersed with deep gasps for air. But at least they were becoming shallower. Easier.

She'd fallen asleep in the bath. That was all. No need to panic. Her body had kicked in and rescued her – even if her brain was still struggling to catch up. She shivered. The water was cold. She must have been in it for hours. Instinctively, she turned her head, looking for her robe and towel.

They were missing.

It took a while for the implications to dawn on her. Not just missing. Taken. She'd dropped them on the floor, just far enough away to ensure they didn't get wet. And now they were gone.

Her head snapped towards the door. It was shut, bolted. She glanced behind her. The room was only a few feet square. There was barely enough space for the bath, and certainly no place to hide.

And so she was quite alone. Except that footsteps had started to echo up from the quad below. Soft at first, but growing louder. Someone – maybe two people – was coming. She felt her shoulders shake, but the footsteps didn't stop. They were heading up the staircase.

To her floor.

2

NICK HOUGHTON ALMOST made it. In the five short minutes since finishing work, he'd managed to confirm his pigeonhole was empty, and was already hustling towards the History Department's exit. He should have been easily outside and heading home. But that would have to wait. Because he'd been intercepted. Just as his hand had reached the door handle.

"Nick. A moment of your time, please."

The diminutive figure didn't pause to confirm he'd been heard. Nick followed him back into the bowels of the faculty. Professor Drockley could have chosen a better location for his office. As the relatively new head of the History Department, most people had expected him to move into one of the building's larger offices. But all the books and papers down here probably anchored him just as securely as his apparent desire to stay away from the centre of things.

Nick maintained a fixed smile as he let himself be waved into an old wooden chair opposite Drockley's desk. The professor didn't make eye contact. Instead, Drockley started to shuffle his papers.

It took a few seconds for Nick to register the problem. The professor didn't know what to say. Or, rather, he did – but didn't know how to say it. After a few more seconds, Drockley passed a leaflet across the desk.

"Interesting new exhibit on at the British Museum."

Nick examined the leaflet. The cover displayed a photograph of a polished, mahogany-brown skull. He knew what it was without a second look. He'd already ordered tickets for the British Museum's main summer event.

"Peking Man," continued Drockley. "I must admit, I didn't think anyone would ever find those bones. But, then again, I suppose there are new ways of doing things now."

Nick nodded. Maybe a little too quickly. "The exhibition opens tonight," he replied, scanning the rest of the leaflet. It didn't tell him anything he didn't already know. Peking Man was a collection of bones of several individuals from the extinct species *Homo erectus*. Although not really his main area of interest, the story of their rediscovery struck much closer to home. Even if it was all just another example of what his father would call cheap tricks and nonsense. Or rather, *dangerous* cheap tricks and nonsense. Nick made a move to hand the leaflet back.

"Keep it," said Drockley, waving it away. "I take it you'll be going?"

"Yes, in a couple of weeks' time. The first few days got booked pretty fast."

The professor gave a mischievous smile. "Does your father know you're going?"

Nick shook his head. "We've not talked about it."

"Quite." The professor let the conversation evaporate. Nick didn't try to keep it going. One thing was certain: he hadn't been invited here to talk about Peking Man. And the professor had stopped shuffling his papers.

"Your father told me you've had your research proposals turned down?"

"No," Nick said. His voice suddenly sounded small. Like somebody had reached into his throat and unplugged the amp. Cutbacks. There were going to be more cutbacks. "I'm still waiting on Imperial."

"It's a pity we haven't any open research posts here at the moment," continued Drockley, seemingly not hearing his answer. "But funding is now so much harder to get hold of."

Nick nodded, and tried to take a deep breath. "I heard there were going to be more redundancies?"

"Yes," said Drockley. "So let me get to the point, Nick. It's going to be difficult justifying your somewhat unofficial position here if I'm getting rid of full-time, qualified members of teaching staff."

"Quasimodo," said Nick.

"Hmm?"

"It's what one of the lecturers calls me. Quasi-student, quasi-teacher." He hesitated, the silence pushing him towards an admission. "I guess I've always preferred the idea of research to teaching."

The professor looked straight at him, his expression serious but with a great deal of sympathy. "I think you'll find most of us prefer research to teaching, Nick. But the government operates under the illusion that universities exist to teach. And, from what I've seen, you're good at it. You *will* be good at it too, once you're qualified."

"I don't enjoy it."

"Perhaps not, but still. There it is. And it's not really all that different to being a proper research student. Quasi, or otherwise."

"Well, I'm still waiting on Imperial," Nick repeated, finding a bit more volume. "And, if necessary, I could stay here on a voluntary basis, and see what happens next year."

Drockley sighed. "Look, Nick," he said. "Your father wants me to keep you in your existing post, and his view still counts for a lot even considering his recent… troubles. But people are going to be upset when the pink slips start being distributed."

Nick struggled to swallow. "Thank you for letting me know," he said. In his lap, he'd folded the Peking Man leaflet so many times that all that remained visible was a company logo in its bottom right-hand corner:

presented by novus particles UK LLP

3

A FEW LAST DROPS of bathwater ran down Kirsten's body. Her wet hair clung to her shoulders and back. And if the water had been cold, then the air was truly freezing. Goose pimples shimmered across her arms and she stood slightly hunched, her arms crossed against her chest as she tried to keep the last remaining dregs of heat close to her body. But all the while, she remained focused on the sounds from beyond the door.

The footsteps were heavy, the voices male. With each upward step on the staircase, she'd hoped they would stop at one of the floors below. But they hadn't. And now they were right outside the bathroom door.

"So the door was definitely locked?" said one of them.

"Yeah," said a second, older voice. "We had to kick it in. The room was empty."

Kirsten was shaking so much that the words took a long time to sink in: *It was locked. We had to kick it in.*

Her attention snapped back to the bathroom door. The barrel was slid into the locked position. But the bolt glinted from within a splintered frame. They could just...

...push it open.

The door started to move. "Fucking hell! Wait!"

Her words should have been shrieked, but instead came out like a distorted cassette tape. Long and low. Each vowel stretched into the time it would have taken to express three or four. As if she had a pint of water sloshing around inside her ears. Not that it mattered. Two policemen stepped in from the corridor. They didn't even look at her. Instead, their eyes roamed around the bathroom, and then they turned their attention towards the door through which they had just come.

Kirsten opened her mouth to say something – to tell them to get out – but her throat had closed tight. It was difficult to breathe, let alone talk. She'd managed to keep one arm across her breasts, and pushed the other flat between her legs. But neither man seemed to have noticed her.

"Hello?"

Again, her words came long and low. She shook her head, and felt the floor surge beneath her as she continued to shiver.

"Doesn't quite match the rest of the Cambridge pomp downstairs, does it?"

One of the officers, the younger of the two, indicated the peeling floral wallpaper and stained yellow carpet. "Think they've redecorated the place since the seventies?"

The older policeman didn't reply. Both were tall. Kirsten dimly noted they were cut from the same cloth. Only their age distinguished them from each other. One looked to be in his early thirties, the other closer to retirement. Both wore police uniforms. And both were ignoring the naked woman standing not four feet from them.

Almost immediately, Kirsten gasped. A dim image of Christmas flashed into her memory. Or rather, three different versions. And a very old story.

Past. Present. Future.

Kirsten swallowed, her body no longer shaking. She turned back to the bath, half expecting to see her own body still floating in it. But the tub was empty.

No body. No water. *No water.*

She turned back to the men, and gripped her chest tighter. Ordinarily, she'd have wanted them gone – for them not to have opened the door in the first place. But now they were in front of her, she desperately needed them to see her.

The younger officer pointed towards the lock on the door. "You've not touched this?"

His colleague shook his head. "No."

"The catches mean it can't just slide accidentally shut."

"Agreed."

The younger man stood, and turned towards the bath. Kirsten stepped dumbly back out of his way. "The water was still in the bath?"

"Some of it had leaked away, but there was a ring of scum around the edge. Someone had definitely been using it. It's all gone now, of course. The plug's still in. We haven't touched it."

"The window?"

"See for yourself."

The younger policeman took a few steps forward and pulled back the blind. He grunted. The window looked out across one of the college quads. It should have given him a great view of the old library, but it was dark outside. Pitch black.

"And the college hasn't heard from the girl for over forty-eight hours?"

Kirsten started to shake again, but this time not because she was cold. Forty-eight hours?

"She didn't turn up for duty on Tuesday morning," replied the other officer. "Porter says she's often late, but not like this. The others on this floor haven't seen her. First reported missing by another bedder at fourteen hundred hours."

Forty-eight hours? Kirsten felt her arms drop to her sides, useless. The men were right in front of her. Neither had noticed she was standing beside them. And there could only be one explanation. She'd seen the movies. Read the books.

She was already dead.

"What did she do, again?" asked the younger policeman.

"College bedder."

"Which means what? She slept with the students?"

The older officer didn't smile. "Emptied their bins. Changed their sheets. Kept the fellows informed of what was happening on the student staircases."

"And what sort of girl was she?"

"Flirty. Some might say cheeky."

"Boyfriend?"

"No."

The younger man stared into the bath. "Many staff live on site?"

"Not nowadays. There's some shift accommodation for porters in the front lodge. But these rooms have traditionally been used by bedders. They're too small to be any use to the students."

"They don't look too bad…"

"Not great if you're paying fees." The older man pointed upwards. "There's also a bell in the roof of this stairwell. It rings at seven each morning, and seven at night. Breakfast and dinner."

"I see."

"Locked-room mystery," mused the older officer.

"Hmm?"

"Missing person. Door locked from the inside."

"It could have been locked by someone using a piece of nylon."

"Difficult…"

"Possible with practice. Students are known for their pranks – and the ones at this place must be cleverer than most. So I suppose my last question is this: who's the last person we know who saw her?"

"A kid called Harold McMahon."

4

NICK ARRIVED HOME to find an envelope waiting for him. It sat on the telephone stand. Placed so he would see it as soon as he came through the front door. So here it was. The last one.

Nick examined the envelope – but didn't pick it up. Not yet. The top left-hand corner bore the logo of Imperial College, London.

"Are you going to open it, or just stare at it?"

Nick didn't reply. Didn't even turn. He could sense his father standing in the doorway to the lounge. He should have made the effort to get home earlier. At least then he could have opened the letter in private. Taken the beating with no one to see him. Now that wasn't going to happen. His father was waiting.

Nick hesitated, then took the letter from the stand. Inside, the answer to his application would be switching between "yes" and "no" until the moment he read it. Like a roulette wheel. Yes or no. Red or black.

"Stop messing around and open the damn thing."

Nick scanned his name again before letting the edge of his thumb slide along the gummed flap. Yes or no. It could be either.

And yet he only needed one to say "yes".

Behind him, his father let out an impatient sigh. They'd both been waiting for this for the last couple of weeks. It was his final opportunity. But, in the end, it was written in the same way as all the others:

Dear Mr Houghton,

Thank you for your recent research application. We read your proposal with interest; however, you will understand that these are difficult times and as such we need to be particularly selective with regards the projects we support. Unfortunately, we felt your research proposal was not quite right for us at the present time and…

Nick didn't bother to read the rest. Wordlessly, he slipped it back into the envelope. So, that was it. His applications had all been turned down. He stood for a couple of seconds, the implications bearing down on him.

His father seemed to read his body language. "You can apply again during the next round."

"Do you expect their opinion will have changed by then?"

"It would be wrong of them to punish you for my mistakes."

Nick didn't respond. Yes, it would be wrong. But the slow accumulation of rejections indicated he was already being punished. Already being driven out.

"I'll find a way round this," his father continued.

Nick didn't say anything. He drifted towards the kitchen and ran himself a glass of water. He drank it in one go before refilling. He'd been to seven interviews. Applied for seven potential proper jobs. The bastards had all smiled, shaken his hand, and listened to his proposal. And then they'd thrown his applications in the bin.

All because of his father's "mistakes".

Nick looked down. His knuckles were white. The tendons clear against the back of his hand. He forced himself to put down the glass before it shattered. He should have stayed at work. The roulette wheel would have still been spinning. He shook his head, and headed towards the lounge.

His father's middle-aged bulk already occupied one of two easy chairs. He held a book loosely on his lap, but wasn't reading. Nick sank into the other chair. He couldn't settle. His father's eyes were locked on him – his face illuminated from above by a solitary reading lamp.

"I didn't see you in the library today."

Nick shook his head. He shouldn't have given any sort of answer, but his response had been automatic. His father closed his book. "If you spent more time studying then you'd be further on with your preparatory research. Maybe that would have impressed them at the interviews."

So it was his fault. Nick took a large mouthful of water. Emptying the glass for the second time. Tension was pulling at the back of his neck, but he couldn't look away. Just as his neck started to cramp, his phone rescued him, buzzing in his pocket. One new message. Ronnie. *Be here now.*

Nick rose to his feet.

"Going out again?"

Nick nodded.

"To see Ronnie?"

Parry, thought Nick. *Just parry.* "He adds a bit of colour," he said, looking down at his phone.

"He adds distraction. Him and his damfool ideas. As I said: you need to focus on your studies. Or would you rather join him on the dole queue?"

Nick felt his brow tighten. Could he just ignore this bullshit?

"You want to say something?"

Parry. "No."

"Well, you look like you do. Perhaps you think I'm wrong? Perhaps you think you could get a better job than the one I secured for you? Just like Ronnie managed with his degree? Not all friends are for life, Nick."

Nick pulled his head back upright. His dad was still glaring at him. "You're not wrong, Dad."

"I'll have a word with Drockley, tomorrow. There may be something I can do."

The trip across London took a good deal longer than he expected. *Be here now.* If Ronnie had actually said where he was, then he might not have taken such a circuitous route. As it was, his friend wasn't at home – and Nick had

been left to take a further thirty-minute journey over to
Russell Square underground station.

On any other day, he'd probably have been sufficiently
pissed off to head back home. But not today. Instead,
Nick pushed his hands into his jacket pockets and waited.
Trying to keep out of the main lanes of pedestrian traffic,
and merge into the background buzz of the ticket hall.

Although it was well into the early evening, there were
still a fair number of people pushing back and forth on
either side of the ticket barriers. Some looked like they
were going into town for drinks; others were likely making
their way back to hotels after a day of sightseeing. Nick
watched for a few seconds, and then headed out on to the
street. He couldn't see the scraggy outline of his friend,
and hoped he hadn't been called out for no reason.

"Hey, you took your time."

Nick turned in the direction of the raspy voice. His old
friend grinned back at him from beside a newspaper kiosk,
tipping a fresh cigarette between his lips. The cigarette
remained unlit, and he allowed it to slip back and forth across
his mouth as he talked. "I thought you weren't going to show."

"Well you could have been more specific with your
directions."

Ronnie leant in closer. His breath stank of hamburger.
"You look like shit."

Nick managed a weak smile as he remembered his
meeting with Drockley. "I think I'm about to lose my job."

"Yeah, right."

"There's going to be more cutbacks."

"Your dad will square it."

Nick didn't reply. In all likelihood, Ronnie was right. But his father hadn't been able to get Drockley to sign off on his research proposal. And he must have tried.

"You just need to chill," continued Ronnie. "Stop worrying about what *could* happen, and start thinking about what *might*."

Nick closed his eyes and pinched the bridge of his nose. He might lose his career. He might have to go on the dole. "So what have you got planned?" he asked. "Drinks, and then some video games at your place?"

Ronnie didn't reply. Instead, he hunted around in his coat pocket and pulled out a couple of rectangular cards. He grinned broadly. Waiting for a reaction. Which he got almost immediately. Because Nick found himself looking at two tickets. Launch night invites to the Peking Man exhibition, complete with security perforation and a skull-themed hologram.

"Where did you get these?"

"Fuck does it matter? We got about twenty minutes to get there before the doors open. You've been banging on about it enough. I assumed you'd want to go."

"Yeah, but…"

Ronnie started to scratch the underside of his jaw. It was a clear sign of nerves. A trademark tell. "Okay. They're from some guy who owed me. Totally legit, I swear. But what does it matter? You want to go. I want to go. Let's go!"

Nick continued to hesitate.

"Oh, fuck it – you know why I want to go, and it ain't about those bones."

Nick started to turn away but Ronnie grabbed his arm. "Look," he said. "That boat? The *Awa Maru*? It was loaded with crates before it set sail. Official documents say it wasn't just carrying the Peking Man specimens back in 1941. Five billion dollars worth of gold bullion and platinum were on that thing. Five fucking billion. So when the Chinks found the boat in the 1970s – after they'd spent millions trying to locate the wreck, by the way – guess what they found?"

Nick shrugged, but he pretty much knew the punchline. Because it was the entire point of the exhibition. The contents of the boat had never sunk. Novus Particles had intervened before the bones had even got damp.

"Nothing," said Ronnie, answering his own question. "The wreck was empty." He grabbed the leaflet, jabbing it with his fingers. "So who's got the gold?"

Nick sighed, and reached for the tickets. In the corner was a stamp he hadn't noticed on his first glance. But its meaning was obvious, both for the tickets, and for his presence at Russell Square. They were part of a batch reserved for academic staff from nearby universities. The same batch he'd been unable to get hold of when they'd been first offered around his department. "So you need my university pass," he said, "or these aren't valid."

Ronnie didn't say anything.

Nick looked in the direction of the British Museum. They could make it. Twenty minutes before the doors opened. A couple of minutes' walk, or a two-week wait. "You promise me you're not going to do anything stupid while we're in there?"

"I promise on your mother's grave."

The Great Court of the British Museum looked nowhere near as good as it had done when it had been newly refurbished. The marble floors were scuffed with the pressing of too much shoe leather, and the glass ceiling was almost completely covered in green and brown grime. But it remained an impressive space. And, in some ways, the frayed fabric of the building perfectly reflected the state of its galleries.

Nick sighed. After the hasty repatriation programme, he didn't come here all that often. There was little of note left on display. Tonight, however, the court hummed with activity – and a long line of people stood waiting to gain access to the central reading room.

It seemed most had dressed for the occasion. Nick glanced down at his outfit, and felt a little embarrassed. Expecting to spend most of the night in an overheated bar, he'd only put on a light jacket to meet Ronnie. It didn't do much to hide the T-shirt underneath. Still, at least his outfit could pass as smart-casual. What Ronnie had on was hardly in keeping with the marble floor of the central courtyard, scuffed or otherwise. The security guard at the main door certainly hadn't been able to hide his smirk.

"Remember," Nick said, coming to a halt some

distance from the end of the queue, "I don't want to hear a single word about NovusPart."

Ronnie scratched at the back of his neck. "Even your dad agrees with me on this, Nick."

"Not a word."

"Yeah, well not talking about it doesn't mean people aren't going missing."

Nick gave his friend a cold glare. "Well I'm still of the opinion that Lee Harvey Oswald shot JFK, and Princess Di's driver was drunk." He paused, swallowed. "And you promised me, Ronnie."

Ronnie didn't answer. He appeared distracted. Nick followed the direction of his gaze. Two women were looking back at them from near the head of the queue. Both were dressed in smart business suits – one dark blue, the other beige – as if they'd arrived straight from work.

"There's no dress code, is there?"

"No." Ronnie took his time pulling his attention away from the women. "No," he repeated, blinking. "Look, you remember back at university, that old fart Webster used to make a big deal of the Rosetta Stone? How it suddenly allowed classicists to decode Egyptian hieroglyphics after years of scratching their fat heads over fragments?"

Nick nodded. The stone was inscribed with a decree written in three scripts, one of them ancient Greek, the others two types of ancient Egyptian. Translating the Greek provided the key to the hieroglyphics, and suddenly all those mysterious symbols on Egyptian artefacts began to make sense. The last time he'd visited the museum, he'd heard two tourists express surprise it was a real object. "Sure. Your point?"

"Well, we ain't going to work out what NovusPart are up to from one or two bits of information. We need to figure it out by overlaps. Ideally find something that brings everything together."

"I'm not interested, Ronnie." Nick turned away. A man and woman had joined the end of the line. Suddenly, Ronnie and he weren't the only ones who looked out of place. While the man had dressed conservatively, his companion had certainly come to be noticed. Bright pink hair, bright yellow jacket, bright green skirt. Of course, it could have been a combo that now passed as vintage, but it was going to give whoever was sitting behind her a nasty headache. As he watched, the man returned his interest with a small wave. Nick turned away, and felt his cheeks flush. Did Ronnie know them?

"The Rosetta Stone's still here, you know," Ronnie continued. "It's one of the few things the dicks running this place haven't given back."

Nick didn't reply immediately. The queue was growing. Which meant inside was going to be rammed. But he'd get to see the Peking Man. It would be worth it. "Well," he said. "Let's go and see what all the fuss is about."

"We got time," replied Ronnie. "I'm going for a piss. Wait for me here."

Ahead of them, the queue started to move. "They're going in…"

"I won't be long. Chill."

Nick swore under his breath as his friend ambled away and down through an archway. The queue continued to move forward.

After five minutes Nick started to get irritated. Around him, the Great Court was rapidly emptying. The excitement was all elsewhere. And he should be part of it.

He looked towards the archway through which Ronnie had vanished, and started to tap his foot nervously. The evening was going to start with a talk about the Peking Man and some high-level discussion about how the bones were found. No doubt whichever spokesman NovusPart had chosen would be allowed to reveal something interesting about the artefacts, but exactly zilch about how they pulled off their now-famous trick. But still, it would have been interesting to have heard it first-hand, even if he'd be able to read the same information in the exhibition programme.

Because Ronnie was right about one thing, even if he was wrong about everything else. It wasn't really about the bones. It was about NovusPart. But after getting hold of the tickets, it looked like Ronnie was going to end up frustrating him again.

Shit. Only if he let him. Taking a last look towards the exhibition entrance, Nick headed down a set of stairs, in the direction of the toilets. He found his friend loitering in the corridor outside the gents'. Rolling an unlit cigarette between his fingers. Like he wasn't in any particular rush.

"What are you doing?"

Ronnie turned towards him, his eyes suddenly widening. "Jesus, Nick. I told you to wait for me."

Nick blinked. "What's going on?"

"Nothing."

Nick didn't say anything. He just waited. Waited for the inevitable scratching around the chin and the jaw. The noise of stubble being rubbed back and forth. The sound of nerves. "What are you doing, Ronnie?"

"Just go upstairs and wait for me, okay?"

"You want me to go in without you?"

"No. I want you to go upstairs and wait."

"And then what?"

"And then we'll all get to know."

Nick felt his stomach contract. This couldn't be happening. "Know what?"

"People are disappearing, Nick. They're disappearing all the time."

5

"RONNIE," SAID NICK, lowering his voice. "You promised me…"

"Just wait, and hear me out on this." Ronnie took a step forward. He slipped the cigarette into his mouth. It wobbled between his lips but just about stayed in place. "We both know NovusPart didn't go down to the bottom of the Pacific to get those bones they've got on display up there. No, they reached back through time, and they snatched them from the *Awa Maru* before it went down."

Nick didn't say anything.

"A lot of us believe they're also snatching people off the streets."

Nick slowly counted to ten. It suddenly felt like someone was pushing down hard on his right eyeball. A migraine was starting. He could no longer breathe freely. "Once you've eliminated the impossible," he said, quietly.

"Fucking A! They did it on Flight 391. They may have done it at King's Cross…"

Nick flinched. *King's Cross.*

"I'm sorry, man. But you need to hear it."

I promise on your mother's grave.

"There's one big difference, Ronnie…"

"Only if you believe the government has the power to stop them – which they don't."

Nick heard himself laugh. He needed to leave. He could come back in two weeks. Sometime when Ronnie wouldn't be in the same postcode, much less the same museum. But as he started to turn away, he stopped himself. "'A lot of *us*'?"

"There's a small group."

"And your plan is to loiter near the toilets?"

Ronnie scratched his chin. The cigarette came close to toppling from his mouth. "There's an important guy from NovusPart in the audience," he said. "We're going to try to kill him."

Nick let the words settle. As they did so, the pressure on his eyeball turned into a high-pitched drilling pain. It transferred across into his temple. He felt his stomach knot, and had to remind himself he was near the toilets. If he was going to throw up, he wouldn't have far to run. "What do you mean," he said, slowly. Trying to take in every word. "Kill him?"

"Relax—"

"You're talking about murder."

"Relax. I said 'try', didn't I?" Ronnie stopped and removed the unlit cigarette before flicking it back between his lips. He was excited and his words were rolling together. Whatever he was planning, it was certainly real. "Because we don't think we can. It's all about the threat. We just need to get close. So fucking close we could breathe down his neck."

"And then what?"

"One of two things. Either they transport the guy to save him. Or they take the potential killer."

A test. Ronnie was talking about a test of his conspiracy theory. "What if you're wrong?" he said.

"We're not wrong."

"And you've got others working on this?"

"There's about a dozen of us. All upstairs. All sitting close to the boy."

Boy. "How old?"

"Eighteen."

Nick nodded. So not a boy. A young man. At least that was something. They weren't all going to end up arrested for attempting to murder a minor. "You think NovusPart will be forced to act," he said. "That they'll reach back in time and either take the kid out of harm's way… or one of your fruitcakes?"

"Yeah."

Nick tried to breathe. Tried to think what to do. "That's a pretty big risk for the assassin."

"Not so big, actually."

"How so?"

"Everybody will be crowded together when they run out. It'll be hard for them to tell who attacked him, so they're more likely to just take the kid. But whatever the outcome – we'll end up with a transportation on tape." Ronnie stopped and pulled a lighter out of his pocket. He lit the cigarette. "I'm sorry to have tricked you, Nick. But this is very important."

"I think you're an idiot," Nick whispered. "And I don't think this is going to work."

"Why not?"

"If this guy is as important as you think, he isn't going to leave as part of a scrum."

"No?"

"No."

"Because it's going to be chaos up there in a few minutes, Nick. Absolute chaos."

A thin line of smoke was coiling up from Ronnie's cigarette. Nick looked up. They were standing beneath a small white box with a blinking red light.

"You ever see how long it takes people to evacuate an old building?"

6

Nᴄᴋ sᴛᴏᴏᴅ ɪɴ the forecourt, the sirens finally fading behind him. He felt sick. He also felt ashamed. He'd run like hell as soon as the fire alarm had sounded. His brain had certainly called on him to try to warn the boy – but its instruction had been quickly overridden by the need to get out of the museum. And there was likely nothing he could have done anyway. He'd have arrived just that bit too late. But more than in time to implicate himself.

Shit. It didn't matter what logic told him, he should have done something.

The other guests were congregating in the forecourt outside the building – their voices merging into a single drone – but it was time for him to leave. He stumbled towards the museum's gates.

He barely registered a pressure on his shoulder, until the smell of overcooked onions enveloped him. Ronnie was at his side again. He was talking at speed, a new cigarette thrusting back and forth in his mouth, but Nick couldn't understand the words. The cigarette fell from Ronnie's lips and on to the ground.

"So, did you enjoy that, gentlemen?"

The voice wasn't Ronnie's. It was hard, and had come from behind them. A couple of black shapes closed in from ahead, cutting off their route. Coldness washed over Nick's face. He turned.

A tall man was standing there. He wore a dark suit, his hair buzz-cut just a fraction too close to his skull. The overall look spelt out "NovusPart security". But not quite. Although the guy was physically big, his clothes weren't off-the-peg. The suit was tailored around his thick frame. And he was also about thirty years older than the two men closing the net around them.

"You're Nick Houghton, right?"

The man beckoned but Nick didn't move.

"And you are?"

"A friend of Ronnie's."

Nick turned. Ronnie was already shrugging an open-mouthed denial, but his eyes were wide, his pupils dilating.

Shit.

"And you're a friend of Ronnie's too. Right, Nick?"

Nick found himself nodding as he looked around. The other visitors had all disappeared back inside. Aside from the odd member of staff at the museum doors, they were quite alone.

"We'd like to invite you to dinner tomorrow night." The man adjusted his footing. He was taller than either Nick or Ronnie, and the movement emphasised the point. However, his tone indicated he wasn't a simple thug. He was at the very least articulate.

"I'm not interested, thanks…"

The man reached forward with a card. "Eight o'clock?"

"And if we don't go?"

"Our security team has already arrested four people tonight. Let's not make it six, shall we?"

7

Kirsten blinked, then shivered. Ice-cold water lapped against her chin. She was back in the bathtub. The police officers were gone. And once more, she was quite alone.

Tap – tap – tap.

I'm going to kill you, bitch!

Kirsten moved her head slightly, turning towards the door. It was open. Wide open. She could see out into the corridor and across it to her room. Had she run a fresh bath? Got back into the tub in some dumb trance?

No. Impossible. Well, at least, very unlikely. She thought back to the police officers. They'd been talking about her disappearance. She could remember it quite clearly. Until it had all been replaced by an incandescent haze. Soft at first, before the whiteness had rushed at her. Until she'd woken. Once more in the bathtub. Once more in the water.

She sat up and pulled herself out in one smooth movement. She stood for a moment or two, water dripping on to the floor. Again, there was no robe. No towel. She took the few short steps into the corridor.

"Hello?"

There was no answer, but at least her words now sounded normal. No longer stretched or distorted. She took a few more steps. She couldn't hear anything. Suddenly she was at the door to her room. She reached out – and her hand slipped straight through the door handle. It just glided through, with only a tingle and shimmer indicating the difference between air and metal. And then she knew she hadn't been dreaming.

She was very much dead.

8

Pulling at his collar, Nick began to regret his choice of suit. The jacket hung loosely from his shoulders. Reflected in the restaurant windows, it gave the impression he was too thin for his height. But the more expensive suit at home in his wardrobe hadn't helped him win a research post. Perhaps an unthreatening look might be enough to gain him some leniency.

He checked the card again. The name of the establishment was written in a highly stylised flowing font, and hard to read. But he was pretty sure he was at the right place, if only because the address and phone number were printed underneath in a more down-to-earth font.

Bellotoni's

He hadn't heard of it before. He didn't spend much time in this part of London. However, he quickly realised he'd not been invited to some cheap pasta house. Although the windows were steamed up by heat and conversation, the interior looked like a portal back to the 1930s. Fine dining from a very different era.

Nick glanced at his watch, and then back along the street. There was no sign of anyone he knew. Although he had a good view of the inside, he couldn't see Ronnie. Or the man from the British Museum. He looked at his watch again. He'd arrived early, but not by much. He'd just have to wait.

He sighed. He seemed to have spent most of the last day waiting and worrying. Of course, Ronnie had been a lot more relaxed. As soon as they'd reached the nearest underground station, he'd been talking as if they'd won some sort of victory. His logic was simple, yet seemed a little naïve: since NovusPart had let them leave, they must have been unable to prove they'd been connected to the plot. But that was assuming NovusPart couldn't just make them "disappear" anyway. And the irony of being worried that Ronnie's conspiracy theory was correct provided Nick with little comfort.

Inside his jacket, his mobile buzzed. He skimmed through the text message. Ronnie wasn't coming. Nick typed a response: *Too scared of that NovusPart guy?*

Nick stole another glance through the restaurant windows. He didn't recognise anyone inside but, then again, he couldn't see all of the tables.

His phone buzzed: *Too scared of your father?*

Nick put the phone back in his pocket. It was nothing he hadn't heard before, but Ronnie usually reserved that particular jibe for when he wanted him to do something he shouldn't. Just like at university. He let a few more seconds pass before glancing at his watch again. Ten to eight. Time to find out what this was all about. Swallowing, he pushed open the restaurant door.

The place was nearly full. A few diners glanced over and allowed themselves a moment of judgement. They no doubt expected to see him ejected pretty quickly and, sure enough, it didn't take the *maître d'* long to notice his arrival. The man advanced as if trying to shoo a stray cat from his garden.

"Do you have a *reservation*?"

"I'm meeting someone," Nick replied, keeping his voice low. "My name is Nick Houghton…?"

At the mention of his name, the *maître d'* blinked in surprise, and then adopted a fixed, professional smile. "Of course; we are expecting you."

Nodding, Nick allowed himself to be led past the other diners and seated at a table near the back of the restaurant, close to the kitchen doors. The position gave him a clear view of the main dining area – but also meant he had to face the crowd. The *maître d'* hovered by his side. It took a moment to realise there were some papers and a pen set out on the table in front of him. Nick glanced at them, and recognised the lengthy, complex constructions of legalese.

"What's this?"

"If you would sign, initial and date the non-disclosure agreement, sir?"

Non-disclosure agreement? Nick flicked through the documentation. From the contract's title and opening paragraphs, he guessed he wasn't to discuss the content of the meeting with anyone. After a moment's hesitation, he scribbled his name at the appropriate points and was left to sit on his own.

His mobile phone buzzed.

Another message from Ronnie. One word: *Bastard*. Frowning, confused, he deleted it and turned his attention back to the table. It was set for two others. They appeared a couple of minutes later. The tall, well-built man from the British Museum, and the CEO of Novus Particles, Harold McMahon.

Nick stumbled to his feet, but remained completely mute. Harold McMahon. The man was in his fifties, and fat. His hair was black, but clearly dyed. Overall, he looked a long way short of the Machiavellian character portrayed by the press. Still, here he was: sitting down at the table. He didn't acknowledge Nick's presence. In contrast, the tall man extended his hand, and gave Nick a warm smile.

"My name is Mark Whelan, Chief Operating Officer at NovusPart. And this is Harold McMahon, our Chief Executive Officer."

For a long moment, Nick remained frozen. Finally though, he shook Whelan's hand and sat down. Both McMahon and Whelan sat with their backs to the rest of the diners. The seating arrangement effectively made them anonymous, except that a few feet away stood a couple of security guards. Both of whom were armed.

Nick stared at McMahon, struggling to find something to say which wouldn't sound stupid. Fortunately, the arrival of the waiting staff covered his silence.

"We took the liberty of ordering in advance," explained Whelan, indicating the tiny portions of salmon being set in front of them. "News of Mr McMahon's whereabouts usually travels fast and, as you found out last night, there are certain groups with whom we're quite unpopular."

Nick continued to flounder. "I don't get what this is all about."

"It's about the fact that five of your friends tried to pull some sort of stunt last night," said Whelan. "But you somehow didn't fit with the rest of the group. In fact, we could only find a connection between you and one of them, Ronald Saunders."

Some sort of stunt. So they didn't know what Ronnie's pals had been plotting. Something hadn't gone to plan. "Okay," he said, feeling some of the tension leaving him. "And the non-disclosure agreement?"

"We don't expect you to tell anyone about the details of this meeting."

"Don't worry," said Nick. His mind focused on his father. "I won't."

"Good, so let's get straight to the point. We have an opening at our company for a researcher. And then you landed in our laps last night. We've seen your CV. You seem to have all the right skills, if not the qualifications."

Nick was about to pick at some of the salmon, but quickly stopped. Was he hearing right? "You're offering me a job?"

"That's correct."

"After what happened last night?"

Whelan nodded. "Especially after what happened last night."

Nick looked at McMahon. The CEO of NovusPart

still hadn't contributed anything to the conversation. He seemed uninterested. Sullen. "And you need a historian?"

McMahon rolled some salmon in his cheek, and glanced towards his operations chief. "Not me. *Him*."

Whelan smiled, perhaps a little embarrassed. Nick's assessment at the British Museum had been correct. The guy's physical size clearly hid an active brain. "I've already assembled a very good team for our new project. However, we have a last-minute vacancy we're looking to fill. Initially on a six-week trial period, with a view to a permanent position."

Nick nodded. "And the others on your team?"

"Most are young men like yourself… but you'll have heard of Eric Samson?"

Nick blinked, surprised. "*Professor* Eric Samson?"

"Yes."

"But he was very vocal… I mean, he wrote a series of articles…" Nick felt his words disappear as he sensed he'd said the wrong thing. McMahon, however, just grunted and continued to eat.

"After Flight 391, Professor Samson wrote a series of articles and papers attacking NovusPart," said Whelan. He didn't sound concerned. "Just like your father did… before his disgrace."

Nick flinched. Disgrace. A much more damning assessment than "mistakes". "My father isn't one of your biggest fans."

"I know," replied Whelan. "He thinks it's immoral that a private corporation has access to our technology."

McMahon stirred. "Tough. We developed it."

"Quite," continued Whelan. "But we know all this because we do a lot of due diligence, Mr Houghton. And we're looking to build a very small, select team."

Nick nodded slowly, trying to buy himself time. Samson was one of those historians who liked to dip in and out of a wide range of periods. But his major interest was alternative history, the TV-friendly stuff. The questions of what might have been: *what if Hitler had died during the Great War; what if the Princes in the Tower had been rescued; what if the Soviets had won the space race?* So it made sense that NovusPart would be interested in him. But still. "Samson works for you?"

"Samson works for us," confirmed Whelan. He let out a short sigh – the first real sign of impatience. The muscles in his neck flexed beneath his collar. "Look," he said. "We know about your father. And we also know about your mother."

Nick felt a line of sweat trickle down his back.

"If you don't want to hear any more," Whelan continued, "we can part on good terms. But your CV is a suitable match with what we're looking for. And it's the only reason you're sitting here tonight, instead of being with your friends."

Nick nodded. "Like you said, only one of them is my friend. And just for the record: I don't buy into all that conspiracy crap."

Whelan wasn't listening. He was already halfway through a dismissive wave. "I think it's rather clear where the lack of brains sat last night," he said, before turning towards his boss. "Should we continue?"

McMahon grunted as he swallowed. He stared out from eyes that looked small against the fleshiness of his face. "You ever met a guy called James Harris?" he asked.

Nick shook his head. "No."

"You're sure?"

"Yes."

McMahon didn't look too convinced. He glanced towards Whelan, and pushed away the remains of his starter. "It's your call. But you're making a pretty big leap of fucking logic."

"Okay," said Whelan, turning back to Nick. "So what do you know about NovusPart?"

Nick hesitated. "You can transport things. Objects. People. From the past into the present."

"And what do you think about that?"

"I think it's probably wasted on putting on shows at the British Museum."

"The Peking Man? That's just a PR exercise."

"Still…"

McMahon took a large gulp of wine. "Don't ask us about the gold," he said.

"I suppose the more interesting question," Nick said, his voice quiet, "is what if, without NovusPart, those bones were meant to have been found by someone else. By taking them from the shipwreck, aren't you altering the timeline? Something you claim not to be doing?"

"Good question," said Whelan. He smiled again, seeming to relax. "And you're right; it's one of the reasons we employed Professor Samson. Basically put, our priority is to eliminate potential changes to the past as per the UN mandate. The present, like the future, can take care of itself."

"A philosophy that justified saving the passengers of Flight 391?"

Whelan nodded, but didn't reply straight away. Instead, he allowed a waiter to clear his plate. Even though he hadn't touched his food, Nick leant back so his own plate could be taken.

"Most of those passengers are now living productive lives," Whelan said. "That's something the press likes to ignore."

Nick nodded, feeling his throat tighten. How far could he push it? He tried to swallow. His father wouldn't forgive him if he didn't take the opportunity to press home at least a few points. "Some of them committed suicide," he said, softly.

Whelan stopped, and took a slow sip of wine. "Which is why we haven't done anything like that again," he said. "Dislocation from the past to the present is too much for some people. They couldn't cope with a world that had moved on by fifty years. All the small things we take for granted such a short time after they're invented. We know we made some mistakes with Flight 391 – but we also learned valuable lessons. And the important thing remains that the timeline isn't threatened, because all events between their transportation and the day they arrived are unaffected. It's the same with the Peking Man."

"But…"

"We're aware that some people, like your father, would prefer this power not to be left in the private sector. And we're aware what we've been doing is controversial, as it poses certain… questions."

From beside him, McMahon growled. "It's a little bit rich to be criticised every day for *not* saving someone's relative."

Again, Nick nodded. Because if you could pull people from an aircraft just moments before it crashed, why not save everyone who died in such disasters? Thousands of survivors, all without any potential paradox. And if you could snatch people from disasters, what was stopping you from taking people off the street? Just like Ronnie kept banging on about. Just like he was trying to prove last night. "As I said, I'm not a big fan of conspiracy theories."

Whelan smiled. "Well, good, Mr Houghton. Because we want to discuss our latest project with you."

9

WHELAN LEANT BACK and took a large mouthful of wine. For a second, the restaurant lights picked out the few flecks of grey in his hair. "It's something Harold and I feel everyone will be able to get behind," he said. "A truly spectacular demonstration of our technology."

Nick felt himself tense. This was the point of the meeting, he could sense it. This was the reason he'd signed the non-disclosure agreement. Everything up to this point was probably fair game. Something to tell Ronnie. Something he could maybe even admit to his father.

"We've created a unique research environment."

Nick's mind blanked. "What do you mean, 'unique'?"

"A replica historical setting – to avoid the problem of dislocation."

For a long time, Nick didn't say anything. Finally, he turned to face McMahon. "But after Flight 391 – we were told there'd be no more human transportations."

McMahon didn't reply. He just turned an indifferent eye to his colleague. Whelan leant forward. "We have a special dispensation. It's a sort of *pro bono publico* spin-off from our other activities. Something that academics can use to talk to people from the past and to answer... points of interest."

Whelan paused as the waiters returned with plates of sautéed chicken liver garnished with fashionably bitter leaves. McMahon looked at his serving like a child might survey a new toy; then he started to slice into his food.

Nick was no longer hungry. Plus, the front of the restaurant was getting busy. A handful of people were milling by the door and the *maître d'* was having trouble clearing them. It wouldn't take long for a protest to form. Or maybe two. One set of people calling for NovusPart to be shut down; another asking for them to intervene in whatever tragedy was personal to them. The security guards flanking their table stepped closer. McMahon and Whelan would probably be whisked out the back; but where did that leave him? Nick forced his attention back to Whelan. "It won't work," he said. "You can't isolate a few people and expect to recreate a historical environment."

"What if we recreated an entire town?"

"No. You couldn't do it. In a plane crash – like Flight 391 – you know exactly how many people died and the envelope of the event is well defined. But there's no way you could pull so many survivors from a disaster zone. You couldn't be certain about who lived and who died. You'd end up with timeline problems."

McMahon spoke up. "I'm glad you know so much about our technology."

"I'm familiar with the arguments."

"Hiroshima?" Whelan asked.

Were they serious? The people who'd been vaporised?

Could some of them have been pulled forward in time?

"No," Nick said, regaining his composure. "It's a case in point. Many people survived very close to the blast. It would be risky. And, anyway, there's lots of footage and documents from that time. There would be no academic interest."

"Please save our daughter!"

The shout had come from near the *maître d*'s lectern. So at least one of the two sides of the coin had arrived. The people who wanted NovusPart to go further. Nick looked over towards the restaurant door. A man was being thrown out. Waiters were moving to guard the entrance. People were gathering outside. The other diners had stopped eating. They probably knew they were now trapped in the restaurant. Until McMahon decided to leave, or the people outside broke in.

Whelan leant closer. "Mr Houghton, you're working at a third-rate university, and we know you've had all your research applications turned down." His voice didn't betray any urgency. He didn't appear to have noticed the mix of anger and desperation forming in the lobby. His eyes remained relaxed, his tone firm. "To my mind, and from what you've said tonight, you deserve better. But we want your situation to be our gain. So can you think of anywhere else, Nick? Somewhere you might be interested in? Somewhere that litters your academic CV?"

Nick flinched.

Bodies. Bodies made of plaster cast. Choking on the ground.

"Pompeii," said Nick. He closed his eyes.

"Dr Houghton…"

"I'm not a doctor…"

"But you could be. And can you think of a better way than by walking the streets of a living, breathing Roman town?"

"You can't be serious."

"Why not?"

Nick winced. "Pompeii had a population of thousands," he said. "More in its hinterland. But there's evidence of only a few hundred bodies. Most of its inhabitants likely fled in the days leading up to the eruption."

"Really?" replied McMahon. He didn't bother to raise his head, concentrating on his food. "Or were they transported? This academic paradise; it's already up and running."

10

KIRSTEN TOOK A deep breath. She couldn't just stay in the corridor. Couldn't spend any more time in the bath. And she was just so damn cold.

Looking down, she knew the door handle wasn't an option. But if her hand could pass through metal, then it stood to reason the rest of her body could follow through a simple barrier of wood and paint. She took another deep breath, and walked forward.

Sure enough, as soon as she lifted her right leg, she felt a soft tingle in her toes. The sensation pushed quickly on through her ankle, and then her calf. She closed her eyes as the tingle reached her hips. Let her weight slowly transfer from one leg to the other. About halfway through the movement, she felt a pressure on her chest… face… neck.

And then she was through. But she wasn't in her room, at least not how she remembered it. And she wasn't alone. A young man was sitting in an easy chair pushed up against one of the walls. A girl sat on the bed, her knees drawn up under her chin. Both were wearing jeans and T-shirts. Both looked like students. It took a while for Kirsten to tune in to what they were saying, but it turned out to be something related to their lectures. They sounded like they were studying maths – or maybe one of the sciences. She didn't understand a word of it.

She ignored them. It was clear her room had been taken over. Someone else's personality had been plastered over the walls. After she'd first arrived, she'd hung a series of posters to remind her of her trips to America. But they had been replaced with movie posters. She didn't recognise any of the film titles, but some of the actors' faces were familiar.

Kirsten felt tears pricking at the corners of her eyes. This change had taken some time. It hadn't been done in the forty-eight hours mentioned by the policeman. Probably not even forty-eight days. If her room had been taken over by students, it likely meant the whole floor was now reserved for them. More than a year could have passed since she...

"Can you pass me my jumper?"

The girl was waving a hand towards her friend.

"How can you be cold?" he said.

"I just am. Look, don't be a dick and pass me the jumper."

"It's the hottest day of the year."

"I suddenly feel cold, okay?"

The lad smirked. "Maybe she's here? You know, the bedder in the bath?" He was clearly enjoying making the girl uncomfortable.

"Quit it. That's too recent to be a joke, right?"

He laughed. "She could be in there: the next time you go take a pee. You could ask her who did it."

"Shit, Lee. You know I'm not happy I got assigned this room."

Lee shrugged. The girl pulled her knees tighter to her chest. "Would you think me stupid," she asked, "if I said I'd already seen her?"

11

POMPEII. THE LOST Roman town, buried under ash and pumice, its inhabitants killed by a mixture of heat and suffocation. The images of its streets and buildings were fresh in Nick's mind. He'd visited the site many times. Walked its pavements. Read the graffiti left on its walls. And now? Could the town and its population be reunited?

Nick leant forward. His forehead creased. The table in front of him could seat about sixteen people, but only three of the places were taken. Aside from himself, a couple of female students occupied the far end of the table. He didn't pay them too much attention. Although presumably in the library to work, they seemed more interested in sending messages to each other on their phones than doing any reading. Occasionally, they issued a stifled giggle. On a normal day it would have irritated the hell out of him. But today wasn't normal.

He looked down and continued reading his favourite book about Pompeii. Written forty years earlier, it had been at the very top of the undergraduate reading list. Back then he'd appreciated its clear diagrams and the fairly dismissive passages about the Italian tourist board.

As a researcher, he still regularly used it to check his own work. So much so, he usually returned the book a couple of shelves above where it should be kept. Just so he would have a good chance of getting hold of it when he needed to. Just like now.

Nick ran his finger down the index, searching for Pliny the Younger – a Roman magistrate, and one of the few people who'd actually witnessed the eruption of Vesuvius first hand. Finding the name, he flicked through to the critical quotation:

> *You might hear the shrieks of women, the screams of children, and the shouts of men. Some wishing to die; some lifting their hands to the gods; but the greater part convinced there were now no gods at all, and they would disappear into the final endless night which had come upon the world.*
>
> *For a time, it grew lighter. However, with sparkling flashes, the fire fell again and we were immersed in thick darkness. A heavy shower of ashes rained upon us, which we were obliged every now and then to shake off – otherwise we should have been crushed and buried.*
>
> *In the darkness, I was convinced by that miserable, though mighty, consolation, that all mankind were involved in the same calamity, and that I was perishing with the world itself.*

The words looked as familiar as ever. He'd read them many times. Somehow though, the account still made his heart race. Although writing some years after the event, Pliny had provided the best record of the disaster. The event wasn't just some date on a calendar. It had affected real people.

He read the extract again. Felt the words burn into his eyes. A man's thoughts transmitted from the distant past. But could he trust them? Or had they been for ever mangled by the actions of NovusPart?

He'd never know. Even though he was familiar with every line, he scanned the page again just to make sure. At least there was no mention of people disappearing into thin air. But what about the reference to sparkling flashes? It had never seemed strange to him before, but was this evidence of transportations?

One of the girls at the far end of the table issued another excited shriek. Nick cast them a wary glance and then picked up another book. He flicked through it until he came to a photograph of a plaster cast of a dog. It had died still lashed to a post. Curled in a ball, the animal had suffocated just before the town had been buried. It was still choking, all these years later.

Nick grimaced. The casts had been made by filling with plaster the voids in the hardened ash left by long rotted-away bodies. The archaeologists who'd first explored the site had recognised the pumice shells as natural sarcophagi. A true miracle, even though the resulting plaster casts were now nothing more than a morbid tourist attraction. And yet only a few hundred remains had been found. Where had everyone else gone? Had they deserted the town in the days before the eruption like so many researchers assumed? Or had they been transported?

Nick shook his head. He didn't know. Didn't know enough about the technology. The debate had always centred on the ethics rather than the practicalities – and NovusPart didn't exactly advertise how they pulled off their trick. Still, Whelan would contact him again soon for his decision. And that raised its own question: because they should have had him arrested, not offered him a job.

Even if it was subject to a six-week trial period.

Nick gave a sigh. Six weeks.

Setting the book to one side, he stood up. His sudden movement caused the two girls to stop giggling. As he turned to the nearby window he could hear them whispering. He didn't much care what they were saying.

Although the number of books in Falconbrook University's library made a good show of it, there was little to be done to hide the fact they were sitting in a cold, concrete shell. It was an unattractive working space – all fluorescent tubes and dry air. Poorly adapted to a world where everything was available online, and people could work from home.

Six weeks.

His mind swung back to the dinner with McMahon. The speed at which that protest had formed. The mix of desperation and anger in those people's faces as they'd begged for the lives of their loved ones.

But did they really expect NovusPart to rescue everyone?

* * *

Nick ate his lunch slowly. He'd headed to a small café just off campus but wasn't enjoying any peace. The food was cheap enough for the place to be busy, and he'd soon found himself penned in by a melee of other students. At least he had a couple of limp cheese sandwiches for company.

And an envelope. It had been waiting for him in his pigeonhole in the History Department. He'd recognised Drockley's handwriting and had assumed the worst. But on opening the letter, he'd found the exact opposite. His contract was being renewed. The paperwork sat before him. All he had to do was sign. Which meant Ronnie had been right. His dad had pulled some strings and again saved him from the dole queue. But now it seemed second best to what NovusPart were offering him.

Nick spread out the flyer from the British Museum on the table in front of him. He focused on the bones of the Peking Man, but all he could think about were the survivors of Flight 391. All of whom were now walking around, just like they'd never actually boarded the plane. Or, at least, most of them were. Some just hadn't been able to survive in the modern world.

"I knew you'd be here."

Nick looked up to see Ronnie pushing through the crowd towards him. His friend fell into the shabby plastic seat opposite before making a grab for the list of specials. He only considered the menu for the bare minimum of time before dropping it back to the table. "You enjoy your meal the other night?"

Nick hesitated. "Why didn't you come?"

"How the fuck could I?" Ronnie said, his voice suddenly loud. "Two cops showed up at my place and effectively revoked my invitation."

Nick put his sandwich down. Ronnie's jaw was set tight. He wasn't scratching at his jaw. He wasn't lying. A few of the other customers – mostly students – looked warily in their direction. "I didn't know," he said. "And after what you pulled at the museum, I think it's me who's owed the apology."

"So what did you talk to McMahon about?"

Ronnie said the name bluntly; Nick felt himself flinch. McMahon. How did Ronnie know he'd met McMahon? He looked towards the exit. He needed to get out of here. They were too close to the department. More importantly, they were too close to his father. "Let's go somewhere else to talk."

"You'd like that, wouldn't you?" Ronnie reached into his pocket and plucked out a lighter and a cigarette. He lit it, and blew out a long plume of smoke. More people looked round. They'd soon be thrown out.

"Ronnie," said Nick, leaning forward. He kept his voice low, hoping his friend would finally take the hint. "What do you want?"

"I want to know what shit is going down. Men like McMahon don't socialise with blokes like you." Ronnie nodded towards the café window. It gave a good view across the campus. Right across to the History Department and the library. "This is a long way from being an ivory tower. Even if you get that PhD you're always banging on about, it ain't going to be worth shit because it's from the University of My Arsehole."

Nick didn't say anything. Part of him hoped the students were still listening. Still, Falconbrook had done for his father – even if he sometimes referred to it as an "academic lifeboat".

Ronnie grinned, knowing his insult had hit home, and then stubbed his cigarette out on the table. He'd left most of it un-smoked. "McMahon must want you for something," he whispered, his breath heavy with tobacco. "And others seem to be taking an interest in you too."

Nick flicked his eyes upwards. At first he thought he meant the other customers in the café, but Ronnie's face was suddenly filled with regret. He knew he'd overstepped the mark.

"What do you mean, 'others'?"

Ronnie fumbled in his coat pocket for his phone and brought up an app. Nick leant forward.

Who's Where. Social media. And he'd managed to appear on its radar. Great.

Who? Nick Houghton. (Falconbrook University.)
Son of Dr Bernard Houghton.
Where Been? Met with Harold McMahon
and Mark Whelan at Bellotoni's Restaurant,
London.
Where Now? University Park, Sunbeam Café.
With Ronnie Saunders.

Nick looked around. Someone in the café must have updated his status to give his current location. Blank faces stared back at him. He checked the screen again. Some of the entries were hyperlinked. He thumbed on to his dad's entry but found it gave no real detail. Just the obvious facts and a short summary of his disgrace. But the lists of people with whom McMahon and Whelan came into contact seemed to be catalogued in extreme detail.

"Amazing isn't it?"

"Yeah," said Nick. "Someone's got too much time on their hands."

"Not someone, Nick. Everybody. Given that it started as a way to find and bump into celebs, this app is actually a private dick's wet dream."

Ronnie sniggered. Nick ignored him. "Well, I don't see my entry getting any longer. I'm thinking of going on a field excursion."

"To Italy? You've been there masses of times—"

"I'm not going to Pompeii again."

Ronnie ignored him. There was real anger in his eyes. "Well my guys from the Peking Man thing have disappeared," he said. "No one's heard from them. They're all missing. Which means they were transported. Right out of the room."

"They're more likely in a jail cell."

Ronnie stood up. He paused and looked around the café. The other customers were still staring, their faces holding a mix of genuine interest and nervousness. "No," he said, firmly. "They were transported. And we weren't. So don't cut me out, Nick. This is too good. We could finally find out what they're up to."

12

KIRSTEN FORCED HERSELF to go on. The last steps into the quad were the worst. She found herself listening for the slightest of sounds. *But no one can see me*, she thought. *No one can see me.*

And yet she still hesitated, starting to shiver.

She'd woken in the bath again. The haze had simply taken her back to the water – like so many times before. But this time she'd moved faster. She hadn't lingered in the corridor. Instead, she'd pushed straight down to the quad.

Her feet found the cold flagstones and again she listened. *But no one can see me*, she thought. *No one can see me. Most of the time.* Because even though the police officers hadn't been able to see her, and the students had ignored her when she'd gone to her room, it was clear that, on some occasions, she *had* been seen. She'd been seen often enough to get a nickname. She'd heard them whisper it. The "bedder in the bath".

But no one can see me, she reminded herself. *No one can see me...*

...because I'm already dead.

Kirsten stopped. She tried to concentrate on the air

passing over her body. She could still feel it. Just like the tears now trickling down her cheeks.

She let out a cry of frustration. There was nothing down here.

Certainly no answers.

But then she saw them. The long rows of black-framed noticeboards covered in flyers about the college's various clubs and activities. Kirsten moved quickly. One of them would tell her what date it was, or at least what year. What she found was better. Faces she recognised, staring at her from a glossy poster announcing an event.

Harold McMahon. Joe "Octo" Arlen. And Mark Whelan.

They all looked older than she remembered – heavier and more lined. She looked at the date on the poster, but it only gave a day and month. She scanned the other notices, and found the university code of conduct, half hidden behind a list of upcoming sports events. Beneath the signature of the university's chancellor was the date. Kirsten felt a cry well up, and she pressed her hand over her mouth. Ten years.

She pulled her eyes away and focused on the poster again. Tried to recall the three men. Yes, that was right. They'd lived over in Rose Court. All on the same staircase. She saw them nearly every day, briefly on days when she'd just emptied their bins. Longer on others when she'd changed their sheets.

Octo the geek. Whelan the soldier. McMahon the slob. Three lads who'd been randomly assigned rooms on the same staircase and, if she remembered correctly, didn't much care for each other.

She drifted forward, bringing the text into focus.

They'd started a business together. Novus Particles. Again she felt tears welling at the corner of her eyes. Ten years? Had all that time passed already?

She wiped her face, trying to read the rest of the notice. They were going to give a talk in the Hereford Lecture Theatre in a few days' time. She examined the photograph.

Octo Arlen beamed at the camera, a mixture of pride and excitement making his ruddy cheeks glow. Whelan had his jaw out like he was having his army mug shot taken. She used to regularly see him in his army fatigues. Playing at soldiers at weekends and working late during the week to catch up on his studies.

McMahon's stare was as dead-eyed as ever, having finally gained the pounds all those empty pizza boxes must have been carrying. For someone supposedly so good at maths, he didn't seem to understand how to count calories.

Smiling despite herself, Kirsten reached forward, groping for the picture. Her hand went straight through it, and she pulled back in sudden anger. Turning away, she looked out into the quad.

A man was looking straight at her.

It took a full ten seconds before Kirsten recovered enough to speak.

"Can you see me?"

He didn't respond. Instead, he took a step forward.

Kirsten only just stumbled out of the way. And no, he hadn't seen her. He was looking at the noticeboard. The poster about Arlen, Whelan and McMahon.

It was soaking wet.

13

IT WAS EARLY. Too early. Nick rubbed at his stubble, and felt his jaw stretch and pop as he yawned. Ronnie didn't live in a great area. It was a conclusion he reached pretty much every time he visited his friend's home. Most of the pre-war terraced houses that dominated the street had long since been converted into flats. Despite the number of people who must be living nearby, the streets were empty, and it only added to the sense of the neighbourhood's dereliction.

Be here now. Urgent.

The message had pinged into his phone almost the second Nick had woken that morning. Or perhaps the message had broken his sleep and his brain was just playing tricks on him. Whatever the answer, he wasn't fully awake. But he was now at least prepared to have an argument with his friend. About what Ronnie had said at the café and, more importantly, about what had happened at the British Museum.

A short set of concrete steps led up to the main door of Ronnie's building. Nick took them two at a time and rang the bell for the first-floor flat. He flexed his fingers. He'd rehearsed what he was going to say. He was ready.

The door didn't open. Finally, a flap of curtain attracted his attention downwards. The occupant of the basement flat – a fat, unshaven guy wearing a vest and shorts – was staring up at him through a window. Nick shrugged an apology and pushed the buzzer again.

Then he noticed the obvious.

The glass in the front door was broken. Nick stared at it. The top section was made up of glass panels – four rows of three. But one of them was missing. The one right next to the lock.

Nick slipped his hand through the hole and flicked the Yale catch, pushing through the door into the small entry hall. He noted there was no glass on the floor, which meant the break wasn't fresh. Typical. It looked like someone had decided to make it easier for visitors to get in without disturbing the rest of the occupants – maybe the fat guy in the basement – or perhaps there'd been a break-in and the landlord hadn't yet got round to making a repair. Whatever the answer, he'd get the full story from Ronnie. If he got the opportunity to ask him anything before he was berated about NovusPart, or whatever else was playing on his friend's mind.

Be here now. Urgent.

Nick headed upstairs and rapped on Ronnie's door. It swung open.

"Ronnie?"

Nick stepped inside and tapped on the bedroom door. He heard only the barest sound of movement in response. "Come on, Ronnie. We need to talk."

More noise from the bedroom. Nick sighed. Back when they'd lived together as students, Ronnie had developed a habit of leaving doors unlocked. At the time it had seemed harmless. But now it just seemed stupid, especially given the damage to the front door. Then again, and as Ronnie had so eloquently put it, "If you have fuck all to steal, it's better to let them know."

Nick knocked again, then moved deeper into the flat. The lounge smelt of stale cigarettes and beer. He made his way through the piles of clutter to the sofa, and then settled down to wait for his friend to surface. A few newspapers were pushed up against the armrest, and he noticed the top copy had an article ringed in thick, red marker. Another report of a missing child.

Ignoring it, Nick pulled out his phone and checked his email. The previous night, he'd started writing his acceptance letter. In all likelihood, he was going to join Novus Particles.

But he still hadn't sent it. And something Ronnie had said to him at the café continued to niggle him. *McMahon must want you for something.* He let out a frustrated sigh. Why did they want him though? There were plenty of academics who had spent their whole careers researching Pompeii. He was a nobody. Why on earth did such a powerful company care about him? He wasn't going to find out without accepting the offer. But did he want to know?

Yes.

Yes, of course he did. Just like he wanted to get to their version of Pompeii.

Nick rubbed his temples. A six-week trial. Just over a month of guaranteed work to balance against the offer from Drockley to extend his *quasi*-contract followed by a good chance of a proper research post. If he looked at the situation logically, then there was no way he'd go. But all he needed to do was press "send" and, when he next met McMahon and Whelan, his *Who's Where* page would be trending for months.

And he'd never hear the end of it from Ronnie or his father.

Nick frowned. *Who's Where.* Saving his email back into "drafts", he brought up a browser page and searched for his own link. It didn't take long to find: it was still trending nearly two days after his meeting with the men from Novus Particles.

Who? Nick Houghton. (Falconbrook University.)
 [More]
Where Been? University Park, Sunbeam Café.
With Ronnie Saunders.
Met with Harold McMahon and Mark Whelan at
Bellotoni's Restaurant.
Where Now? 46 Westburn Avenue, London.

Nick followed the link to his father's page. It was still a stub, but it told the ugly truth of his disgrace in just a few simple words: *Found to have plagiarised the works of several Chinese academics.* That was how his father had written so many papers in such a short space of time. All summarised in a single sentence. No one had bothered to update his entry. Which was unsurprising. Given his father had disappeared off the academic radar, there was no reason to suspect he'd make any waves in the virtual world now.

Nick switched over to McMahon and Whelan's *Who's Where* pages. His meeting with them was already way down their list of engagements. However, no one seemed to know where they were at the moment, and several flags had been raised asking people to keep a lookout.

Losing interest, Nick skipped back and refocused his attention on his own log. It gave his current location: 46 Westburn Avenue, London.

His page was telling people he was at Ronnie's.

Instinctively, Nick glanced around him. His friend hadn't appeared from his bedroom. He took a few steps to the window, but the street outside remained deserted. He glanced back down at his phone – and flinched at the sound of an incoming call.

"Hello?"

"Nick?"

"Yes."

"Mark Whelan." His voice was firm and confident. "You've made a decision?"

Nick hesitated. NovusPart. He turned to the lounge door, half expecting to see Ronnie staring back at him. "Yes… I mean, not yet. Not quite."

"We'll need an answer soon."

Nick tried to keep his voice quiet. "It's a big step."

"So you've had time to think about it?"

"Yes. But you're asking me to give up a full-time post."

"I once heard a footballer say he'd give up his entire career for one game at Wembley."

"Yes, but…"

"What exactly is your role at Falconbrook anyway?" asked Whelan. "It seems you're caught in some form of academic limbo? Sustained by your father?"

"I—"

Whelan cut him off. "It doesn't matter. Where are you?"

Nick glanced at the bedroom door. "At a friend's."

"If you'd prefer to talk later…"

"No." Nick got to his feet and checked the bedroom door. It remained shut. He closed the door to the lounge, and kept his voice low. "I want to talk now."

"Very well," said Whelan.

"I need to know why you've done this. Why Pompeii?"

"I thought we'd explained…"

"You called it a pro bono spin-off. But sorry, I don't buy that."

Whelan gave a slight chuckle. "Glad to see you're not naïve, Mr Houghton. And you're right; we do intend to turn a profit on the venture. A substantial one."

Nick felt his shoulders slump. "It's a tourist attraction, isn't it?"

"No," said Whelan, his voice suddenly losing its humour. "That much I can promise you. The site will be closed to the public – and for good reason. But you can imagine, I think, the value at which we could retail a bottle of genuine Roman wine? Or a fresco? Or some jewelled metalwork? And that's before you start thinking about the television revenues…"

Nick already knew what was coming next. "Gladiators?"

"They are part of the picture, certainly," replied Whelan. "But fights won't be the only attraction."

In truth, it didn't come as much of a surprise. He had no doubt that people would watch. And at least Whelan had given him a direct answer – not evaded the truth like some corporate automaton. But perhaps there was something that NovusPart hadn't considered. "I'm not sure you'll be getting what you expect," he said. "Gladiators were highly trained and very valuable – fights weren't often to the death."

"Well good," replied Whelan, "because we don't have an endless supply. And, as I said, they won't be the only attraction. But the real question is this: do you want to live among the people you've studied your whole adult life? Or do you want to have your nose in a textbook while our project makes your endeavours redundant?"

Nick gripped the phone tighter. "I want to say yes."

"And the only things stopping you from saying 'yes' are your father… and the matter of working for Novus Particles."

Nick felt himself falter. NovusPart. He thought about the small protest at the restaurant. He thought about his father. "They're not minor issues."

"No one's saying they are."

Nick looked down at the sofa. He saw the thick red mark surrounding the newspaper article and immediately knew there was another question he needed to ask before committing. And it all revolved around Whelan's "due diligence", and Ronnie's insistence that people were going missing. "My mother died when I was ten."

"I thought you said you didn't go in for conspiracy theories."

"She was in King's Cross when the terrorists attacked it. No bodies were ever found." Nick paused. Swallowed. "I just want to know."

"That was twelve years ago, right?"

"Yes."

"Then I'm not sure how I can answer you. We can't transport objects or people in the last thirty years. We've been pretty transparent with everyone on that issue, even if some people don't believe us. Near-past transports are inherently risky. The odds of survival, pretty mediocre. We can't even grab particles from those sorts of horizons."

"I just needed to ask before I made my decision."

"I didn't mean to be insensitive," continued Whelan. "But there are lots of incidents like the one that killed your mother every year. Lots of accidents in which bodies are never found."

"I know," said Nick, again. "But if she was transported..."

"Then we wouldn't know about it until a few years down the line."

"But could you rescue her? If you wanted to?"

Whelan paused. "Do you know how many requests we get from people who want us to save their relatives? Do you think we would be able to save them all?"

"No."

"Good. Because despite what the crackpots might tell you, people only have one chance to live. Which is a good thing, Nick, because the world doesn't have the resources to provide for two. And it would be cruel, wouldn't it? To be zapped into the future, only to find your baby boy a full-grown man? Maybe it would be different if we could reach back a few hours. But thirty years? Isn't that too much for people to pick up where they'd left off? Didn't Flight 391 prove that? Isn't that why we've gone to such lengths to create our Roman bubble?"

Nick suddenly felt a lump in his throat. It made it difficult to swallow, or speak. "Yes."

"So, this opportunity of a lifetime we're offering you: what are you going to say?"

It was time. And he had his answer ready. He took a deep breath. Tried not to think of what his father would say. "I'm in."

"Good. We'll be in touch."

The phone went dead. Nick continued to hold the phone as if Whelan might call back. Finally he headed for the hallway. "Ronnie!"

No answer. He rapped on the bedroom door, then pushed it open.

The room was empty. The bedcovers were thrown back, the mattress and pillows still showing the impression of a sleeping form. Nick looked about, confused. A cup of coffee sat steaming on the bedside cabinet.

Which meant he hadn't been gone long.

Nick hurried out of the flat and moved down the steps

at speed. How much of his conversation with Whelan had Ronnie overheard?

When he opened the front door, he realised he'd made a mistake. There was a man waiting on the pavement. No, there were three. And Ronnie wasn't among them.

The man in the centre of the group spoke first. "Mr Houghton," he said. "We'd like a word."

14

"CHICKEN OR FISH?"

Nick couldn't help but be disappointed by the question. For one thing, it didn't fit with the plush interior of the private jet. The stewardess smiled amiably and waited for his answer. If he'd been on a commercial flight, her eyes would have already been filled with impatience but, given how few people were on board, she probably had more than enough time to deal with indecisive passengers.

"Just water," said Nick, feeling his tongue sticking to the roof of his mouth. He'd forgotten how much he hated flying. The drone of the engines and the dry atmosphere of the cabin always seemed to give him a headache. He could feel a new one starting to drill into his temples, and it hadn't been helped by the requirement to give a blood sample before they'd taken off.

He rubbed at the crook of his arm. "How long until we land?"

"Not long now, sir." It was the same answer he'd been given half an hour ago; the same vagueness with which she'd answered his question about where they were heading. He let his head fall back into the soft beige leather of his seat.

Six weeks. He'd potentially given everything up for just six weeks of gainful employment. Nick rapped his fingers gently against the armrest. The throbbing in his temples seemed to turn up a notch as he went back over the last argument he'd had with his father. After all, if it all went wrong, he'd have to crawl back home. And hope everything else fell into place rather than smashing to the ground.

Six weeks. Nick massaged the back of his neck, trying to loosen the muscles in his shoulders. No, all things considered, he needed to make this move permanent. Whatever he found when the plane landed, he needed to impress McMahon. Needed to impress Whelan.

Not that either of the two NovusPart bosses were travelling with him. He glanced around, casting his eye over the four other passengers: two men, a woman and a small child. Most of the seats – about twenty in total – were empty. The aircraft wasn't laid out as generously as he'd seen in some magazines, but it was clearly expensive. About a third the size of a jumbo, the interior had a single column of seats running down each wall. They were more like easy chairs than normal airline seats.

"Put that down!"

Nick glanced over his shoulder. The woman and child were sitting in the rear of the cabin. From the sound of it, the boy's patience with the flight had finally run out. He was maybe eight or so, and had been remarkably quiet up until this point. The woman – probably his mother – looked to be in her late thirties. She was thin, almost gaunt. Her blonde hair was tied back into a tight bun, perhaps in an effort to keep herself looking young.

Nick turned back towards the front of the plane. The two men flying with them looked like NovusPart security. Both were thick-set, and hadn't moved since they'd sat down.

"Sir?"

The stewardess had returned with his water. It was in a short, thick-rimmed glass more suited to holding liquor than anything softer. A couple of pills were set down beside it. Nick took them to be another round of antibiotics. The third since he'd been picked up from home. A quick flush of his system, they'd said, while they checked his blood sample. Which was all fine, given the risks involved. He swallowed the pills with a quick gulp, turned back to the window and looked down over the sea.

The thought of going to a foreign country had been enough to trigger his latest headache. He'd only realised after they'd passed three or four road signs that they were heading towards an aerodrome, and he'd be expected to board a plane. Which should have been obvious, if he'd stopped to think about it. After all, NovusPart couldn't exactly build the new Pompeii in Britain. Not where every little bit of gossip made the local news.

Nick reached into his pocket for his phone and glanced briefly at the screen before pushing it back. The display confirmed they'd been airborne for three hours, and he had no messages. Not even any reception. Of course not, he thought. They were thousands of feet in the air. The realisation caused another twinge of pain through his right eyeball.

"Sir?"

The stewardess again. She was holding out a slimline media player. Nick glanced at it, but years of avoiding campus leaflets meant he didn't bite.

"Sir, this is your inflight entertainment."

"I have a bit of a headache coming on."

"It's a present from Mr Whelan."

Six weeks to make an impression. Nick grunted and took the device. As soon as he did, the stewardess disappeared back up the aisle. Confused, he pressed the headphones into his ears. The player had several audio files loaded on to it, and Nick half expected to find some cheesy briefing from McMahon or Whelan. He selected the first track. There was a hiss of static, and then a voice started to speak. In Latin.

His initial reaction was to laugh. Although he recognised the words, the pronunciation was off; like someone reading aloud without any background in the Classics. But then it clicked. The voices belonged to Romans. Real Romans.

Brief snatches of dialogue, the voices those of men, women and children. They were saying their names, where they were from, what they did for a living. It didn't sound much like the Latin he'd been taught at school, or the vulgar idiom of the graffiti on the walls of Pompeii. No, this was an earthy vernacular. Latin spoken as a man from the East End of London might speak Cockney.

Nick listened to the tracks several times. On the first pass, he was just happy to hear the voices. On the second, he noticed the strange use of inflection and rhythms. On the third, he started to pick out common phrases.

He suddenly needed another drink. A real one. Because it was true. McMahon had done it. And he was on his way to a place where there were real Romans. And not just any Romans. People from the heyday of the Empire. Nick searched for the stewardess.

Where the hell was she?

"I'm going to be a Roman soldier!"

Nick looked round. The young boy had come to stand by his seat. He held a short foam sword in front of him. Nick leant forward. "That's great," he said. "Do you think they'd let me join the army too?"

"Noah!"

The boy's mother was out of her seat. Her pale features were drawn tightly together. She didn't even look at Nick. Instead, she took hold of the young boy's shoulders, and started to pull him away.

"Hi," said Nick, trying to make eye contact. "Your boy seems quite excited about our trip."

The woman's eyes narrowed. "You're going to New Pompeii?"

Nick raised his eyebrow slightly. The blood in his temples continued to thump. "Nick Houghton." He held out his hand. The woman ignored it.

"Maggie Astridge," she said. "And this is Noah."

Nick smiled at the boy, letting his arm drop. "You've been listening to the recordings too?"

The woman shook her head. "No – we don't speak Latin. Robert and I will have interpreters."

"Robert?"

"My husband," she said, as if the fact was obvious. "The project architect." She looked like she was about to say something more, but caught sight of his media player. "If you're listening to those recordings you must be Professor Samson's replacement?"

Replacement? Nick shook his head. "I'm going to join Professor Samson's team," he said, suddenly uncertain. He needed to change the subject. "Do you know how much longer we're going to be in the air?"

"We should be almost there!" piped up Noah. He lifted his foam sword and pushed it into Nick's shoulder. The action was too quick for his mother to prevent, but there was no force behind the blow.

"Have you been there before?" asked Nick, smiling at the boy.

"I had a preview before the rabble moved in," Maggie replied, "but this is Noah's first time. We were meant to arrive two weeks ago, but someone got a cold, didn't he?"

Noah suddenly looked as proud as his mother looked irritated. "Yes, he did!"

Nick's smile wavered as he tried to ignore the possibility that his own blood test might delay his arrival. Maggie started to look a little embarrassed. Like she wanted to stop talking and get back to her seat. Behind her, the stewardess reappeared.

"Okay, everyone – can we all get back into our seats for landing, please!"

15

"THE INTERESTING THING, therefore, is that the Big Bang provided the first temporal momentum."

It was about ten minutes into the lecture, and Kirsten was already lost. As soon as her eyes had fluttered open, she'd left the bathroom and headed for the lecture theatre. Just as she had so many times before.

She never knew how many months had passed between visits. If she'd be early, or years late. Every time she woke up she was in a different – well – time. But on this occasion, as she'd stepped into the quad, she'd seen the lights burning in the auditorium and had known she would make it.

Yet she didn't even know why she wanted to be there.

Maybe she didn't. Maybe it was just the promise of seeing some familiar faces. As it was, Octo Arlen was doing most of the talking.

Kirsten smiled. Arlen looked uncomfortably at the large audience, his cheeks drained of colour. But whatever the reason for him taking the lead, he now stood before an audience of about fifty people explaining his theory of virtual particles. Whelan and McMahon both sat to one side. Whelan looked stern and attentive, almost like he was on the verge of giving a salute. McMahon, on the other hand, didn't seem to want to be there. He was slumped in his seat and appeared distracted.

"Okay," continued Arlen. "I'll try to summarise." He paused, before reaching for some water. His hand was clearly shaking. "I'm sure you're all aware that you cannot empty a glass jar."

Kirsten felt her eyebrows rise, and she glanced at the rest of the spectators. Quite a lot of them looked as confused as she felt. Then again, few of them appeared to be scientists. This was an audience drawn from the great and good of the college. Some were maybe in charge of funding. Perhaps a lot was at stake.

"Sure, you can tip out anything you've put in the jar," continued Arlen, his voice cracking and uncertain. "You can suck all the air out and create a vacuum. But the jar still won't be empty. All you'll have is a jar of empty space. And space isn't empty. It's like a pond, teeming with life." He paused. Swallowed. "What we have, in fact, is a jar that at any one time is full of 'particle pairs', which appear from the vacuum, and then annihilate each other before we have opportunity to measure them."

Kirsten blinked. Now she was really lost.

"This theory of 'particle pairs' was first hypothesised in the twentieth century during the heyday of quantum physics. Hawking theorised that you'd only see these 'particle pairs' at the boundaries of black holes where they're created on either side of the event horizon – meaning one is sucked into the singularity whereas the other escapes.

You will all have read the news stories when this was first observed by the James Webb Space Telescope. But the real mystery remained." Arlen seemed to be finally finding his rhythm. "Where do these particle pairs come from?" He waved his hand towards Whelan and McMahon. Neither man acknowledged his gesture. "All matter was created during the Big Bang. Novus Particles promotes the theory that this matter wasn't just ejected outwards in space, but was also propelled forward in time. The matter we see is only that which is travelling forward in time at the same rate. The particle pairs we observe in the vacuum are those travelling either more slowly, or more quickly, than our native matter. We zip past them – or they zip past us – just long enough for us to theorise about their existence. The black-hole effect identified by Hawking is merely the impact of a gravitational singularity slowing down a particle's forward temporal movement to a speed that we can observe."

Arlen was about to continue, but a loud cough at the back of the theatre stopped him. "Okay, Octo. If all matter is just simply stuff travelling forward through time, how does it all stay together in one place? Why doesn't it just fly apart?"

Arlen took another mouthful of water. A look of irritation passed over his face. "I'm sure you'll agree that two spacecraft travelling at twenty thousand miles an hour are still able to gradually come together and dock."

"I think I can see where this is going," said another voice from the crowd. Kirsten tried to locate it, but the source was lost among a sea of greying hair. "The conclusion of your theory is that time travel becomes possible… but you fall foul of the same logical test as everyone else. If time travel is possible, where are all the time travellers?"

A ripple of laughter. Whelan and McMahon shifted uncomfortably in their seats. Arlen's face, however, flashed with a mix of embarrassment and anger. Kirsten remembered him as quite a nervous youth; it was clear he wasn't ready to deal with hecklers. "The Big Bang threw particles forward in time," he repeated. "I think it's perfectly possible for a particle pair to be taken from the past – or the present – and taken into what we perceive to be the future. But a particle pair existing in the future cannot move into the past. They would be swimming against the tide."

"So no time travellers?"

"No. Not moving backwards anyway."

"But you'd still end up with paradoxes," the voice persisted. "Therefore, the question still holds. If you take someone from the past, you will alter history. And, if you're right, it would *already* have been altered, and we would probably know about it. So where are all the time travellers, Octo?"

Arlen glanced behind him for help but neither Whelan nor McMahon responded. But then he smiled. Almost as if a new thought had sparked in the recesses of his mind. "There could be exceptions," he said, finally relaxing. "For instance, what if you only took people with no futures. Say those about to die and whose bodies would never be found? How could they impact on history?" He paused. The room had fallen silent. "After all, they'd already be dead."

Kirsten started to shake. A white mist had started to thicken in front of her eyes. Which meant her time here was running out. But she could still see enough of the theatre to notice that McMahon was suddenly alert. He was leaning forward in his seat – mouth slightly open. *They'd already be dead.*

"I was speaking hypothetically, of course," Arlen continued, suddenly breaking into nervous laughter. His voice became distant as Kirsten felt herself floating away. "That isn't what NovusPart are proposing. But as the great Roman philosopher Seneca once wrote, 'There is no genius without some touch of madness.'"

There was silence. Finally, a single voice called out: "And what *are* you proposing?"

"Power, gentlemen." Whelan got to his feet. "If you can slow particles from a faster temporal stream into our own, then we can effectively create matter. And from matter flows energy. We're basically looking to solve the world's energy crisis. Let Dr Arlen continue, please. We'll take questions at the end."

16

Nick had only just screwed his eyes shut when a light tap on his arm forced him to open them. Wincing at the pain in his head, he followed the point of Noah's finger. Bathed in the orange light of the descending sun, he saw a Roman villa.

He squinted. His migraine was a lot worse, and the small turn of his head was enough to make his surroundings spin. Noah leant forward to say something, but the boy's voice was lost in the incessant thump of the rotors above them. Rotors. Nick shuddered. After their initial flight, he, Maggie and Noah had boarded a helicopter. The other two men hadn't joined them for the second part of the journey.

The small aerodrome where they'd made their pit stop revealed they'd been heading into old Soviet territory. The buildings had been nothing more than concrete bunkers – and they'd been set among a grey, decaying urban sprawl. It didn't take much to imagine a golden hammer and sickle once adorning the sides of the buildings. Or a statue of men saluting the revolution.

Nick glanced at his watch. They'd been in the air another couple of hours. The helicopter engine now seemed to be in perfect time with the beating inside his head. He needed something to distract him. He stared out of the window and tried to concentrate on the villa below.

The building was set among vineyards, with larger crops of cereals nearby. A simple, narrow track led away from it and disappeared down a valley. There was no sign of any other properties. The track itself stopped at the villa entrance. There was only one way in or out.

Nick paused to swallow the bile collecting in the back of his mouth. There was a good chance he was going to be sick. He could feel his stomach churning. *Swallow*, he thought. *Breathe. Then swallow. And concentrate on something*. He slumped forward – letting his harness take his weight.

The villa looked newly built, its whitewashed walls topped by a flow of soft red tiles. It seemed well laid out, made up of two large adjoining wings with front and rear façades. The arrangement created a central, private courtyard. As the helicopter came in lower, it became clear the space was being used as a car park for about half a dozen khaki-coloured Land Rovers. And there was a large, black satellite dish pointing upwards from the villa's roof.

So much for authenticity. Nick sat back and tried to relax, but the helicopter was vibrating like a washing machine on full spin. Opposite him, Maggie mouthed something but he couldn't tell what she was saying. Instead, he just gave her a thumbs-up and waited. It didn't take much longer for the rotors to start whipping up dust. A few bumps almost made him vomit, but then the landing skids made contact with the ground. Once. Twice.

He'd made it.

"Okay folks!" shouted the pilot. The doors clicked open. Nick didn't wait to be helped. He pushed the door outwards and stumbled to the ground. He took a couple of steps – and felt nausea wash over him. But he wasn't sick.

Not yet, anyway.

"I thought you were going to spew!"

Nick smiled weakly at Noah. Behind him, Maggie was the last to leave the helicopter. The pilot remained at his controls.

"Is this it?" Noah sounded tired, but his head bobbed around, his eyes taking in their surroundings. He looked both confused and disappointed. His mother didn't seem interested in trying to cheer him up.

Slowly, Nick tried to find his bearings. The helicopter had landed at the front of the villa. He pushed at the ground with his foot. They were standing on Grasscrete. It was a purpose-built helipad, but one that wouldn't be obvious to a casual observer.

Shielding his eyes from the setting sun, he peered towards the building. The villa's entrance was nothing more than a large archway in its front wall. Through it, he could clearly see the Land Rovers in the courtyard beyond. There wasn't any other obvious way in or out. Nick squinted. There was somebody heading towards them.

"Maggie! Noah!"

If he hadn't been in the grip of a migraine, Nick would have laughed. Mark Whelan was heading towards them; the NovusPart COO was wearing a dull white toga. It didn't look like he knew how to wear it, the cloth flapping around his body, caught up in the rotor wash. "Come on. Let's get you inside!"

Whelan let Maggie and Noah scurry past him before moving to block Nick's path. "I'm glad you decided to join us," he said. "I think you're going to enjoy the next few weeks."

Nick forced a smile. It caused another spike of pain to shoot through his temples. "Hopefully I'll be here for longer than that."

Whelan didn't confirm or deny it. "You have a phone?" he said.

Nick nodded.

"You don't need it here. You probably noticed we were blocking your signal from the moment we picked you up?"

Nick shook his head. He hadn't noticed, but now the lack of messages made sense. "You seem to have found a nice, isolated location."

"We have a good agreement with the locals. They're more than happy to give us the privacy we require." Whelan paused, as if mulling something over. "We weren't entirely straight with you when we last met."

Nick braced himself, but then remembered what Maggie had said. "Professor Samson?"

"Yes. He left the project some months ago."

"So you see me as…?"

Whelan glanced over his shoulder, but Maggie and Noah were long gone. "A lot of people attached to this project think it can already be classed as a success," he said. "After all, the buildings are finished and the people are living in them. So McMahon wasn't too bothered when

Samson upped and left. But his absence effectively leaves us blind, and lots of people are waiting for us to fail." The operations chief paused. "You want to do your research, which is fine. Because what you find may help us detect any issues with this imperial idyll."

"You're worried about trouble?" Nick blinked. The ground seemed to be spinning.

Whelan started to shepherd him towards the villa. "The people of Flight 391 weren't put in a glass box," he said. "They weren't tricked into thinking they'd somehow survived the crash. What we're doing here is different; we can't afford to make mistakes. We needed someone who has a bit more understanding of the Roman world."

"That's a lot of work to get through in just six weeks."

"Don't focus on the timescale," said Whelan. "It's not important. In my experience, people are either useful, or nothing more than dead wood. And it won't take long to figure out which category you fit into."

Nick felt another twist of pain ratchet through his skull. "That's not very reassuring," he said. His mouth suddenly filled with saliva. He was finally going to vomit. There was no stopping it. Whelan waited until he'd finished without showing any sympathy. "Travel sickness?"

Nick nodded, saying nothing.

"Well, let's get you inside," Whelan continued, as if nothing had happened. "It's in both our interests that you make the best of it."

* * *

It only took a loud growl from his stomach to wake Nick the next morning. Incessant nausea had stopped him from eating anything the night before, but now his body had reset. It was ready for a good meal.

He rolled on to his back and sat up. Although he'd drunk plenty of water before going to sleep, his tongue felt dry. He could taste the grittiness of the aspirin he'd taken to dull his migraine.

He glanced around. He hadn't taken much notice the previous night, but his room looked more like a budget hotel than the inside of a Roman villa. The realisation was disappointing. The flat-pack furniture might have been obtained from the nearest IKEA. All plywood and pine. The walls were painted a simple cream, and the only hint of character came from a single painting hanging on the opposite wall. Four large blocks of primary colour.

Character maybe, but not interest. He still seemed a long way from Pompeii.

Nick let a sigh escape his lips. He got out of bed and walked into the small en-suite bathroom. A couple of white plastic cups sat by the sink, each wrapped in cellophane. He pulled one free and filled it with water.

When he returned to the main room, he saw that someone had left him homework. There was a small desk up against the far wall, on it a pile of paperwork. Nick stepped across and started to leaf through it. A series of reports, drawings and maps.

The first report looked like a design manual. The sketches were rough – not detailed designs – but each page showed a different element of the town. From a basic layout to concepts for bathhouses, temples and water systems. Another document showed the elevation of several buildings.

Nick recognised each element. Most had been taken from the ruins of Pompeii. But others looked like they'd been taken from Rome, Ostia, or even the forts and villas that had been left dotted around the British Isles, Turkey and the northern coast of Africa.

The name "Robert Astridge" was on most of the drawings, inside a title block that ran along the bottom of each page. It was accompanied by specific reference codes, and a small box documenting the approvals. Nick thought back to the plane. The woman – Maggie – had called herself "Astridge".

Designed by Robert Astridge. Approved by Professor Samson.

Nick stiffened. Some of the drawings were missing Samson's signature. He went back through the pile, checking each one. Most had been signed off by both Samson and Astridge, but about thirty per cent had only been approved by the architect.

Nick shook his head and pulled out the last document. It turned out to be a large map, too big for the desk. He stepped across to the bed to open it out. He found himself looking at a large-scale town plan. Again, Samson's signature was missing from the approvals box. His mouth pulled into a slight smile when he noted the map's title: *New Pompeii*.

Nick tried to pick out the detail from among the

general arrangement. The town was longest on its east–west axis, with a curtain wall surrounding it. Eight gatehouses – five along its north wall, and three along the southern – marshalled its defences. The forum was located in the south-west of the town, and a large oval amphitheatre was set into its opposite corner.

Just like in Pompeii.

The rest of the town was laid out around a simple grid pattern. The effect created solid blocks of buildings between the roads. It, too, resembled what was known about the layout of the real Pompeii. And yet there was something odd about it that he just couldn't place.

What was it?

Nick softened his focus, letting his eyes wander along the grid. At the centre of the map – slightly off-set to the north – was a building shaded red. He ran his finger down to the key. *The House of McMahon.*

Arrogant prick.

"Nick? You're feeling better?"

Nick turned to find Whelan filling the doorway. The NovusPart Chief Operating Officer was still wearing his toga. However, without the interference of the wind, he at least now carried it with some degree of authority.

"Yes, thank you."

"Good. You'll be pleased to know your blood samples all came back clear, so you're free to travel to the town." He nodded towards the plans. "Astridge thought you might want to review those, seeing as you didn't seem to be taking in much last night."

"Thanks."

Whelan was holding a small bundle of clothes, which he tossed on to the bed. The action made Nick painfully aware that he was wearing only his boxer shorts.

"Leave all your belongings in this room," continued Whelan. He was already turning to leave. "Once you're dressed, come down to the control room for a final briefing. And some breakfast. It's just off the courtyard."

Nick nodded, but waited until the other man had left before starting to dress. The clothes he'd been provided with were basic: a tunic, a leather belt and sandals. Nick laid them out on the bed, considering them each in turn. It was apparent he'd not been considered worthy of a toga. Still, as he wasn't officially a Roman citizen, he could live with the snub.

He picked up the tunic first. It immediately stirred up the image of overenthusiastic historical re-enactments in muddy fields. He sighed. The potential to end up looking like a Sunday Roman was very real, and something he was keen to avoid. At least he couldn't look worse than the men paid to stand outside the Colosseum dressed up as gladiators.

But he could come close. Nick hesitated for a few more seconds before pulling the tunic over his head. It was the same dull white colour as Whelan's toga, but he was pleased to find the wool was at least smoother than he'd anticipated. Still, he had to roll his shoulders a few times to get it to fall into a comfortable position.

After tightening his belt, he found the most important

item on the bed had been initially hidden from view by the rest of the clothes. A small pouch, filled with money. He tipped the contents out into his hand, and counted the coins. They were good replicas. Nick tied the pouch on to his belt. He was ready.

17

THE ROUTE DOWN to the courtyard should have been pretty straightforward, but Nick had been shown to his room the previous night by one of Whelan's security guards, and the mental image he'd constructed of the villa wasn't quite as clear as he'd thought. Somehow, on the way down, he'd taken a wrong turn.

Given the modest size of the building, getting lost was some achievement. Nick turned back the way he'd just come – past what looked like a children's nursery and several medical offices. He soon came to a halt again. A man was watching him from one of the side rooms, and Nick's scowl quickly turned into an embarrassed grin. "Hi," he said. "I'm looking for the courtyard?"

The man didn't respond. He was in his thirties, and was wearing one of the same off-white tunics that Nick had been given. He took a couple of steps forward. The light from the corridor caught the mottles and pocks covering his face.

"I do not speak your tongue," the man said in perfect Latin.

Nick nodded dumbly, his mind whirring. This was a

Roman. Not in New Pompeii, but right here. Right now. "I'm sorry," he said, stumbling over his words and hoping they sounded intelligible. "Do you understand me now?"

The man smiled. Like he was speaking to a child learning to talk. "You're one of the new arrivals?"

"Yes."

"And you're looking for the others?"

"I guess I'm lost."

"Aren't we all?" He nodded down the corridor. "You need to be along there, and to the right."

"Thank you."

The man edged back into his room and shut the door. Nick watched dumbly. His mind was bubbling with the questions he could have asked. Should have asked.

Damn it!

He'd frozen. But he'd expected all the Romans to be in New Pompeii. Not here. Not now. Shit. He'd probably get another opportunity. Fuck, he'd *better* get another opportunity.

Nick cursed all the way to the courtyard. As soon as he stepped into the open air, a security guard directed him towards a doorway marked CONTROL ROOM/SHOWROOM. He wondered what sort of show he was going to be treated to.

The room was dominated by row upon row of video screens. Their glare was sufficient to plunge the rest of the room into relative gloom, and it took a few moments for Nick's eyes to adjust but, once they did, he realised that the screens were showing security-camera feeds. And not from the villa.

This was his first glimpse of New Pompeii.

Nick felt his breath grow shallow, his jaw slacken. Each screen showed a different view of town life. And there they were. The people of Pompeii. Moving around the streets of their new home. Eating. Drinking. Buying bread. Rolling dice. Just going about their daily lives. And the fact he'd not really spoken with the first Roman he'd met suddenly didn't seem to matter.

"You like my town?"

Nick heard the words but didn't acknowledge them. It took many more seconds before his attention zeroed back into the room. Maggie, Noah and Whelan were standing next to a tall, thin man. He was completely bald, with a satisfied smile on his face. And from the look of the video feeds, his smugness was entirely deserved.

"Yes," said Nick, his throat dry. "I can't wait to visit."

"Well, it's a few hours by horse. Have you ridden before, Mr...?"

"This is Nick Houghton," cut in Whelan, stepping forward. "Nick, meet Robert Astridge, our project architect."

Nick nodded in acknowledgement, and offered his hand.

The architect shot a glance at Whelan, his grin turning sardonic. "I take it you're here to replace Professor Samson?"

Replace. That word again. Nick glanced at Maggie. She'd been given a longer, female version of his own tunic. A heavy shawl covered her shoulders.

"Yes," he said.

"Well, I don't see your role as being that relevant, to be honest. Samson's work was almost complete – you can't keep on advising about the historical details of a town when the buildings are occupied, can you?" Astridge let out a short bellow of laughter, almost as if something had just struck him. "Patrick is going to love that you're here!"

Patrick?

Maggie shook her head and gave an impatient sigh. "At least you look a bit more human today, Dr Houghton."

"Thank you. But you can drop the doctor part... it's still something of a work in progress."

"I see. It seems odd to have replaced an eminent professor with a student, doesn't it?"

Nick swallowed, not knowing what to say. Certainly Whelan didn't appear to want to cut in and justify his appointment. He needed to change the subject. Quickly. "Someone mentioned something about a briefing?"

"So, Nick," said Whelan, taking a step forward, "what do you think the most important thing is, in making all of this work?"

Nick's mind cycled quickly, trying to find an answer that wouldn't make him look stupid. The buildings? The logistics? The technology?

No.

The people.

It always boiled down to people. He looked back at the screens. Thought about what this all meant from their perspective. "You brought them here just before they were about to die," he said, letting his thoughts click into place. "They would have seen the eruption. Felt the earthquakes in the days leading up to it. Maybe seen the ash fall. So when they woke up here, they would all want to know what had happened."

"Spot on," replied Whelan, smiling. "It's all about the story. Anybody going into and out of New Pompeii has to remember it, and stick to it. We've tried to keep it simple. The people here think they're still in Pompeii. A good three-quarters of the town is physically similar; the eruption and tremors account for the changed landscape beyond the walls."

"So no volcano?"

"And no sea either – we're inland."

Nick felt his eyebrows rise, but didn't say anything. The strangeness of the town map suddenly made sense. Pompeii had been a trading port. But there was plenty of evidence that Pompeii and the neighbouring town of Herculaneum had experienced their fair share of sea-level changes. So it wasn't entirely implausible...

"The Italian peninsula is in chaos," Whelan continued. "Travel between towns is prohibited. They have to stay in the town and make the best of it." Whelan's voice rose, as if taken in by the story himself. "By order of the Emperor."

Nick nodded but said nothing. He already had about a dozen questions, but they would probably be best answered when he got to the town.

"The good news is that the populace were so shell-shocked they believed the story straight away," said Astridge. "We've got them all settled into their new homes. And most people are in similar standards of accommodation to that to which they were accustomed."

"How's the economy working?"

Whelan turned to Astridge. "You see, Robert? I knew our new historical advisor would get to the nub of the issue." He turned back to Nick. "We're getting there," he said. "Pompeii seems to have made its money mainly from wine."

"And garum."

"Yes. Quite. But once the vineyards and olive groves are up and running, we can take their wine and oil, and in return give them anything they want. But we're supporting the economy externally for the time being."

"What about us?"

"You didn't find your little pouch of money?"

"That's not what I meant…"

"We have a house at the centre of town."

"The House of McMahon?"

"Yes. It looks Roman on the ground floor, but is in fact a central control station similar to this villa."

"Great," said Nick. "But, again, with due respect… you said all the population is from Pompeii. But *we're* not. What's our story?"

Whelan smiled. "We're their saviours, Nick."

"What?"

Astridge chuckled. "Sent by the god-emperor himself, Augustus Caesar."

18

IT WAS ONLY mid-morning by the time they were ready to go to New Pompeii but the sun had already baked the air dry. Nick was glad to discover that he wasn't expected to ride a horse. Outside the villa, a convoy of eight wagons had converged, most of which were filled with wheat, beans and fruit, while others contained a variety of iron tools and implements presumably to help support the town. The wagon at the back of the column was empty apart from two benches that ran the length of its parapets. Nick initially struggled to clamber up into it, but soon found himself being given a boost by a NovusPart security guard. The Astridge family joined him a few minutes later, the architect sitting up front with the driver, with Whelan the last to arrive.

The operations chief was the only one who didn't require any assistance getting into the wagon. He simply vaulted into the back. As he sat down, Nick noted Whelan had opted to lose the toga and instead just wore a tunic. He was also wearing a black leather wrist-guard, which encased his right forearm. Its only decoration was a series of metal studs that marked out the shape of an eagle.

Nick glanced towards their driver, a NovusPart employee. They didn't seem to be going anywhere fast. The wagon remained stationary, the two mules fidgeting in their traces. "You don't use labour from the town to drive the wagons?"

Whelan shook his head, and started to fiddle with the straps on his wrist-guard. "We don't allow anyone from the town up here," he said. "Too much risk they'll see something they shouldn't."

"But the guy in the villa?"

Whelan's eyes narrowed. "You met Felix?"

"He didn't tell me his name."

"He looks like he's had the pox."

Nick nodded. "I bumped into him, yes."

Whelan paused, considering. "We transported him five years ago. Part of the vanguard we used to test the business model. He was a merchant, owned a small fleet trading spices and ore, and so was able to give Samson decent insights into the top brass. Difficult to know what to do with him now. You probably heard his voice on the tapes."

Nick shrugged. He might have done. But Samson's recordings had contained so many voices he'd need to listen several times before he'd be able to remember them all. From the front of the wagon, Astridge stirred. "Ironic that the first Roman you meet is the main reason your predecessor left."

"Oh?"

"Well, how could he continue to give me advice when I could simply ask Felix?"

Nick frowned. "The opportunity to speak to these people must surely have been enough to keep him here."

"Like most academics, Samson took any chance he could get to stroke his own ego. Let me give you an example, *Dr* Houghton. What would you say the people did when Vesuvius first started erupting?"

Nick hesitated. *Dr* Houghton. It was clear Astridge wasn't going to let it drop. And he could also tell where his line of questioning was leading. Whatever he said would be wrong, because Astridge would know the definitive answer whereas he would just be guessing. But the architect was waiting for an answer. As was Whelan. He had to prove he knew his stuff. "The traditional view is that a few people stayed, but most fled."

"You mean they left their houses to be looted?"

Nick didn't answer.

"The problem is one of hindsight," said Whelan, cutting in. "If there's an earthquake, sure, you run outside and wait for it to stop. But do you abandon everything permanently *on the chance* there might be a second or third? No, of course not. So most people stayed. They hired people to fix their houses, and they tried to make the best of it."

"And when the volcano erupted?"

"Where would you go? Where would be safe?"

Pliny's words flashed into his mind. *I was convinced that all mankind were involved in the same calamity, and that I was perishing with the world itself.* "Inside the town walls," Nick said.

From the front of the wagon, Astridge gave a slow clap. Whelan ignored him, but the sarcastic gesture seemed to amuse his wife. Noah laughed too, but Nick doubted he got the joke. "The town's population actually grew just before the eruption," Whelan said. "People didn't flee the town; they fled towards it, even people in outlying farmsteads. And running through deep ash is not easy; I can assure you of that. They congregated in the forum, and the temples, and the amphitheatre, and they waited for the storm to pass."

"I suppose that made it easier for you."

Whelan nodded. "The targets were all clustered in a few places when we transported them."

"And you managed to transport pretty much the whole town?"

"Yes."

A thought nagged at the back of Nick's mind. "But the plaster casts?" he said. "In the Naples Archaeological Museum?"

"We failed in about two thousand cases," replied Whelan. He gave the fact neutrally, like he was taking inventory.

"There are only about a thousand recorded remains."

"And a lot more bodies under the unexcavated areas of town. The ash cloud made things difficult."

Nick paused, mulling things over. The wagon still hadn't moved. "And, despite all this, Samson left?"

Whelan gave a shallow smile. "We don't know why he left, Nick. But he did, and that's why you're here."

"I told you," said Astridge, trying to stop Noah from leaning over the edge of the wagon. He waited for his son's protests to stop before continuing. "He left because he no longer had a monopoly on answers. So, Dr Houghton, if *you* could use this town to answer only one question, what would it be?"

A few points of interest immediately spun through Nick's brain, but there was only one really worth asking first. "The date of the eruption," he said.

Astridge and Whelan both looked at him, clearly confused.

"There's some debate," Nick continued. "Because although the traditional date of the eruption is the twenty-fourth of August, there's evidence it happened later." He felt his voice weaken. "Though I guess to transport them you would have needed an exact date."

Whelan shifted on the bench. "That's not actually how our tech works, Nick. We just find the general timeframe and then look for the radar spots to converge and blink out—"

"Evidence?" interrupted Maggie. "Such as?"

At first Nick didn't answer. Whelan's remark was the most he'd heard anybody reveal as to how NovusPart's technology actually operated. But finally he settled back into his groove. It was time to stroke his own ego, as the architect had put it.

"Mainly it centres on the types of food archaeologists have found in people's homes. Pomegranates, and so on. But there were also some coins found that were minted *after* the eruption."

"Well *Professor* Samson never brought this up," said Astridge. "And neither have the people here. They would have said something, don't you think?"

Nick felt his cheeks redden. "As I said, it would just be a question to which it would be useful to have an answer. It does seem a bit of a coincidence though that the volcano was said to erupt the day after the festival of Vulcan. Almost as if the August date was being used to make a political and moral point."

"Well, as Robert says," said Whelan, "it doesn't seem to be a problem. Although insights like these are no doubt useful."

From the front of the wagon, Astridge allowed a sigh of contempt to escape him. Nick struggled for something else to say. Something more abstract that couldn't be as easily challenged. "It would also be useful to get to know about how people lived at the bottom of the social pile," he said. "Away from the Plinys and Senecas of the Roman world. For example, one of the best sources we have about ordinary Roman life is actually nothing more than a joke book."

"A joke book?" Maggie turned her attention on him, a slight smile on her lips. "Would you care to give us one? To pass the time before we get under way?"

No. No he wouldn't. But now Noah was looking at him expectantly. Shit. "Okay," he said, taking a breath. A funny Roman joke. Which was a stretch. Most didn't translate particularly well. "Okay," he said again, trying to focus on an anecdote he'd recited during a recent tutorial. "So an absent-minded professor, a barber and a bald trader are walking to Rome. On the way, they have to camp overnight in an area known for bandits so they each agree to take a turn standing watch, and the barber takes the first shift. However, he soon gets bored and decides to shave the professor's head. Once his watch ends, the barber wakes the professor who scratches his head and says, 'Oh that silly barber! He's only gone and woken up baldie by mistake!'"

Nick managed to laugh even though he was joined only by Noah. Astridge gave him a withering look. His own bald head was already growing red in the mid-morning heat. "Hilarious, Dr Houghton. Hilarious."

19

IT WAS ANOTHER five minutes before the wagon pulled away.

Any number of alternative Roman jokes had already come to mind, none of which would have caused any offence. But Nick remained silent and waited for the convoy to pick up some momentum. Fortunately, it didn't take long before two men on horseback drew level with them to provide some distraction from his faux pas.

Nick recognised one as a security guard from the villa, though both had adopted the uniform of a Roman cavalryman. They looked fairly impressive with their mail tunics and bronze helmets but their legs dangled inelegantly. It took a while for Nick to determine the reason – stirrups had been unknown to the Romans, and without them the men had been left to wobble between the four horns that jutted up from each corner of their saddles. Still, if the men's presence was to provide security, then the thin lances held out in front of them would prove more than effective. As would the short-swords and daggers at their sides. But it did beg another question. "Have you had any problem with violence?"

Whelan cast him a sideways glance. "Not really."

"But won't it look odd to the locals that we've got our own guards?"

"No," replied Whelan. "It fits the story." He waited a few seconds before continuing, the wagon's speed and the unevenness of the road forcing him to take a firm grip on the wagon's side. "You've got to keep in mind, Nick, we're not going to their Pompeii. *We* haven't travelled in time. They have. They're living by rules we create, in our town."

Nick nodded. The Italian peninsula in chaos. Travel between towns prohibited. Yes, it fitted. It was sensible that each convoy was guarded – every ounce of food protected.

"You've had no problems convincing the people we're gods?"

"Technically we haven't claimed to be deities."

"Just the agents of one?"

"Precisely. And we've specifically chosen a god these people already believed in, the deified Emperor Augustus. Sent to protect them in their darkest hour."

Nick remained silent.

"You're not convinced?"

"Roman religion is relatively opaque."

"Go on."

"Well, most modern religions are centred on just one god. But in another two thousand years, our descendants may look back at our culture and think we worshipped any number of deities: Santa Claus, the tooth fairy, even Batman. It doesn't necessarily follow that the Romans believed in all the gods they wrote about. Especially not a real man – emperor or not – who was deified after his death."

Whelan considered this. "Well, fortunately, we tested our story on a small group before we transported the rest of the population."

Nick nodded. A sensible move. "I presume your reconstruction includes the Temple of Fortuna Augusta?"

"Yes."

"And you've reinforced the message how?"

"With smoke and mirrors. It didn't take too much, to be honest. Felix knows that's all it was, of course, but the rest of the population seem to have fallen for it. After all, when you've been sucked out of the jaws of hell and then prodded and poked by our medical teams... Well, let's just say we didn't really have to invoke Clarke's Third Law."

"Clarke?" Nick knew he must have looked confused, but he didn't try to hide it. "I'm not familiar..."

"As in 'Arthur C.'. The science-fiction writer. 'Any sufficiently advanced technology is indistinguishable from magic.' Samson wouldn't shut up about it. You'll understand when we get there."

Nick nodded. The wagon was meandering through the bottom of a shallow valley. On either side, more villas had started to appear. Many looked occupied, and each had a small patch of farmland surrounding them – mainly given over to vines. Other villas along the route were still being constructed. At first he tried to examine the design and origin of each one, but the exercise soon became repetitive. It was the people, not the bricks and mortar, that he really wanted to see. He remembered that Astridge had said that the journey would take several hours by horse. His eyelids drooped.

"Dr Houghton?"

Nick started awake. Astridge was waving lazily in his direction from the front of the wagon. How long had he been asleep? "Sorry," he said. Both Maggie and Noah also looked half asleep. Maggie's face had burned pink. He shifted on the bench to see what the architect was trying to show him.

A dark stain rose above the horizon. Smoke. Nick let out a soft whistle. Smoke – from small fires – all mingling together as it rose into the air. Soon the road widened. He began to make out the northern wall of New Pompeii.

And suddenly there it was. A sight no one could have seen in over two thousand years. Pompeii, brought to life. But it wasn't like anything he had expected. In several places its northern wall had been breached – collapsed inwards. And the stone he'd been expecting to be grey and mottled was instead scorched orange and black.

"Just like it's been hit by pyroclastic flow," said Whelan. Nick noted with some satisfaction that Whelan had a line of saliva on his chin. He wasn't the only one to have nodded off.

The wagon had started to kick up more dust, a thick, dirty-white powder. Nick ran a finger along the side of the wagon and identified the substance pretty quickly. Ash. He turned in his seat. Sure enough, the fields around them were also covered in fine cinders, which grew thicker the closer they got to the town.

"From what you said – and the plans back at the villa – I pictured it differently." He swallowed, trying to stop himself coughing as dust hit the back of his throat. "Something a bit more finished?"

Astridge snorted. "Why would we build something that never existed?"

Nick felt his cheeks flush. But although the architect had been blunt, he was right. "The earthquake in AD 62," he said. "Pompeii was left in ruins, and there's evidence that they were still fixing things when the volcano struck in 79."

"I think you're finally getting it," said Whelan. "And the volcanic damage also plays into our hands."

"Because the northern parts of the real Pompeii aren't yet excavated? So it gives you a ready-made excuse for any parts of the town that aren't quite right?"

Whelan nodded. Nick returned his attention to the town wall. At one spot the scorching was less severe, and the natural grey of the stone was almost visible. It seemed to mark out the shape of a man. Although too small to make out clearly, a few dots of colour and cloth indicated that people were kneeling in front of it. "What's that?"

Whelan leant forward and smiled. "That's where Augustus Caesar stood when he deflected Vulcan's power."

"Seriously?"

"It's part of the smoke and mirrors. Good spot, by the way – most people miss it. We got the idea from Hiroshima."

The Hiroshima shadows: where people's bodies had momentarily protected the surfaces behind them from the flash-burn of the world's first nuclear attack. In some ways, a grisly phenomenon to match Pompeii's own plaster casts. But whereas the plaster casts were just something to be gawped at by tourists, here people were kneeling in front of the northern wall like they'd found the spot where Christ had risen. So did they actually believe the restoration of the town was the work of Augustus Caesar?

As they drew closer to the town they started to pass people standing by the side of the road. Romans. Nick tried not to stare. Each face was intent, watching the food convoy as it passed. Some approached, but the armed escort pushed them back.

"You don't stop them leaving the town's walls?"

"How can we?" Whelan shifted on the bench, looking out towards the town wall. "It's not a prison. But where can they go? We own all the land around here, and the perimeter alarms warn us if anyone gets too far. We shoo them back with nothing more than the power of a Roman army uniform and a loaf of bread. You could describe them as being our flock – and they're sheep that are pretty damn scared of the imperial eagle."

Nick nodded. They were rolling towards a stone gatehouse consisting of three archways – the largest at the centre.

A handful of pedestrians wandered ahead of them – back and forth – through the archway on the left. However, Nick's attention was being drawn to the solid, square tower looming to one side.

"I take it you control the towers and the curtain wall?"

Whelan shrugged. "Don't worry, Nick. We're perfectly safe. You won't need to leap to Mrs Astridge's rescue."

"I should hope not," said Maggie, who had woken up. Nick didn't appreciate the humour but before he could reply he was forced to make a grab for the side of the wagon. The convoy was coming to a halt. From the unordered deceleration and protest from the mules, it didn't look like the driver had expected to slow down so soon.

Nick looked past Whelan's shoulder. A short, fat man had appeared from the gatehouse, and was blocking the way. He wore a tight, badly fitting scarlet tunic, and he spoke in a loud voice with his head raised, not looking directly at the convoy. Rather, he was looking upwards and away – as if the convoy's business was somehow beneath him.

"No wagons are allowed inside the town walls between sunrise and sunset," he shouted. "By the order of the aediles."

Ah, not beneath him. Now Nick understood the man's strange posture. He was just some unfortunate soul who'd been instructed to repeat a proclamation. But Whelan clearly wasn't in the mood to receive orders. He started to get down from the wagon and signalled for Nick to follow. The two cavalrymen brought their horses forward to flank them. Time to put the power of a Roman military uniform to the test.

Whelan came to within a few inches of the fat Roman before turning to Nick. "What did he just say?"

Nick repeated the proclamation in English. "Presumably, you know the aediles? The magistrates in charge of running the town?"

"Yes," said Whelan. "They report to us, as does the *duumvir*. But I wasn't aware of any new rules."

Nick felt a bubble of frustration burst inside him. Aediles. And their de facto bosses, the *duoviri*. All already elected and in position. He needed to get to grips with how this version of the town was set up and fast. "Well this seems to be one of their customs officials," he said. "Checking goods into and out of the town."

A slight wobble of fear rippled around the official's jowls. He kept glancing at Whelan or, more specifically, at the black leather wrist-guard covering his forearm. Why did he seem scared by it?

"Ask him if he knows who we are."

Nick followed the instruction. The official stammered a positive response.

"Good," said Whelan. "Tell him we want to get past."

Nick hesitated. He needed to make an impression. Needed to show he could be useful. "Isn't this just them getting back to normal?" He paused, choosing his words carefully. "Or is it your intention to micro-manage things?"

Whelan glowered, then relaxed. "Good point," he said and turned back to the wagon. Astridge was staring at them. The architect looked sullen. He would clearly just have pushed past if he'd been on his own. "We'll walk the rest of the way," shouted Whelan. "The guards can wait here with the convoy until it's allowed in."

Nick translated Whelan's order for the customs official. The fat man immediately broke into a relieved smile and gave a short bow. Not that Whelan noticed. He was already heading through the gate and into the town.

20

A PART FROM THE odd pedestrian, the gatehouse was quiet. Nick had expected more bustle, but the first buildings they passed looked derelict. A few were little more than piles of rubble, covered with canvas. Others looked like taverns and food stalls that had simply not been reoccupied. Nick glanced back to the road leading out of town. Perhaps without a continuous stream of trade, they'd been permanently abandoned.

"This isn't one of the more interesting approaches," explained Astridge, who was walking with his wife while Noah ran ahead. He wasn't addressing anyone in particular, but rather gesticulating at the buildings in the manner of a tour guide. "If we'd orientated things a bit differently, we'd enter via the forum… It's something we're thinking about changing."

They'd entered the town by one of the central gates along the northern wall. If Nick had been in the real Pompeii, he'd have called it the Vesuvius Gate. And yet they'd not travelled past a volcano. Because there wasn't one. And this wasn't the real Vesuvius Gate.

Shit. He needed to get the real Pompeii out of his

mind. If he was going to be of use to Whelan then he couldn't just rattle off familiar information, because it was now suspect. And if the design manual was anything to go by, then "Augustus Caesar" had made use of many different bits and pieces of Roman architecture to repair as much of the town as he could following the eruption.

Picking up his pace, Nick tried to catch up with Whelan. The man was clearly in a hurry. Fortunately, the road was almost dead straight and, from the plans he'd seen, ran all the way to the southern wall. Indeed, he could just about make out the Stabian Gate on the other side of the town. Or what would have been the Stabian Gate. If he'd been in Pompeii.

Nick cursed and wiped sweat from his brow. Even though he was no longer walking in direct sunlight, it was baking hot. According to the plans he'd seen at the villa, the streets between the gatehouses were the widest in the town, but they were still only about three metres across. Alleyways leading off them were narrower still. All in all, the street plan created plenty of shade between the buildings. There was just no movement of air to cool things down. The roads themselves, though, were a good match to those found in the Pompeii he knew – right down to the trademark high kerbs and narrow pavements. They made no sense in a modern town, but here they seemed perfect.

He instantly felt better. He was really here, surrounded by real Romans. What did it matter if the scenery wasn't perfect? He inhaled deeply – and quickly regretted it. The ash and volcanic black rock of the pavement hid a layer of litter, which had accumulated along the kerb edge and was starting to spread like a web across the road. The further into the town they walked, the more there was: matted straw, rotten food, and animal dung. The smell started to get worse. Piss and shit. Some of it likely human.

The unpleasant smell brought to mind the city drawings. Astridge had stayed true to Roman plumbing – which probably meant only the grandest houses would have running water. Somewhere, possibly close, would be a communal toilet where he'd be able to see the true face of Roman society. But, in the middle of the night, wouldn't it be easier to sling your piss into the street than walk to the local convenience?

Of course it would. Nick tried to focus on where he was putting his feet, but couldn't stop his eyes wandering to the buildings that lined the street. The walls looked freshly painted, but they were already covered in a thin layer of soot and dust, as well as graffiti. Some were election slogans for candidates for the posts of aedile and *duumvir*. Others were nothing more than badly drawn phalluses.

Nick broke into an involuntary schoolboy smirk. The real Pompeii was riddled with penises. Most academics argued they were just symbols of good luck or good fortune; others said they pointed in the direction of the nearest brothel. Maybe he could catch someone actually drawing one, and ask them just what the hell they thought they were doing.

"Come on, Nick!"

The others were waiting for him about fifty metres

ahead. Noah was waving at him to come along. Maggie was examining her sandals with obvious disgust. She scraped them against the high kerb while Noah, bored of waiting, ran ahead again, pointing at everything and shouting their names.

The kid's in Disneyland, Nick thought. *And, despite everything, aren't I?*

To modern eyes, the entrance to the House of McMahon looked unwelcoming. It certainly didn't appear to be a residential property. Its whitewashed façade was tall and narrow, and it had no windows apart from tiny slits, which sat just below the red slope of its roof. It could have been a prison but for two features: an open doorway leading into a dim corridor, and a couple of small shops operating from cubicles on either side of the main entrance.

Whelan and Astridge strode through the doorway. Maggie hesitated at the threshold, as if suddenly uncertain, but Noah pulled her forward. Nick hung back to examine the terracotta pottery and jewellery fronting one of the gloomy shops. He couldn't make out the stallholder in the dark interior.

"Nick!"

At Noah's shout Nick drew himself away and stepped into the corridor. It immediately felt cool after the heat of the street. He noticed that the entrance could be blocked using a solid oak panel. Presumably it was swung across to close the house up at night. During the day, however, the door to the House of McMahon was left unlocked. But that didn't mean it was unguarded.

Looking down, Nick chuckled. The floor of the passageway was lined with an intricate mosaic of a big, black hound. Underneath were written the words of warning that had served property owners well for at least two thousand years. *Cave canem*. Beware of the dog.

Nick stepped over it and out into a square atrium. A shallow pool dominated the centre of the space, and the soft patter of its fountain was enough to mask the bustle of the street beyond. Overall, it looked like a pretty good match for the idealised townhouse drawn from the ruins of Pompeii – except the paintings lining the walls gave a rather vivid depiction of the eruption of Vesuvius rather than the more typical idyllic scene. Perhaps to scare the locals when they came visiting.

The pool – the *impluvium* – had been positioned directly below an opening in the roof, which allowed in both light and presumably rainwater. A staircase in the far corner of the atrium led upwards to the balconied first storey above. There were several rooms off the atrium itself; if this was modelled on a typical Roman townhouse then at least one of these would be the *triclinium*, the dining room, and the one opposite the front door would be the *tablinum*, the place where a Roman man conducted business. That in turn would lead into the *peristylium*, an open-air courtyard with a garden at its centre surrounded by a *peristyle* or open colonnade, off which would be the kitchen. Eager to find out, he started to walk around the atrium.

"Hey!"

Nick turned at the sudden bark. A stocky man was addressing him in English. Presumably a NovusPart employee, despite his tunic. Nick realised that Whelan and the Astridges had remained close to the entrance. What had he done wrong?

Cave canem. The dog at the door.

"It's okay," said Whelan, placing a hand on the man's shoulder. "Dr Houghton is just exploring his new environment."

"Well, Dr Houghton can wait like everyone else. People don't just wander in from the street."

Nick nodded apologetically and walked back to the others. He returned by way of the far side of the pool so that he could glance into the other rooms leading off from the atrium. Most were small, and appeared to be bedrooms. Maybe one of them would turn out to be his.

The porter coughed loudly, as if to make a point. Nick followed the man's stare downwards. He realised he was standing at the end of a trail of dirt. The rest of the group had all removed their sandals. They were now wearing leather flip-flops, which they'd taken from a pile by the entrance. Nick checked back along his path. Sure enough, he'd trodden detritus from the road into the atrium – and all the way around the pool.

Astridge allowed himself a sneer. "So much for our historian. Ah, Harold!"

Nick turned to find McMahon had entered from the garden. The NovusPart CEO didn't offer a greeting. He was wearing a white toga, which contrasted starkly with his dyed black hair. At his shoulder was a much younger man – from his slight build and general demeanour, he looked to Nick like a fellow post-grad rather than security.

"Good journey?" asked McMahon.

"Yes, apart from the last few minutes," Astridge said. "They've stopped wagons coming in during the day." He glanced towards Whelan. "We decided to accept it."

"Good," replied McMahon. He lumbered forward, shrugging his toga back up on to his flabby shoulder. It carried the purple stripe of a senator. "It was bloody chaos here when I turned up. My convoy got stuck behind a grain wagon. You've built the streets far too narrow!"

"I've built the streets just as they are in Pompeii," replied Astridge.

Both men went silent. McMahon seemed to notice his new member of staff for the first time. Nick shifted his feet, uncomfortable under the man's gaze. McMahon nodded at him. "Well now we can take advantage of some new advice." The CEO didn't seem aware of the mood that had swept over the room. "I have business to discuss with Mark. Patrick" – he indicated the young man beside him – "can give you your first tour of the town."

21

"To be honest, I don't know why you're here."

Nick had barely stepped on to the road before Patrick made his first pointed observation. He decided not to respond. It was clear this guy's nose had been put out of joint, and any effort spent trying to correct it would be wasted.

"We don't need another interpreter," Patrick continued. "And the town is up and running. I don't think we need any more historical advice either."

Nick didn't say anything. It was clear Patrick was just out of university. They were probably about the same age – both belonged to the generation who'd left university when there were no jobs. A degree in a dead language probably hadn't done much to help.

"I was brought here to assist Professor Samson."

"Well, he's not here."

"Do you know where he's gone?"

Patrick shrugged. "No. But as he didn't get on with Astridge, it wasn't much of a surprise." He pointed to a nearby junction. "Well, where first, Dr Houghton?"

Nick didn't respond. The news that Professor Samson had left continued to rattle around his brain. Something wasn't right. Finally he managed to bring his focus back. "How about the forum?"

As they travelled further towards the civic centre, the number of buildings increased: shops, houses and taverns. He recognised a few from the design manual. As with the buildings near the Vesuvius Gate, most showed signs of damage, or were partly covered in white canvas to keep the heat and rain at bay. Others were simply piles of rubble.

And then there were the people. He hadn't taken much notice of the few they'd passed on the way to the House of McMahon, but now he couldn't help but stare. Men, women and children buzzed past them. The variety of faces and the quality of their clothes matched the variation in the buildings. And the narrowness of the street funnelled all the activity together into a hubbub of heat and noise. He'd always thought the Roman way of mixing housing for the poor and rich together would be a good thing to see replicated in a modern city. But to be poor here must be terrible. Constantly reminded of the vast wealth of those living next door.

"Overall, I think we've done a good job," said Patrick, in English. A few pedestrians glanced in their direction, clearly detecting the strangeness of his words but saying nothing. "Though I'm sure you'll be able to tell us otherwise."

Nick didn't respond.

"Sure, we have a few problems – but they're getting less severe. The town will soon be self-sufficient and then we'll be able to spend more time studying it, not just trying to fix it."

Nick nodded. He doubted the town would ever be self-sufficient, but he'd be pleased to be proven wrong.

"Have you noticed their stature?"

"Yes."

The Pompeians were short. Nick realised that he'd noted it subconsciously on their arrival, but as the crowd grew his own usually rather average height became more noticeable. Both he and Patrick were about half a foot taller than even the tallest Roman. The throng was also reasonably young; he spotted few faces that looked over forty, at least by modern standards, and the proportion of children and teenagers was high. And there was something else. The Pompeians were staring back at them. As they passed, clusters of people lowered their voices, glancing at them out of the corners of their eyes.

Nick felt his stomach tighten. These people might be quiet now, but did McMahon have enough men if they turned into a mob? Even with all his tricks, and the imperial eagle? Maybe. Maybe not. He didn't particularly want to find out.

"So you translate for McMahon?"

Patrick nodded. "Yeah. When he's in town. He doesn't speak any Latin. But, then again, he doesn't actually go out much."

"And the people have accepted their new surroundings? They're not suspicious?"

"Of course they're suspicious! But at first the shock kept them quiet, and now they seem to be making the best of it. Wouldn't you? Most of them thought they were going to die. They should be grateful." He continued in a more lively tone. "And here's one of our bathhouses!"

Patrick turned the corner and swept his hand towards a large building. Men and women were milling back and forth from between the small shops built into the side of the structure. Similar to a Roman townhouse, thought Nick. Nothing to be seen from the outside, and no space wasted. About halfway along was a doorway through which only men were passing. He could hear the dull echo of activity inside. He remembered the words of one of his tutors: "If you want to understand Rome you must see its baths." And there they were. Right in front of him.

"It would be good to go in..."

"Maybe later, Nick. Remember, you have plenty of time. The forum's this way."

Patrick started to head towards a giant stone arch between the baths and the building on the other side. Despite his host's eagerness, Nick hovered for a moment. There was a temple near the bathhouse. In some ways it was the focal point of this whole charade: the Temple of Fortuna Augusta. It was typically Roman, with a front-facing portico of five columns supporting a triangular gable that jutted out over the building and its promenade. If he'd been on his own, he would have taken the time to go in. Maybe tomorrow, when Patrick wasn't looking over his shoulder. He noted that few Pompeians seemed to be giving the temple a second glance. It was odd that they weren't flocking to the temple of their supposed saviour.

"Finally restored, I suppose," Nick said. "After being

damaged in the earthquake of AD 62?"

Patrick chuckled. "Yeah; all adds to it. Augustus' temple restored to its former glory."

Through the archway the narrow street spilled out into the large, open space of the forum. Nick exhaled deeply and stood frozen, ignoring the people flowing past him. Although not as grand as the reconstructions he'd seen of Rome's civic centre, the forum still reflected the essence of something that had continued long after the fall of the caesars. Like St Mark's Square, the Grand Place of Brussels, or the long, grassy strip of Washington's National Mall, this was a place where citizens could come and *know* the power of their city.

Astridge's buildings rose to different heights all around the square, but the arrangement of columns, porticos and flanking walls gave the illusion the area was fully contained by a single, interlocking structure. And, unlike the more modest baths and the townhouses, these buildings oozed wealth. Though still capped by a flow of red tiles, they were built of stone, not brick. And there wasn't a trace of damage from the volcano.

"You think we've done an okay job now, Dr Houghton?"

Nick nodded dumbly. He wasn't really listening; he was trying to identify the various buildings. Lining them up in his mind with the ruins he had seen at the real Pompeii, and with artists' recreations from academic works. He stumbled forward.

The Temple of Jupiter stood to his immediate left, dominating the northern end of the forum. As with the

Temple of Fortuna Augusta, a flight of steps led upwards to a platform surrounded by tall, white columns. Inside would be statues of Jupiter, Juno and Minerva. However, unlike its counterpart near the bathhouse, this temple buzzed with activity.

A small crowd waited at the bottom of the steps. The people were quiet, looking expectantly upwards. Several men were standing at the front of the platform. The priest – if that's what he was – wore a full toga, an additional fold of fabric covering his head. Three other men, close to him, were stripped to the waist. Another man was kneeling.

"Can you see it?"

Nick followed the direction of Patrick's finger to the top of the steps. Yes, he could see it. Blood was starting to trickle down the steps. If they'd come a few minutes earlier they might have seen the full ceremony; it was clear an animal had just been slaughtered. The man now kneeling at the top of the steps was trying to divine some sort of message from the poor beast's entrails.

"What have you managed to observe about their religion?"

Patrick shrugged. "Very little. It doesn't interest me. That's your field, Dr Houghton. And good luck with it."

"But surely as someone with a background in the Classics…"

"Eh?"

"You know Latin and Greek?"

"Well, I do now – but my background is in French and Italian."

Another odd choice. But then Nick thought about the recordings. Would a bunch of classicists be that useful? Was it better just to employ general linguists, who didn't have the tendency to speak as though they were quoting Cicero?

"Astridge built several temples," continued Patrick. "But the Pompeians only appear to be interested in this one, another by the Marine Gate, and the one over there."

Nick glanced across the square. He could see the roof of another large temple just outside the main area of the forum in its own enclosure. From the city plans and his knowledge of Pompeii, he knew it was just as large as that dedicated to Jupiter, but it also came with its own colonnaded courtyard. "The Temple of Apollo."

"Yeah. They seem to do most of the sacrifices here, most of the wailing over there."

Nick grimaced, not impressed with his guide's attitude. Religion was central to these people's lives. But with no definitive religious text, no one had any real knowledge of how it all worked. It would be his main task to find out.

With the crowd at the Temple of Jupiter still waiting for their divination, Nick let his gaze roam round the forum. At the far side stood the various civic buildings: the law courts of the Basilica, and the offices of the town council. He'd need to find out how each of these buildings was actually being used. Because no matter how impressive these replicas were, it was the people that mattered here. Everything else was just pastiche.

Nick turned back to Patrick. As he did so, he spotted

a man out of the corner of his eye. The man seemed to be watching them but, before Nick could fully focus on him, he turned and scurried out of the forum.

"Something wrong?"

"I think we've caught someone's interest," said Nick.

Patrick didn't seem to be concerned. "Not unusual. We attract a fair bit of attention. Everyone is waiting for the next miracle."

22

KIRSTEN LET HER mouth break the surface of the water. The freezing cold nipped at every inch of her body. She didn't react to it. The feeling, which had once felt like a thousand needles, no longer caused her any discomfort. She was used to it. She'd woken in the bath more times than she could remember, and now she didn't even feel the need to move.

Yes, she could walk along the corridor; but there would be little point. She could walk down into the quad. Take a look at the noticeboards to find out the date. Listen to some student banter, if anyone was passing. And yet, no matter what she did or where she went, eventually she'd be overtaken by the white haze and brought back to the bath. It was inevitable, and she didn't want to play any more.

Slowly, she let her face slip below the surface and watched as a series of bubbles streamed up from her mouth. She held on for as long as she could, waiting for her body to exhaust its oxygen – and then pushed back to the surface. Why did she need to breathe, if she was already dead?

"You're sure?"

Kirsten turned her head. She was in no rush. These weren't the first people she'd encountered in the bathroom, and they wouldn't be the last.

"Yes. I can see her. She's there. We might not have much time."

They could see her. Kirsten's attention suddenly shifted. Her movement drove a small tide of water over the bath's side and towards the two men standing beside her. Or rather one man and a youth who looked barely out of his teens. Perhaps a student, he seemed to be fixing his attention on her face... and further down. There was a flicker of a smile for just a fraction of a second. The other man beside him was also looking, but clearly not seeing.

"Get on with it then!"

The student leant forward. He wore a pair of round, horn-rimmed spectacles. Their reflection just showed an empty bath. "What is your name?" he asked.

"Kirsten. Kirsten Chapman."

The student repeated what she'd told him.

"Anyone could have found out her name," said the other man. "It was in all the papers."

The student didn't shift his focus. "Mr Black is such a cynic," he said.

"I almost lost my job on the first day," Kirsten said quickly. It was the first thing that came to mind, but something that would have been long since forgotten. "I was late."

Again the student repeated what she'd said. The other man froze. This Mr Black. His eyes widened. "Shit."

"We need to ask you some questions," continued the student. "Do you remember what happened to you?"

Kirsten shook her head. "I think I was killed. Someone killed me in the bath. I can't remember who—"

"Do you remember Harold McMahon?"

Tap – tap – tap.

I'm going to kill you, bitch!

The words echoed in the room, but Kirsten guessed only inside her own head. Neither the boy nor Mr Black reacted. "No," she said, stumbling over the memory. Letting the water lap around her. Suddenly feeling its icy temperature. Suddenly realising she could be seen. "I mean, I don't know. No, Harold couldn't have…"

"Think carefully. What do you remember?"

"Nothing. Just a voice."

"What did it say?"

"'I'm going to… kill you, bitch.'"

The student relayed the information to Mr Black. The man looked unimpressed. "That could be anyone. We need evidence. Tell her to be more precise."

"I don't understand." Kirsten pushed forward in the water, taking hold of the bath's edge. The first wisps of white had already begun to encircle her. Her voice had started to distort. Long and low. Stretched and warped. She was going to lose them. The first people she'd spoken to in years. "Who are you?" she asked. "What the hell is happening to me?"

"We're here to help. We need you to answer our questions—"

Mr Black stepped forward. "Don't waste time!"

"What do you remember about Harold McMahon?"

The wisps were getting thicker. Turning into clouds. Blocking her view of the student. But still she could see that flicker of a smile. He wanted to help her. "I used to clean his room. He lived in Rose Court."

"When did you last see him?"

"At the Hereford Lecture Theatre. The thing about NovusPart. Octo, Whelan and McMahon were there."

"Impossible," said Mr Black, his tone firm. "That lecture occurred several years after she disappeared."

The white was all around her. The student faded. She needed to explain. "I was there," she said. But her words were now losing their volume. As if she was listening to herself from another room. "I can move around the college... but only when I..."

The student reached forward. Through the white. He took hold of her arm. Her skin flexed like jelly, but his hand didn't pass through it, and his grip was tight. Mr Black watched and clearly saw. His mouth dropped, and he stopped talking.

"You're becoming more tangible with each passing phase," said the student. "Your time is getting closer. We may only have a few more opportunities to help you, so be prepared to talk to us again."

The white haze had almost taken her. She felt herself sinking back into the water. "Do you think Harold McMahon killed me?"

"Unfortunately," said the student, his smile finally fading, "you're not dead yet."

23

"SO, WHAT DID you think of your first taste?"

Nick looked at the two black olives rolling round in his palm. In truth, he didn't like them. But he was trying to put off reaching for the snails. Without their shells, they looked like fat, greasy slugs. Luckily though, he looked up before answering, because from his expression it was clear that McMahon was talking about the town, not the meal. Nick shifted on his left elbow. The small movement provided some relief to his aching arm. Around him, the others continued to eat.

The *triclinium* of the House of McMahon was set out in the traditional manner – three large, flat couches arranged in a U-shape around a central, knee-high table. He was lying diagonally across one of the side couches with Patrick on one side of him and Noah on the other. Maggie and Robert Astridge lay on the couch opposite. McMahon and Whelan occupied the base of the "U".

Six guests. Some way short of the optimum nine preferred by the Romans. But although they hadn't arranged themselves according to social status, Nick had to concede it was a decent enough approximation of what historians knew about Roman dining. He reached for his wine. "To be honest, I'm struggling to take it all in."

McMahon snorted. Beside him, Whelan refilled his goblet. Next to one another, it was clear the men were almost the same age – although Whelan had clearly kept himself in better shape. Nick flicked another olive into his mouth.

He'd arrived to find McMahon had arranged a formal dinner to mark his first day. He'd assumed they'd be served a hotchpotch of Roman clichés. But there'd been no dormice yet. Instead, the dining table heaved with dozens of pewter dishes filled with pickled fruit, mushrooms, quails' eggs... and snails.

Feeling queasy, Nick followed Whelan's lead and took a sip of wine. Like the food, his drink had been heavily spiced. Still, it was perfectly adequate and would probably help him sleep. Whether it would sell on the international market as NovusPart hoped was another matter...

"It would be useful to see Professor Samson's notes."

McMahon grunted. "We want you out on the streets, not stuck inside reading."

"You can access Samson's work via the intranet," said Whelan. "We just need to get you a terminal set up. But yes, your main role will be outside."

Nick smiled. "I'm also looking forward to visiting the baths."

"Huh," McMahon said, mumbling through a full mouth. "Each to his own."

"The Central Baths are the best," said Astridge,

somewhat lazily. Like he wasn't going to explain his reasoning without being asked.

Nick knew that the Central Baths hadn't been finished when Vesuvius erupted. And yet, not only were they now finished, but also open. Completed, despite the destruction wrought elsewhere in the town. Similar, in a way, to the restoration of the Fortuna Augusta. "Thanks for the tip," he said, finally. "But I guess the real interest will be in how they were used, rather than the buildings themselves."

Astridge gave a patronising laugh. "The buildings are what make this entire thing work."

"All I meant was that the people—"

"—belong to the town. Not the other way round. They go to the baths to get clean. Big mystery."

"Yes," said Nick, not wanting to be put off his stride, "but in some ways the baths are more important than the forum. It's where people meet, chat, do business, conduct politics."

"Or so your textbooks tell you. It'll be interesting to know what you think after you've stripped off next to a sweaty Roman."

From beside him, Noah giggled. Whelan reached forward and threw a chickpea in the boy's general direction. It bounced harmlessly away, and seemed to take some of the tension with it. "We've noticed they're very popular," the COO said, his tone calm. "And the illusion relies on both the buildings *and* the people. It's not a competition."

On the opposite couch, Astridge looked annoyed; his bald head had noticeably reddened. But he didn't continue the debate. Nick tried to repair the damage. "Well, the

Forum Baths certainly looked impressive. Indeed, I can't help but wonder about the cost of all this?"

He flicked his eyes towards McMahon to direct his enquiry. McMahon snorted, shovelling food into his mouth. "The cost is immaterial. It's worth every penny."

"It's less than you might think, actually," said Astridge, wiping a sheen of sweat from the side of his head. Nick saw the architect look at McMahon; it seemed the man was waiting for permission to continue. McMahon waved lazily and Astridge continued. "The land here is cheap. We had plenty of cheap labour. The town isn't constructed to modern building regulations – apart from this structure and a few others – and we didn't have to pay any infrastructure costs. The most expensive element was the communication lines between here and the villa – and the security perimeter."

"Still…"

"Noah!"

Nick turned quickly – reacting to the shrillness in Maggie's voice. For a second, he thought the boy must be choking. Then he caught sight of Noah slipping a snail between his lips. The boy grinned at his mother. Nick smiled, but didn't fancy eating anything else. He was already starting to struggle, and this was just the starter.

He looked across the table. There was far too much food for the six of them. His companions had also stopped picking at the food. Even the last few remaining snails didn't attract Noah's interest. Finally, McMahon signalled for the main course.

Maggie issued a long sigh. "So when do we get to check our emails?"

Just like the Land Rovers and the satellite dish at the villa, the mere mention of email was sufficient to burst the illusion. *They'd* travelled in time, Whelan had told him. Not us. And yet, with all the real Pompeians he'd seen today, Nick was finding it hard to keep that in mind.

"At the moment we're only allowing secure communication between us and the villa," replied Whelan.

"You think I'm going to sell an exclusive?"

"We want a controlled launch." Whelan's tone was firm. "There are still certain political challenges we need to overcome."

McMahon snorted. "Fucking idiots. They give us permission for something, and then try to stick their oar in. No doubt we'll be forced to bring a few of them here eventually."

Nick raised an eyebrow. On the couch opposite, Maggie looked like she wanted to argue the point, but she stopped short on catching sight of the pig. Carried by the porter and a female chef, the animal was still attached to the roasting spit. Its skin was crisp and blackened, and the room was soon filled with the smell of seared pork. Nick regretted eating so many olives. Especially when the carcass was set down on the table – its head facing towards him.

The porter retreated back to the atrium but the chef remained. She was a fairly young woman, and the only other member of staff – other than the porter – that Nick had seen at the House of McMahon. She was probably attractive, when she wasn't red-faced and sweating from hours in the kitchen. Retrieving a long, serrated knife from her belt, she sawed through the pig's stomach – spilling its intestines on to the table.

McMahon roared with approval. Nick couldn't have spoken even if he'd wanted to. Only after a few gut-wrenching seconds did he realise that the entrails were sausages, and the surrounding organs were nothing more than soft-roasted apples and pears, covered in a thick red sauce.

A decent trick, and one he'd read about. Still, he would have preferred not to have seen it performed without warning. He glanced at Maggie. She looked like she was about to be sick. Noah was beside himself with laughter. The chef winked at the boy and started to carve the meat.

"We're doing *this* again," shouted McMahon. He shoved a handful of steaming pork into his mouth. "Your fucking faces!" Nick noted Maggie's wince, but it was obvious McMahon didn't feel the need to temper his language in front of Noah.

"Better than the dormice?" Whelan's question didn't get a response. He turned to Nick. "We tried eating mice on our first stay here," he said. "You know, how the Romans did? We spent weeks fattening up the buggers in little clay pots. What were they covered in?"

"Honey," said Astridge. His expression was one of extreme distaste. "And poppy seeds."

24

MAYBE THE DEEP rumble wouldn't have woken him, but the high-pitched squeal certainly did. Nick tried to bury his head deeper into his pillow. It didn't work. He was awake – or at least, somewhere just below the surface of sleep.

Groaning, he rolled over. An ache extended down his back. He'd drifted off soon after the previous night's meal had ended, the wine dulling his senses just enough to allow him to ignore the thinness of the mattress. But now he could feel each of the bed's wooden slats, and they introduced him to another side of Roman life. Was this level of authenticity necessary in NovusPart's guest bedrooms? Budget hotel furnishing would have done just fine.

Another piercing screech forced Nick up on to his elbows. It was much closer this time. Glancing around dumbly, he couldn't quite place it and his thoughts returned to the preceding night. By the time they'd finished eating it was dark, the only light thrown by a dozen or so oil lamps. With nothing else to do, and with polite conversation already strained, everyone had stumbled in the directions of their beds.

Nick stretched and gave a shallow yawn. His room was small, one of the cubicle-sized rooms just off the atrium. It was only large enough for the bed, but a shutter over the doorway at least gave him some privacy.

Another rumble echoed through the house. This time it was accompanied by the clatter of hooves. The source of the noise clicked into place. Wagons. Wagons moving around the town.

Nick yawned again and pulled himself out of bed. He slipped on his tunic and pushed his feet into his sandals. The leather seemed to find all the sore spots on his feet. As he stood and tightened his belt, a more important message came from his bladder.

Stumbling out into the atrium, Nick shielded his eyes from the light pouring in through the opening in the roof. Fortunately, he didn't need to pollute the atrium's central pool, or go to one of the town's public latrines. He headed through the *tablinum* and towards the kitchen, in the far corner of the colonnade surrounding the garden, where a toilet had been built to typical Roman specification. It was little more than a bench above a cesspit, hidden by a curtain. Astridge had seemed particularly amused by it when he'd pointed it out the previous night but as far as Nick was concerned it was fine. Or it would have been. If the chef hadn't already started preparing breakfast.

She stood at the counter, carefully pitting olives. She looked as if she was concentrating hard, and probably wouldn't have noticed him standing there if he hadn't dallied so long. But his uncertainty seemed to attract her attention – her eyes suddenly flaring as though she hadn't expected to be disturbed.

For a moment they just stared at one another. The chef looked a lot better than she'd done the previous night. Her hair was no longer greasy, and she had that just-rolled-out-of-bed look. Her lips were pursed together as if trying to comprehend something that didn't make sense. "You're up early," she said in English.

Nick hesitated. From the atrium came the sound of heavy clattering, almost as if someone was trying to break in through the front door. Then he understood. "The shops," he said. "Opening up for the day."

"You'll get used to it."

Nick nodded. The toilet was just a few steps away, but there was no way he could use it while the chef was still standing there. With just that tatty bit of curtain separating it from the rest of the room. But the bowls of food she was preparing looked almost finished. He'd just have to wait. He looked around the kitchen, trying to ignore the pain in his bladder.

The remains of the roasted pig lay on a table. Cold and covered with a layer of congealed fat, it didn't look anywhere near as appetising as it had the night before – but he could still smell the spices. Suddenly feeling queasy, Nick pointed at the bowl of olives. "Our breakfast?" he asked.

"They're for Mr McMahon."

"So no chance of one or two going missing?"

"No."

"Well, they say it's a poor cook that won't lick the spoon."

The chef gave him a lopsided grin. "Only if they're prone to misquote Mr Shakespeare," she replied, her eyes narrowing. "So why are you here? Apart from to get in my way, that is?"

He looked once more at the curtain hiding the toilet.

"Are you some sort of spy?" The chef's eyes were bright and mischievous. "Brought here by McMahon to keep an eye on me?"

"No," said Nick, suddenly stumbling over his words. "No, I'm filling in for Professor Samson."

"Oh." From her tone of voice, it didn't sound like she'd been expecting that answer. "So you're some sort of doctor?"

Nick hesitated. "Yes. Well, trying to be anyway."

"Well I have a sore throat, and I'm not sure what to do about it."

"I'm… I'm not that sort of doctor… I…"

"That's a pity," she said, her eyes suddenly wide like a puppy. "Because I had questions about *other* things too." She waited a moment, just long enough for his cheeks to flush. "So what's your name? I didn't catch it last night."

"Nick Houghton."

The chef wiped her hands on her smock and held one out. "Mary Kramer," she said. "So I hope you have a sense of humour, Dr Houghton? You didn't look impressed with the pig."

Nick suddenly felt like he was about twelve. "It was very… inspired."

"Well, help yourself to some cold cuts for breakfast." She gave a final grin, and picking up the bowl of olives from the worktop, left the kitchen.

Nick forced himself to wait until he was sure she was gone before reaching for the curtain. It was only then that he heard her voice in the distance, which made the situation truly desperate: "He's in the kitchen."

Whelan appeared at the door, looking well rested. He was dressed in a short-sleeved tunic, which barely seemed able to cope with the girth of his upper arms. Just like at the dinner the previous evening, he wasn't wearing the leather wrist-guard he'd worn on the trip from the control villa. "You're up," he said.

"Yeah," replied Nick, trying his best to sound relaxed. "The wagons…"

"At least none went past in the night. You sleep okay?"

Nick nodded.

"Well you look like shit," Whelan said.

Nick indicated the curtain behind him. He was going to have to say something. Wetting himself was hardly going to get him anywhere fast. "I was just about to…"

"Don't," replied Whelan. "That's just so we have something authentic for visiting locals. You can use the facilities upstairs."

Upstairs? "But Astridge…"

"This is the kitchen, Nick."

Nick nodded, trying to quell the rising irritation. In less than a day, he'd managed to tread crap in from the street and had now been caught trying to urinate in a food-preparation area. Not a good start. He ran a hand through his hair. It felt heavy against his scalp.

"Once you're settled in, we'll get you somewhere better to sleep."

Nick tried to think of something to say. He needed to get back on the right track. Needed Whelan to get to the point, so at the very least he could go and find the facilities upstairs. "I intend to do some exploring today."

"Good. I trust from what you heard last night you now understand my problem? Why we brought you here?"

Nick nodded, although he wasn't sure that he did.

"The biggest threats I can see are arrogance and complacency. This place is currently working, but that doesn't mean it's *worked*."

"So I can just go where I like?"

"Sure."

"And you're fine with that."

"We have ways of keeping an eye on you… and sorting out any trouble you may cause."

"Then I guess I'll head back to the forum, and see where I end up."

"Okay, but report back here at midday."

Nick hesitated; something else was playing on his mind. "What if there's trouble?"

"Relax." Whelan grasped the leather buckle of his belt. It was identical to the one around Nick's waist. "This contains a GPS chip and a simple alarm. When any of us leave the house, the security system tracks our movements. You saw all the CCTV back at the villa?"

"Yeah…"

"Well there you go. In the unlikely event you get into

trouble, just take hold of the buckle and squeeze. We can get to anywhere in the town within a few minutes. So there's no need to worry. Have fun, Dr *Houghton*."

At first Nick thought Whelan was making another sly dig at his lack of qualifications. But the emphasis was on his surname, not his title. And there was something in Whelan's eyes...

"I need a Roman name, don't I?"

Nick had intended to head straight back to the forum. He'd wanted to start piecing together the functions of the various buildings, and how they were being used. But every step seemed to bring something new into view, and mostly something unexpected.

He shivered, but not through cold. Now he was used to his physical surroundings, the everyday details were coming into much clearer focus than on his initial tour. Whereas Patrick had whisked him past the streams of people in order to get him to the town's civic centre, he could now hover and observe the Pompeians at his leisure. And it was already clear that the surrounding streets were going to be of much more interest than the buildings of the forum.

He came to a halt at a crossroads. In front of him, a woman was making an offering at a small shrine. Which god she was dedicating it to wasn't entirely obvious, but she seemed devoted to her duty nonetheless. And what would his students have thought of that? For it to be normal to worship not inside a church or temple, but just at a small, community site. Completely open, and with no one laying special claim to the words of God.

Nick started to walk across to the shrine as soon as the woman had departed. He quickly thought better of it, and moved away. After all, he didn't want to cause any offence. And, if the past was indeed a foreign country, it would probably be easy to make a cultural faux pas: the Roman equivalent of showing the soles of your feet in Thailand. For the time being he would just have to observe – taking in the town, and reporting back to Whelan. But would he find anything wrong? Anything critical to say? Because one thing was for sure: he'd already seen enough to know he wanted to stay a lot longer than six weeks. But that didn't mean they would let him if everything was going to plan. Nick swallowed, feeling a sense of frustration. Clearly everyone, including Whelan, would want him to come up with nothing meaningful – then they could breathe a sigh of relief and get on with their project. But where did that leave him?

Back home with his father?

Nick pushed the thought to the back of his mind, and continued to the south-west corner of the town and through the Marine Gate. The view was just as he thought it would be, the countryside beyond stretching out for miles.

He walked down a ramp and felt his sandals sinking into grass where there should have been water. Just as Whelan had told him, New Pompeii was landlocked. However, the harbour's retaining walls still rose behind him. Astridge had even gone to the trouble of adding metal rings on to which boats could be tied. In the real Pompeii, this area would have been alive with activity – with amphorae and people coming to and from the town from as far afield as India. And yet he was the only one here.

"They say the sea vanished during the disaster."

Nick turned. He wasn't alone. A customs official was standing behind him, dressed in the same scarlet tunic his colleague had worn at the northern gate. But his post made a mockery of his uniform. There was no sea trade for him to manage.

Nick remembered the name that Whelan had told him to use. "Decimus Horatius Pullus," he said, by means of introduction. The customs man just grunted in response.

"There used to be hundreds of men employed here to haul goods from our docks," the man said.

And now they're doing nothing, thought Nick. Or they'd be rebuilding the town. But that was only a temporary employment.

"I see the supplies now come in from the north."

The customs official grimaced. "Yes. The men help unload our supplies at the walls, now the wagons aren't allowed into town. There's talk of building a new road round to this side of town to keep the northern access clear of trade." He looked at the rolling fields and sighed. "A pity for all those with their money in garum, eh?"

25

"I CAN SEE HER."

Kirsten gasped. The student was sitting a few feet away from the bath. Mr Black stood behind him. "You're still here…"

"It's been several months."

"I'm sorry."

"Don't be," said the student. "It's not your fault." He paused, his face momentarily full of regret. "We don't think we were fair with you before. You had questions. We needed to ask ours."

She opened her mouth again, wide. Trying to pop her ears. She always sounded so odd. "You can see me?"

"Yes." The student tapped the steel rims of his sunglasses. Mr Black remained silent. "Nothing to do with these. Just a gift, like playing football, or the piano. I see things others don't."

"What's happening to me?"

"You should already know that, Kirsten. You said you went to the NovusPart talk at the Hereford Lecture Theatre?"

Kirsten nodded. It made the bathwater ripple.

"Arlen's speech became quite famous," continued the student. "It made the mainstream media. Can you think why, Kirsten?"

"It was about time travel." It was the only bit of the talk she remembered.

The student's smile broadened. "Hence the question asked by the media: where are all the time travellers?"

"They said it was only possible to move forward… not backward."

"True enough. So, the question should have been: where are all the *missing* people?"

For a beat, Kirsten didn't respond. A few of the dots connected. "Whelan said it wasn't about people travelling in time at all. He said they were trying to make power. Electricity."

"They may well have been, at first. But just as Fleming didn't go searching for penicillin, NovusPart soon figured out that if you could locate and pull forward enough particles at the same time, and at the same rate…"

"…You could move a person."

"So on the one hand they had a very expensive way of generating power and, on the other, the power over time and space. Which do you think they found most attractive?"

"So I'm being moved forward in time too quickly."

"Perhaps. We think with you the process went wrong. That you didn't just appear where you were supposed to. Instead, you've skipped forward like a pebble skimmed across a pond."

Kirsten felt a weight being lifted. The student looked

pleased with himself. At least she now knew something about what might have happened. She looked downwards at the ripples around her. "The water?"

"Yes. It's dense, and pushes right up against the edge of the skin. We think it might have made it very difficult to judge the edge of a person's body."

"Might?"

"We don't know exactly how McMahon's tech works."

"I'm surprised it's allowed."

"If it were up to us, it wouldn't be."

"But isn't it dangerous?"

"Surprisingly not."

"But what if someone was about to do something important? Something great? And they were then winked out of existence, like I was?"

"You're talking about screwing with the timeline," said the student. "A lot of conspiracy theorists say it's already been done, but who would be in a position to tell? Any amendments to the past become the new reality. And NovusPart claim they avoid the problem by only snatching people about to die. Say, those about to be killed in a plane crash." He said this with a meaningfulness that Kirsten didn't understand.

She felt her throat tighten, and found herself thinking about what Arlen had said in the lecture theatre, and the expression on McMahon's face.

Tap – tap – tap.

I'm going to kill you, bitch!

"But I wasn't about to die," she said. "I was taking a bath."

"Yes," said the student. "The 'bedder in the bath'. The college suppressed the stories when they eventually closed off these rooms. But a ghost? One that could be seen so regularly? And at the same college as McMahon perfected his tech? So you see, Kirsten – we need to know why, thirty years after he left college, McMahon wanted you dead. Why he risked using his tech to murder you. It could be the key to stopping all of this."

"I don't remember what happened." Kirsten paused. "But I can't believe Harold would have killed me. He was a slob yes, but just a kid."

The student took a deep breath. "As I said once before, unfortunately, you're not dead."

"You were just saying that McMahon murdered me."

"You won't live for very long when you finally arrive where you're going. So, you see, although you're technically still very much alive – you've already been murdered. It's just the trigger hasn't yet been pulled."

Behind the student, Mr Black stirred. There were footsteps on the staircase. Several people were approaching.

"We've been here too often," said Mr Black. "They've found us!"

The student was no longer smiling; his tone became urgent. The hammering of feet on the stairs was getting closer. "Listen, you may not believe us about McMahon, but what we're telling you is true. He wants you dead. You need to think why he would do that. Your answer is very important."

The footsteps reached the top floor just as the white

haze started to circle. They'd run out of time. Mr Black was moving towards the door. The student continued to sit and stare. Waiting for her answer.

"I don't know!" she shouted. "He should have been grateful! I saved his life!"

26

REPORT BACK HERE at midday.

Nick was having trouble keeping to Whelan's timetable. His trek back from the Marine Gate had been interrupted several times, his focus distracted by the sights and sounds. The Pompeians had only been within its walls a matter of weeks, but they were already hard at work. In every street he'd heard the chipping of stone and the sawing of wood. And it turned out planning a ruined town didn't just cover up for any mistakes Astridge and Samson may have made; it also gave people something to do. Demolition, building, decorating. In a few months the skeleton built by NovusPart would be completely encased in living Roman skin. It wouldn't just be a replica; it would have become real.

For what seemed like the thousandth time that morning, Nick came to a halt. A ragged man was performing a simple cup-and-ball routine to the obvious delight of a group of children. It was the first bit of community activity that fitted with his mental picture of old Pompeii: the close community of Naples merged with the colour and spice of

Marrakesh. Because until that new civic skin was finished, the place lacked that certain depth of Roman character he'd been expecting.

The performance complete, Nick turned towards a *taberna* on the other side of the street. He watched a few moments, trying to pick out the customs and rules, and then approached, his stomach growling loudly.

The entrance to the *taberna* was wide – its shutters pulled back to expose an L-shaped bar. The servery enclosed the staff while giving customers a good view of the many goods on sale – all of which were kept in large terracotta bowls sunk deep into the bar's countertop.

As he approached, Nick noticed the owner had painted the words "*Avis incendiaria*" – "Firebird" – above the doorway, but the sign was already in danger of being over-written by daubed electoral slogans: *The drunks of the Firebird endorse Merula as aedile!*

Roman politics at its sarcastic best. Nick grinned. However, his smile dropped when he spotted the bar's main decoration. A bronze lamp hung from the ceiling. Although not obvious from the street, it was in the shape of a naked man holding a knife, sporting a penis the same length and girth as the rest of his body. And one the bronze man looked like he was about to cut off with his own knife.

"Yeah?" asked the owner. The man didn't turn round from the stove at the back of the shop.

Nick looked down at the counter. The different bowls contained fava beans, walnuts and raisins. Did he just ask for one of each? He glanced around. There were a couple of other men in the bar. They were staring at him. They knew he was a stranger but, for the moment, it didn't matter – because Nick could see what they were eating.

"I'll have the same as them," he said.

"Eh?"

Nick winced and repeated the words – concentrating on his pronunciation and trying to imitate what he'd heard on the recordings. The owner mulled over his request, and then served up a helping of baked cheese topped with honey and a handful of raisins.

"How much?" asked Nick, reaching for his purse.

The man's eyes narrowed. "You're paying?"

Nick nodded, uncertain. "Sure."

The owner looked thoughtful. Like he was trying to weigh something up in his mind. "It's on the house."

Nick hesitated, wondering whether to accept. Finally he nodded and took his food to an empty table. It smelt good and he took a tentative bite. It didn't disappoint. He'd probably be able to spend six weeks just sampling the food.

"The Isis crowd are making a lot of noise again."

Nick looked up. Another man was now standing at the bar, but he didn't seem to be ordering anything. Straining to listen, Nick tried to make his meal last longer than it should have done, but he needn't have bothered. The owner cocked his head in Nick's direction. The signal ended the discussion. Swallowing the last of his food, Nick pushed himself off his stool and headed for the exit.

* * *

He arrived back at the House of McMahon to find a small group of people huddled around the main entrance. Something was clearly going on inside. He cursed, instantly regretting his decision to stop at the *taberna*. He pushed through the crowd and on into the atrium.

The House of McMahon had been transformed while he'd been away. The frescos depicting the eruption of Vesuvius were now shimmering – like the fires were still erupting from its crater. And the entire house reverberated with a low, deep rumbling. It took more than a couple of seconds to figure it all out. But although his attention had immediately been distracted by the paintings, his focus should have been on the underside of the balcony, from where spotlights were being directed downwards. Probably picking up some sort of reflective pigment that made the lava look like it was moving. There was clearly some sort of speaker system hidden away too. Or at least, a very heavy bass.

All so simple, and yet probably all so magical.

Nick walked around the central pool to the entrance of the *tablinum*. Inside McMahon was sitting on a small wooden stool, which looked like it barely had the strength to support his weight. Patrick stood to his right and Whelan to his left. A couple of security guards – dressed as Roman sentries – flanked the group. Nick caught Whelan's eye; the man glared at him and placed a finger on his lips.

Three Romans stood in front of McMahon, one slightly ahead of the others. Although Nick couldn't see their faces, it was clear the lead man was both short and thin. His tunic hung off him, while the two men with him were significantly more squat and muscular.

"And you will take our message back to the town council?" McMahon asked.

The lead Roman looked towards Patrick, who provided the necessary translation. "Yes," he said finally, his voice nasal and high. "We meant no disrespect, and certainly did not want to interrupt the flow of supplies into the city."

"Good. You may go."

The three men bowed low, then started to back away. Nick quickly walked from the doorway, not wanting the men to think he'd overheard. As they passed him, the lead man glanced in Nick's direction and his thin features immediately furrowed. Nick watched them head back to the street, then returned to the *tablinum*.

McMahon was grinning; Whelan appeared more sombre. *Report back here at midday*, he'd been told. And it now looked like he'd missed an important meeting with the locals.

Whelan beckoned him over. "You're early," he said.

Early?

"We decided to call one of the aediles in," continued Whelan. "To remind them they need to inform us of any new rules."

Nick nodded. The weasel-faced man who'd just left hadn't appeared very impressive. He'd expected more charisma from an elected official. "No watch," said Nick, raising his arm to show the white ring encircling his wrist.

"You'll get used to it," replied Whelan. "So what do you think of our little show?"

"Impressive."

"Bullshit," said McMahon. He pushed himself from his stool and rearranged his toga, fishing the purple stripe out from its folds. "We could vomit on the floor and these people would worship it for years."

He didn't wait for a response, but headed towards the stairs, followed by Patrick. Whelan watched the pair go before continuing. "A key advantage of Clarke's Third Law is that relatively simple things continue to astound," he said.

"Well, I once thought Wi-Fi was magical – but now I get pretty annoyed as soon as it's not available."

Whelan turned to him, his eyes narrowing. "Quite," he said. "Fortunately, we have a range of tricks. Most of which we haven't yet used."

Nick said uncertainly, "Did you need me for this?"

Whelan shook his head. Around them, the shimmering walls had once more turned solid, and the rumbling was replaced by the slow patter of the pool's fountain. The magic was over. For the time being, at least. "Maybe later," he said. "But you'll be pleased to know I've arranged something for you this afternoon to hone your language skills."

27

Nick found the Astridges at New Pompeii's main crossroads. No matter which way anyone proceeded from this crossroads, you'd eventually come to a gate leading out of town. But this time he'd only be following Astridge a couple of blocks further south to the theatre.

He ran his hand through his hair, and found it heavy with sweat. People were streaming steadily past him. No doubt many would be heading for the theatre, like he was. Some might be going to see the gladiators practise at their barracks, or to worship at the Temple of Isis. Everyone rubbed up against each other in this part of town. Nick remembered the conversation he'd overheard at the *taberna*: *The Isis crowd are making a lot of noise again.* However, any uncertainty he had slowly ebbed away as he waved at Noah.

The boy returned his greeting enthusiastically. Maggie wrinkled her nose at his approach. Astridge gave him a cool nod. Two guards stood alert at a polite distance. Nick eyed the men cautiously. They would hardly help them fit in.

"Great. You made it." Astridge's words were spoken without warmth. "The performance should be starting in about forty minutes." He turned and headed in the direction of the theatre. Nick followed. He didn't think the show would be starting to such a strict timetable. After all, the Romans split their day into twelve even hours – which were necessarily longer in summer than in winter. Nothing would be run all that precisely.

"There's a number of temples in this block of buildings," commented Astridge, dryly.

Nick nodded, but otherwise didn't respond. Just like the original, New Pompeii had been built with two theatres, one open-air, and the other covered. They nestled within a cluster of buildings in the south of the town that were not as grand as the forum, but nevertheless provided the town with a secondary focus of activity.

"We copied the layout from Pompeii, of course, but the juxtaposition of the temples and theatres is a bit unsatisfactory, don't you think?"

Nick smiled to himself. Another test of his knowledge. "They may hold the occasional religious ceremony in the larger theatres," he said. "Especially given the additional seats. Have you seen any yet?"

"Yes."

From the architect's tone, Nick guessed he'd just robbed Astridge of a bit of trivia. Still, he didn't want to get into any further disagreement, especially since Whelan wasn't around to referee. He turned his attention towards Noah. "So, have you been exploring?"

"Yeah," the kid shouted. "We've been to the forum."

"And have you visited the amphitheatre?"

"No… but that would be great!"

Maggie frowned at her son. "Please don't encourage him, Mr Houghton."

Nick fell silent, focusing his attention on the people in the crowd around him. A surprising number of them showed signs of disease or deformity. One man seemed to have rickets. He wondered if NovusPart was doing anything to help them.

"Here we are!" announced Astridge, sweeping his arm out in front of him.

The theatre itself was relatively small. They entered via a short passageway and soon found themselves at the foot of a horseshoe of tiered stone seating. It faced directly on to the square bulk of a wooden stage and its backdrop – all of which was open to the elements and the afternoon sun. Nick eyed the tiers, noting that many people had already taken their seats. The stepped seating looked steep and difficult to climb, but at least it was littered with cushions to make it more comfortable.

Astridge led them to the front row and they took their seats. It didn't take long before a few murmurings of discontent began to come from behind them, loud enough for the architect to take notice. It was clear he didn't appreciate the cause.

"Women sit at the back," Nick whispered. He pointed up, and now they saw the crowd was segregated. Women at the back. Men at the front.

Maggie wrinkled her nose. "I'm not a second-class citizen, Dr Houghton."

Nick nodded, but didn't remind her that she wasn't a citizen at all, and never would be. She lacked the basic requirement of full Roman citizenship. Behind them, the murmurings grew louder.

"We'll get a better view from the top," said Astridge, rising. The architect didn't wait to hear Nick's opinion, and started to climb. The others followed, and they settled into their new seats at the top of the tier, Nick and Maggie flanking Astridge, Noah next to his mother. After a few minutes Nick was squirming, but only partially due to the heat of the sun which was now searing his scalp. The people sitting lower in the stands were continually glancing over their shoulders to stare at the strangers sitting in completely the wrong part of the theatre, their guards looming behind them.

And yet if Astridge was conscious of the stares and whispers, he didn't show it. Instead, the architect leant closer to Nick. "Whelan brought you here to find faults with my town."

"No," Nick replied. "He just wants a second pair of eyes on the street."

"Bullshit. I've put a lot of effort into this, Dr Houghton. And I'm not going to let some trumped-up student pick holes in it."

"That's not my intention."

"Good. Because as I understand it you're here for only six weeks."

"Well, hopefully it will be for longer than that."

"Is that what Whelan told you?"

Nick hesitated. He could feel his cheeks burning. The sooner the performance started the better. "The trial period is six weeks," he said. "With a view to a permanent contract."

"And that decision will be McMahon's. And I'm damn sure that if I don't wear the right-coloured tie, then neither do you."

Nick held back a caustic reply, looking down at the seats below. The people of New Pompeii were watching them. "Aren't you in the least bit curious to know what these people think of us? If they suspect anything?"

Astridge wiped sweat from his forehead. "How can they possibly comprehend what's going on?"

"These people aren't stupid," said Nick. "They can see and hear, just like us."

"But they lack the benefit of two thousand years of evolution."

"Haven't you been to the Colosseum? The Pantheon? What they built with concrete has lasted a lot longer than the office blocks put up in the 1960s."

"It's easy to forget about their slums, isn't it? And we've already had a few of the new buildings they've put up themselves collapse. Hardly master builders."

Nick opened his mouth to respond, but stopped when there was movement from the stage. An actor had appeared – a big, beefy man. He brought his hands together in five slow claps and instantly had the audience's attention. Within a few seconds, Nick knew they were going to be watching a comedy. And he also knew Maggie wasn't going to enjoy it.

Sure enough, a series of stock characters began to roll out. An old man appeared and started making lewd suggestions towards a young woman. Nick waited for the dialogue to reach its crescendo, and counted down the seconds before the older man's wife would come on stage to scold him. Now the son. He, in turn, looked longingly towards the girl…

Despite knowing all the jokes, Nick found himself laughing along with the crowd. Two-thousand-year-old slapstick humour and farcical dialogue were one thing, but there was something about a good knob joke that was pretty much universal. And the language was getting increasingly crude. All in all, it was an interesting mix of classical theatre and the bawdiness of the Roman mime.

Nick turned towards Maggie, interested to see her reaction. Sure enough, she looked disgusted. If they'd been watching a melodrama or tragedy, she could just have sat there as if watching an opera without needing to understand the details. But it was all too clear what was happening down on the stage – and Maggie was trying her best to protect her son from it. It didn't take long for Astridge to lean in close. "We're going when there's an interval."

"Fine," said Nick, concentrating on the actors. To one side, a man dressed as a god tiptoed into view. Probably waiting to intervene in a helpful manner. "I'm happy to wait for the *deus ex machina*."

28

KIRSTEN WOKE AND felt herself slipping down. The water lapped over her face, and bubbles streamed upwards towards an indistinct light.

She should have been used to it, but this time was different. It felt like she was drowning. She was under the water and slipping fast. Instinctively she shot out a hand, groping for the side of the bath. She found nothing but water and air.

Because she was falling. Not drowning. *Falling*. It took a couple more seconds for her brain to register the new sensation. But her stomach screamed a clear message that gravity was pulling her down. Far too fast to be sinking through water.

She was falling through air.

Kirsten screamed. She felt a jarring pain. Starting in her left ankle, then tearing into her calf and thigh. She screamed again as the pain reached her hips and back. Her head lashed backwards and her skull smacked down. She heard herself cry out as the breath was forced from her lungs.

She sucked in air. Tried to sense if anything was broken. It didn't feel like it. Although rattled, she seemed to be in one piece. She was lying in sand, in what looked like a circular pit. Above her, light swirled and twisted. It took a while to realise that more people were falling into the sand around her. Men. Women. Children. All wearing the same expressions of terror as they plummeted through the air.

Kirsten stared around the pit. It was huge, its stone walls lost in darkness except where spotlights shone down, nearly blinding her, but it was open to the sky; she could see stars above her. It certainly didn't look like any part of the college grounds. No, she was a long way from Cambridge. And she was visible. The other people in the pit could see her. She was real. No longer the body in the bath.

She gasped. A man was crawling towards her. He was dragging his legs behind him. They looked broken, probably from the landing. He was wearing a bright shirt and shorts, clothes that wouldn't have been out of place on a beach. She looked around. Many of the other people were also wearing summer outfits.

Kirsten started to get to her feet. Others were already standing. They waved at her, grinning. The expressions of confusion and terror on their faces had been replaced by a growing sense of relief.

The spotlights dimmed. Kirsten blinked. Although difficult to see, there were clearly people circling them. They were dressed in black, and some were carrying long sticks. Prowling around the edges of the pit. Like a pack of lions hunting antelope.

Fuck.

They weren't sticks.

Kirsten started to scrabble away, heading for the wall.

They've got swords.

"Where do you think you're going?"

The words echoed out of the darkness. A man stepped forward. He held a large, angular handgun and was pointing it directly at her. His stern expression turned to one of adolescent amusement. He'd noticed she was naked. "What? Looking to join the mile-high club, were you?"

Kirsten took a few steps backwards. The man leered, his gun still raised. His eyes flicked between her breasts and crotch.

"You think you can get away from me, bitch?"

Behind her, a shot rang out. The other men with rifles were holding back. But the men carrying swords were moving in. Each wore a metallic mask, twisted into an expression of fury.

Kirsten turned back to the man. He waved his gun at her. The message was simple. She wasn't going to be allowed to get away. He was going to keep her in the killing zone so the men with swords could have their fun. So he wasn't the primary source of danger. She turned to see a woman standing in the centre of the pit – the arena – long blonde hair halfway down her back. She was gazing upwards, her arms open, screaming for help even as the swords closed in. Other people were starting to run.

She looked frantically from left to right. She froze. In the shadow of the wall stood McMahon. He wasn't looking at her. He watched the action with no emotion, and certainly no empathy. Mark Whelan stood close by, his brow furrowed.

She was already dead.

"Trying to work it out, bitch? Wondering when you're going to wake up?"

Kirsten snapped her attention back to the man. Back to the gun. The student had told her she'd already been murdered. All that was needed was for the trigger to be pulled. And there it was. Right in front of her. Her days of wandering the college were finally over.

But the man didn't seem to be in a particular hurry. He looked around, and relaxed the grip on his weapon. "How about you give me a show?" He waved his gun. Grinned. "Spread 'em."

"Go fuck yourself."

For the first time in a long time, Kirsten recognised her own voice. And she didn't regret her choice of words. If this prick was going to kill her, then he could just do it. Because there was only one way out of this.

She charged forward. Tried to ignore the dizziness ringing around her skull, and focused instead on making a last ditch dive to the right.

The man just laughed and jerked his gun up so that it pointed directly at Kirsten's head. "*I'm going to kill you, bitch!*"

Kirsten didn't wince. Didn't even close her eyes. She heard the hammer pull back, and the crack of the shot. She felt the bullet hitting her forehead. Tingling as it passed through and out the back of her head.

She didn't know if the man fired a second time. The white haze had already started to surround her. Moving across her vision and taking her away.

Like a stone, skipping across a pond.

Maybe she hadn't stopped bouncing yet.

29

H<small>E'D ONLY JUST</small> drifted off to sleep when the first wagon rumbled past. It came as a soft approach of thunder that only just faded before the next one came. The pattern continued until the first rays of light pierced into his room. Groaning, Nick levered himself up and pulled on his tunic.

A tablet computer sat on the cabinet beside his bed. On arriving back from the theatre, he'd viewed it with some irritation and left it switched off. However, after an uncomfortable night on his Roman bunk, it now seemed easier to accept its intrusion. He reached for the device, and waited for the screen to load.

What he found was limited. Most of the icons – internet, email and settings – were ghosted out. How long that would remain the case, would likely be down to Whelan. However, he'd at least been provided with a direct link to Samson's notes.

The bastard had written everything in Latin. Nick frowned. This wasn't going to allow him an easy view into the professor's thinking. He'd need to translate it line by line. But that wasn't the most irritating aspect. Instead of using modern words where no Latin equivalent existed, Samson had taken the convoluted approach of *describing* anything invented after the fall of Rome. Simple words – computer, telephone, aspirin – became entire sentences of Latin. *Extract of willow bark distilled and pressed into disks, ingested for the relief of pain.* It was going to be very hard work.

He first tried to make sense of the index. It looked as if Samson had focused on two main areas, starting prior to the creation of New Pompeii with what might happen to the timeline if they carried on with the project. Nick read a few paragraphs but quickly realised Samson had been working at a very theoretical level. And none of it was very interesting. After all, the population of Pompeii *had* been transported. What was done was done, and there was no going back.

The second thread was more interesting. Just like Whelan had said, NovusPart had transported an initial batch of Pompeians and Samson had spent a long time interviewing them before transporting the rest of the town. One name stood out from among the others: *Felix.* The man he'd met at the control villa.

Nick read a few of the entries, and then felt his stomach start to grumble. It would take him a long time to get through, and was probably a task best left for the evening. After all, there was now an entire town to interview. Putting the tablet back on his bed, he wandered into the atrium in search of breakfast.

Just like the day before, he appeared to be the only one up. The front door was shut, the house secure from intruders. Nick stood for a moment, letting the patter of the atrium's fountain soothe away his tiredness, before he made his way through to the *tablinum*.

The House of McMahon's main room of business wasn't as grand as the atrium but it did have the benefit of a large map of New Pompeii painted on to one of its walls. The details were scant – an illustration of roads and main buildings rather than a detailed, modern town plan – but after two days of exploring, every feature on it now seemed very real.

The surrounding countryside was also sparse, showing only the location of the main agricultural villas and a few tracks. A large residential villa sat on the town's northern approach. Nick thought back to the journey from the control villa, but couldn't remember such a structure. Perhaps McMahon was planning a summer retreat to complement his townhouse?

Whatever the answer, the hinterland surrounding New Pompeii was clearly a work in progress. Given that McMahon received Pompeians in this room, he wasn't going to reveal too much. The control villa looked like all the others – isolated maybe – and screened by the surrounding hills. But the map showed no indication of its helipad or real function.

"Where do you intend to go today?"

Nick turned quickly. Patrick was standing behind him.

"I'm not sure."

"Heading back to the forum?"

"Maybe." Nick paused, uncertain. There was clearly something else playing on the translator's mind.

"Look," said Patrick, finally. "It appears I was wrong.

Whelan told me you're not here to do any translation work."

Nick offered a conciliatory smile, thinking about the awkwardness he still felt towards the spoken form of Latin used here. "I think that comes as a relief to both of us."

"I'll have to find time to give you a proper tour," Patrick continued. "Probably in a couple of days, once I've got Whelan and Astridge set. You know: the temples, gladiator barracks, amphitheatre. You name it."

Nick nodded. In a couple of days, he'd probably have seen everything anyway. But the offer seemed genuine. "Thank you. They say you don't understand Romans until you've been to the baths…?"

"Excuse me, sir?"

Nick ambled to a halt. He'd only just left the House of McMahon, and was heading south towards the forum. Although this was one of the town's wider streets, there wasn't much room to pass the man now standing in front of him. Sure enough, as he stepped to one side, his path was blocked.

It was the same man who'd been watching him and Patrick in the forum. There was determination in his eyes. And they were locked directly on him. Like he was a target.

"Hi," Nick said. He gave a friendly smile, but it wasn't returned. He shifted his gaze skywards, moving his left hand to the buckle of his belt. But he didn't call for help. Not yet, anyway. "Looks like another nice day?"

The man didn't follow his glance. "You will come

with me. My master – Manius Calpurnius Barbatus, the *duumvir* of Pompeii – wants to see you."

The man spoke without moving his lips, his mouth slightly parted to reveal broken teeth. It took Nick a few moments to work out but, when he did, it only added to his discomfort. The man's lips were missing. It looked like they'd been cut off.

"Okay," replied Nick, trying to repress a shudder. He dropped his hand from his belt. This was clearly a slave. A fact about New Pompeii he suddenly realised he'd been trying to ignore. Because as well as transporting Roman citizens, NovusPart would have also rescued slaves. And slavery, something that was utterly abhorrent in the modern world, was never going to be extinguished in their attempt to recreate Pompeii. "I'd be happy to see him."

They walked in silence for ten minutes, heading into the north-east quadrant of the town. Straight into one of the zones which hadn't been excavated in the original Pompeii. Which meant he was walking into an area built entirely from the imagination of Robert Astridge.

Their destination was a building that looked much like the House of McMahon. Whereas the townsfolk gave the NovusPart base a wide berth, this one seemed to be a centre of activity. A long queue snaked out of its doorway, but Nick wasn't taken to join the end of it. His escort took him straight inside and along the atrium corridor.

At the threshold to the house proper, a porter was stationed inside a cubicle, his feet poking out, and acting as a rudimentary gate. The slave stepped around them and waved Nick past. A small, scrappy dog yapped to announce their arrival, and Nick couldn't help but flinch at the animal's sudden appearance. He heard a few people at the head of the queue mutter in tones of amusement and frustration. Unfortunately, he wasn't able to pick out individual comments. Not that they'd be very complimentary. After all, he'd just jumped ahead of them, and there was no telling how long they'd been waiting.

"Stay here."

The slave headed towards the *tablinum*, its entrance hidden by a blank wooden screen. Nick turned back towards the doorway. He was being closely watched by the porter, and remembering his first night at the House of McMahon, he quickly removed his sandals. This done, he surveyed the rest of the atrium. Just like at the House of McMahon, the roof opened at its centre directly above a shallow pool. However, the area was clearly being refitted. There was the smell of wet plaster and paint, and decorator's equipment was scattered around. The layout was also subtly different; while McMahon's mansion was long and thin, this one was notably wider, allowing for what looked like a second atrium off to the right. Whoever owned this property had clearly acquired the building next door, and was knocking the two properties through to make an even larger house. Which only confirmed his view that the transformation of New Pompeii was well under way.

A man walked towards him from the *tablinum* followed by the slave. This must be Manius Calpurnius Barbatus, the *duumvir*.

"Cato? This is the man from the northern gatehouse?"

The slave nodded. Barbatus gave Nick a cursory glance. Even when compared with the rest of the Pompeians, the *duumvir* was short. But he was stocky, his rounded shoulders giving him a look similar to that of a bulldog. And he also had something else which most of the population didn't yet possess: age. This was a man clearly in his fifties or early sixties, his skin wrinkled and flecked like an old oil painting.

Nick smiled cautiously. Barbatus, however, was already heading back to the *tablinum*. Nick followed. The *duumvir*'s main room of business was nothing like McMahon's; it had been embellished with painted columns framing scenes from Greek myth. Without thinking, Nick ambled to a halt. The decoration created the illusion of both grandeur and space; and all in the deep red and black of classical Pompeii.

The *duumvir* hadn't stopped, but had carried on through the *tablinum* into the traditionally more private space of the garden beyond. Nick glanced behind him before continuing. If the people in the hallway hadn't liked him jumping the queue, then they'd be mad as hell if he was seen in the relative privacy of the *peristylium*. Fortunately, the wooden screen meant they wouldn't see the further snub.

And as it was, the garden was anything but private. Just like the house, it was more of a building site than a finished home. The wall through to the next-door property had been dismantled, and several columns lay on the ground, presumably ready to be erected in another location. A deep pit marked the location of a planned pool.

Barbatus led the way to the back of the property, where a shallow niche had been cut into the rear wall at about chest height. It had two shelves built into it, the upper one housing a painting of three figures and a snake. The lower shelf held an oil lamp, and a few crumbs of bread. The *duumvir* inclined his head slightly, then reached forward and tossed a crumb into the lamp's flame. He waited for Nick to do the same.

"I don't know why it's out here," said Barbatus, nodding at the family shrine. The action emphasised his thinning mop of grey-blond hair. "The idiots renovating the house thought it was a suitable spot. Soon, I'll have it moved back into the atrium." He gestured towards the painting of the three figures. "It's adequate in summer, but I think they'll be cold in winter."

Nick smiled, but kept quiet. He was only just about understanding, struggling with Barbatus' pronunciation. He'd need to do his best to imitate it. The last thing he needed was to sound like he'd done at the *taberna*.

"So tell me," Barbatus said. "Are you a god, or simply one of their helpers?"

For a second, Nick's mind went blank, trying to recall Whelan's preferred script. "I've been brought here to advise," he said, his Latin still sounding clunky even if the *duumvir* didn't noticeably react to it.

"Interesting. And your name?"

Nick hesitated. "Decimus Horatius Pullus," he said,

pronouncing each syllable as clearly as he could. Barbatus listened politely, but raised his eyebrows sceptically. Nick suddenly realised that the *duumvir* – one of the most important elected officials in Pompeii – was not wearing a toga but just a simple off-white tunic. Why?

"A good Roman name."

"Yes."

"Well, Pullus, I've heard about your intervention at the northern gatehouse. Thank you for telling your friends to obey the rules set down by the new aediles."

"It was nothing."

Barbatus issued a deep sigh. Frustration. Disappointment. Maybe somewhere between the two. "Really? Your friends would have just pushed through that gatehouse and ignored our man."

"As I said, I'm here to advise."

There was a flutter of movement from the *tablinum*.

"Father? Father, I…"

Nick turned to find two women standing at the entrance to the peristyle. One was young, and wearing a modest *stola* and *palla*. The *stola's* sleeves completely covered her arms, and its hem reached the floor as she walked. The other woman hovered in the background and, from her dress, was presumably another household slave.

"Begone, girl," shouted Barbatus, suddenly angry. "Haven't you seen the length of the queue?" He waited for the girl to retreat before giving Nick an apologetic shrug. "My daughter. Too silly to stop and think for a moment. Just like her mother."

Nick nodded, but didn't pass comment. "I'm still a little puzzled as to why you brought me here."

"Invited."

"Pardon?"

"I *invited* you here."

The *duumvir* continued to smile politely, but his voice was firm. Nick hesitated. "I didn't feel like I had much choice."

"Surely gods can choose where and when they go?"

Nick didn't answer, but felt his cheeks burn. He was being played with.

"Still," continued Barbatus, "no matter. Perhaps Cato was a little too aggressive. That is the fault of many a slave. You give them an instruction, and they carry it out. But I'm still pleased you're here."

"Why?"

"Simply put, you're new and I wanted to meet you. From what I've been told you've already taken a keener interest in our town than many of your friends. And that makes you stand out."

Nick nodded. "Even in its current state, it's a fine town."

Barbatus ignored the compliment. "You came in on the northern road?"

"Yes."

"And how did you find your journey?"

Nick swallowed. He needed to remember the script. "As you know, chaos has consumed much of our land. The roads between the towns are very dangerous. I myself travelled with a guard."

"Yes, this calamity has changed everything." Barbatus laughed humourlessly. "You know, the money still rolls in from my estates, but I don't know when I'll next see them. And here we are – eating bread from a nearby villa I'm not even permitted to visit."

"Things will no doubt improve."

"Good." Barbatus leant closer. "Because the people elected me *duumvir*. So, this should be my town. But for the moment, it's your people that run things."

A sudden thought struck Nick. Something that had first occurred to him at the gatehouse, but which he'd not had chance to ask Whelan. *Duumvir*. There should have been two of them, the *duoviri*, running Pompeii as an equal partnership, with the aediles below them. "And your counterpart?" asked Nick. "The other *duumvir*?"

"You tell me," replied Barbatus. "Quintus Valerius Bibulus is in Rome."

"He travelled there before the eruption?"

Barbatus stared at him blankly. "So have you brought any news from the Senate? Any word from our Emperor?"

Nick shook his head. "No."

Barbatus shrugged. "No, I thought not. You see, other than the odd proclamation, we've heard nothing from the capital. And yet, since our return, I've been writing regular letters to Titus."

"I'm sure he's very busy."

"He'd make time for me. We're close personal friends." Barbatus' eyes narrowed. "Maybe my letters aren't reaching him."

"He'll be receiving letters from across the Empire."

"So he's alive, then?"

Nick didn't reply. He knew he needed to get out of this conversation. Because if Whelan hadn't yet wanted him attending meetings with the aediles, then he'd surely not want him meeting the *duumvir* on his own. Especially if Barbatus was asking detailed questions about their back story.

"As you say," Nick said, "we continue to receive the Emperor's proclamations. And I doubt the god-emperor Augustus would have saved a town as small as Pompeii only to let Rome fall."

Barbatus nodded, smiling. "Good point." He leant forward again and slapped Nick's shoulder. "You know, I really thought I was going to die when Vesuvius turned to fire. But now the memory of that terrible day is falling away like the ash did from my hair. And I'm sure my letters will get through to Titus eventually."

Nick smiled sympathetically. Whelan might be pleased with the smoke and mirrors at the House of McMahon, but he couldn't have anything up his sleeve to compare with the real thing. The shaking of the ground and the first waves of heat. It must have been truly terrifying. It was probably the key trick that made New Pompeii work. "His reply may already be on its way."

"Indeed, and we shall talk again later." Barbatus issued a short, loud laugh. "Cato! Show our guest back to the street!"

* * *

Nick hadn't gone far before a shout made him turn back. He was being followed by a woman, and she was running hard. It took a moment for Nick to recognise her but, as she got closer, he saw she was the slave waiting on Barbatus' daughter.

"Look," said the woman, gasping, "we don't know who you are, but my mistress needs to speak with you. Meet her at the Temple of Fortuna Augusta at noon!"

Before Nick could respond, the slave was already dashing back to the house. He hadn't even had time to ask her mistress's name.

30

CALPURNIA.

Nick had cursed himself more than once since he'd been given the message. *He hadn't even asked her name.* But of course he hadn't needed to. Because he'd met her father: Manius Calpurnius Barbatus.

His daughter would be called Calpurnia. It was that simple.

Nick hadn't covered much ground since leaving Barbatus' mansion. After retracing his steps back to the main *via*, he'd pushed on to the forum and spent most of the morning exploring the buildings and watching the people using them. Then, as the sun had reached its zenith, he'd slipped out of the forum's southern access point, headed through the entertainment quarter, and circled back to the Temple of Fortuna Augusta.

It was not as imposing as the temples in the main forum dedicated to Jupiter and Apollo. Its position outside and to the north of the forum, opposite the Forum Baths, belied the fact that its patron had obviously spent a large amount of money on it. And yet the temple remained surprisingly quiet. Those walking past gave it a wide berth. Some eyed it – or perhaps him – with suspicion. But there it was. A good replica. And, he had to admit it, a credit to Astridge.

Nick eyed the stone arch over the main entrance to the forum. He couldn't see Calpurnia. Nor could he see her approaching from the north – her most probable route from the House of Barbatus. He glanced at his wrist, again forgetting he wasn't wearing a watch, and then looked back at the temple. Maybe she was already inside?

Nick headed up the steps and found the temple's portico deserted. Statues of the goddess Fortuna and Rome's first emperor, Augustus, guarded the shadows of the interior. Nick continued past the colonnade and through the ceremonial doorway. Again, no one. He shivered, suddenly cold.

"They're gone."

The voice was soft. Nick turned. Calpurnia stood inside the doorway. She was wearing her *palla* loosely as a hood.

"Calpurnia?"

"Yes, Not elder, nor younger, nor wiser, nor dumber. Just Calpurnia, daughter of Manius Calpurnius Barbatus. I'm pleased you came."

Barbatus' daughter looked about twenty. As she stepped forward, the light from between the columns swept over her mid-section and revealed a distended stomach. Was she pregnant?

"Our great emperor," she said, tilting her head towards the statue of Augustus. "A great man followed by a tyrant, a madman and a stuttering fool. And yet every caesar has been made into a god by our grateful Senate."

Nick swallowed. Hard. This Calpurnia was clearly no fool. "Perhaps best not to mock a god in his own temple," he said.

"Why? Do you see anyone here?"

Nick looked about him, even though he knew the answer. The temple was deserted. The Temple of Fortuna Augusta. Associated with the man who was meant to have saved Pompeii. And yet no one was here.

No one.

Calpurnia smiled, perhaps detecting that she had managed to sow at least one seed of doubt. "Nor at Vespasian's place in the forum," she added. "And why do you suppose that is?"

Nick didn't say anything. He already had his answer. Because there was a contradiction at the heart of Whelan's script. The god-emperor Augustus was a political machination. Perhaps some people in the provinces believed in his divinity – at the edges of the Empire and far from Rome. But did anyone here actually think a man could be voted into heaven?

"Pompeii was busy on the day Vulcan turned against us," continued Calpurnia. "A lot of people are now saying the old gods were reminding us of their importance."

"And yet Pompeii still stands."

"Yes, it does. But emperors come and emperors go. Not so long ago, we had four in a single year. We don't really know if the imperial family are still alive. So who do you choose to worship when all around you are falling? Augustus? Or Jupiter?"

Nick thought about Whelan's story. He needed to remind her of the proclamations. But he also sensed Calpurnia didn't really want to talk about the imperial family, or even religion. No, there was something else troubling her. "This isn't why you asked me here," he said. It was a statement, not a question, yet Calpurnia nodded all the same.

"I bet my father told you about his estates," she said, still seemingly distracted. "And his money, and his house. You see, his only concern is getting all of those things back under his control. He notices who owns things, and who controls things."

"He is a *duumvir*," said Nick. "Surely *he* controls things."

Calpurnia laughed. "He's a *duumvir*, certainly. But no, he doesn't control things here. So he summons you to try to find out why. But that doesn't interest me, because I have more important things to occupy my mind."

"Such as?"

"Why are the chickens so large, and the carrots orange?"

For a couple of seconds, Nick didn't take in what she was saying. But then it broke across him with a force that made him close his eyes. It was the detail that they could never hope to get right. Astridge could reconstruct the walls of the buildings, but not their contents. They could reproduce the costumes, but not wear them in the correct fashion. And they could provide pots and pans but the food they put in them just wouldn't be the same. The chickens should have been small and scrawny, the carrots any number of colours – but probably such a dirty white they'd more closely resemble a parsnip than its modern cousin. And could any of that be explained by an erupting volcano?

Calpurnia seemed pleased she'd put him on the back foot. But he couldn't leave her with the impression she was right.

"So you're worried about the contents of your stomach?"

It was a good line. Better than he'd have come up with if he'd had time to think, and delivered with just the right amount of sarcasm. Which meant it was now Calpurnia's turn to hesitate. She turned away and towards the statue of Augustus. For a second, she seemed frozen under the full glare of his imperial majesty. The image of a man who'd died old but remained young; his hand held out as if calling and commanding all at the same time.

"I'm not wrong," she said, turning to leave. "I'm not wrong."

31

*T*AP — TAP — *tap.*

"You've done it?"

Kirsten opened her eyes, but found herself standing in thick, white fog. Suspended in motion, unable to sense whether she was drifting in air, or floating in water. But she could at least recognise the voice. Strong, controlled, smooth. *Mark Whelan.* And he was so close he could have been talking straight into her ear.

"Yeah."

McMahon. Also close by, and somehow all around her.

"So there's no longer any threat," Whelan said. "Nothing that can be used against you?"

McMahon didn't reply.

"We agreed this was the right thing to do," Whelan persisted. "We agreed we couldn't let this continue. This was your idea."

"Yeah."

"So what's the problem?"

"I really thought he'd become our Augustus."

32

THE ENTRANCE TO the House of McMahon was blocked, the wooden door closed and secured on the inside. Nick knocked. From within, he heard approaching footsteps. Finally, the door opened a fraction.

"Oh," said the porter. "It's you."

Nick thanked him and started to squeeze past. However, the dog-at-the-door took tight hold of his bicep and thrust a squat finger towards the doorframe. "You see that?"

Nick pulled his arm free. The porter seemed to be indicating a bit of graffiti scratched into the doorframe. A roughly cut grid, like a tic-tac-toe table. "I didn't do it," he said, smiling in what he hoped was a disarming manner.

"Huh," came the gruff response. "Look harder."

Nick peered at the grid. It had been cut deeply into the wood. But the closer he got, the less it looked like the material had come from a tree; it looked synthetic. And that meant the grid wasn't there by accident. It could almost be a number pad on an ATM machine.

"If I'm not here, then the code is 391391."

Nick nodded. But there was one problem. "The keys aren't numbered."

"They're always laid out the same," said the porter.

Nick waited for the porter to re-secure the entrance and then followed him along the corridor to the atrium. The house appeared deserted. "Where is everyone?"

"Maggie and Noah are in the garden. McMahon's about somewhere."

"And Whelan?"

"No. He's out with Patrick."

Nick let out a frustrated sigh. His initial reaction after meeting with Calpurnia had been to hurry back and make a report. But with Whelan gone, he maybe had a little more time to get his thoughts in order, and to pick out the more important aspects of his two morning meetings.

He glanced briefly at the balcony encircling the upper floor of the house, and then pushed on towards the *peristylium*. He found Maggie and Noah sitting together in the garden. She was holding him in a tight hug.

"I thought you two were going out today?"

Noah looked up at him, his eyes red. Nick immediately regretted the comment. The boy had been crying. Maggie wasn't holding him in a soft embrace. It was more like she was restraining him, her face screwed into tight anger. "The wanderer returns," she said. "I take it you're still enjoying this place my husband has created?"

Nick measured his response. "What happened?"

"We went out for a little walk this morning. Robert took us to the forum, back round to the theatre area and then on to what he called the gladiator barracks. It was full of whores. Rutting." Maggie's eyes narrowed. "So we went to one of the temples and found an angry mob outside. On the way home, we stopped at a street café – and again found ourselves surrounded by whores and pimps. This entire town is little more than a brothel."

Nick nodded. The exact number of *tabernae* and brothels in old Pompeii was something that classicists liked to argue about. Estimates for the latter ranged from about forty down to just one. The only thing that was certain was that the Roman attitude to public sex and nudity was at odds with the modern world, just like they'd seen at the theatre. But what was it that Maggie had just said about a mob?

"Where was the trouble?" he asked. "Which temple?"

"That's all you can say? *Which temple?* Not: 'I hope you're okay, Maggie'?"

Nick didn't reply, immediately feeling guilty. Noah was just looking at him, his eyes swollen. Disneyland had obviously turned a bit sour.

"It was that one by the theatres," Maggie said finally.

Nick blinked. The Temple of Isis. It tied up with what he'd heard at the *taberna*. He sat on the bench next to Maggie and Noah. He felt he needed to point something out, even if he was probably going to get another earful. "Have you ever been to Barcelona?"

"Yes," she said. "But I don't see—"

"It's a nice city isn't it?"

"A little too commercial for Robert and me."

"And the tourist guides tell you not to go to certain areas?"

Maggie snorted, suddenly understanding his argument. "I appreciate what you're saying, Dr Houghton. But we're not going out again. And the porter will keep the door shut while we're here."

Nick again looked at Noah. He looked frightened, his face damp with tears. All the excitement seemed to have been taken from him. And yet there was something else in his eyes: confusion. Nick opened his mouth to say something but before he could speak, footsteps echoed from the atrium.

McMahon stood at the threshold to the garden. The CEO was persisting in wearing a toga. Now that Nick had seen Barbatus wearing a tunic his appearance looked all the more odd, even if he was the representative of a god.

"I take it you're the one who's walked crap across my floor again?"

Nick nodded dumbly, realising he was still wearing his outdoor sandals rather than the clean flip-flops which were probably waiting for him by the door.

"Patrick and Whelan aren't back yet," McMahon said.

"No…"

"Good." A NovusPart guard had appeared behind McMahon. He was dressed as a cavalryman. Did that mean McMahon was leaving? "Stay with these two. Astridge has gone out to inspect a few architectural problems."

"Are you going somewhere?"

"I doubt that's any of your business."

Nick hesitated. "We still need to discuss my work here…"

McMahon considered this for a moment. "Talk to Whelan."

Nick had to wait another couple of hours before Whelan returned with Astridge and Patrick. He spent the time mainly in the garden, doing his best to amuse Noah with a simple game of dice.

All the time, though, he was going over his meetings with Barbatus and Calpurnia. Trying to work out what he could say so he would at least have something useful to report – while at the same time not overplaying what had happened. After all, Astridge was convinced that he'd been brought here to find problems, and would certainly think it suspicious if Nick came up with any so soon after his arrival. And that was another paradox about why he'd actually been brought here: *Damned if I do, damned if I don't.*

Settling on what he was going to say, he waited another few minutes before going to find Whelan, time which he used to bring his game with Noah to an end without it appearing like he was abandoning the boy. Then he headed through to the atrium to find the others holding an impromptu conference near the pool.

"Dr Houghton," said Astridge on seeing him. "Being paid to play with Noah?"

"He was a bit upset—"

"Which is why my wife is here. So, have you found any evidence that our illusion is about to collapse?"

Nick looked round the group, annoyed by the

architect's attitude. "I met one of the *duoviri*," he said.

Whelan immediately turned to him. He was once more wearing his leather wrist-guard – perhaps he only wore it when he was in town. "You were asked to get a view from street level, Nick. Not to interview people we already know."

"I wasn't interviewing him. He sent a guy to get me."

Whelan's eyes narrowed. "Did he threaten you? You didn't activate your belt."

"There was no need. It didn't feel... I mean, I didn't feel in any danger. Barbatus put it down to a misunderstanding."

Whelan remained silent for a moment. Patrick hovered in the background. With nothing to translate and McMahon gone, his presence was somewhat superfluous.

"Interesting. There's only one of them, of course. The other *duumvir* chose the wrong time to take a holiday. So what did he have to say?"

"He just wanted to thank me for what I said to you at the gatehouse."

"Oh?"

"Respecting their decision not to let wagons in during the day."

"And that was it?"

"Pretty much. I guess he just wanted to meet the new face."

Astridge snorted. "Insights like these are certainly worth top dollar."

"He also told me he's been writing to the Emperor."

Whelan raised an eyebrow. "Yes, he's very keen to tell anyone who'll listen that he knows Titus. And Vespasian? Did he mention him too?"

Nick shook his head. "No, but it's interesting in the sense that I've always thought of Pompeii as being self-contained."

"And anything from the street?"

Nick hesitated. He wanted to say something about Calpurnia, but something was nagging at him. Some small doubt. "Only in a bar," he said. "Something about trouble at the Temple of Isis." He turned to Astridge. "But I guess you already know about that."

He'd expected a swift rebuttal, but none came. Instead, the architect cast a sideways glance at Whelan. So it was clear Astridge did know about it. And it was sufficiently important to neutralise his condescending attitude.

Whelan cleared his throat. "Let's talk upstairs."

The instruction was unexpected, and clearly aimed only at Nick. Whelan didn't wait for a response. Instead, he headed across the atrium and up the staircase. Nick followed.

Whelan's room was at the top of the stairs. On Nick's visits to the bathroom, the COO's door had always been shut. The room was simply laid out, and reminded Nick of the control villa. It was like a hotel room, a high-end one. Everything was plush and comfortable, except for an exercise bike and bench press.

Whelan waited just in front of his desk. He unstrapped his wrist-guard and dropped it to the floor. "I think it's fair to say that Astridge irritates me just as much as he does you."

"He's done a fantastic job here," Nick replied, trying

to be diplomatic. He let his attention wander to the walls. Hanging quite innocently beside a small wardrobe was a photograph of Joseph Stalin. The old Soviet leader was walking alongside a canal with two other men. All wore military uniforms from the Second World War.

"But as you remarked, understanding buildings isn't the same as understanding the people who use them. And it's always best to know what your opponent may be thinking." Whelan paused, perhaps trying to formulate the right question. "What do you know about Isis?" he said. "Patrick can't tell me much about it."

Nick remembered the translator's dismissive comments about religion. "It's essentially a cult brought over from Egypt," he said. "They worship the goddess Isis, the wife of Osiris, god of the underworld."

"And the Romans allowed them in?"

"The Romans' general approach was to integrate with other cultures. Greek gods, Persian gods, Egyptian gods. Clearly, it ebbed and flowed. Augustus tried to re-establish traditional Roman deities but the general pattern was to make conquered peoples part of the Empire – and that meant accepting their gods."

"That somehow doesn't fit with crucifying a certain man on the cross, or feeding his followers to lions."

"Romans can believe in more than one god. Christians don't. So the rejection wasn't entirely one way." Nick paused, but didn't give Whelan time to interrupt. "You've got problems at the Temple of Isis?"

Whelan grunted. "You've probably noticed we've got a

lot more people in the town than we have jobs for them to do. Building work keeps some of them occupied but most just loiter on the streets. They now seem to have got it into their heads to make their way over to the Temple of Isis in the early afternoon. There have been some scuffles between those using the temple and people who have a problem with the rites that go on over there."

"The worship of Isis is essentially about the annual flooding of the Nile, and the fertility it brings. You know, cycles of life. Rebirth. Life after death."

"Ironic, then, that people have taken a dislike to it."

Nick frowned. The same photograph of Stalin was also hanging on the other side of the room, to one side of the double bed that occupied most of the floor. Even at this distance, it was easy to spot there was a big difference. An extra man. While the picture near the wardrobe showed three figures, the one near the bed had four.

"The guy fell out of favour and was edited out of the shot," said Whelan, following Nick's gaze. "Soviet censors were playing with photos a long time before computers came along."

"Interesting choice of subject," Nick said.

"Well, I read a lot about Stalin at university. And the photo is more of an in-joke. It reminds me not to take accusations that NovusPart is playing with history too seriously." Whelan paused. "But you were telling me about Isis?"

Nick nodded. "Yes. I would say the situation is probably more to do with rejecting foreigners at a time of crisis." His hand trembled as a sudden thought occurred to him. The Temple of Fortuna Augusta had been empty. As was Vespasian's temple in the forum. "How prepared are we if we're faced with a Roman mob?"

"At the temple?"

"No," said Nick. "Here. At the house."

"There's been no trouble here," replied Whelan. "Do you have reason to suspect there will be?"

Nick shook his head. "No, but as I said, mobs – especially Roman mobs – attack people they see as outsiders. Just like they're doing now at the Temple of Isis. So the real question is: do you have enough men to maintain order?"

"We have superior weapons, Nick."

"But…"

"How many British soldiers kept hold of India? How many conquistadors destroyed the Incas? How many Romans subdued Gaul?"

Nick didn't answer, and Whelan slowly smiled. "Just keep your ears open," he said. "And, if necessary, we'll break out the guns."

33

KIRSTEN DIDN'T SCREAM. She knew what was happening. Her brain registered the fall, and she braced for impact. After hitting the floor she immediately rolled on to her side and pushed herself up on to her feet. Ready for whoever was waiting for her.

But there was no one. Not a soul.

She was quite alone. And she wasn't in the pit. No spotlights. No men with guns. No men with swords.

The relief was overwhelming. Her shoulders heaved, and the tears started to well up. But she didn't let them run down her cheeks. There would be time for that later. First, she had to find out where she'd landed. Because although she wasn't in the pit, it didn't look like she would be going very far.

Stone walls surrounded her. She was in a small vault, perhaps a basement. Just a few metres square, with only one way out: a solid wooden door.

So where was the light coming from?

Kirsten looked up. The ceiling was way out of reach and didn't quite fit with the stone walls. It looked modern, plastered and painted a simple cream. The light shone from a small window at its centre, revealing her only companions: a collection of toys lying on the floor. Dolls, action figures and a small set of cars.

Letting out a shallow breath, Kirsten crossed to the nearest wall and lifted her hand. She had to test something. She reached out, and touched the stone.

The tips of her fingers brushed against the rough-cut granite. She pushed. The stone resisted. Her hand didn't pass through. She pushed harder still. The stone didn't give way. She was back in the real world.

There would be no more second chances.

She woke to the sound of approaching footsteps. Next came a rattle of keys. The door swung open.

The man who had opened it was small and scrawny, something not even his heavy canvas coat could hide. He stepped into the room and looked directly at her. He looked more annoyed than anything. Irritated.

Kirsten got to her feet. She didn't say anything. Should she tell him her name?

No. The man was fumbling in his coat. For a second Kirsten felt like running but instead she froze. *He's reaching for a weapon.* It was enough to stop her muscles from responding. She wouldn't be able to get away this time.

Instead the man pulled out a small walkie-talkie. "Yeah," he said. He spoke out of the side of his mouth. "I'm down in the basement. Another paradox just landed."

There was a screech of feedback, and the echo in the

basement made it hard to understand what was being said in return. Kirsten waited.

"I'm telling you we've got another one," continued the man. "No," he said, letting his eyes pass over her. "No. Not a child." The man paused as another screech of noise filled the room. "I'm telling you, she ain't a kid." Another pause, another screech. "Just tell Mr McMahon he needs to get down here and sort out his mess."

34

IT WAS PROBABLY yet another passing wagon that brought Nick to the surface of sleep. This was getting tiresome. Groaning, Nick sat up in bed and reached for his tablet.

He'd been reading late into the night, and the glare from the screen probably hadn't done him any favours. And what he'd read certainly hadn't let him drift off easily.

In what had probably been a late-night moment of doubt, Professor Samson had admitted to being out of his depth. The Latin had been so beautifully constructed that the few sentences from his notes had completely caught Nick off guard. So much so, he'd been compelled to read the section several times. But in the end, they made perfect sense. Because NovusPart had first hired Samson due to his expertise on alternative history, not because he had a specific interest in Roman life. He'd kept on advising them in the same way he'd made his TV programmes – rapid research from secondary sources – all patched up with first-hand interviews from the first tranche of transportations. But the notes contained a clear admission. He'd been afraid of making mistakes.

Nick rose and started to dress. Did it matter?

He didn't know, but it certainly made it more important to finish reviewing Samson's work. First though, he needed to see some more of the town.

Stepping into the atrium, Nick paused to detect any sign of life. He'd not heard any movement during the night, even though the noise from the street had disturbed him several times. Which likely meant McMahon hadn't returned. He made his way towards the kitchen.

Mary was at a table, stripping a cooked chicken carcass from the previous night's meal. Nick stared at her for a few seconds. Her look of concentration mirrored his own grim expression. She looked up and gave him a friendly grin. "Caught me again!" she said. "Are you sure you're not a spy?"

"Quite sure," he said, smiling. "Those beds aren't exactly comfortable."

"Authentic though, eh?"

"Probably. You've got one of the rooms upstairs?"

"Sure."

Nick glanced upwards. "Above the atrium?"

Her expression was teasing. "Is this your way of getting an invitation to see my boudoir, Dr Houghton?"

"No… I…."

She wiped her greasy hands on her apron. "Relax. I think Whelan may be testing you. Waiting to see if you pluck up the courage to ask for better accommodation."

"Patrick has his own apartment in the town."

"Yeah."

"I suppose it's easier to learn the language, if he's out among the people."

"It's also easier to have sex with the local girls."

Nick was embarrassed. But she was probably right. And she likely knew all sorts of other things by simply being around McMahon and Whelan. "So how long have you worked for NovusPart?"

"Oh, a while now. I was originally Professor Samson's PA, until he left. Then McMahon tasted my cooking and… well, I kind of got stuck in the kitchen."

"He certainly seems to like his food."

"Oh, yes. The challenge here is that Samson insisted on no potatoes."

Nick nodded, thinking about the colour of carrots. If only NovusPart had gone that little bit further. Or perhaps if Samson hadn't just studied when and where different foodstuffs had first started to be eaten, but had gone on to examine what they would have looked like.

"So have you found anything interesting?" said Mary, returning to her task. She seemed intent on rescuing as much of the cooked meat as possible.

"Lots," replied Nick. "But I'm sure I've just scratched the surface." He pushed his hand through what was getting increasingly lank hair. "I've quite a few pet theories I'd like to test over the next few days."

"Theories? I thought you were a historian, not a scientist?"

"There are an awful lot of things we don't know…"

"Such as?"

"Well, for starters, Pompeii is known for the number of phalli drawn all over the town." He felt himself start to blush. "Some say they point the way to the nearest brothel, others that they're symbols of good luck…"

"Oh." The chef stopped tearing at the chicken. "Well I thought it was just that young men liked drawing willies. Just like they do on every school textbook and toilet wall." She paused. "There's a lot of young men in Pompeii, you know."

Nick nodded quickly. "Well yes," he said, his cheeks now burning. "But the point holds that a lot of what we know about Ancient Rome is just based on professional judgement, rather than known facts."

"You mean guesswork?"

"Something like that."

"But surely the details are less important than the general sweep?"

Nick hesitated. "That's pretty deep."

"It's something your predecessor used to say."

"Samson?"

"Yeah. For him, it was all about 'cause and effect', 'cause and effect'. And who cares about the pots and pans, when men are fighting for their crowns?"

Nick nodded, thinking about Samson's notes. "Well, I disagree," he said. "Take Caligula, for instance. There was relatively little written about him during his reign. But we know he enacted political reforms and ordered the construction of several aqueducts. So he didn't spend all his cash on wild parties. Everything written after his death may have been exaggerated to justify the way in which he was murdered."

"The Richard III effect?"

Nick nodded. Though he wasn't overly familiar with

that period of history, he knew it was still dangerous to refer to Richard as a usurper anywhere north of Chesterfield – and that Shakespeare's character was very much influenced by being written under the dynasty that had toppled him. "So you're a Cousins' War type of girl?" he asked. Mary looked at him blankly. "The Wars of the Roses?"

"No," she said, suddenly laughing. "Samson did a TV show about Richard III and what would have happened… you know, the two princes in the tower?"

Nick smiled, something suddenly occurring to him. "Well, you never know; perhaps NovusPart took them?"

He'd said something wrong. The amusement had gone from her face. "You shouldn't make jokes like that, Nick," she said. "McMahon would be angry if he heard you."

Nick nodded, suddenly feeling foolish. "Sorry."

"It's okay," she said. "Just be careful." She smiled at him. For just a fraction too long. "So Caligula wasn't mad after all?"

"Oh, I didn't say that," said Nick, relaxing again. "He started out as the golden boy of Rome. A direct descendant of Augustus, and the son of the famous general Germanicus. But the way he was killed? The way his legacy was poisoned by hundreds of writers? No, by the end, he must have gone absolutely mental to have been so hated."

The remainder of the morning brought nothing but frustration. Avoiding the pull of the forum, Nick pushed into the streets surrounding the House of McMahon.

Trying to find the shops, homes and *tabernae* in which he could observe the people going about their business. And maybe start talking to a few of them, too.

Unfortunately, it wasn't going to plan. After an hour of wandering back and forth, he approached a man who'd just finished taking a long drink at a water fountain. The man quickly darted away. Indeed, the more Nick thought about it, the more his presence reminded him of detergent dropped into a pan of oily water. The rush to give him space was almost palpable.

So how was he to get to know them if he couldn't get close?

"Don't you know it's dangerous for a mouse to talk to a lion?"

Nick turned. He was being addressed by a man standing at one of the many shrines that had been set up at the junction of two *viae*. His clothes were rumpled and worn, as if he'd spent one too many nights sleeping on the street. And yet he wasn't cowering away like all the others.

"Surely the mouse would be too fast for the lion to catch?"

The vagrant grinned. "But if he was caught, then the mouse wouldn't get to meet another lion, would he?"

Nick nodded, smiled and approached the shrine. The man indicated downwards. There was a collection of dice and tablets near his feet. Getting closer, Nick saw that these objects were the man's property, and not part of the shrine itself. So he wasn't a vagrant, but an itinerant fortune-teller. One perhaps unlucky enough to get trapped inside Pompeii by the eruption.

"You're making offerings to Mercury," said Nick, indicating towards a roughly moulded statue. It sat inside a niche cut into the building next to the crossroads. Ready to accept any and all offerings.

"I am here to allow access to his wisdom," replied the man. "Although my services are, of course, nothing when set against your access to the almighty Augustus."

Nick hesitated. With the difference in language and pronunciation he couldn't quite tell if the man was being sarcastic. But this was the only person who seemed willing to talk to him. Nick pointed towards the dice. "Perhaps you could provide me with advice, and I will see how accurate your readings of the gods are?"

Nodding, the man reached for a small pouch tied to his belt. It jingled with coins. He held it out and Nick added a couple of coins to the collection.

Payment made, Nick crouched alongside the oracle and scattered the five dice across the pavement. He noted they were real knuckles, probably sheep. Their edges were marked with simple Roman numerals, scratched into the bone, possibly with a metal blade. It looked like a new set.

As soon as the dice stopped rolling, the oracle reached for his tablets. He made a great show of checking and counting the dice before finding the right combinations on his chart. His expression changed as he moved from concentration to epiphany. "Take care when moving the rock," he said, his voice suddenly full of melodramatic zeal. "Because when the sun shines, the most dangerous scorpions seek shade."

Nick smiled. He knew the combinations on the chart gave only a limited series of possible outcomes, and the one he'd just been given was almost the same as that which he'd read at a site near Turkey. "And will I be able to avoid the scorpion's sting?" he asked. "Or will I end up being an unlucky mouse?"

"You are a lion," said the man. "Not a mouse. And take care not to mix the words of a god with a simple parable. But, yes, I can answer your question."

Again the purse was offered. This time, Nick didn't bite. "I already know the answer," he said. "I'm simply here to test the services you're offering to the other mice."

The man smiled, though this time with a breath of irritation. Nevertheless, he picked up the five knucklebones from the floor and offered them to Nick. Nick rolled them again and waited for the tablets to be consulted.

The oracle's face turned sombre. "You will survive, but with sacrifice."

"Thank you." Although he was crouched down, Nick could see out of the corner of his eye that he was being observed by a small crowd. But now he'd played along, he needed to take the chance to ask some questions of his own. He was just about to pose the first when the oracle shrank back against the wall.

Puzzled, Nick turned and found the slave owned by Barbatus standing behind him. Cato's teeth were bared behind the mess of scar tissue. "The *duumvir* would like to know if you're free to attend a gathering tonight."

Would like to know. The words had almost been spat.

Maybe Barbatus had decided to beat some manners into the slave. Nick winced at the thought. It certainly hadn't been his intention to cause any trouble. "Thank you," he said. "I would be delighted."

35

KIRSTEN SAT NEAR the door and waited. The man in the heavy canvas coat had returned only once. He hadn't brought McMahon. Instead, he'd tossed a pile of clothes in front of her – jeans, T-shirt, jumper – and placed a wooden tray on the floor.

Food.

A bowl of hot stew and a piece of crusty bread. She'd rushed to it immediately but, given it was the first food she'd tasted in years, it felt strange to eat. On every swallow she felt like she was going to choke – and it took a long while for her body to remind her gullet of how to transfer solids from her mouth to her stomach.

The clothes also felt odd. Somehow restrictive and unnecessary. But they also held the coldness of the basement at bay, and made her feel more human. More civilised. Less like a lost animal. And less of an object in her jailer's eyes.

With the food finished, Kirsten got to her feet and crossed the basement to the door. It looked and felt solid. She started to hammer on it with her fists. Loudly.

It didn't take long before she heard his footsteps.

Kirsten moved quickly, and sat on the floor at the far side of the basement. As far as she could from the door, near the toys. She pretended to play with them, pushing the toy cars around with the tip of her finger, cradling one of the dolls. Like a child.

The door to the basement opened, carefully. The man in the canvas coat stood behind it. He rubbed his eyes like he'd been asleep. Maybe she'd woken him. Maybe that explained his look of irritation.

He watched her playing with the toys, and Kirsten looked back and smiled. She didn't say anything. She just looked at him. Opening her eyes wide, and keeping her focus at a slight upward angle. Then she turned back to the toys, and continued to play.

"Keep it down," said the man, his voice cold. He backed out. The door closed, and she heard it lock. She started to count. She knew how many seconds were in a minute, and how many seconds were in an hour. When she got to just short of four thousand, she'd start to hammer on the door again. Louder and louder until he came back. And again he'd find her playing with the toys. On the other side of the basement, far from the door.

But not the third time. On the third visit she'd be standing close to the hinges. And the frustration at twice being awoken would have long since turned to anger. And the door wouldn't open carefully, it would open wide.

And then she would get out.

36

As Nick approached the House of Barbatus, he noticed the main door to the street had been left open. But this time there was no queue waiting for a chance to see the *duumvir*. Instead, a thick din of conversation and laughter came from the corridor leading to the atrium.

Nick hesitated on the threshold – listening to the voices echoing out into the street. He'd not told Whelan about the invitation. But then again, he'd not seen the operations chief that day. And with no clear rules on what he could and couldn't do, it seemed sensible to take advantage of the opportunity.

Not that it would put him any closer to the ordinary people of Pompeii. After all, the *duumvir* would hardly have invited just anyone off the street. No, inside the townhouse would be a collection of powerful locals. Which would be useful but potentially less interesting than getting to know the class of people below them.

Idiot. Don't look a gift horse in the mouth. He started along the atrium corridor. The noise became louder with each step. But when he finally reached the porter's cubbyhole, everyone fell silent. There were about thirty

Romans staring at him, men and women in their best togas and *stolae*. Despite the invitation, those inside clearly hadn't been expecting him.

He glanced to his left. Barbatus' sentry was standing guard, the curtain to his station tied back. It indicated he'd be there for the rest of the evening. But although the porter's chin had already jutted forward, he wasn't making any moves to stop him. Nick took a couple of steps forward. Forcing a smile, he kept his hands as loosely as he could by his sides – but he could already feel his fingertips shaking. Where the hell was Barbatus?

"Pullus! Welcome! Welcome!"

The bellow had come from the far side of the atrium. The *duumvir* stepped out from the crowd. The porter shrank back into his hole. The other guests remained quiet.

Nick glanced around the atrium, trying to kill the seconds before Barbatus reached him. The ongoing renovation work had been hastily covered by draped sheets and wooden screens. But the atrium was also filling up with pieces of furniture – including a metal-strapped wooden chest, which had been placed at the head of the *impluvium*. There for all to see, and something that shouted this was a rich man's home.

"Pullus!"

Barbatus slapped him hard on the shoulder and broke into a wide grin. "I'm pleased you could attend our little party."

It was clear Barbatus wasn't really talking to Nick. He was addressing his other guests. A soundbite to assuage their suspicions, and show them their leader remained in charge. And he had a big audience. Apart from the thirty or so people standing around the central pool, undisturbed laughter indicated there were more in the garden of the *peristylium* beyond. Perhaps seventy or eighty guests were packed into the house – and that didn't include the slaves bobbing and weaving between them.

"Thank you for your invitation," said Nick, following his host's lead and projecting his voice.

"Not at all. Drink! Get this man a drink!"

From the crowd, a slave darted forward with a goblet of wine. Nick took it, and then realised everyone was waiting for him to taste it. Rather theatrically, he took a small mouthful and nodded his appreciation. Indeed, it was a good drink. Much better than the stuff served at McMahon's dinners.

"Good," continued Barbatus. "Now, let's get you away from the door."

They took a few steps further into the atrium, but the atmosphere remained tense. Just as Nick began to rack his brain for something to say, a small man appeared at the doorway to the *tablinum* and made his way across to them. It didn't take long for Nick to place him: the weasel-faced man he'd seen at the House of McMahon. Up close, he looked about twenty years younger than the *duumvir*. "Lucius Salonius Naso," said the man. "Aedile."

Nick smiled back. "Decimus Horatius Pullus."

"A good Roman name."

Barbatus snorted. "Well, we won't go into that again. You met my daughter at the temple."

It wasn't a question. Either Calpurnia had told him, or he'd had her followed. Either way, it was obvious Barbatus knew. "Yes. At the Temple of Fortuna Augusta."

"No matter. You are here now and that is good. Come through to the garden and have a few of our figs."

The other guests continued to stare as Nick followed Barbatus and Naso through the *tablinum* and into the garden beyond. As he suspected, the *peristylium* was filled with people. Some were standing under the colonnade, concentrated near tables of food. On one of the walls a half-finished fresco of what looked like a plump, nude Venus was beginning to emerge. Otherwise, the ongoing works were less well hidden than in the main house. The view into the property next door had been left unmasked. It looked like additional rooms were being constructed.

"I'm building private baths," Barbatus said. "Now we have decent running water, it seemed only wise."

Nick felt the academic side of his brain tick over. There'd been a lot of debate as to whether the private water supply in Pompeii was working at the time of the eruption. From the excavations, it was thought that at least one bathhouse had been out of action. But did the rich have access to their own separate supply? Or had that also been damaged in the earthquake of AD 62?

"Augustus works in mysterious ways," said Naso, almost to himself. Even with his unfamiliar accent, it was clear his comment was laced with irony. "He protects only a fraction of the town, but manages to fix our pipes."

Nick didn't say anything, but felt himself wince.

Because although the tourists milling around old Pompeii probably didn't notice, what they were actually seeing were buildings that had been damaged well before the eruption. Which probably made the place these people found themselves in all the more wondrous.

"Do you have any idea, Pullus, how frustrating it was to have a glorious bathhouse and no water to put in it?"

Nick nodded, but his thoughts were quickly evaporating. As had happened in the atrium, conversation was slowly fading as the other guests caught sight of him.

"It was something I'd bugged Titus about," Barbatus continued. "Perhaps you don't know, as you're new here, but there was an earthquake – oh, about twenty years ago now. Left half the town in rubble, and everyone had to use the public fountains. We'd not got halfway through rebuilding by the time the ground started shaking again..."

Barbatus let his words trail off. Looking round, Nick noticed Calpurnia at the far side of the garden. She was sitting at the corner of a long table, leaning back and probably trying to get some relief from the weight of her stomach. His analysis at the temple had been correct. She was pregnant. It was also clear Barbatus wasn't going to facilitate a second introduction. Instead, he led him back across to the niche, and they went through the motions of thanking the household gods. Once finished, Barbatus moved them on towards a long trestle table pushed up against the peristylium's rear wall.

The *duumvir* picked a few figs from a pewter plate. Naso appeared at his shoulder. "We should meet again tomorrow," said the aedile, "rather than now."

Nick saw that Naso's eyes were in continuous movement, checking each person within the peristyle. Likely calculating if they were close enough to hear what they were saying. Possibly considering if they were judging him by association. Barbatus didn't seem to care.

"You know, Pullus," he said. "Every day, I see dozens of people in this town. They either come to my door for an early audience, or meet me in the forum as part of my public duties. Naso sees just as many."

"But no one's seeing me to complain about the state of the roads," added the aedile, his voice strained.

Nick reached for a fig. The fruit stuck against the dryness of his mouth. He was forced to take another mouthful of wine just to swallow it.

"Look," continued Barbatus, "we invited you here to share our concerns."

"You have regular meetings with us…"

"But you are someone who appears to have better hearing than your friends."

Nick reached for a second fig, but didn't eat it. He let it rest in his palm, in part so he had something to hold. "I'm not sure I'll be able to help… being new here myself."

Naso leant forward. "We're growing concerned about the town's security."

Nick was about to deflect the comment – to again fall back on the script – but something in the aedile's eyes made him pause. "From what I've seen, the town seems to be well run. Considering what's happened."

Naso sighed and turned to his host. "This is a waste of time."

Barbatus ignored him. "People are starting to wonder where their food is coming from. And their money."

"But there's plenty of food. The market is full..."

"Of course there's plenty of food. But for how long? People used to be able to see healthy crops in the fields, the ships, the merchants. They used to know where it was coming from, and that their supply was secure."

Nick laughed. A cliché had come into his mind. "I don't know where the sun goes each night," he said. "But I bet you it will rise tomorrow."

"True. But, as *duumvir* and aedile, we're expected to provide for this town. And yet we don't know where our money is coming from. Most of my guests here are hoarding coin, not throwing parties."

"And certainly not organising games for the arena," Naso added, his voice growing increasingly reedy.

"These are real concerns, Pullus. And we want you to take them back to your people. The crust of civilisation is thin, and the people will react if it is broken."

"Most of the Empire has been in flames."

"And yet no one can see a mountain looming above the town," Barbatus said. "Nor can they see any ash or smoke in the sky. Where is the threat, Pullus? Where are the burning fields?"

"Fuck this," whispered Naso, his voice likely carrying further than he had intended. A look from Barbatus caused him to lower it before he continued, "Do you know what happens when people find a focus for their fear? They attack. They attack their leaders." He glanced at a nearby slave. "They attack their masters. And they attack monsters – whether they are real or not."

Nick felt a sharp pain shoot through his temple. "Are you making a threat?"

Barbatus slapped Nick on his arm. It took a second for him to realise the *duumvir*'s attention was focused over his left shoulder. He turned to find Calpurnia heading towards them.

"Three things," said Barbatus, directly into his ear. "The first is we shall speak again. The second is she's no longer married. And the third is that she's only had two births. So although she's old, the field is still fertile."

Both Barbatus and Naso quickly beat their separate retreats. By the time Calpurnia reached Nick, the *duumvir* and the aedile were already chatting with other guests.

"Pullus," she said. "I hope you're well?"

"Yes—"

"I thought I'd rescue you from my father's politics… and Naso." Her nose wrinkled. "The man's a trader, you know."

Nick nodded, noting her distaste. "Your father said people were worried about whether the food will continue to arrive."

"No. That's his interpretation. Everyone can see the villas going up around the town, and that the fields are starting to produce crops. What really worries *him* is who's running things here. And what really worries *them* is that they can't queue up outside your door."

Nick didn't say anything. Whelan had told him they'd wanted to take a back seat, to let the people here run things for themselves. But that didn't appear remotely possible – not for a long time, anyway.

"But some people have more pressing problems," continued Calpurnia. "My father makes all his money from his estates. Some around Pompeii, others nearer Rome. We're from a very old family. The vines here are already doing well, though we could do with more rain. But Naso doesn't have any land – he makes his money from industry and moneylending."

"So Naso is new money, your father is old. He's the *duumvir*, and Naso's an aedile. But new money normally beats old, given enough time."

"Oh, I don't think Naso will be aedile for very much longer. Not when his cash flow stops. Unless you're planning to support him in perpetuity."

Nick glanced across to Naso. The man looked anxious.

"Garum," said Nick. He caught a brief smile cross Calpurnia's lips and knew he was right. "No port. No water. No fish. No garum."

"He used to make the best in the town. You know, his villa was filled with paintings of his bloody fish sauce. But now the money flows from you people. Just like you control our food supply. And everything else we need." She pointed to the table. "From these figs, to the bricks, to the paint that goes on to our walls."

Nick tried not to confirm or deny anything she was saying. "You're pregnant," he said, trying to change the subject.

"Yes. My father thinks my husband is dead."

"He didn't arrive here with everyone else?"

"No. But that's not unusual... almost everyone can name someone who is still missing."

Nick couldn't think of anything to say. He kept silent, all the time thinking of the plaster casts in the Neapolitan museum.

"I doubt we'll hear anything before the baby arrives," Calpurnia continued. "My father still hopes we'll soon start getting regular news from Rome. Did he mention he knows the Emperor?"

"Yes..."

"The ironic thing is that my husband wanted to see the Festival of Vulcan, and I didn't. Yet when the time came, off he went to Herculaneum with his brothers."

Although he didn't want to, Nick baulked. Herculaneum. In its own way, the town was even more of a miracle than Pompeii. But whereas generations of excavations had made Pompeii famous, most of Herculaneum remained buried under feet of rock. Not pumice, or ash. Rock.

"You think he's dead too." She spoke slowly, trying to read his expression. "By the gods... you *know* he's dead."

"No," replied Nick. But it was simple really: if Calpurnia's husband hadn't been in Pompeii, then he hadn't been transported. But to have been in Herculaneum? The poor man must have died in agony. "I've heard stories, that's all."

Stories? No. He'd seen the bones. The plaster moulds of Pompeii were popular with the tourists, but they always seemed somewhat ghostly. Detached. By contrast, the skeletons from Herculaneum were twisted from the heat that had first folded their limbs close to their bodies, then stripped the flesh from their bones, and finally made their brains boil and their skulls pop.

They were still screaming, all these years later. Nick took another heavy swig of wine. It hit the back of his throat hard, and made him cough. "I'm sorry," he said. But Calpurnia had already turned her back on the other guests, just quickly enough to prevent anyone seeing the tears welling at the corner of her eyes. Her stoical mask was suddenly gone. For a second, her entire body shook. But, before Nick could say anything, she regained her composure.

"I suppose I should thank you," she said. "For removing my doubt. My father is right. He is dead, and I am no longer married." She held her stomach. "I only carry a part of him now, if it survives." She turned back to face him. "So tell me, Pullus. Tell me again how we managed to survive by the will of a dead emperor?"

Nick didn't say anything. He stared ahead, feeling each glance from the other guests like a needle. From the direction of the atrium, Barbatus glanced at him and, for a horrible moment, Nick thought he might come over. But his host was beaten to them by a small boy, who ran across the garden and came to a dead halt in front of Calpurnia. He identified the boy's mother pretty quickly, a woman nearby who was straining to collect her child – but a man held on to her arm. Holding her back.

The boy pointed to Nick's watch-strap mark. "Are you one of the people with the white wrists?"

Nick hesitated. "Is that what you call us?"

The boy nodded, before changing tack. "Some people are saying we've travelled in time."

As Nick felt his jaw fall open, Calpurnia leant down and shooed the child away. "A lot of people want to know the truth," she said. "And, in a way, I think by lying to you a few moments ago, I think I may have got to some of it."

"How do you mean?"

"My husband didn't miss the Festival of Vulcan," she said. "It had long since passed when we felt his wrath. Which means, if the festival had just finished as you people claim, then maybe Augustus can control our calendar too."

"I don't know what you want me to say."

"I want you to tell me the truth, Pullus. Just the truth. Because while this place you've brought us to could be mistaken for Pompeii's twin, many areas of the town are wrong."

Nick struggled for his words. "The volcano... Augustus..."

"And then there are the empty houses."

"What?"

Calpurnia stopped, suddenly uncertain. "That's the first time you've sounded genuinely confused," she said. "You don't know about the empty houses?"

"No."

"The empty townhouses."

"Empty? Or just unoccupied?"

"Empty," she said. "There are dozens of houses with no owner. And who would leave so many empty houses, when there are so many crammed into tenements? Few people have noticed them, Pullus. But my father has. And when he found out, he only asked one question. Over and over."

"And what was that?"

"'Who else is coming?'"

37

NICK STUMBLED OUT on to the street and came to an immediate halt. It was dark. Really dark. As the door to the House of Barbatus slammed shut, what little light there had been was also extinguished.

He'd stayed longer than he'd intended to, his discussion with Calpurnia ending once Barbatus had decided to introduce him to some of his other guests. Then the entertainment had started. A pantomime of dance and music, lit with simple oil lamps that hadn't done much to lift the early evening gloom.

By the time torch-bearing slaves had started to arrive to accompany their masters home, it had become clear he would have to negotiate the streets on his own. Not that Barbatus had been happy about it – he'd offered him a bed – but the short walk back to the House of McMahon at least offered him the chance to clear his head of all the wine and figs.

Taking a few deep breaths, Nick started back to the main *via*. He knew the way, even if he could hardly see it. And he'd staggered back from enough student parties to trust his homing skills. One foot in front of the other and…

He almost fell to the ground, only stopping himself

with a quick lurch from his right leg. Yes, the pavements were high, the road low. And, most importantly, the paving was uneven. Adjusting his footing, Nick lifted his feet higher than was natural and continued on his way.

On each side of him, the walls of the townhouses and shops loomed high and close – cutting the sky down to just a narrow, dark strip. Looking up, he couldn't see any stars, let alone the moon. And of course there was no street lighting. Or any other lighting. The houses all turned inwards, guarding their light as if it might be stolen.

Nick stopped. Should he return to the House of Barbatus? Admit defeat and ask for lodging? He glanced behind him, startled as a wagon creaked its way past. He paused for a moment – waiting for it to move out of earshot – then noticed that, even though the town was dark, it wasn't silent. Laughter and shouting echoed into the street from behind closed doors. And all around him was the sound of more wagons in distant streets. Of work, of activity.

No. He would push on. He just needed to let his eyes get used to the dark.

Sure enough, after a couple of minutes, he reached a crossroads. Left or right? He went left, forcing himself to walk slowly so he didn't trip over any unseen hazard. It didn't work.

It could have been anything. A pile of rotting food, a slick of vomit, or perhaps just some horseshit. Whatever it was, it provided sufficient lubrication for his feet to slide out from under him.

For a few seconds, he thought he'd broken his lower back. "Shit!"

As he got back to his feet, a dark shape appeared beside him. It took a moment to realise it was a man. His breath stank, real pig breath pushing right into his face through a set of badly broken teeth.

"So much for you gods, then?"

The man laughed fiercely. Nick stumbled and the high kerb bumped into the back of his heels. He went down again. Another bite of pain shot up from the base of his spine.

"Here – let me help you, god."

The man reached down and yanked Nick upwards.

"Thanks," he said. "Pullus."

"Urgh?"

"My name. It's Pullus."

"Zeus, Mars, Minerva, Juno... Pullus."

Snaking his arm out of the man's grip, Nick thanked him again and continued on his way. After a few steps, he looked back. The Good Samaritan had already been consumed by the pervading darkness of the street. But Nick knew he was still there – somewhere. After all, he could still smell the breath and...

Crack!

A sickening odour of shit and piss erupted around him – and a few droplets of liquid ran down his shins. From above, a pair of shutters clattered shut.

Great.

Ignoring the pain in his back, Nick pushed on. He really needed to get back to the House of McMahon; it would take him no more than ten minutes. He tried to keep in the very centre of the road – keeping a good watch above for more flying sewage.

Another wagon came into view. It had just turned into the street from the junction ahead and was now rolling towards him. Cursing, Nick hopped up on to the pavement and took a position between two high windows.

A sudden glint of moonlight allowed him to see the driver's face. Not for long. Maybe just two or three seconds and then he was gone. But Nick recognised him almost instantly. The scars of a face ravaged by the pox. The Roman from the control villa.

Felix.

Nick stumbled down into the road, watching the wagon disappear. Hadn't Whelan said he wasn't allowed into town? Yes, he was almost certain. But there he was, driving a wagon and delivering supplies.

Nick took a couple of steps forward while feeling for his belt. He needed to know where Felix was heading. He wouldn't be able to stop the wagon, but if he could toss the buckle into the back then at least Whelan would be able to track its movement. However, as he slipped the belt from his waist, the dark shape of the Good Samaritan moved out of the shadows. The man blocked his path and pushed his face close. "You're one of them, aren't you?"

Nick tried to pull away, but the man shoved him in the chest. He felt the belt slip out of his hand. Further along the *via*, the wagon continued to rumble away. "I really don't know what you mean," said Nick. "Look, I'm just trying to get home."

The man used his other arm to grab Nick's shoulder. "You're from the house that runs things here. Everyone knows you control our food."

"The aediles—"

"Are two pale shits." The man issued a barking laugh, which stopped almost as suddenly as it started. "You run things. So why do you keep me down, and give others so much?"

Nick tried to wriggle free but couldn't. The wagon had turned into another street, the noise from its wheels dissipating with every passing second. And there wasn't anybody around to help him. Could he shout for help? Would anyone in the surrounding houses even hear him?

And would they venture out to help a stranger anyway?

The man clearly sensed his lack of focus. He let go of Nick's chest – and then drove his fist in just below the breastbone. With the air forced from his lungs, Nick's legs buckled, but the man kept a tight grip on his shoulder and held him upright. Stopped him from falling beside his belt and its emergency alarm.

"Look at me!" he screamed. "You'll fucking look at me!"

Nick opened his mouth but couldn't speak. He had no air. He looked down. He needed to get to his belt.

"I thought I was going to die that morning," the man shouted. "I was down on my knees. I couldn't breathe. It was like I was in a baker's oven. But I wasn't. I was in the street – being covered by ash."

"Wait…"

"I thought I was going to die! And then I'm in some

sort of camp, with all these strange people around me. People like you. Tall, and speaking in some godforsaken tongue! So tell me, god, man or whatever you are – is it true? Are we already dead?"

The man started to laugh. Not the barking madness of a few minutes earlier, but the belly laughter of a man who'd finally got the joke. "It's true what they're saying, isn't it? We're in Elysium!" The man's face twisted. "So why do *they* get to live for eternity in their big houses – and I end up sleeping in my own piss!"

With the dam of frustration broken, the man threw another couple of punches. Nick put his arms up to deflect the blows, but they came too fast. He slid down to the pavement.

38

KIRSTEN STRUGGLED TO catch her breath. She knew where she was. The basement had turned out to be under the student lodgings in Chaderton Court. Which meant she hadn't even left the college. She'd emerged only a few hundred metres from her own staircase.

She stopped for a moment and allowed her body to recover. Her lungs were still burning from the effort of her escape. She rubbed her right shoulder. It was probably already starting to bruise where she'd rammed the man in the canvas coat aside.

She tried to relax. He'd still be locked away where she'd left him. Hollering to get attention just like she'd done. But with one big difference. There was no one to hear him.

She glanced around. Chaderton Court was unlike the rest of the college, built in a gothic style at odds with the classical sandstone and columns of the front quad that separated it from the city beyond. It was clearly early evening; it was still just about light enough to see outside, but the student rooms were slowly lighting up. Getting out was going to be easier said than done. The college sat right in the middle of the city centre but it was surrounded by a high stone wall. At this time, most of the gates would be closed. She would need to head for the front quad, and then get past the porters guarding the lodge.

Suddenly she heard voices heading her way. Shouting.

The man in the canvas coat was still locked up. But he had a walkie-talkie. He must have called for help.

39

NICK WOKE, AND immediately wished he hadn't. His ribs had taken the majority of the beating, but a dull throbbing also extended from his jaw all the way up to his right temple and a stinging sensation cut across his legs and forearms. He touched his face gently, and felt the ache turn into a lancing pain. A couple of teeth felt loose.

He let his eyes open. He wasn't lying in the street. Instead, he was on the hard floor of a building. He twisted and pushed himself up on to a sore elbow. Someone had laid him on a pile of cushions, but his makeshift bed must have moved in the night, leaving him resting on nothing more comfortable than a wooden floor. He swore and tried to drag a few cushions back underneath his body, but they provided only limited comfort. He was going to have to stand up.

It was clear he wasn't in the House of McMahon. The room was small, a large bed had been pushed up against one wall, and a few odds and ends of furniture were squeezed in around it. In many ways, it looked like a studio flat. Except there was no kitchen or toilet. Just a small brass piss-pot at the end of the bed.

The realisation pushed down hard on his bladder. Groping for the pot, Nick hitched up his tunic and took careful aim. There was liquid already in it. His own piss would just have to add to the mix. It was only when he'd finished that he realised his belt was missing. It made his tunic look like a mini-dress.

"You're not dead, then?"

Nick turned, hot liquid soaking the tips of his fingers. There was a woman in the bed. She was buried deep among the sheets and pillows, staring up at him with sleepy eyes. Nick tried to engage his brain. He slowly put the piss-pot back on the floor, and wiped his hands across the back of his tunic. She'd spoken to him in Latin. She was Roman.

"No," said Nick. "Not quite." He stumbled for something to say. The woman kept staring at him. "Thank you for helping me…"

"You can thank Canus when he gets back. He dragged you in off the street."

Nick nodded, tongue-tied with embarrassment. All he could hear was the settling froth from the pot. He gestured towards it. "Sorry."

The woman shrugged. "Better there than on the floor."

"This is your… apartment?"

The woman's eyes narrowed. "You've not been here before? Canus said you were a friend."

Canus? Nick racked his brain. Had he been introduced to a Canus?

A sudden movement at the door answered his question. It opened, and Patrick stepped through from a stairwell.

He gave Nick a look of concern. "Glad to see you're still in one piece."

The woman laughed. "His body may be, but I don't think his brain is. He doesn't know who you are!"

Patrick grinned and strode forward, taking hold of Nick's right hand and giving it an exaggerated shake. "Appius Seius Canus. Pleased to meet you. And you are?"

Nick pulled his hand away, unimpressed by Patrick's attempt at humour. "Pullus."

"So what happened?"

Involuntarily, Nick's gaze flicked to the bed. The woman rolled her eyes. "You boys talk, I'm staying here."

"Well, I'm needed at the forum this morning," said Patrick, looking towards her. "Perhaps I could meet you later?"

For a few seconds the woman didn't move, but finally she got the hint that Patrick wanted her to leave. As she slid out of the sheets, she muttered something under her breath. It sounded offensive, but Nick couldn't hear through the noise of blood beating in his ears. The woman was naked, and didn't seem in a particular hurry to retrieve her *stola* from the floor. She finally pulled it on over her shoulders, and swung the door shut behind her.

"If your face wasn't so bruised, I'd say you'd gone a rather fetching shade of red."

Nick shrugged and pressed his fingers into the side of his face. Another jab of pain shot through his jaw. "Not very modest, was she?"

"Different culture. Most people's homes consist of just one room, so there's little mystery about what's under everyone's tunic." He laughed. "You'll get used to it, especially once you've been to a bathhouse."

"Bathing must be segregated," Nick replied, unimpressed. "Pompeii bathhouses had separate areas for women, and sometimes they had completely separate buildings."

"Yes," agreed Patrick. "But have you been to one of their communal toilets? I can assure you that they have no problem taking a shit together."

Nick nodded, wanting to change the subject. "Was she...?"

"No. If you were going to ask if she's a whore, then the answer is no. She works in a bakery. We got talking a few weeks ago and then decided to break bread, so to speak."

Nick smiled, trying to ignore the pain from his ribs. "Well, be careful. She won't wait until you've got down on one knee before she claims you as her husband. Roman marriage is based on cohabitation. Although I'm a bit surprised that Whelan and McMahon..."

"They don't know. And I'd prefer to keep it that way." Patrick's face had turned to stone. "McMahon thinks of these people as his puppets. He doesn't mind the security teams paying the odd visit to a brothel, but I'm sure he'd be pissed off if he thought I was actually in a relationship."

Nick's smile turned into a grin. It was worth the pain. "And are you? In a relationship?"

"I'm serious, Nick."

Nick's throat was suddenly dry. "Okay," he said. "I won't say anything."

Patrick grunted his thanks. "So what happened last night?"

"I was mugged."

"Clearly. But you should know Whelan went apoplectic. You caused us a lot of trouble. We sent some men out to find you."

"I was unconscious in a gutter…"

"Well your belt was in a rather seedy bar."

The GPS tracker. So, it did work. If he'd only managed to get it into that damn wagon.

"Our men beat the shit out of the guy who took it from you," continued Patrick. "He couldn't tell us where you were, but I found you a couple of hours later and dragged you back here. I figured it was probably better for your safety than handing you over to Whelan. Even though you've seen I had other things to do last night."

"I'm sorry."

"You were out pretty late."

Nick opened his mouth to answer, but stopped short. They would already know where he'd been. The GPS system had probably been recording his movements since he'd arrived. "I was invited to a party."

"And you didn't think to mention this to anyone?"

"I got the invite in town. I didn't think I needed to sign in and out."

Patrick considered. "This is a great town," he said. "But basic precautions still apply, Dr Houghton. Just like in every city on earth, you just can't wander around the streets when people have been drinking in the sun all day."

Nick couldn't help but feel embarrassed. He'd been caught out like a naïve tourist. And after what he'd said to Maggie. But still… "I think we have bigger problems," he said.

"You're sure?"

Nick nodded, but he'd grown less certain with every step he'd taken back to the House of McMahon. It had been dark. He'd been drinking. And he'd seen the guy for just a few seconds. From the side. So, no, he wasn't sure. And if he'd been in a court of law, it wouldn't have stood up to any sort of scrutiny. But if New Pompeii was built on an illusion, then nothing could be allowed to break it. And from the look in Whelan's eyes, he understood this perfectly well. After all, it was why Nick had been brought here in the first place.

"I think it's highly unlikely," Astridge said. The architect stood on the far side of the atrium, his attention focused on the roof line above the *impluvium*. Almost as though the current discussion wasn't worthy of his attention.

"This isn't an architectural issue," replied Whelan, coldly. "It's a security matter. So, first, we need to confirm it."

Nick watched Whelan head towards the atrium stairs. Beside him, Patrick gave him a look of sympathy. The translator probably knew that, whatever the outcome, it was bad news. Because if Nick was right about Felix, they had a security breach. And if he was wrong, then he'd be on a slow flight back home – and Whelan would be looking for another replacement for Professor Samson.

It didn't take long for the operations chief to return, a tablet computer in his hand.

And it was clear it was bad news.

Wordlessly, Whelan handed Nick the tablet. On the screen was a mugshot of Felix. The Roman stared back at him, dead-eyed. The man at the villa. The man driving the wagon. The man on the screen. All the same. "Yes," said Nick. "That's him."

"Are you sure?" asked Astridge. "He's a fairly swarthy fellow."

Nick felt his cheeks burn. How many times did he need to confirm it? "It's the same man."

"Great." Astridge walked around the pool to join them. "Fantastic! The town's working brilliantly – and it's all going to be screwed up by a 'security matter'."

Whelan ignored him. He took the tablet back and tapped at the screen for a few moments. It chimed in his hands. "Well, the villa staff have just confirmed it. He's missing. So we can presume Nick is correct, and Felix is now in New Pompeii." Whelan frowned, his mood visibly darkening. "Harold is also on his way back."

Astridge cocked his head towards Nick. "Maybe one of your recommendations could be that he employs some decent security, and stops relying on toy soldiers."

Whelan drew himself up to his full height and took a step towards the architect. "Give me a reason."

Astridge didn't move. Despite Whelan towering above him, he grinned smugly. For a second, Nick thought Whelan was going to punch him.

"Do we know why he'd want to be here?" asked Nick. No one replied. Astridge continued to smirk. Nick turned to Patrick. "Well?"

The translator shrugged. "There could be any number of reasons. He might just have been curious. He might be trying to find his family."

Nick thought back to Samson's notes. Felix had been part of the vanguard, transported five years before the rest of the town. To test the system and prove the business model.

"Well, he can't be allowed to find them," he said. "For starters, he'd be older than they'd remember." He thought back to the party. The kid who'd asked him if they'd travelled in time. It had been like someone had taken a sledgehammer to this whole charade. And now there was a guy walking around town who could prove as much. "We need to find him as soon as possible."

"Okay," said Whelan, taking back control of the discussion. He suddenly looked a lot calmer. His emotions back under control. He turned away from Astridge. "Okay. So we need to find him."

"Where do his family live?"

"They don't. They're dead. He lived alone in the north of the town. Alone with a dozen slaves, obviously; he was a wealthy man. We'll send men there, but the building he used to own is occupied. We gave it to another family. And, anyway, surely he'll know that's the first place we'll look."

Nick didn't say anything. Had Felix's family not been transported? He thought about Felix's mugshot, his pox-riddled face, and wondered if NovusPart had similar photos of everyone in Pompeii.

"Well that gives us some time," said Patrick. "The security cameras have facial recognition, don't they? We haven't used it yet, so it could be a good test."

"But only if he goes to one of the key sectors," replied Whelan. "We could be waiting a long time, and then be left to hope he looks in the right direction."

Astridge snorted. "So how do we find him? Any ideas, *Dr* Houghton?"

"I think I know," Nick said.

40

I THINK I KNOW.

Why had he said that? Nick cursed as he made his way down the *via*. With a cold, academic eye, it probably just about made sense. Felix could be anywhere. But there were two types of places most Pompeians would go to regularly. The first were the bathhouses. Whelan had covered those with a contingent of men ready to make a quick interception. The second, and the more likely, were the *tabernae*. People needed to eat.

In Pompeii, the poor went out to eat; the rich stayed at home. Which meant Felix would be almost guaranteed to be out in the streets at certain times of day because now he had nowhere to go. But it also posed a problem. Because with so many people to be fed there were scores of establishments catering to them, and at peak times the main streets were bustling. It would take a long time to find their man – Nick had already tried half a dozen *tabernae* without success.

He looked down at his palm. Whelan had given him a small photograph of Felix to jog people's memories. Some more "smoke and mirrors" to help with their search. Sure enough, every time he'd showed it, he'd seen the surprise on people's faces. But it had mainly related to the quality of the image rather than any hint of recognition. And they'd all soon retreated behind a screen of silence. Just like they'd done when he'd tried to talk to them about their everyday lives. Simply put, the Pompeians didn't want to talk to him. Not about how they spent their day, and certainly not about a face they didn't know.

Mice don't talk to lions.

He'd needed to come up with a new tack.

And so he'd headed east.

If Felix wanted to eat over the medium to long term, then he'd need to find work. Without a family, he'd be on his own. Nick allowed himself a tight smile. The eastern side of town had been taken over by blacksmiths, bakers and fullers. Their workshops and stalls started to appear from between the townhouses and apartments only a few blocks from the fringes of the civic centre. And if someone was looking for a job, this was probably where they'd come.

Nick glanced into each workshop as he passed, trying to keep his attention from being drawn by the activity of the people inside. He soon found it wasn't just people who were working. The doors into one bakery gave him a good view of a couple of mules grinding corn between two large, circular stones. The animals were being forced to walk in a tight circle, rods across their backs the only thing providing the required force on the stones. The smell from the ovens though proved more than a little distracting.

But not for long. In just a few strides, Nick caught

the stench of stale urine. A couple of pots had been left outside a fullery, presumably for the use of passers-by who wanted to donate, or possibly sell, their piss. A cloud of flies buzzed around them. Nick felt his lip curl, especially when he noticed that a large townhouse had been built in close proximity. Rich and poor. Shoulder to shoulder.

"Pullus!"

The shout had come from the other side of the street. Nick recognised the reedy tone. Naso.

He raised a hand to acknowledge the call, and then headed across to the aedile.

Naso stood with about half a dozen other men. They all looked like they were prepared to throw a few punches, if need be. The workshop they were standing outside was shuttered. Naso thumbed towards it. "They owe me money," he said, loudly. "Half this town owes me money."

Nick nodded. As well as controlling the garum supply, Calpurnia had told him the aedile had a sideline as a moneylender. Nick made a mental note to raise the issue with Whelan. After all, he didn't have a good understanding of how NovusPart was distributing cash to the Pompeians – and how that might be affecting the local politics. But at the moment that took a lower priority than finding Felix.

"What are you doing on this side of town?"

Nick flashed the photograph. He got the same response from Naso as everyone else. Surprise, then nothing.

"I thought you might have been heading to the arena," Naso continued. "The guards there tell us it's off limits – even though I've told them I'm an aedile!"

Nick shrugged. He'd almost reached the final blocks of housing and workshops before the large open space surrounding the amphitheatre. He could just about see the low oval profile of the building set tight against the town's curtain wall. The only thing clearly visible was a massive stone ramp leading towards the top of the structure. "There must be a good reason for it."

"Well, our gladiators grow fat and lazy, while their swords go rusty…"

Nick smiled. "Are you saying you're going to pay for some games?"

Naso's face suddenly froze. He pulled Nick away from his men and towards the centre of the *via*. "No," he said. "Definitely not." He gave a nervous look back at his employees, probably hoping they wouldn't expect him to pay for their entertainment. Especially if he was starting to watch his cashflow. "I just want to know if it's in good order. So we can get some games on, if we need to."

"To quieten the mob?"

"Precisely."

Nick nodded. "It looks like a fine building. I doubt it will be left empty for long. I've heard the games at Pompeii were particularly good."

Naso's eyes narrowed. "Yes, but then I suppose you've heard about the trouble with our neighbours? We don't seem able to get away from that night."

Nick grinned. He knew games in Pompeii had been banned for several years after a series of riots. Just like with certain football clubs, it seemed a bad reputation was hard to live down – and all too easy to live up to. "You held about two events per year?"

"Yes," said Naso, his expression a mix of pride and mournful reminiscing. "We have one of the best arenas in all the Empire." He nodded towards it. "When your people finally let us inside."

"I'm sure it won't be long."

"We know you're keeping animals in there."

Nick blinked. "Really?"

"The people round here can hear them at night."

Nick didn't respond, making another mental note.

"Perhaps we'll get to see some lions," Naso continued. "Like they have in Rome. They're building a new arena there, you know. Or they were. Barbatus has seen it. He says it's more like a mountain than a building. And it's not even finished yet."

41

KIRSTEN WOKE IN the bath.

The coldness of the ceramic made her gasp, and she quickly wrenched herself out. Standing in the bathroom, she ignored the sharp ache in her shoulders and cramp in her neck. After all, they were sensations that told her she was still alive. And there was no water around her. She wasn't wet, and she hadn't woken up floating. There'd been no white mist and she'd not come back to it from any netherworld. For once she had chosen to be here. She held out her hand, pushed against the wall. She remained solid.

She needed a plan. The previous night, with the man in the canvas coat and his associates out looking for her, she'd had no real choice. The odds of her getting out of the college past the porters had been pretty low, and she didn't know where she would have gone. Yes, she'd done the right thing. Retreated to a place of safety, the part of the college she knew best. But now she needed to leave.

She opened the bathroom door and looked out on to the landing. The rooms didn't appear to be occupied. She remembered the student saying that the college had shut off the floor to stop the stories about the resident ghost.

"You've heard about NovusPart? They've lost one."

Kirsten's breath caught in the back of her throat. The voice echoed up from the stairwell where it opened into the quad below. Just like she remembered from when she'd lived here. Private conversations, funnelled and magnified.

"What do you mean… lost?"

"A paradox. Last night. Landed in the basement, like all the others. Except this one wasn't a child. It was a woman."

"And they let her go?"

There was no response. Whoever was talking had moved away from the sweet spot.

Kirsten waited, but the voices didn't come back. She peered through the bathroom window. The coldness of the bath had woken her early. The sun was only just climbing into the sky, and the roof of the old library looked damp with dew.

They were still looking for her. She edged down the landing and reached the top of the stairs. They didn't know she was still in the college. But they were looking for her.

And they would be able to see her.

Her breathing grew shallow. She started to walk down the steps, gently, to minimise any noise. Alert for any movement or sound.

They were looking for her.

But they weren't going to find her.

Kirsten smiled. She had two leads. Mr Black, and the student with the horn-rimmed glasses. She knew what they looked like. She had to find them. And then maybe she'd get some answers. Maybe she'd get her revenge on Harold McMahon.

She reached the foot of the staircase and ducked into the post room, nearly tripping over a stack of newspapers. She picked up a copy and looked at the date, and felt her legs start to buckle. Thirty years. She'd lost thirty years.

For a moment she concentrated on her breathing, then scanned the rest of the front page.

NOVUS PARTICLES ANNOUNCE TRAGIC SUICIDES OF SURVIVORS OF FLIGHT 391

Flight 391? She vaguely remembered the story, a plane that had gone down with no survivors. But that had been around the time that she'd been born, twenty— No, fifty years ago now. There were several passport-sized photographs of the dead passengers inset within the columns of text. One face leapt out at her, a young woman with long blonde hair. She looked familiar, but Kirsten couldn't place her. She looked around but the quad was empty. She quickly scanned the article.

So they'd done it – they'd transported people before the moment of death. And now NovusPart were claiming that some of the passengers had committed suicide. She looked at the blonde woman's face. This woman had first died before she was born, and had been transported while she was trapped in that damn bath. And now she was dead again. How could she be familiar? Kirsten closed her eyes – and then she knew. She saw the woman's face again, her mouth open, screaming as the men with swords closed in. Suicide? No, they'd been butchered in that pit. Perhaps she was the only one who knew.

She had to keep moving. Kirsten looked down at her clothes, the T-shirt, jumper and jeans given to her by the man in the canvas coat. Hopefully she just looked like a student. They'd be expecting her to try to get through one of the gates, so she wouldn't go for them. Not yet. And if she was going to find out more about Mr Black and the student, then this was where she needed to be.

She left the post room, walking around the quad and towards the chapel. Turning right before its doors, she pushed on through the sandstone cloisters and out across the lawn, heading for the library. She couldn't stay outside. Eventually someone would ask themselves why she was wandering around the college.

She suddenly slowed her pace. Because she also knew how college security worked. Staircases might be left open, but rooms were locked. And key buildings were always secure. There would be an entry system, and who knew how complicated it might be in this time. She wouldn't be able to just walk into the library. She kept going, back around the edge of the lawn and into the gardens. Waiting for the first students to arrive.

42

NICK WAS STILL some distance from the House of McMahon when the sweet smell of oil and ripened fruit stopped him in his tracks. He had searched for Felix in the workshops around the amphitheatre without success. So he'd gone back to Plan A: checking as many eateries as he could in the hope that he and the Roman would eventually cross paths.

In a *taberna*, a woman was serving customers from behind the counter. She looked harassed, moving rapidly between two stoves. A few men were sitting in the back, playing dice. One gave a loud bark of laughter. Clearly the man had achieved a good score.

"Well? What do you want?"

Nick pointed at a wedge of a round Roman loaf. He watched the woman hack it free, and handed over a couple of coins. Pushing bread into his mouth, he laughed as he caught sight of another phallus carved into a table. As he edged around the side of the bar there was the sound of the dice being thrown again, followed by another celebratory bark.

Nick turned. Amongst the group was a man who wasn't playing. Instead, he was just quietly eating. Looking in something of a daze. As if his world was gone.

Felix.

Nick quietly moved back towards the street. Taking hold of his belt buckle, he squeezed it tightly. The leather vibrated in response. And that was it. A simple input, and a basic output. Whelan and his men would be on their way. He just needed to find a place to wait.

The nearest decent position was next to a water fountain. He walked over and took a long drink of water before scooping some into his hair. As he turned back, he realised Felix was now standing at the exit to the bar. The Roman waited on the threshold – probably letting his eyes adjust after the relative gloom of the *taberna* – and then started walking north.

Nick looked up and down the street. There was no sign of Whelan. Which meant he'd just have to follow and let Whelan track his belt's GPS. But after a few paces he realised the task was going to be difficult. He'd never tailed someone before. From watching late-night TV shows, he knew he needed to be close enough to keep his target in sight. But how far should he hang back? If he made a mistake he'd either be spotted or his quarry would get away. And Nick knew he stood out. The Pompeians were watching him, some casually, most openly.

Fortunately Felix didn't seem to have noticed. He continued walking north and entered a residential area. Perhaps he was looking for friends, hoping they would shelter him. All Nick needed to do was see which house he went in to. Felix turned into another street; he had walked about halfway along the *via* when a woman who was passing suddenly grabbed his arm. Nick saw Felix spin around, his face taut, then relax in recognition. He leant close to the woman, talking urgently. Nick felt the blood drain from his face.

Felix was talking to Calpurnia.

43

W HELAN WOULD BE on his way. And he'd have a
contingent of security staff with him.

Shit. The street was heaving with people, and Whelan's
people would no doubt approach from both ends, trapping
Felix. So all Nick had to do was wait. But then he looked
at Calpurnia again.

How did she even know him? Of course, Whelan had
said that Felix had been a wealthy merchant. It wasn't
surprising that he knew the *duumvir*'s daughter. Nick
edged back to the house behind, making sure he kept
the pair in view. Even from this distance, it was clear that
Calpurnia was shaking. Her face was drained of colour
and, while Felix was doing all the talking, it didn't look
like his words were registering. There was too much shock
on her face. Too much disbelief.

She knew him. A person she thought had been lost,
suddenly brought back to life. And she could probably see
he'd aged slightly faster than he should have. Which meant
she would know something was wrong.

He stumbled forward, his legs and brain not quite in
sync. Despite this, he was within a few feet before they

noticed him. Felix was the first to react.

"Are they coming for me?" The Roman's face was set. He seemed resigned, like he was expecting it.

"Yes," said Nick. "They'll be here any minute."

Felix looked up and down the street. There was no sign of the encroaching net. "I thought I'd have more time," he said. He gestured at Calpurnia. "You need to let her go."

Nick hesitated. Calpurnia remained frozen, her eyes fixed on Felix. "I think it would be best if we all stayed here and waited," he said.

"They'll kill us, you know."

Nick shook his head. "No. You'll be returned to the control villa."

"No. They'll kill me, and they'll kill her too."

"I don't think…"

"They'll kill her."

Nick didn't say anything. He felt his throat contract.

"I thought I'd have more time," Felix repeated. "But if they come for me now, they'll take us both."

"You'll be taken back to the villa," Nick repeated. "They'll speak with her separately."

Again, Felix looked up and down the street. Nick followed his gaze. There was still no sign of Whelan.

He was going to run.

Instinctively, Nick felt his legs brace, ready to give chase. But Felix didn't move.

"I'm the only one left, you know," he said. "There were about ten of us, at first. One by one, we escaped. But I held on."

"The others," said Nick. "What happened to them?"

"They were hunted, and killed. By your Whelan – and McMahon."

"Why would they do that?"

"What do you do with a slave who's too old to be of use?"

You gave them their freedom, thought Nick. And let them die on the street. But he didn't quite believe it. "You're sure?"

"I saw the bodies. We were shown the bodies. And we were told quite clearly: run, and end up dead."

"Then why do it?"

"Because I am not their slave."

Nick looked up the *via*. There was still no sign of Whelan but he could hear a commotion in the distance. Something was getting closer.

He looked back at Calpurnia. She seemed a world away from the confident young woman he'd spoken to at the Temple of Fortuna Augusta. But would they really kill her? He thought about what Patrick had told him. *McMahon thinks of these people as his puppets.* Not people. Puppets.

Nick grabbed Calpurnia's arm. "You have to leave," he said. "Disappear into the crowd."

"But…"

"Calpurnia!" Felix shouted. "You have to go!"

A few people turned in their direction, but most were now flooding away as a group of men appeared at the far end of the street. Nick counted ten in all, each wearing the uniform of a Roman legionary. NovusPart security. Whelan was at their head. He raised his arm and the metal studs of his black leather wrist-guard glinted in the sun.

"Calpurnia," repeated Felix, "you must go! Now!"

She didn't move. If anything, her expression grew more determined. Maybe she thought being the *duumvir*'s daughter would be enough. Maybe she thought she was more important than she really was. Maybe she thought she was still a Roman, rather than already dead.

"Calpurnia," said Nick, keeping his voice barely above a whisper. He needed to say something to make her go. "Go now, and when we next meet…" He hesitated. Felt the words gather at the back of his throat because he knew there was only one thing he could say. "When we next meet," he repeated, his voice suddenly calm, "I'll tell you the truth."

44

TAPPING AT THE keyboard, Kirsten let out a frustrated sigh. She wasn't getting anywhere fast. Mr Black was proving to be elusive. The only lead she had didn't appear on the college staff list. She was now clicking through photographs of past alumni and lecturers, trying to spot two familiar faces.

Although the main door had required a pass-card, getting into the college library hadn't been difficult. The first two students to arrive had been female, and she hadn't bothered attempting to duck in behind them. Odds were they'd know she was a stranger, and pairs were always less vulnerable than an individual. She'd finally fallen in behind a young man who was all teeth, glasses and acne. A last minute dash to the door, and the presence of mind to stand that bit too close to him was all that had been required. The next task had been working the slimline computer – at first she hadn't even recognised it for what it was – but it had turned out to be a lot easier than she'd been expecting. Previously, she'd struggled with computers, unable to remember what commands to type at the blinking prompt. But this one seemed intuitive.

Like someone had actually thought about how it would be used.

She still wasn't going to find him, though. The realisation was crushing. She'd searched through all the fellows, research students and temporary teaching staff. She ran a search for her own name and followed a link to a news story. She was described as "missing". Not murdered. Missing. There was a photograph of her parents at a press conference, flanked by grim-faced policemen.

Kirsten suddenly felt sick. She started to shake, her entire body suddenly caught up in the realisation that her parents had spent the last thirty years not knowing where she was. Why had she not thought about them? Why had she not even considered…?

They'd be in their seventies. Kirsten let out a strangled yelp, then panicked. *Had anyone heard her cry?*

She glanced over her shoulder. It was difficult to tell if she was alone. The computer stations were butted up against one wall, and the rest of the floor was occupied by a scattering of bookshelves and desks that made gaining a clear view across the floor almost impossible. All she could hear was the soft drone of the air-conditioning units.

Kirsten waited a few moments before turning back to the screen. She needed to find her parents. To tell them that she was okay. But thirty years?

She caught sight of her reflection in the computer screen. She hadn't aged a day since she'd first stepped into the bath. She was still a young woman, in her twenties.

How the hell would they cope with seeing her again? The shock might be enough to…

From somewhere in the distance there was the sound of a chair scraping back, the sound of approaching footsteps. She looked over her shoulder, and saw one of the two girls who she'd seen arrive at the library. The girl was staring at her.

Kirsten turned back to the computer.

She knew she was running out of time.

45

Nick was resting in his room when he heard voices from the atrium.

McMahon was back. And he was with Whelan. Nick hesitated behind the shutter. McMahon didn't sound very pleased, and what Whelan was saying in return was so terse he could barely hear it.

Nick moved closer and tried to peer through a gap between two shutter slats. McMahon and Whelan were standing near the atrium pool.

"I thought you'd dealt with this." McMahon waved his hands as if to emphasise the point. He looked pale, his skin clammy. Whelan said something in response, but it was inaudible. "I want to know who this guy is!"

Again, Nick couldn't pick out what Whelan was saying. And only being able to hear one side of the exchange meant he couldn't build up much sense of the conversation. But surely they knew who the "guy" was? Hadn't Felix been at the control villa for years?

Felix... Calpurnia had only just merged back into the crowd when the NovusPart guards had circled their prey. And then Whelan had finally revealed the true function of his leather wrist-guard.

It was a Taser.

And every single Roman who'd been watching had seen Felix writhing on the ground under a stream of blue lightning.

Smoke and mirrors, Nick thought. He hadn't seen what had happened next. Felix had still been convulsing when he'd been dragged away. Where had they taken him?

Whelan crossed the atrium to the staircase, smacking the ball of his fist into his palm. And now he could be clearly heard, calling for Astridge. McMahon followed him. "I want Harris found," McMahon said. "I want him found, and I want him removed."

"I'll take care of it."

"I want him dead."

Nick swallowed hard. *Harris*. He edged back to the bed. *Harris*. McMahon had used that name when they'd first met. Asked him if he'd ever met a James Harris. But dead? They actually wanted him dead?

It could have just been a figure of speech. But something was ringing deep in the back of his head. Something that told him that McMahon wasn't fooling around.

"Harold!" The architect's bellow echoed in the atrium. It didn't contain any concern. Rather, it was laced with the thick treacle of disdain. "Great to see you back, but I think Mark has now brought his little problem under control."

Nick looked back towards the shutter, but couldn't hear Whelan's reply. Instead he saw a flutter of movement. He lunged for his tablet. The device had only just flickered to life when the shutter was wrenched open.

"Yes," said Astridge, grinning down at him. "I thought I'd seen him come in here."

Nick assumed an open-mouthed expression he hoped would be mistaken for academic confusion. It seemed to work, although McMahon cast him a guarded look as he joined the other men in the atrium. He kept tight hold of the tablet, his shield against an accusation of eavesdropping.

"Working hard after his exploits, no doubt."

McMahon turned towards Nick. Drops of sweat were gathering on his brow. "Find anything useful?"

"Only that Professor Samson didn't really know much about Roman history."

The grin on the architect's face grew wider. "Really? He was always lecturing me on the subject."

McMahon grunted. "We didn't appoint him specifically to work on this project." He tilted his head towards his operations chief. "Mark has filled me in on what happened. But what I really want to know is: how much did you just overhear? We all heard you shuffling around in there."

Parry. Nick held up the tablet. "Shit," he said. "Look, I've just been chasing some guy across town the night after having the shit kicked out of me." He paused, trying to look suitably embarrassed. "I wasn't working. I was asleep."

McMahon gave a sudden snort of laughter. "Well, you seem to have earned your pay cheque. And proved Mark right."

Proved Mark right? Nick glanced at Astridge and saw his confusion mirrored on the architect's face.

"Ironic though," said Astridge, his voice wavering,

"that Whelan brings you here to point out my mistakes, and you end up reporting his. Now if you can just tell him how to sort out the rest of the disorder in my town…"

"This is *our* town."

Nick shrank back as McMahon turned to the architect. "This is our town," he repeated. "Mine and Mark's. And you work for us. Just like Nick. So don't forget that."

Whelan let a few seconds' silence hang in the air before speaking. "The town is quiet tonight," he said. "But we're still having regular problems outside the Temple of Isis. And the town's authorities don't seem particularly interested in doing anything about it."

Nick nodded. "Have you spoken with Barbatus?"

"We've sent him a message. But as I said, he doesn't seem too interested in getting involved. But Roman mobs were frequent. How did the emperors cope?"

"Some put soldiers on the streets…"

"We don't have enough men – and I don't want to dilute the power of the imperial eagle by using it too often."

"Then it boils down to the old cliché of bread and circuses."

"The people are well fed."

"So you need to entertain them. They're bored – and frightened."

Whelan considered this. He turned to McMahon. "We could bring forward our launch events?"

"Fine. It's your call. Yours and your young advisor's."

46

KIRSTEN SWITCHED OFF the computer and headed for the stairs. Her brain was only just overpowering her instinct to run. After all, she didn't want them to know what she'd been researching. But the voices had been clear and loud. The girl had left the library soon after Kirsten had seen her staring at her. And now she was back with a couple of porters in tow.

"She was in here," said a female voice. "I've not seen her before – and with the news saying that stuff about a madwoman on the loose…"

"You did the right thing."

Kirsten sprinted up the single winding staircase, which led to all four levels. She headed to the third floor and ducked inside, trying to hide among the bookshelves while peering through the windows that overlooked the lawn.

More porters were coming. At least another two. Four to search the building. She had to keep hidden. Or else be taken back to NovusPart. To be dealt with once and for all in that pit.

In her time, the porters had all been ex-policemen and she had no reason to think that wasn't the case now. Old and grey, but not stupid. And trained to search a building. Kirsten looked round the floor, and saw nothing but shelves. There was only one door, back to the staircase. She had nowhere to go. She was going to be caught.

Footsteps echoed in the stairwell but continued up to the top floor. Ex-police, she thought again. They'd keep two downstairs, while the others swept the building from top to bottom. One guarding the stairwell while the other searched the floor. But maybe they only had four porters on duty. Which meant only one person to sweep the rooms while the other stayed on the staircase.

It was her only chance. Kirsten edged away from the door to the back of the room in perfect line with the exit. She crouched, trying to peer through the bookshelves. If the porter came in and moved right, she'd go left. If he came in and went left, she'd go right. Try to keep behind him as he made his sweep.

A couple of minutes passed before her plan was put to the test. The door swung open and a large, fat porter took a couple of steps into the room. After a few seconds, he went right. Kirsten moved in the opposite direction, hugging the back wall and then slipping down the side of a bookcase. The porter continued his sweep. He didn't find her.

As the door snapped shut, Kirsten felt herself exhale. She crawled over to the windows and saw four figures crossing the lawn, back towards the lodge. But she couldn't go yet. They'd still be looking for her.

After ten minutes her terror had turned to boredom.

She looked along the shelves. The nearest held scientific journals; she moved on quickly, idly pulling out bound up copies of a history periodical. Then she saw them: *College Life*, the annual college magazine, row upon row of issues. From battered copies decades old, to the crisp clean volumes of the previous year.

Her fingers trembled as she searched for the correct year. Each magazine had identical content: a brief overview of the previous year; news from fellows and old members; clubs and society events; obituaries; and a matriculation list. She paused at a page of photographs. One shot showed three young men: McMahon, Whelan and Arlen stared back at her.

She put the issue to one side and started to look at the years following their arrival at the college. She paid particular attention to the matriculation photographs, the group shot of all the new students taken in each year. She scanned each photograph in turn, taking her time, but also in a hurry. Alert for any sound of footsteps on the stairs.

But they were already too late. Because she'd found him. The student by the bath. The one who had spoken to her.

Kirsten gripped the magazine tighter. The door to the staircase had opened. Light footsteps. She heard the door shut, but whoever had entered was now walking in near silence. She was being hunted, and she had no idea which way she should feint.

She braced herself to run. Perhaps if she caught them by surprise she might get past. But it was too late. A man stepped in front of her. He was holding something to his ear, a flicker of a smile on his face.

"Yes, Marcus," he said. "She's just where you said she would be."

47

"Making any progress, *Dr* Houghton?"

Nick stopped by the pool. He'd been heading towards the street when the chef had appeared in the atrium. Mary was grinning at him, her cheeks slightly flushed, holding a small bowl of fruit and nuts. He presumed she was on her way upstairs to McMahon.

"Sort of… I'm actually heading out for breakfast."

"Something wrong with my cooking?"

"No," said Nick, just a little too quickly. "But it's my job to…" He let his voice trail off. From the look on her face, she was clearly teasing him. He would only end up digging himself in deeper if he tried a witty response. "I've never seen you out in town," he said.

"No." Her eyes narrowed as if she was trying to work something out. "So, are you getting any closer, Dr Houghton?"

"Closer to what?"

"Working out what makes the people tick."

Nick shrugged. In truth, he wasn't. But he'd only just started, and a project of this size would take a lot of time. If he'd be given enough was another matter entirely.

Mary laughed, and made for the stairs. "Well," she

said, "don't spend too long trying to solve the past, when the real riddle is working out the future."

Nick watched her go. Working out the future. Pop psychology that sounded good but didn't make sense. As Cicero wrote, if you don't know your history, you remain for ever a child.

Which would have been a good response, if he'd thought of it sooner. Nick headed for the atrium corridor. The next time he bumped into Mary, he'd have to raise it with her again.

He headed to a nearby *taberna*. No matter the impact on the chef's professional pride, eating out provided him with the best opportunity to get close to the people he was meant to be monitoring. He could hear what people were saying without them scurrying away like he had the plague. And very occasionally he got to speak with them directly.

"Excuse me?"

Nick looked up from his bread. A man and woman were standing in front of him. From their dress it was clear they weren't wealthy, but they weren't slaves either. Ordinary Romans. Well, as ordinary as they could look, living fifteen hundred years after the end of their Empire.

"Yes?" Nick said. He had sat at the end of the bar, with his back to the street – just in case he needed to make a quick exit. But these Romans didn't look aggressive.

"You're one of them, aren't you?" asked the man. He pointed at Nick's white-banded wrist.

"I don't know what you mean…"

"We can tell. By the way you talk."

And the way he looked.

"We wanted to thank you for saving us," said the woman, cutting in. "We all thought…" There were tears in her eyes. "We all thought we were going to die."

Nick put down the last of his bread, not really knowing what to say. "Augustus saved you," he said. "I'm just here to do his bidding."

The woman smiled with sympathy. As if she was complicit in his lie. She reached forward and took hold of his hands, bowing her head. A couple of tears trickled down her face. "You are good people," she whispered.

Nick looked about him, slightly embarrassed. He slid his hands from the woman's grip. A couple of the other customers were nodding in agreement; however, the majority seemed unmoved. One man bristled with hostility. Which meant, although Nick wanted to speak with the pair further, it was probably time to leave.

"Thank you," he said, getting up from the counter. He looked round the bar again. He desperately wanted to be able to talk freely with every person he saw staring back at him, but every one of them would only respond to him as a stranger.

A sudden thought struck him, a memory from his undergraduate days. At the time, he'd not really understood it. "It is impossible to measure something without affecting it." The guy who'd told him the line had been studying physics, and his statement related only to the smallest particles of matter. But that same phenomenon was going to end his research. Because he'd come to find the people of Pompeii, and he'd found they weren't really here. They'd already been lost in the ash of the volcano.

"Pullus!"

Nick stumbled back on to the street. He could tell the people in the *taberna* were already talking about him. The hum of conversation was almost drowned out by the noise from the street. But not quite.

"Pullus!" It was Patrick, with Maggie and Noah. A couple of NovusPart security guards were walking a few paces behind. "We were told you'd be out here."

Noah was pulling at Maggie's *stola*. The kid looked like he'd been cooped up for too long. He could probably use a trip over to the amphitheatre to burn off some energy. The Astridge woman didn't seem to notice.

"I seem to recall you comparing this town with Barcelona, Dr Houghton. Did you get beaten senseless there, too?"

With all that had happened, Nick had almost forgotten his encounter with the Good Samaritan. But the bruises were probably still visible on his face. And from the look on Maggie's, she seemed determined to remind him.

"I guess I was tempting fate."

"You certainly were." Maggie tipped her head towards her guards. "Fortunately, Mr Whelan provides us with protection when we want to go into town. Mind you, we're not here to hang around the forum, or take part in an orgy." She turned her full glare on him. "That's where you were, wasn't it? Some sort of Roman party? Patrick told me they found your clothes on the floor of a whorehouse."

Nick felt his cheeks flush. Before he could reply she had turned, dragging Noah with her, away along the *via*. The guards followed in her wake, but Patrick stayed close. "I said 'seedy bar'," the translator said, somewhat defensively.

Nick nodded. "Well, you can at least understand her being protective of her son."

For a second, Patrick looked confused. "Oh, Noah? Sure... right."

"You don't agree?"

Patrick shrugged. "It's nothing to do with me." He pointed down the street. "Whelan asked me to say 'thank you' for your good work yesterday."

"Really?"

"Yeah, I think you've managed to impress him, which is no mean feat."

"So what's my reward?"

"He said you could do with a bath."

It was only mid-morning, and Nick followed Patrick expecting that they would be turned away. In Pompeii the bathhouses would have been closed until about midday. But the Stabian Baths were open; another indication that New Pompeii was different to its namesake.

"We asked the aediles to keep these places open longer," Patrick explained. "To distract people from some of the remaining problems, including the Isis situation. Of course, as representatives of Augustus, we don't have to pay."

Nick nodded, and followed the interpreter into a changing room where about a dozen men were in the process of getting undressed. The sound of voices and splashing water echoed from the rest of the building.

Nick removed his sandals and stepped barefoot on to

the changing room's intricate mosaic floor. A beautiful image of an octopus stared up at him from the tiles, mythical sea creatures floating around its tentacles. All he had to do was take off his clothes, but that was easier said than done. He struggled to remove his belt and swore under his breath. Although he'd wanted to see how the Roman baths worked since he'd arrived, the process of going inside didn't exactly fit with any modern ideals of modesty. He pulled off his tunic and stuffed it into one of the many niches that lined the walls, making a mental note of the number scrawled above his niche. He looked over at Patrick, careful to keep his gaze at eye level.

"What happened to Felix? Was he sent back to the control villa?"

Patrick looked at him with heavy eyes. "No, Nick. That's not how McMahon likes things done. And Whelan generally makes sure things don't go wrong twice, if you catch my drift."

Nick nodded, understanding. "They're all just puppets, right?"

"Something like that."

"And it doesn't bother you?"

"Of course it does. But I'm not going to feel too upset about what happens to someone who should have died two thousand years ago."

Nick didn't reply. The translator's logic didn't assuage his feeling of guilt. He followed Patrick through the low door at the far end of the changing room, trying to push thoughts of Felix to the fringes of his mind, remembering that at least he'd managed to save Calpurnia from getting caught.

Calpurnia. He immediately regretted thinking about her.

"So what do you think?" asked Patrick.

The exercise yard was noisy and stank of sweat mixed with olive oil. There were men lifting weights; others sparring. Shouting as they won some small victory, and letting everyone know defeats weren't their fault. Around the edges of the main pool stood a huddle of stalls, mainly selling food. Their owners hollering about what they had for sale, above the splashing of the water.

It was all there. A Roman bathhouse in full flow.

And no one seemed to have noticed them.

"Let's speak in Latin," Nick said.

The translator looked amused. "Going native?"

Nick shook his head. Patrick didn't understand. On the street they were obviously outsiders. But although he'd come in here feeling completely exposed, their "emperor's new clothes" were an effective disguise: they were lost among all the other naked apes.

Still, there were still some things he wasn't prepared for. They made their way to the main pool, and Nick scowled as he saw the water. He reminded himself that Astridge had recreated Roman plumbing. The lack of circulation meant an accumulation of soap fat, oil, scum and phlegm dotted the water's surface. He didn't even want to think about what else could be in there.

"I'm not going in that water," Nick said.

"Fine – let's go and get scraped."

Patrick indicated a side chamber. Inside were a

collection of knee-high rectangular tables, each manned by a slave. The translator slid on to the nearest one, stomach down. Nick clambered on to the table next to him. Two slaves came over and started the process of oiling and then scraping their skin using hook-shaped metal strigils.

"Roman exfoliation," Patrick said. "Maggie would be very impressed."

"There's an old anecdote about the baths," said Nick, feeling the pressure of the metal pushing against his shoulder blades. The smell of the oil was starting to irritate his nose. "It goes something along the lines that an emperor visits the baths and sees a man scraping his back against a wall. The emperor finds out he's too poor to own a slave to do it for him, so gives him one. The next time he goes, ten men are stood scraping themselves against the wall. So the emperor tells them to scrape each other."

"Very good. From that joke book?"

"Yes." Nick paused, feeling the strigil scrape away at the tension in his muscles. "Back at the house, I heard McMahon talking about a man called Harris."

Patrick didn't respond.

"He seemed quite obsessed with him."

Patrick turned his head as his slave pushed heavily against him. The skin on the translator's back was pushed up like a wave and deep into his shoulders. "Best not to talk about that," he said, in English.

"It would be useful to know," Nick persisted. "So I don't put my foot in it with McMahon."

Patrick let out a heavy sigh. "Okay – but you didn't hear it from me, right?"

Nick nodded.

"So a few years ago, we kept on hearing about a guy called James Harris. Who was he? Who knew him? Who had he spoken to? McMahon was quite worried for a time but then announced he'd dealt with the problem."

"When was this?"

"A while ago… I'd only just joined. I had to answer a ton of questions about him. Which would have been easier to answer, if I'd actually known anything about the guy."

"Well," said Nick, "it looks like he's back."

48

"YOU LOOK SURPRISED."

Kirsten stared into the eyes behind the horn-rimmed spectacles. It was the student. Except he was no longer a teenager. Or a student. His hair was thinner and there were clusters of lines at the corners of his eyes.

"I don't think I ever introduced myself." He put the small phone he'd been carrying into his pocket, and extended his hand. "James Harris."

Kirsten didn't accept the gesture. She lifted the magazine. "That's not what it says in here."

"No," he replied, his tone even. He reached forward and took the magazine from her, replacing it on the shelf. "But sometimes it's better that people don't know who we are, or where we've been."

"You're working for McMahon?" she said.

The student – James Harris – smiled patiently. "Why would you think that?"

"You said he'd snatched me into the future. I didn't expect you to be part of it."

"Well, I don't work for Novus Particles."

Kirsten didn't say anything.

"Now," said Harris, looking towards the door, "if we wait another ten minutes, I'm assured we can get you out of here."

49

THE NICHES WERE empty, their tunics and sandals gone. Nick looked about, seeing Patrick looking as confused as he felt. Other patrons were dressing and undressing around them – all seemingly unaware of their predicament.

"Where's the attendant?"

The man who had been guarding the changing room had disappeared.

"There he is." Patrick pointed at a man who had appeared in the entrance. Nick didn't recognise him. Was he even the same guy who'd been on duty when they'd arrived? Nick realised he didn't know. He hadn't been paying any attention.

"Where are our clothes?"

Patrick's voice was perhaps a bit too aggressive for a man who was naked.

"Someone must have taken them," replied the attendant. He didn't sound at all bothered. Then the edge of his lip curled upwards, and Nick realised it was a scam. "Citizens can buy replacements for a small fee."

So that was it. Pay the fee, boys, or lose your dignity on the way home. Nick didn't fancy the latter. But replacement clothes were probably going to be expensive. And that was their other problem. They had no money.

"How much?" asked Patrick. Others were now listening to the conversation. And more men were entering from the main door. But they weren't undressing.

They were circling.

Nick found himself being shepherded closer to Patrick. It took far too long for it to dawn. It wasn't a scam.

It was a trap.

The attendant grinned. "Citizens can buy replacements for a small fee."

"You've already told me that."

"You're no citizen."

Instinctively, Nick looked behind him. The circle of men had grown tighter, and the attendant's face had lost its self-satisfied smile. His expression was grim.

Naked or not, it was time to leave. "Let's go," he whispered. "As quickly as we can."

"No," said Patrick. He still didn't seem aware of the danger. His attention was focused on the attendant. He'd not noticed the other bathers starting to scramble. Grabbing their clothes and running for the door. "Do you realise who we are?"

"Patrick!"

Nick grabbed the translator's arm, spinning him round. But the men wouldn't have let them run anyway. Without a spoken order, they lunged forward – some aiming at Nick, others for Patrick. It didn't take long to wrestle them both to the floor.

Nick tried to resist but couldn't. Two men held his shoulders. Another couple sat on his lower thighs, holding his ankles. Slowly, his legs were pulled out into a "V".

To one side, from where Patrick was being held, Nick heard a voice. It was a smooth, controlled tone, which barely echoed around the chamber.

"The Greeks believed that, when Uranus was overthrown, they cut his balls off with a sickle and cast them into the sea."

Nick immediately tried to wrench himself free but couldn't. He felt the *thump-thump-thump* of his heart, but no amount of adrenaline was going to shift the weight now pushing down on him. His entire body had been locked down. All except his genitals.

"And from his blood and semen, the whole gamut of life erupted from the oceans, and a new era was born…"

The thug holding his right shoulder grinned down at him just as the speaker appeared in his line of sight. He was holding a small metallic blade, which looked a lot like one of the strigils used in the steam room. Not unlike a sickle.

The man disappeared from view. Back to Patrick.

"Some people here think of you as gods," he continued. "They think you saved us from the mountain. But I don't think this is Olympus… and your shrivelled, wet dicks don't look too godly to me. So should we see what happens when we throw your balls into the water? Will any new life spring forth?"

"You're all going to die for this!"

Patrick. Nick ignored him. They were in no position

to make threats. "Let's just talk this through, okay?" His voice sounded weak – his chest squeezed by the pressure on his shoulders. The man with the sickle came and stood over him. He leered down.

"And what do you have to say to me?"

A few lines of argument came to mind. He rejected most of them. "We're not like you," he admitted. "We're not from Pompeii, and we're not Romans. But we never claimed to be gods…"

The man knelt down in front and below him – inside the "V" of his legs – the sickle resting on his knee. "Go on…"

"We can give you money," said Nick. "What do you want? To be aedile? *Duumvir?* We can arrange that."

"Nice speech, Cicero; but I don't believe it." The man reached forward and grabbed Nick's balls. Bunching them between his thumb and forefinger. Squeezing and stretching.

The vessels connecting to his testicles pulled tight. Nick opened his mouth to scream, but couldn't. The man slid the curve of the sickle underneath him. He lifted the blade a couple of centimetres, allowing the edge to bite into the underside of Nick's balls. Nick felt them trying to contract. But they couldn't go anywhere. And it just made the pain worse.

"Wait…" Nick whispered. The hammering in his chest was getting louder. He heard the first few missed beats as his heart started to motor like it was running low on gas. He swallowed dryly, and registered blotches of red and purple in his vision. He was going to die. They wouldn't just stop at emasculating him. They were going to kill him. Make an example of him. Probably drag his neutered body through the streets so everybody could see there was nothing to fear from the men of Augustus.

The sickle lifted higher. Nick sensed the deepening of the initial cut, but only allowed himself the merest grimace. He felt blood running down between his thighs. His head lolled. He was about to faint, and tried not to shake. It wouldn't take much now. Perhaps just one flick of this psycho's wrist.

"Do you have anything to say to me, god?"

Nick opened his mouth, but didn't speak. His head was swimming, and he didn't have anything to say. He couldn't see the corners of the room. Didn't know if there was any CCTV. And without his belt, he couldn't call for help.

Nick could feel a small pool of blood forming around him. But the man suddenly hesitated; looking at his men and then skyward. Nick's heart continued to pound, but suddenly he understood. They weren't sure.

They weren't sure he wasn't a god, and that there wouldn't be some divine retribution. Nick looked at the men holding him down. They were all staring at their boss, clearly uncertain. He might still have a chance. *He just needed to work out what to say…*

But as he opened his mouth, the man reached forward with his free hand, and touched Nick's bruised cheek.

"You can be injured," the man said, his tone still calm.

"Stop," said Nick, suddenly finding his voice. But the men holding him down were no longer fearful. Whelan's smoke and mirrors had suddenly dissipated, even though the steam from the bathing chambers seemed to be encircling them.

"Please stop," he said again, closing his eyes.

"*Do you hear me? You're all going to fucking die for this!*"

Patrick. In his terror, the translator had shouted in English. The man with the sickle looked puzzled – not understanding the words, but hearing their venom. He pulled the sickle away. Nick opened his eyes just as the changing room filled with the sound of Patrick's screams.

It stopped almost as soon as it had started. The poor bastard had probably lost consciousness. Nick turned his head, trying to see, but not quite pulling Patrick into view. It would be his turn next. He'd only been granted a temporary reprieve. Around him, the thin, hazy wisps of steam were getting thicker. But above the beating of his heart came a new sound: sandals on tiles, and metal on flesh.

Shouting. Screaming. Confusion.

Vengeance.

There were no longer any men holding him down.

It took a while for Nick to respond. He flailed on the floor, and then pushed himself to his feet – glancing down at the bloody mess in his groin and then dumbly towards where Patrick had been.

The translator was hidden by a scrum of men. Nick stumbled forward, but a man grabbed his wrist. Whelan.

The Chief Operating Officer looked him straight in the eye. There was no sympathy, only pure, unadulterated anger.

"Harris," he said. "What do you know about a man called Harris?"

50

T HE DRIVE FROM Cambridge to London was a long one. Kirsten stared out of the window. Harris didn't try to engage her in conversation. He stared ahead and concentrated on the road.

For the first time in years, Kirsten felt herself relax. She breathed out slowly and settled back against the headrest. It was a trip she used to make by train, visiting her parents...

Kirsten sprang forward in her seat. Her parents had lived in Hammersmith. But where would they be living now?

"What's the matter?"

"I was just thinking about my parents."

"You've been floating in that bathtub for the best part of thirty years."

"They'll be in their seventies now." Harris didn't respond. "My sister will be nearly fifty."

"I'll take you to them when we're done," he said. "One more day won't matter."

Kirsten nodded, uncertain.

"We're nearly there," Harris continued. "Don't beat yourself up. It wasn't your fault."

Kirsten didn't answer. She turned back to the window. They had reached Cambridge's outer suburbs quicker than she'd expected. In thirty years the city had sprawled – what had once been out-of-town shopping centres were now surrounded by new houses. The shops looked like they'd seen better times; many were shuttered, or had large "sale" signs in their windows. She half expected Harris to provide some commentary about what had happened while she'd been away, but he remained silent. The first real landmark she recognised was the botanic garden.

"You didn't use to be able to drive this way," she said. "It was for buses."

"No longer needed, now so few people drive." Harris paused, as if contemplating further explanation. "It's an expensive way to travel." He pushed down on the accelerator and nudged his way onto the last stretch of road before the motorway.

Kirsten looked in the wing mirror. Somehow, she knew she'd never be coming back.

51

Nick woke. He opened his eyes and immediately registered the pain between his legs. He reached down and felt rough stitches.

His stomach heaved. He waited for the feeling to pass, and then allowed himself a hysterical giggle. At school he'd been hit in the groin by a cricket ball. As he'd lain prone on the ground, with his mates laughing all around him, his teacher had shouted, "Don't rub them! Count them!"

So Nick counted. One. Two.

His testicles felt about three times larger than they should have – but they were both there. He was still intact. The relief almost overwhelmed him.

From the décor, he was back at the control villa. He tried to remember the events following the attack, but they were a haze. He tasted vomit at the back of his throat. He struggled to swallow, and rolled on to his side. The movement pushed his right leg against his wound and he quickly rolled back, trying to find a position that wouldn't cause him any more pain.

There was a breakfast tray on the bedside cabinet. A croissant, a pot of jam and some fruit juice. Nothing that needed to be heated. Probably placed there so he could wake up at any time, and didn't have to go stumbling about the villa looking for something to eat.

Beside the tray lay his tablet computer. On it was a handwritten Post-it note: *This is what we did.*

He really didn't want to know.

When he next woke his room was bathed in the half-light of either twilight or dawn. How much time had passed? He pushed himself up in bed. Tried to ignore the pain.

He didn't know how many people Whelan had in the villa, or if any of them had visited him while he'd slept. The cold breakfast still lay on the bedside table. As did the tablet and its little note. *This is what we did.*

Nick reached for the tablet and turned it on. The screen lit up. Whoever had left it for him had set it on a video file. For a moment, Nick hesitated. Did he really want to know?

No. No, not really. But he pressed play. The footage showed the interior of the Temple of Jupiter. Had they executed someone?

No. He was being shown yet more smoke and mirrors. A small crowd had gathered inside the temple, not on its steps as would be normal practice. In his short time in New Pompeii, he hadn't found time to go inside the largest of the religious sites. The temple interior was dominated by three statues – Jupiter at the centre, with the goddesses Minerva and Juno on either side. They looked down over their subjects, reminding Nick of the Lincoln Memorial. The gods were watching a man in a chainmail suit.

From the size of him, it must have been Whelan. Sure enough, as the video continued, he was the only NovusPart man missing from the rest of the group. McMahon was to one side with Astridge. In the crowd stood Barbatus and Naso, surrounded by well-dressed Pompeians. Probably the townsfolk who commanded a vote. There were no women in the crowd. He didn't see the man who'd tried to mutilate him. Nick focused on Whelan. A chainmail suit. He guessed what was about to happen before he saw it. Chainmail. Smoke and mirrors.

Electricity.

Sure enough, from the four corners of the temple shot sudden streams of lightning. Whelan reached out with his arms and seemed to catch it. The electrical charge spiralled around his arms, passing harmlessly over his body.

A Faraday cage.

Even to a modern audience, the trick was pretty spectacular. And it gave a very strong message to support their claim to god-like powers: just like Jupiter, Whelan had the power over the most frightening force in the ancient world. Even if the people working for him had been shown to be mortal.

Nick felt a sudden surge of rage. He flung the tablet across the room. It hit the wall opposite, but dropped – somewhat disappointingly – undamaged to the floor.

For a few seconds, Nick's chest heaved. Then his rage turned to confusion. A sound came from deep within the villa; one that confirmed he wasn't alone.

A baby crying. It was an incongruous sound. Whose baby was it?

He suddenly couldn't move. He looked over at the discarded tablet. A Faraday cage.

He swore. The attempt to reinstate NovusPart's smoke and mirrors policy may well have worked. But it had also brought into clear focus the town's failed premise.

He'd been told he'd have the opportunity to walk the streets of a living, breathing Roman town. To speak with real Romans, and to find out how they'd lived. But that wasn't what NovusPart had achieved. They'd simply taken a group of people and made their superstitions real. Which meant the town's religious practices had been altered. It meant no one had wanted to talk to him as they might a neighbour. And it meant men jealous of their power had tried to remove it with a sickle.

So, yes, he could write a thesis. But it would only ever be about what happened to the people of Pompeii after they'd been transported. Not how they lived before the eruption. *You can't measure something without changing it.*

"You're awake."

Whelan was standing in the doorway, his features taut. "Yes," Nick said, feeling his throat tighten.

What do you know about a man called Harris?

"You saw the video?" Whelan asked. Now he was away from Pompeii, he'd taken the opportunity to wear modern clothing. However, the neatly pressed shirt and chinos indicated he wasn't in the mood for relaxing.

Nick nodded.

"Good. You'll be pleased to know it had the necessary effect. The man behind the plot – someone who evidently failed to be elected aedile – has been handed over to us by your friend, Barbatus."

"What will happen to him?"

"I'm not sure yet." There was a glint in Whelan's eye. It suggested that, whatever he had planned, he was going to enjoy it. And Nick guessed the man wasn't going to get much of a trial. Not even a Roman one. Because out here, NovusPart could pretty much act how they wanted. Their word was law; and there was no accountability. They truly had the power of the caesars.

"Thank you for letting me know," Nick said, his voice wavering. He hesitated. *What do you know about a man called Harris?* "So what does this mean for the town?"

"It means nothing." Whelan's smile disappeared. In the background the baby was crying. Nick wished it would stop. "It means NovusPart has suffered an accident and we've taken appropriate action." Whelan took a few steps into the room. "I take it you're not going to sue us?"

The power of the caesars. "No."

"Good." Whelan was silent for a moment. Nick knew what was coming. "I need to ask you something. McMahon's pretty pissed off about it."

The baby's cries were getting louder. Like it needed its mother.

"What do you know about a man called Harris?"

Nick shifted on the bed, his legs bumping into his

bruised genitals. The resulting wince of pain hid what might have been an incriminatory reaction. "Nothing," he said.

Whelan mulled this over. It wasn't clear if he believed him or not. "Did you meet anybody from the government before you came here?"

"No."

"You're sure?"

"I was trying my best not to tell anybody about this. Not my friends. Not my father."

"That's what I told McMahon." The muscles in Whelan's brow remained tense. He didn't look convinced. A drilling pain erupted in Nick's right temple.

"I think I'm just about okay to travel," he said. "I take it I'll be flown out on the next helicopter?"

"No," replied Whelan. "You're staying here."

Nick hesitated. Considered the illusion around him; and knew it wasn't anything but smoke and mirrors. "I want to leave."

"No," replied Whelan, his tone firm. "Not yet."

Again, Nick hesitated. Although the swelling was starting to subside, his stitches didn't look all that professional. And he didn't even want to think about the possibility of infection. Gangrene. "I need to get to a hospital," he said.

"We've found a mole in our supply lines," Whelan replied. The operations chief let the news sink in slowly. "A man carrying a message to an agent Harris supposedly has right here, in New Pompeii."

Nick felt his throat wobble. "An agent?"

"Yes."

"And what did the message say?"

Whelan roared with laughter, and the tense atmosphere was suddenly broken. "You think I would tell you?"

Nick felt his cheeks turn crimson. "Sorry."

"Don't be." Whelan continued to chuckle. "At least we've established you're no Ace of Spies."

"So when can I go?"

Whelan smirked. "We've delayed the next shipment to give us time to check the remaining staff at the supply depot," he said. "The next helicopter will arrive in a few days. Then we'll get you out of here. Though I'd hope to see you back, once you've had time to consider things."

Nick shook his head. He didn't want to go back to the town. Not after what had happened. No, he just wanted to go home. Back to his father, and his teaching. But there was something he did need to know. "What happened to Patrick?" he said, swallowing hard.

Whelan hesitated, but his voice didn't waver. "He's no longer here."

"He's dead? If you'd arrived a minute sooner..."

"I mean he was transported, Nick. Him and most of the men holding him down. I saw them all sucked out of existence. He's been taken at least thirty years into the future."

Nick didn't reply. Deep in the villa, the baby continued to scream. NovusPart had transported Patrick?

"But...?"

"I can't answer your question, Nick. Maybe there was

some glitch." Whelan paused, his expression betraying his own frustration at not knowing. "The only thing we know for certain is that you'll have to wait thirty years to get your answer. And there are no witnesses to it from the town. We killed everyone who wasn't transported." He started to leave, then turned back. "Apart from you, that is."

52

"*R*ONNIE!"
     Nick hurried out of the flat and moved down the steps at speed. How much of his conversation with Whelan had Ronnie overheard?

When he opened the front door, he realised he'd made a mistake. There was a man waiting on the pavement. No, there were three. And Ronnie wasn't among them.

Nick's foot started to tap. It was his only release valve. At the desk in front of him sat the man who'd met him on the pavement outside Ronnie's flat. A man wearing round horn-rimmed spectacles.

For what seemed like the hundredth time, Nick felt the urge to swear. To let out his anger, even though he knew it would all be directed inward. After all, he'd let them take him so damn quietly. But that didn't stop him running through the incident in his mind. Thinking about what he could have done differently. But as soon as he'd realised what was going on, it was too late. He'd been taken to a black four-by-four, and then driven deep into the city. Now he was seated at a bare desk in a sterile office.

The two goons who'd acted as his escort had both

gone, but probably not far. The occasional shadow moved back and forth behind the frosted glass that made up the interior wall of the office. Opposite him the man with the horn-rimmed spectacles just kept staring.

"Mr Houghton," said the man. His voice was soft. He looked like an accountant, and sounded like one. The men outside: they were something different. "Two nights ago, you met with Harold McMahon and Mark Whelan."

Nick felt his cheeks burn. Fortunately, enough of his brain remained engaged for him to keep silent. After all, speaking didn't make much sense when he didn't know who he was speaking to, or where he'd been taken. He felt the first push of pressure across his right eyeball. He needed to parry.

"You ate smoked salmon, followed by chicken."

Nick didn't say anything. His hands remained still, but only because they'd been shaking so much in the car. His foot continued its incessant tapping. He couldn't keep it under control.

"We're presuming they offered you a position at Novus Particles," the man continued. "Possibly at their new attraction: this New Pompeii?"

Nick felt his lips part just enough to let his interrogator know he'd hit the right spot. The man slid a piece of paper across the desk. The hard black type of the title drew his attention: NOVUS PARTICLES UK LLP ANNOUNCES NEW PROJECT.

"Go ahead," said the man, nodding at the paper.

Nick hesitated and then let his eyes fall to the page. It was a press release.

Continuing its strategy of identifying new ways of using its Temporal Technology, Novus Particles has announced a new facility to be known as New Pompeii.

New Pompeii will operate as a closed entity. It has been operating for several months under appropriate local and national governance and supervision, and constitutes a working replica of the Roman town of Pompeii. Using the latest NovusPart Temporal Technology, the population of ancient Pompeii have been moved to the site and are now living happily in their new home.

There are two principal purposes to New Pompeii. The first is to allow primary research into the life of a Roman town. This work is being led by Professor Eric Samson (formerly of Durham University). Results will be published on a not-for-profit basis for the benefit of museums and universities across the world.

The second is the export of unique Roman products including, but not limited to, wine, pottery, art and foodstuffs. There may also be opportunity to televise authentic gladiatorial combat and Roman theatre.

"New Pompeii reflects the full potential of our Temporal Technology and demonstrates a world-class research proposition," said Harold McMahon, Chief Executive Officer of NovusPart. "For our investors, value will be leveraged across multiple platforms to generate sustained growth and drive significant long-term value. This will include film, television, interactive media, live entertainment, and consumer products."

Driven by technology developed at Cambridge

University, NovusPart is looking to diversify away from power generation. The New Pompeii franchise is well suited to this strategy and is in strong alignment with NovusPart's existing strategic priorities for continued long-term growth.

Nick pushed the paper back across the desk. At least that gave him something: he could talk about what was written on it. He just needed to concentrate. Make sure he didn't say anything stupid. He rubbed at his temples, and felt the first drill of pain shoot down into his neck.

"Interesting that they're calling it a 'closed entity'," the man said. "I'd have thought they'd have made a killing if they'd opened it up to the paying public."

Nick felt his brow rise. "A tourist attraction?"

"You disagree?"

"I don't think it could work that way."

"Really?"

"Most people still struggle with *Mickey la souris*," he said. "You think they'd cope if everyone spoke Latin or ancient Greek?"

"Still…"

"And how would people react to seeing wives as young as ten or twelve, or young boys being openly, and legally, courted for sex?"

The man considered. "A closed entity then. Which begs the question: what exactly are they doing there?"

Nick motioned towards the press release. "It all seems pretty clear."

"You don't see anything wrong with televised gladiatorial combat? You don't think the networks would object?"

Nick shook his head. "We're effectively talking about looking through a portal into the past. If they have gladiators, then yes, people will watch in their millions and I doubt any TV network would have a moral problem with that. It is, after all, what they do."

The man tilted his head to one side. "It would be awkward to grant them modern civil rights, wouldn't it?"

Nick shrugged. He looked back towards the frosted glass. Saw a shadow pass behind it. "So am I under arrest?"

For a second, the man's eyes seemed to flicker. But only for the briefest of seconds. "You may find it difficult to leave," he said.

"On what basis are you keeping me here?"

"Your association with a known drug dealer is not a secret, Mr Houghton."

Nick hesitated. Ronnie? "What have you done with him?"

The man didn't respond, and Nick closed his eyes. Remembered the broken glass of his friend's front door, and the empty bed. Had he simply been messed around, or was something else going on? He looked back at the man, and then glanced down at the press release. "Go on," he said.

"Let's start with basics. What do you know about NovusPart?"

"They're a power company."

"Really? I would suggest they lost interest in that quite quickly. The moment they figured out they could use their tech for something far more interesting, in fact."

Nick didn't say anything.

"So you think there's nothing wrong with it? A private company able to manipulate the past?"

"You tell me."

"You don't think they should be stopped?"

"Why should they?"

"If you look at all the opinion polls, they'll tell you that a majority of the public want NovusPart closed down. They share the same view as your father, that it's too risky to let a corporation have control over the timeline."

Nick didn't say anything.

"So why do you think the politicians ignore it? Why isn't it an issue? Okay, let me put it another way." The man paused. The rattle of Nick's foot grew louder. "How did Tiberius become emperor of Rome?"

Nick's mind blanked. "I don't understand."

"Sure you do; it's an easy enough question."

Parry. "He was chosen heir of Augustus."

"Interesting," said the man. "Then Tiberius must have been Augustus' son?"

"No," said Nick. "He was his stepson. But I can see where you're going with this…"

"Enlighten me."

"Augustus had no sons. Tiberius only became emperor because everyone else…"

"Yes?"

"They all died," said Nick, trying to keep his voice neutral. Academic. "Marcellus, the first in line, and then

Augustus' grandchildren: Lucius, Gaius and Posthumus. Oh, and Tiberius' brother, Drusus."

For a moment the man didn't say anything. He just nodded. Looked down at the press release. Looked back across the table. "That's a lot of bad luck," he said. "And the next emperor? Didn't Caligula have any older brothers?"

"Yes," said Nick. "But they died before Tiberius."

"But I'm confused: Caligula inherited the empire jointly with a young man called Gemellus, didn't he?"

"Yes," said Nick.

"And what happened to him?"

"He died."

"And Nero took over after the Emperor Claudius. But Nero was an adopted son, whereas Claudius also had a biological son called Britannicus."

"Yes," said Nick.

"And what happened to Britannicus?"

"He died."

The man sitting opposite gave a satisfied smile. "You see how easy it is to pluck the strings of power? It's just, back then, they controlled the future by taking action in the present. Now, NovusPart controls the present by manipulating the past."

Nick thought of Ronnie. Thought of all the conspiracy theories he'd spouted. "You can't be serious," he said.

"Why not? Why do you think every previous generation has had its political titans, and yet we're run by a bunch of timid sheep? Where are the people who bestride our stage? Where is our Disraeli? Our Churchill?

Our Thatcher? Why have they suddenly all gone missing?"

Despite himself, Nick chuckled. Some of the tension left him. His foot came to a sudden rest. "Missing people, eh?"

"No," said the guy. His eyes had narrowed to small points of black. "Not missing. Taken."

Nick looked towards the door. Was this all so much bullshit? Was he actually under arrest? Or had he just been taken by the same fruitcakes who'd hatched the plot to kill the young man at the British Museum? "I don't buy into conspiracy theories."

"Well you should do," replied the guy. "Because you're in one."

Nick felt his grin subside. The flicker was back in the man's eyes. Dancing back and forth. But this time not excited. Just angry. "I was just five years old when I saw my brother transported," the man said. "Five. But I can still see him reaching out to me as he was sucked from existence. He was something of a prodigy. And he didn't want to be a pilot, or an astronaut, or a fireman. He wanted to be prime minister. Maybe he made it. But maybe he also made an enemy of NovusPart. And maybe they changed how things turned out."

The guy was serious. He believed it. This wasn't idle chatter. The threat was real. "What do you want me to do?"

"I want you to accept their job offer."

"I already have."

"Good."

"But you need to understand," said Nick. "The position is… there's a six-week trial period."

"Then you'd better impress them," said the man. "Keep your nose clean, wait for me to contact you, and then maybe together we can find out what they're really doing in New Pompeii."

Nick nodded. But the man hadn't finished. "There's one other question," he said. "One I can't believe you haven't asked yourself."

"The others at the British Museum…"

"That's right. A team tried to kill Whelan's son."

Nick gasped. He hadn't known who the "young man" was. "I was something of a patsy."

"It doesn't matter," replied the man. "All the others were transported. Sucked into the future, along with Whelan's son. But not you."

"I told you, I was there by mistake."

"Not really a problem for NovusPart though, right? You were part of the problem. The solution was simple enough. They should have taken you along with all the others. You were a threat that should have been eliminated."

"So why didn't they take me?"

"NovusPart can't perform near-past transports. They have to wait thirty years. So the decision wasn't taken on the night of the Peking Man exhibition. It's going to be taken in the future, not the present. So at some point between now and then, you must affect the timeline in some way that means you can't be moved."

"Like what?"

"That's the mystery. And the interesting thing is: they don't know themselves. Not yet. And maybe not for a long time. But it's clear you're no longer a pawn. You have value. And so they pull you close, Mr Houghton. Somewhere where they can keep an eye on you."

Mr Houghton. Nick hesitated. "You haven't told me your name," he said.

"Everyone just calls me Harris."

53

They hadn't transported him.

They hadn't transported him from the British Museum when they'd taken all the others. Nick thought back to Ronnie's empty bed. The steaming cup of coffee. Had they taken him as well? Just like they'd taken Patrick and the men who had attacked them at the bathhouse?

The bathhouse. Nick squirmed. He'd not been transported from there either. Maybe Harris was right, and he was too important to the timeline. The puzzle remained though: what was he expected to do? And did Whelan or McMahon have any idea?

He shook his head. A few days. Whatever was expected of him, it would almost certainly happen in the next few days. Before the helicopter came. Before he left New Pompeii. Because whatever he was going to end up doing, it surely wouldn't happen in the control villa. No. At some point soon, he'd be heading back into town.

He needed to think. Needed to work out the punchline before the joke was told. Or else just let the events unfold and risk finding himself expendable. Because even though Harris had told him he was no longer a pawn, the most valuable chess piece could find itself sacrificed if the situation was right. And whatever had happened to him in the last few days, he certainly didn't want to die.

Perhaps the thought of his own death should have made him flinch, but this time it didn't. He reached for the tablet. The machine had been placed back by his bed while he'd been sleeping. He was simultaneously annoyed that he'd not managed to break it, and also glad that he hadn't. Because although he couldn't see all the facets of his situation, there was one big question that formed part of the puzzle: *what had happened to Professor Samson?*

The answer might not be relevant – but for the time being it was his only way forward. Unfortunately, Samson's notes continued to be an unyielding and frustrating read. It was as if Samson had just wandered around the town scribbling down anything that caught his eye. Worse were the tangents; there was a long entry concerning what would have happened if Hitler had been killed prior to 1933. Several pages were dedicated to potential outcomes. Almost as if he'd started to research a new TV show. Which might have made sense, if it wasn't such a well-worn topic. He skimmed several more pages, then stopped when a line caught his eye.

[[CHECK HANDWRITING]]

Nick focused on the tablet's screen. In the paragraph below the line a German word had been spelt incorrectly, and the sentences around it didn't make sense.

[[CHECK HANDWRITING]]

He smiled. Samson's notes had been typed up by someone.

Someone who was having trouble reading the originals.

That made sense. From what he'd seen, NovusPart didn't wave their hi-tech gadgets around in front of the locals. The smoke and mirrors was all low-tech stuff; maybe so they could keep upping the ante. Which meant Samson's notes had probably been first written on paper – or maybe even wax tablet.

Somewhere, therefore, were the original notes. Perhaps they would make more sense than the version on the tablet. Perhaps they contained information that didn't make the official cut.

There was a sharp knock at the door. It opened and a man wearing a white coat entered.

"You're awake," he said, simply.

"Yes."

"I'm Dr Chappell. I'm here to check on you." He walked over to the bed and started examining Nick's injuries. "It's all healing well enough," the doctor said, after a few minutes of prodding and manipulation. "It's probably okay for you to start moving around."

Nick tried to keep still as Chappell worked between his legs. He wasn't particularly gentle. "Is there any sign of infection?"

"No." The doctor sounded almost insulted.

Nick nodded. He heard a familiar cry in the background. "We have a new addition to our family?"

The doctor looked up. It seemed to take him a while to register the crying baby. "Yes," he said. "He arrived on the morning of… well, you know. When you were…"

Nick nodded, shifting on the bed. "So…?"

"So, what?"

"So who does it belong to?"

"His name is Julian. He's come here as a little brother for Noah."

Nick blinked, trying to work out what he'd just been told. "Adopted?"

"Yes, the same as Noah."

Nick didn't reply, his mind whirring. "Thank you."

"No problem."

Chappell left. Nick let his head fall back against the pillow. But he didn't keep it there long. He issued a deep growl and pushed himself to his feet, breathing through the pain, and walked over to the room's small desk.

On it were the design manual and maps he'd been given on his first arrival. He took the large town plan and spread it out on the bed, searching until he found the House of McMahon. It had the letters "HoM" inked in its lower left corner. He scanned the other houses and found two more marked with letters. "HoA" and "HoS". Both were near the House of McMahon. He could only guess what the acronyms meant, but House of Astridge and House of Samson seemed to fit.

All three were clustered in the same quadrant of town, separated by a couple of blocks. An easy walk. But he was a good five-hour ride away. That plan would have to wait.

He returned to the desk and fetched the design drawing for the amphitheatre. Next to it were a couple of alien structures, unknown to Pompeii. The first appeared to be made up of several large cages marked simply, CATS. The second, HOLDING ROOM.

A knock at the door. A NovusPart security guard stood on the threshold. "Whelan wants you."

The control room was as he remembered it, dominated by video screens. Whelan stood before them. But the screens weren't showing views of the town. Instead, McMahon and Astridge stared back, the wall of the *tablinum* of the House of McMahon clear in the background. The group looked like they were already deep in conference.

"Nick," said Whelan. "Are you well enough to join us?"

Nick walked forward. "I'm fine," he said. On the screen, Astridge didn't appear too impressed he'd been included in the discussion. McMahon looked pale and clammy. Of course, it could have been the screen playing tricks; the architect's bald head also appeared slightly too purple.

"The Temple of Isis has been destroyed," Whelan said. "We've got reports of other damage coming in from all over the town."

Whelan had said he'd cut the supply line to hunt for Harris's spy. That would mean disruption to the food supply. *And when the boats stopped arriving from Egypt…*

"A mob?"

Astridge nodded. "I was out with a couple of the men at the covered theatre. The street seemed to empty – and then there was a surge of people. It all happened really fast…"

Frustration clearly bubbled under Whelan's otherwise

calm exterior. "I saw something similar when I was out in Tunisia."

"Was the trouble just at the Temple of Isis?" asked Nick.

"No," replied Astridge. "There was other vandalism…"

"Vandalism? Where?"

"Some of the statues in the forum. They've been defaced. Literally."

"The statues of Augustus and his family?"

"Yes."

Whelan paused, suddenly thoughtful. "The question is: how do we respond?"

"You need to get the food convoys rolling," said Nick. No one answered. "You'll have riots if they think there are going to be shortages," he continued.

"Logistics isn't a tap," said Whelan. "We can stop things quickly enough, but starting them again takes planning. The food will start arriving again within forty-eight hours."

McMahon gave a deep sigh, then coughed. His breathing was heavy. "We should make an example of someone. Crucify a few dozen in the harbour."

"Precisely," said Astridge. "Your smoke and mirrors routine has failed, Mark. Now is the time for action or else we risk losing control of the town."

McMahon grew paler. "We can't lose control of the town," he said. There was silence. Astridge grinned with satisfaction. But warning bells were ringing in Nick's brain.

"Roman citizens were never crucified," he said. "It could trigger all-out civil unrest."

McMahon snorted. "The Roman emperors were brutal."

"And most of them ended up murdered."

Astridge gave a short, patronising chuckle. "So what do you suggest, *Dr* Houghton?"

Nick took a deep breath. "If we can't give them bread, then let's at least give them circuses. We need to stick to what we agreed last time: distract them."

"We could put on another show at the theatre," said Astridge.

"No," said Nick. "The best way would be to cement our relationship with the existing hierarchy. We need games at the amphitheatre, and we should strike some sort of new leadership deal with Barbatus. Offer him some real power and influence to give him an incentive to rule with us – not just sit on the sidelines, like he's been doing up till now."

Whelan considered this. "That's your recommendation?"

"Yes."

"We can get the games going very quickly."

"Good."

"Which means we just need someone to talk to Barbatus to strike this deal, man to man." Whelan stared back at McMahon and Astridge. "So the question is: which one of us should go?"

Nick didn't hesitate. He hadn't been transported. There was still some purpose to his being there. And from what Whelan had just said, the helicopter would soon be on its way. So the hourglass had been tipped. The sand was falling.

"I'll go," he said. "I know Barbatus. I can speak the language. And I know how these people think."

5 4

"So you aren't employed by NovusPart?"

"No."

"And you have nothing to do with McMahon?"

"No." Harris adjusted his spectacles, shifting them higher on his nose. "I know people who work for them, of course. It took me a while to figure out they were 'landing' people at their old college – amongst friends – rather than the NovusPart HQ." He paused. "The distance, I suppose, provides some degree of deniability."

Kirsten nodded. They were now in the heart of London, but she didn't recognise the city she had once called home. There seemed to be a lot more skyscrapers than she remembered. The remaining Victorian buildings trapped between them – including the one they were in now – looked like they were just waiting to be torn down. Harris had led her up to a drab office where they now sat, quite alone.

Kirsten let out a deep, pent-up breath and looked around the office. It probably wasn't where Harris normally worked. It was too empty. There was a desk and a couple of office chairs. A leather sofa had been pushed up against the back wall, with only a coffee table for company. A frosted glass wall separated them from the rest of the open-plan floor, which appeared to be deserted.

"So what are you going to do about it?" She felt a flare of anger when Harris didn't reply. "Surely kidnap and attempted murder are illegal," she said. "Even in the future?"

"The situation is not at all straightforward," Harris replied. "And technically we're in the present, not the future."

"But the police…?"

"Are in McMahon's pocket."

"The government…?"

Harris didn't reply, just raised his eyebrows as if to underline her naivety. Kirsten swallowed hard. "So I'm just to go home like a good girl and be grateful?"

"Not exactly. There are certainly things it would be useful for you to know before you continue your life… and we hope you'll be able to tell us a little something about how the world once was."

Kirsten waited a few seconds, regaining some of her composure. "So how did you find me?"

Harris allowed a smile to flicker across his lips. "As I said, we've got people working at NovusPart… and at your college. The porter who let us slip by at the gate?"

Kirsten nodded, understanding.

"Still, it's interesting," continued Harris. "You reappeared almost exactly thirty years to the day that the 'bedder in the bath' went missing."

"Thirty years…"

"Yes. The boundary of McMahon's power over the past." Kirsten shrugged. "But why can't he pluck people from today or yesterday? Surely that's easier?"

"No, we understand it's actually quite the opposite. The further back in time, the longer they have to track the trajectory of the particles. Transporting from a few minutes ago would be like catching a bullet."

"But if they could..."

"Don't worry," said Harris, interrupting. "We know NovusPart has tried short-range pulls on animals – lambs, we believe – and failed. Made quite a mess... but at least it made a good moussaka."

"How far can they reach back?"

"The best estimate we have is five thousand years."

"All very interesting," said Kirsten. "But not very useful."

"All information is useful."

Kirsten didn't reply immediately. She remembered what Harris had told her. "McMahon must have wanted to kill me from the beginning?"

Harris smiled again. "Kill you?" he said. "A bit melodramatic, don't you think?"

Kirsten frowned. "You said I'd die. You said it was just a matter of pulling the trigger."

"I'm not sure I said any such thing."

Tap – tap – tap.

I'm going to kill you, bitch!

"I don't understand..."

"We've been looking for evidence that McMahon has been using NovusPart to tamper with the timeline. To remove people for his own advantage. Just like you."

"No," said Kirsten, her eyes losing focus. She saw the

pit, and the open mouth of the screaming woman. "I was going to be killed. I saw them. You warned me, and I saw them. I saw them killing the others."

Harris's face hardened. "What do you mean, 'others'?"

55

SHE TRIED TO tell her story calmly, but in the end just blurted it out. A stream of words, punctuated by tears: the hard landing in a circular pit. The man stepping forward from the darkness. The single shot. McMahon leering in the background. *I'm going to kill you, bitch.*

Harris listened intently, impassive. "This is new information," he said, his voice calm.

"No," said Kirsten. "You told me—"

"That you were going to be taken from the timeline."

"No," replied Kirsten. "You told me I was going to die."

"My memory is quite clear."

"You and Mr Black…"

"Me and Mr *Who*?"

Kirsten slumped back in her seat, unbelieving. "I'm telling you the truth," she said. "There were about fifty people. They looked like they'd been taken from a plane. On the way back from holiday. The guy with the gun even asked me if I'd been looking to join the mile-high club. And then at the college I saw a newspaper… there was a story about survivors from a plane crash committing suicide, and I recognised one of the photographs. It was a woman. But she didn't commit suicide. I saw her die in that pit."

"NovusPart has only ever admitted to taking one group of people. A plane crash over the Atlantic." Harris picked a thin slice of plastic from his desk. It lit up and he started to work its surface with his fingers. Kirsten realised it was a new type of computer, one without a keyboard or separate screen. Harris spun it round and showed her some faces. He used his thumb to skip through them. Kirsten gasped. The man with the broken legs and the screaming woman.

"Yes," said Kirsten, softly. "These are the people I saw in the pit. They were butchered."

"Then you are indeed mistaken," Harris said. "These people committed suicide."

"I saw them die."

"And I saw them in the morgue," he countered. "In a secure government compound."

Kirsten leant forward in her seat, suddenly angry. But she was interrupted by a knock at the door and the arrival of another man.

"Marcus is on the phone," he said. "He wants to speak with you."

56

FOR THE FIRST hour of their journey back to New Pompeii, all Nick heard was the grinding of gears as the Land Rover made short work of the bumpy road leading away from the villa. He'd expected to have to go by wagon and endure each bump in the road being transferred to his groin. But speed was required, and Whelan had pressed one of the control villa's horseless carriages into service. It was doing a damn fine job. And a reasonably comfortable one.

Nick glanced over at the NovusPart COO, but Whelan just stared at the road ahead. He was in his tunic, the wrist-guard back around his forearm. Nick hoped there would be no reason for him to use it.

"A lesser man wouldn't go back." Whelan's voice was quiet. Nick hadn't seen the operations chief so uncertain before. "It would have been safer for you to stay at the villa and wait for the helicopter."

Nick nodded. "Something tells me I'll be okay."

"Really? What?"

Nick took a deep breath. He almost didn't want to say it. Just in case it sounded foolish. "I wasn't transported from the bathhouse," he said. "Just like I wasn't transported from the British Museum."

Whelan didn't respond.

"I'm right, aren't I?"

"Six people came to kill my son that night," Whelan said. "But the people pushing buttons in the god-knows-when only took four of them. The other two? A historian with an interest in Ancient Rome, and a general waster."

"So why did you bring me here? Why not Ronnie? Or both of us?"

"We told you the truth at the restaurant, Nick. At the time, we were looking for a replacement for Professor Samson. So when I saw you hadn't been taken, I asked myself, 'Why not?' What were the people in the future trying to tell me? Then I saw your CV. Let's just say this is the sort of coincidence that doesn't just happen. It was clear we needed to employ you. The message was received and understood."

"So I'm going to do something important," said Nick. "Something that means I can't be transported."

Whelan laughed and Nick felt his heart momentarily freeze. "You'd think so, right? Maybe you've already done it. Maybe identifying Felix was your big contribution to NovusPart."

Nick mulled this over. Felt a stab of pain in his groin. "If I'd been on my own in the bathhouse, then not being transported might have been a sign I was no longer important. But you took Patrick. Another clear signal: there's something left to do."

"Well, I hope you're right, Dr Houghton. Because there are various ways in which you can contribute to history. It might just be that you think of something. A random, off-hand remark that helps someone else find a solution to a problem. Or it might be something less pleasant. Those people pushing the buttons in the future? They've already proved they don't mind your getting hurt. Have you ever heard of dying for a cause?"

"You came here alone?"

Nick nodded, although he wasn't telling the whole truth. Whelan had sent a couple of guards to accompany him. He'd said they were for his protection but he had sensed they were there to make sure he kept his word. They were nothing but a frustration. He'd intended to head over to Barbatus' mansion via the House of Samson, but their presence had made that impossible.

Still, that didn't mean they had to come with him every step of the way. On the final approach towards the queue snaking out of the *duumvir*'s door, Nick had told them to wait at a distance. So yes, he was now alone. But help wasn't far away.

Barbatus stood at the back of the atrium, surrounded by men wearing heavy armour. They were all carrying swords, likely forged in the workshops on the eastern side of the town. He'd walked straight into a fortress – and it would have been unwise to arrive with an armed escort. He'd made the right call.

The *duumvir* looked at him for a long time. "I must

admit, I didn't expect to see you again," he said.

"I guess I was lucky."

"Well that depends on your point of view." A few of the men behind Barbatus chuckled. Despite what Whelan had said, they'd clearly heard what had happened at the bathhouse. "So why are you here, Pullus?"

Nick paused. Whelan had given him strict parameters. He couldn't promise too much. Couldn't deliver too little. And the sand in the hourglass was slowly trickling away. "There's been a lot of disruption in the town. We need it to be brought under control."

"We warned you, and you ignored us."

Nick thought back to the party. *They attack their masters. And they attack monsters – whether they are real or not.* "That's why we've come to you now."

"And you expect me to do what, exactly? Stand in front of you? Allow the people of this town to associate me with you and let me take a share of their anger?"

"We were hoping to come to some sort of arrangement."

"You mean you were hoping I'd call out the city watch."

Nick opened his mouth to speak, but Barbatus waved at him to keep quiet. "So what are you going to offer me?" he asked. "More money? More land?"

"We want to hand more control back to the town," said Nick.

"Oh, spare me, Pullus. This isn't a town; it's a prison. The ash cloud has gone. The roads are clear. But every time we send out riders, they are stopped by legionaries who send them back."

"Augustus…"

"Ah, yes! Augustus! The first god-emperor! You know, Pullus; I once saw a man who called himself a god. He would argue with Jupiter in his temple. It was a fairly one-sided conversation, as you can probably imagine, but we would all just stand there and watch. No one dared say he was crazy. The Emperor Gaius killed people on a whim, you see. For his amusement."

Nick nodded, understanding. "You're talking about Caligula?"

The *duumvir*'s face twisted in anger. "Caligula?" His voice was now ice cold. "Only cocksuckers use that name now. Men who became brave the moment 'Little Boot' was safely in his mausoleum. Men who didn't have to watch their wives and mothers raped, or their friends and brothers executed."

The academic side of Nick's brain was ringing loudly – *Barbatus met Caligula* – but the rest of it was registering a slow pulling fear in the pit of his stomach. It was different to the immediate terror he'd felt in the bathhouse. Because the men around Barbatus were wearing armour and carrying swords. And the *duumvir*'s house looked like a fortress. Which meant they were going to war.

But whatever he was meant to do for NovusPart, it was unlikely that they intended him to die here and now. There was still time. "We haven't acted like the Emperor Gaius," he said.

Barbatus chuckled. "Tell me about Felix," he said. "He was a good man, so I'd just like to know: did you have a reason to kill him, or was it done on a whim?"

Nick's mind blanked. Maybe dying wasn't on the cards, but that didn't mean he had to blindly follow a path leading nowhere. He needed to find a new tack. "The town stands," he said, trying to keep his voice firm and controlled. He looked at the men around Barbatus. Most stood steadfast but some were looking distinctly nervous. Like they weren't sure the *duumvir* was making the right call. After all, they didn't know everything that had happened in the bathhouse. Whelan hadn't left anyone to report the transportations. There was still some room for doubt.

"Caligula was no god," Nick said, trying to push home the point. "But, then again, he did nothing to prove it. But you each felt the heat of the mountain, didn't you? The shaking of the ground? The wrath of Vulcan? And yet you all survived."

"Then take control of the town yourself," Barbatus said. "What do you need me for?" The *duumvir* looked around at his men. His words seemed to have the necessary effect. The uncertainty had been brief.

"Let me tell you a story from Rome," the *duumvir* continued. "A Roman legion once brought a northern 'king' back to the city. The soldiers were expecting him to act just like all the other defeated barbarians. He'd see the majesty of Rome, compare it with his mud huts back home, and quickly fall to his knees. Quaking at the sight of Rome's power. But this one didn't. He stood in the centre of the forum, and told Emperor Claw-Claw-Claudius to fuck right off."

A few of the men behind Barbatus started to laugh; they'd clearly heard the tale before. But Nick hadn't.

He swallowed uncertainly. "Any sufficiently advanced technology is indistinguishable from magic," he whispered.

Barbatus took a few steps forward. He leant in close. "That's right, Pullus. That barbarian king had no idea how we built our aqueducts. And I don't know how you pull off your little miracles. But know this: I'm no barbarian. And I'm not awed. So you want control of this town? Too late. It's mine. I didn't leave when the earth shook twenty years ago, and I didn't leave when the mountain pelted us with rock either. So if you want it, you'll have to take it from me."

In the *duumvir*'s anger, Nick saw his new tack. Not money, or land. "When I last spoke with your daughter, I offered her something."

"What?"

"I offered her the truth," said Nick. "And somehow, I think we could find it together."

57

NICK LET OUT a long, low whistle. It was clear Barbatus had acquired yet another neighbouring townhouse. What Astridge had designed as a neatly organised home for a modest Roman family was now a warren of rooms. All of which seemed to be alive with people and filled with chests of coins and swords.

"We'll leave by the back."

Nick nodded. The *duumvir's* building work meant there were now several ways into and out of his stronghold. They could leave without passing the two NovusPart guards who'd escorted him there. And his trip around town would go unrecorded in other ways too; he'd given temporary charge of his belt to a household slave. However, it soon became clear they wouldn't be heading straight to the House of Samson.

Barbatus stepped down into the street and immediately took a road north. Nick hesitated before following, trying to get his bearings. Yes, they would miss the House of Samson by a few blocks. Unless Barbatus planned to make a late turn. But he didn't. And the men with the *duumvir* didn't allow him to catch up with his new host. For those watching, the symbolism was clear: they weren't walking together. The *duumvir* was keeping the association between them light, not wanting to stand between the mob and the men of Augustus.

They reached the Vesuvius Gate and Barbatus stopped as soon as he'd passed through the outer wall. He'd only brought a handful of his men with him, but most remained at a courteous distance. The only one the *duumvir* seemed to talk to at any length was his household slave, Cato.

As Nick approached, he thought back to Caligula and his immediate predecessor, Tiberius. Both had promoted their slaves and freedmen to powerful positions. Some of them had been even more powerful than the senators. And they'd been extremely loyal because they owed their position to their master's patronage. Even in the face of tyranny.

So was Barbatus running Pompeii on the same model?

Maybe he was. Because there was another group at the gatehouse, a rag-tag assembly of men carrying swords. The city watch were now guarding the main trade route into and out of the town. And in the distance, Nick could just about make out some horses approaching. Heading directly past the spot where there should have been a volcano.

The *duumvir* started to walk into the long grass that butted up against the town's northern wall. Nick didn't want to follow. He hadn't been told where they were going, and he'd seen enough movies to know bad things happened in lonely locations. But he'd made his decision. He followed. Within a few steps, he realised what he was going to be shown.

The only clue he needed was the rancid stench of rotting meat. It seeped into his nostrils, and made his guts twist.

A pile of bodies, none of them longer than a man's forearm. Like small leathery dolls in the ash-covered grass. They looked like they'd known nothing but a few short days of terror and hunger. Some had been scavenged by animals; one was missing its limbs, its stomach open, its guts spilled.

The traditional way Romans dealt with unwanted children. They left them outside the town walls to die.

"You can understand it, of course," said Barbatus, his voice low. Respectful of the graveyard around them. "They are poor, their future uncertain. So the people bring them out here."

Nick said nothing. He looked away from the crèche of empty eye sockets staring up at him.

"You offer me a way to get to the truth," Barbatus said. "But what I want to know is simple: why do you people keep bringing children here, when there are so many unwanted already? Why keep good homes empty, when people are living on the street? Why lock us in our town, and cut us off from Rome?"

Nick nodded dumbly, but his mind was racing. The nursery in the control villa. The crying baby. NovusPart were bringing children here. And it solved a puzzle posed by the man known as Harris. It was all around him. The way NovusPart could take people from the timeline, and then hide them away without the need to cut their throats: *you took them while they were young. And you hid them where no one would look.*

Maybe some of the missing were out here with the unwanted Roman babies. Maybe others had been given to employees of NovusPart – like Noah and Julian. But whatever the answer, they'd been taken out of the equation. The political titans of the present, reduced to children.

"So the empty townhouses," continued Barbatus. "What do you suppose we'll find there?"

Nick turned to the *duumvir*, feeling his time was close. "Let's go and see."

Barbatus smiled like he knew he'd won. "The closest is only a few blocks away. The people in the neighbouring buildings reported it to us. They thought it was unfair that such a fine property remained empty."

"And what did you do?"

"Nothing. Life's unfair. I was going to give it to Calpurnia. Until some ignorant cocksucker tried to dig their way through the walls. Underneath the brick and plaster is a metal skin."

"Metal?"

"Yes," said Barbatus. "Not iron or bronze. Something new."

Nick nodded. Another question ticked off the list, and another explanation conveniently erased. The empty houses weren't meant for the people of Pompeii. They'd been designed like the House of McMahon. Secure housing, for whomever McMahon invited to the town. Or forced here. He swallowed hard. "There's a particular house I want to go to."

"Oh?"

"There was a man who lived here. A few blocks south and east of your own home."

Again, the *duumvir* grinned. "You mean your predecessor?"

Nick stared blankly ahead.

"There have only been two men from your camp that have shown any real interest in this town. You, and an older man. He seemed like the big chief in the days after the calamity."

"Samson?"

"Was that his real name? Anyway, it soon turned out he wasn't such a big man. And then you arrived to pick up where he left off."

"Do you know what happened to him?"

"He was murdered."

Nick faltered. Murdered. "You know this for sure?"

"This is my town, Pullus. I know what goes on here."

Nick believed him. NovusPart had murdered Felix, and they'd killed Samson too. But why? It was time for a gamble. He looked towards the sky. The sand was falling. "I think there's something in his house which could be useful."

Barbatus glanced back towards the gatehouse. "Then lead on."

58

"WHEN WE LAST met," Harris said, "you told me you saved Harold McMahon's life. Would you care to elaborate?"

Kirsten hesitated. It seemed like a lifetime ago. The memory was distant, almost dreamlike. And now she was starting to doubt herself. What had really been happening while she floated in the bath for all those years?

She breathed in slowly. It hadn't taken long for Harris to return to the office; his phone call with "Marcus" had been brief. "I was always late for work," she said. The words came slowly, but then gathered pace as she let them form in her mind a piece at a time. She had to get this right. Had to make sure she got every detail correct. "Even though I lived in college, I struggled to get out of bed on time. The day I saved McMahon, I was late."

Kirsten stopped. Harris leant forward, and indicated she should continue with a roll of his hand. "I went to empty his bin. If they were in but didn't want to be disturbed, the students left their bins outside their doors. But McMahon hadn't done that. So I went in – and there he was. Sitting at his desk. Choking. He'd been eating peanuts, and one had got stuck."

"You helped him?"

"I hit him hard on the back until he coughed it up."

Harris leant back. That flicker of a smile had returned. "That's why McMahon wanted to remove you from the timeline," he said. "That's why you emerged as a paradox."

"Because I saved his life?"

"Because if you'd been any other bedder, his bin would have been emptied on time – and he would have died at his desk."

"I don't understand."

"No one knows about you, Kirsten. Nobody knows about that little incident with the peanut. You're not even a footnote in history." He paused, thinking. "I bet you took that bath not long after you helped him."

Kirsten nodded. It had been the evening of the same day.

A look of triumph crossed Harris's face. "He needed to take you out of history at a point just after you'd saved him, and before you told anyone about that incident, so that no one else would know to come along later and take you out just before you saved him. If he'd left you alive, you would forever be a gun pointed straight at his head."

Kirsten drew in a sharp breath.

Tap – tap – tap.

A knock at her door. He'd come to her room. Maybe to say thank you. So he'd known exactly where she was, on one of the most memorable days of his life.

But now she was back. A gun. Forever pointed at McMahon's head. She looked back at Harris. "So are you going to kill me now?"

For the first time, Harris looked uncertain.

"Kill me?" repeated Kirsten. "To kill McMahon?"

"Oh, I see. You think we'd go to all this trouble to save you, only to go and kill you straight away?"

"I don't know."

"Understandable. But no, that's not our intention."

Kirsten shifted in her seat.

"Relax," he said. "We don't have the technology to rip you from the timeline. Only NovusPart can move people forward, out of time, and McMahon keeps the company in the hands of a select few. And the tricky thing is that, when you move someone who had a future from the past, you make changes. The people of Flight 391 had no future. They all died, never to be seen again. So they appear and NovusPart knows what they did to bring them there. But when you move a person who wasn't meant to have been moved, you create a paradox. You rip away the future, and the reason they were transported."

"In other words," said Kirsten, filling in the blanks, "Harold McMahon may not know he ordered my transportation."

59

"I've been there before. There's nothing of interest inside."

Nick nodded, but ignored what Barbatus was telling him. Cato and a couple of the *duumvir*'s guards walked behind them. "You've never been upstairs though, right?" he said.

The *duumvir* didn't answer. Nick turned a sharp corner into a narrow street, and found himself facing the House of Samson.

Unlike McMahon's base of operations, this townhouse didn't have any shops built into its frontage. Instead, the cubicles on either side of the main door seemed to be small homes. Or rather, hovels. A flight of stairs led up from a side alley. Nick looked upwards. There were more cubbyholes in the building's upper floors, accessed by a fragile wooden walkway. Each one was shuttered. Typically Roman. No space wasted. And it was an arrangement that meant Samson would have had plenty of real-life Romans living right on his doorstep. Enough study material to keep him going for years. He would never have just left voluntarily.

Nick approached the shuttered front door. He pressed

his hand against the solid wood. They wouldn't be able to break through it. But they didn't need to. Just like at the House of McMahon, a grid was etched into the doorframe.

Nick tapped in the code. 391391. The door didn't shift. Behind him, Barbatus seemed impatient. What code would Samson have chosen? He tried again.

2

The wood didn't give any indication it had sensed his input. But could it really be this simple?

4

Whatever, it was the best place to start.

0879

The twenty-fourth of August, AD 79. Doomsday.

The door clicked open. But before he could smile in triumph, something sharp pushed into the base of his back. Nick felt hot breath in his ear. "If there's anyone in there waiting for us," said the *duumvir*, "then the last thing you'll see is my sword pushing out through your stomach."

Nick didn't respond. He walked forward, pushing aside the heavy curtain that hung across the entrance. The atrium corridor was longer than that at the House of McMahon, and the light from the street was blocked out when the curtain fell back into place behind them.

The house was empty. Looking around the atrium, Nick was unimpressed. The house was a shell, with only a thin layer of plaster on the walls. No mosaics, not even simple ones. And it smelt damp. The floor plan echoed that of the House of McMahon, a set of wooden stairs leading upwards from the corner of the atrium.

Nick let his eyes follow them to the balcony, and noticed the opening above the pool was covered with a steel grate – presumably to stop intruders climbing in over the walls. Behind him, Cato and Barbatus started to whisper to each other. The slave was dabbing at his mouth with a corner of his tunic. Without lips, saliva dripped from his teeth. It wasn't clear what they were saying to each other.

"I wonder if they're all like this?"

Barbatus glanced at him, his eyes narrow. "You mean you really don't know?"

Nick didn't reply. He walked around the pool to the *tablinum*. Plants were growing in the garden beyond, so at least some attention had been given over to getting the house ready for permanent occupation. He turned back to the *duumvir*.

"I still think we'll find the truth here."

Barbatus didn't look convinced. "Do you remember what I said? Whichever direction you head out of town, soldiers turn you back. Most of the people accepted your story as a consequence of the disaster. It was Calpurnia who asked me, 'What exactly are they hiding?'"

Nick didn't reply. He walked back into the atrium, scanning it for clues, but nothing was leaping out at him.

"So we found the villa, and your giant metal mosquitoes."

Nick felt the ground shift beneath him. "They're called 'helicopters'."

"They bring everything here – the food, the money, the iron and the bricks. They even brought you. They seem to be the only way in."

"And out."

"Really? The only people we've seen leave are the men who control the mosquitoes… your 'heli-cop-tors'."

Nick nodded. "How many of your people know about the villa?"

Barbatus shrugged. "That information only matters if I let you go, and your people ask you." The *duumvir* let his eyes flick upwards. "So let's finish exploring. If it's true you know nothing about these houses, you can just set up a meeting with your people and I'll leave you alone."

"All right." The wooden stairs flexed under Nick's feet. It was the first time Barbatus had expressed any interest in meeting with McMahon and Whelan.

The layout of the upper level of the townhouse also mirrored that of the House of McMahon. Four rooms led off the balcony above the atrium. A narrow walkway extended out around the peristyle. Nick moved to the first room – the equivalent of Whelan's – and pushed open the door.

Someone had been living here. Probably Samson. Behind him, he sensed Barbatus prowling.

"I'm told there are rooms like this at your villa." The *duumvir* entered, then stepped into the en-suite bathroom. There was the sound of running water. "Clever," he shouted. "The water is hot. I shall have to tap the spring."

Nick made no comment. With the *duumvir* distracted, Nick started searching the bedroom. Cato was an unspeaking presence behind him, breath continually whistling out of his always open mouth.

And then he found them. A collection of notebooks in a neat stack underneath the desk. Nick started to flick through one. Sure enough, it contained Samson's original notes. The handwriting was appalling, but the content matched what he'd already read on his tablet. And there were additions. Little notes in the margins.

"What's this?" asked the *duumvir*.

Nick turned, and found Barbatus examining a large flat-screen television attached to the wall. He was also holding a tablet computer, and had started to give it an exploratory shake.

Nick walked over and switched on the television. It showed views of the town, directly fed by NovusPart's security cameras. He picked up the remote control and flicked between camera angles.

"You know how to work this?" asked Barbatus. He didn't look shocked. It was almost as if Nick had shown him something completely ordinary. "You've seen something like this before?"

"Yes," said Nick. "McMahon has a similar device."

"It's a trick. A very clever trick."

"An oracle," said Cato, clearly more impressed than his boss. "And one that actually works."

"Yes," continued the *duumvir*, suddenly thoughtful. "And I can see the advantages. He can see where everyone is… See where the crowds are starting to turn nasty. Ha!"

The security feed was showing the forum, where a large crowd was standing outside the Temple of Jupiter, witnessing another sacrifice to the gods.

"Look at those fools," said Barbatus. "Slaughtering bulls like they mean it. We could put the haruspices out of work at a stroke!"

Nick smiled inwardly, reminded of the politicians back home when they turned up to the occasional church service – usually at Christmas or Easter – while clearly having no appetite for organised religion. "What about those worshipping at the Temple of Isis?" he asked.

"Those bastards had better keep a low profile."

"There have been problems at the temple?" He was interested to see how Barbatus would spin the disturbance Whelan had told him about.

"Yes. As Naso told you, when things are going badly, people look for someone to blame. And people getting on their knees in front of an Egyptian goddess put themselves at the top of the list."

"They don't seem too happy about worshipping the Emperor, either. There are no crowds at the Temple of Fortuna Augusta or the Temple of Vespasian…"

It was clear Nick had touched a nerve. Barbatus issued an audible growl. "You forget I've met the Emperor," he said. "He's real enough." After a pause, the *duumvir* shook the tablet. "And what does this do?"

"Give me a second," said Nick. He took the device and flicked it on. When the tablet loaded, he realised it had all access rights enabled. The video screens, maps of the town, the GPS tracking system… and the internet. He could even get on to his email. Look at *Who's Where*.

He tapped the screen and brought up his profile.

Who? Nick Houghton. (NovusPart.)
Currently working for NovusPart.

Where Been? [Expand]
Where Now? Unknown. Probable location: New Pompeii.

"What are you doing? Show me!"

Nick looked up. Barbatus was visibly angry, his face red. And then it clicked. The television may have been an alien system, but at least it was easily understood. After all, it was like looking into an oracle's pool. But a tablet computer... the internet... They were going to take some explaining.

He opened the GPS mapping application. Dots appeared on the screen. "The system tells you where certain people are at any one time," he said.

"Show me the full town."

Nick zoomed out, then turned the tablet round to show Barbatus.

"Thirty," the *duumvir* said. "You have thirty people."

Nick saw that he was right. The GPS system was tracking thirty people. There would be more at the villa. Maybe another twenty or so. Not many more. So that made perhaps fifty people. Not enough to hold the town.

And Barbatus knew it.

60

"T ELL ME ABOUT Harold McMahon."

"I don't understand."

"Sure you do. What was he like?"

"He was just a kid."

"Talented?"

"He was at the best university in the country…"

"If Cambridge only took geniuses, then it would be a fairly empty place. Most people there just make up the numbers. Especially now it's gone back to being a rich kids' finishing school."

Kirsten hesitated. "I didn't see any of his work, I just emptied his bin."

"But what was your impression?"

"He was lazy. He wasn't often in his room but when he was, he stank of alcohol and takeaways. He must have missed a lot of lectures."

"Did you speak to him?"

"He didn't say much. I got the occasional grunt of thanks."

Harris considered this. "What was his relationship like with Whelan?"

"Whelan was the exact opposite. He was almost always out. Whenever I *did* see him, he was either dressed like a soldier—"

"Officer training corps?"

"Yes." Kirsten smiled at a memory. "Or he was exercising. I remember once going into his room to change his bedding. He was doing sit-ups. He carried on the entire time I was in there. By the time I left I could tell the strain was killing him – but he wasn't going to give up."

"A strange pair to run a company together?"

"They'd been allocated rooms in the same court."

Harris was silent for a few moments. "They both had rich parents," he said. "Whelan's father was old money. Had ties to the government. McMahon senior made a more modest fortune from machine parts."

Kirsten nodded, but there was a doubt nagging at her. "Aren't you going to ask me about Joe Arlen? Octavian?"

Harris looked back at her, his face blank.

"I always heard them referring to him as Octo," she explained. "Everyone expected him to win the Nobel Prize. I suppose he's done that by now, hasn't he?"

Harris smiled, sympathetically. "Joe Arlen isn't important. He retired to live the simple life, à la Howard Hughes. We hear from him occasionally, but no one's seen him for years."

61

"ARE YOU ALL right?"

Nick looked up. He was back at the House of Barbatus in one of the cubicles leading off an unused atrium, a guard at the door. Calpurnia stood looking at him from the doorway.

"You don't look frightened," she said.

Nick let out a breath. "I'm not," he replied.

"Then you're crazy."

Nick gave a shallow smile. He felt for his belt, which was now safely back around his waist. "I think for the moment your father needs me. He already sees the advantages offered by the tablet."

"Knowledge is easy to acquire, Pullus."

"Not so easy to use."

"Now you sound like a Greek," she said, not without a hint of contempt. She considered him awhile. "Do you know much history?"

Nick's smile grew. "A little," he said.

"Well then you'll know that when we first went to war against Carthage, Rome had no fleet. Not one ship. And certainly no sailors. But by the time we'd won, we controlled the water from Hispania to Persia."

Nick didn't reply. Barbatus' dismissive attitude of Calpurnia seemed more and more ridiculous. She edged inside. The guard posted on the door looked over his shoulder then turned back to stare out over the abandoned atrium. It was clear Barbatus was occupied elsewhere, and until the meeting with NovusPart was brokered, the game continued. Despite what Calpurnia might think.

"You're keeping yourself busy."

Nick looked down at the notebooks he had brought from the House of Samson, and nodded. The professor's use of convoluted Latin was made more complicated by his terrible handwriting. But they would tell him more than the sanitised version on his tablet. Even if a lot of the information was turning out to be rubbish. Because Nick had been right about one thing: Rome hadn't been the professor's first love, not by a long shot. He seemed obsessed by the Third Reich. And one question in particular that seemed to come up again and again. What would have happened if Hitler had died prior to 1933? Who would have taken over?

Goebbels? Goering? Hess? Himmler? Or none of the above? Would they simply not have been able to embody the same toxic mix of hope and hatred? Would the darkest chapter in world history simply not have happened?

"The work of my predecessor," he said, indicating the notebooks.

"Ah, yes. He wanted to know about everything we did before the ash started to fall."

"Your father thinks he was murdered."

"He was. I saw the body."

Nick hesitated. "It was brought here?"

"Yes." She paused. Examining him. "What does the name 'Perkin Warbeck' mean to you?"

Nick shrugged. "It sounds familiar, but I can't quite place it. Why?"

"Your man was found with a wax tablet. Most of the writing had been ruined. But there was one bit that made sense: *Who is Perkin Warbeck?*"

Nick let the cogs in his mind rotate, but came to no conclusion. Calpurnia seemed to detect the blankness in his face. "When we last spoke," she said, this time in ancient Greek, "you offered me the truth. But you don't know it, do you?"

It took a while for Nick's brain to switch tracks. To place the language and decipher her pronunciation. The guard at the doorway glanced again over his shoulder. Nick caught his look of puzzlement. He clearly didn't speak Greek.

"I did what I thought was right," he said. "And I still hope to find what you're looking for. What we're both looking for."

Calpurnia smiled. "You speak better Latin than you do Greek."

"Perhaps. I didn't know what would happen to Felix."

"I believe you."

"I just couldn't take the risk they'd hurt you."

"But you could take that same risk with him?"

Nick winced. "I didn't mean it like that." He tried to change the subject. "Your father seems to inspire loyalty in his men."

"Yes, they are loyal," she said. "But only because they are scared of him."

"Scared?"

Calpurnia continued to smile, but her eyes suddenly seemed to lose their focus. "Tell me, Pullus. What sort of town do you think Pompeii is?"

Nick shrugged. It was a miracle. An archaeological miracle. But as for the type of town it had been at its peak, he simply didn't know. A jewel in the crown, or another pebble on the shore?

"A trading port," he said. "A town where the rich took their holidays."

"One thing that rich men like is security," Calpurnia said. "And trade brings violence. So let me ask you another question. What sort of a man do you think the emperors trust to run such a place?"

Nick didn't reply.

"You maybe don't know, but my father was first elected when I was just a baby. The men in charge of the town at the time tried to stop him. They invited my mother to a dinner party – and then they wouldn't let her leave. Unless my father withdrew from the race."

"Your father got elected though, didn't he?"

"Yes."

"And your mother?"

"They killed her."

Nick hesitated, but he sensed the story hadn't quite finished. "And the men who did it?"

"My father scraped a small hole in the ringleader's skull. He did it slowly. Carefully. Kept him alive and screaming. Then he filled his cranium with molten lead until it flowed out through his eyes." For a second, Calpurnia's gaze met his, and Nick felt his entire body shudder. Her voice sounded so cold. So detached. But, of course, she wasn't speaking from memory. Someone must have told her. Let her know Barbatus had allowed her mother to die, and then had gone on to murder his opponents. "The Emperor Gaius once said: 'It's not enough they die; they have to feel themselves dying'."

"Caligula was a madman."

"The Emperor Gaius was once *duumvir* of Pompeii, just like my father is now. And if he doesn't get what he wants, it will end badly for you."

"He'll attack us?"

"He'll butcher you, and all your friends."

Nick looked towards the guard. "Then I'd better not fail."

62

"D<small>O YOU THINK</small> he does it often? Take people from the timeline?"

Harris didn't reply.

"But you think there were others, don't you? Like me?"

"Undoubtedly. Just not very often, and so damn difficult to prove."

Kirsten hesitated. "Why do you say, not often? How can you be so sure?"

"How would McMahon know he wasn't removing someone who'd done something that was to his own benefit? Like you, for instance. The risk would be too great. Every time he rolls the dice, he risks losing everything."

"And then what?"

"Pardon?"

"After I'd been taken. What did you think they were going to do with me?"

Harris paused a second. "The news is full of people claiming to have been dumped on the streets of London."

"And no one cares about that?"

"Most have been proven to be crackpots. The same people who a few years ago would have been claiming they'd been abducted by aliens. No, what's more interesting is the quantifiable phenomenon of people going missing. Kids mainly. After all, a child that goes missing creates a lot less consequential disruption than an adult. They are quickly forgotten."

Kirsten's lip curled. "Not by the parents."

"No. And you're right that a few parents manage to keep their loss in the headlines for years. But several hundred children go missing every year, and what do you hear of them?"

Kirsten quietly shuddered in her seat. There was something beneath Harris's cold reply. Anger.

"This is personal for you, isn't it?" she said.

Harris didn't respond.

"Who did NovusPart take?"

Harris didn't reply.

"Did McMahon take your son?"

"No," came the soft reply. "He took my brother."

Kirsten didn't say anything. The words of the man in the canvas coat rattled through her mind. *No. Not a kid. A woman.* She had surprised him. And the only distraction they'd provided was a handful of toys. Something to play with, after the paradoxes emerged.

"They reach back and remove people when they're children," she said, her eyes losing focus. And they must still be doing it, because they were keeping the basement in Chaderton Court under close observation. They were waiting for their prey to arrive. "But if they're only children..."

"They used to say you can kill a man, but you can't kill an idea. Except now they can remove a person before they've even conceived of that idea. Remove anyone who would shut them down."

Kirsten didn't say anything. There was something nagging at her: McMahon probably didn't know she'd been transported because the action had removed the causation. The timeline had been altered.

"Will you come with me," she said. "To see my parents?"

Harris's eyes dropped to the desk. No words. But he'd said everything.

One more day won't matter.

"You won't, will you," said Kirsten. "Because you can't."

"They died about eight years ago," replied Harris. He didn't look up. "I'm sorry."

Kirsten swallowed. Her breath suddenly coming too fast. "And my sister?"

"The same."

"How?"

Harris looked up, his eyes heavy.

"How?" Kirsten repeated, barely containing her anger.

"A bus crash."

"You said you were going to take me to them…"

"I meant the memorial garden," said Harris. "You'd been through a lot, Kirsten. I thought it would be best to tell you after you'd at least orientated yourself."

"So you had my best interests at heart?"

"Probably not. But I didn't keep you in the dark to hurt you."

63

IT WAS THREE hours before Barbatus reappeared, the tablet in his hand. Cato wasn't with him. It suddenly felt like there was more sand in the bottom of the hourglass than at the top. The helicopter would soon be on its way.

"Contact your people," the *duumvir* said, handing the tablet to Nick.

Nick turned it on and activated the communications app. He figured the best person to try was Whelan.

The COO didn't answer the first time. Or the second. But on the third try, his brawny face appeared on the screen. The background of the image indicated he was in his room in the House of McMahon. If Whelan was surprised to see him, then he hid it well. "Nick," he said, almost casually. "You have news?"

"Yes," Nick said, in English. "I think I'm making progress."

"And just how did they get hold of a tablet?"

"I told you these people weren't stupid."

Whelan grunted. "Barbatus is with you?"

Nick nodded, and tilted the tablet towards the *duumvir*. Ready to translate.

"I hope you've had time to consider our offer."

The *duumvir* glared down at the screen. "I have."

"And your answer?"

"I think we need to discuss the terms in more detail."

"We have nothing to talk about. You can either join us, or we cut off your supply of cash. This isn't a negotiation. Perhaps Nick – Pullus – didn't explain it to you properly. We want you to help us take back control of the town."

Barbatus gave a shallow grin. Like a wolf baring his teeth. "Really? You wouldn't like to discuss your villa? Where your metal mosquitoes land?"

Whelan shook his head, remaining calm. "No. They're none of your concern. And I'm very disappointed you've been told about them."

Nick hesitated, then completed the translation. Barbatus listened to his words carefully, but didn't register any discomfort. "No, I disagree," replied the *duumvir*. "Because right now my men are taking control of your villa. So maybe they'll soon fly one of those mosquitoes into town."

Emotion registered on Whelan's face. It was brief, but Nick saw it. Whelan's eyeballs bulged. "You're making a serious mistake."

"Really?" answered Barbatus. "Because a bird can only tease the cat when he's out of reach. And you're flying very low, Mark Whelan of NovusPart. Very low indeed."

64

WHELAN CALLED BACK ten minutes later. Barbatus held up his hand – a clear signal not to answer.

"You think me foolish."

Nick felt the urge to nod. "I'm not sure you have all the facts," he said. "Whelan is a dangerous man."

Barbatus shrugged. "He doesn't look it. He looks soft."

The tablet started buzzing again. Once again, Barbatus indicated he shouldn't answer. "What do you think he's been doing? In between finding out his villa is under attack, and calling us back?"

"Probably checking out your story," said Nick.

"I'd ask you to contact the villa, but my men won't know how to use these devices. And I don't know how many of your men are alive, or in a position to help. Which means Whelan is either calling to tell us my attack failed, or else he wants to meet."

Nick tried to run through the scenarios in his mind. If Barbatus was worried about the outcome, he didn't look it. "The men at the villa were armed. It wouldn't have been easy for your watch."

"I didn't send the city watch," replied Barbatus. "I sent fifteen gladiators."

Nick felt himself go pale. Gladiators. Men trained to kill. Another thought hit him. "You must have sent them before I got here."

Barbatus seemed pleased that his tactics had been understood. "The bonus prize is that Whelan sent the woman and her boy back there. Probably to get them away from the riots."

Nick felt his stomach clench. Maggie and Noah had been sent to the villa? He glanced down at the tablet, and saw himself reflected in the screen.

He looked a mess. Stubble, grease and fear. "The woman, Maggie," he said. "Will she be safe?"

"Of course. I'm counting on it." Barbatus pointed to the tablet. "The next time that thing goes off, I want you to answer."

The tablet suddenly seemed heavier. Should he try to explain? Warn them?

Calpurnia appeared in the doorway. Not wanting to intrude, but clearly curious. He'd offered her the truth, and then not provided it. What would become of her if Barbatus lost? A woman on her own, with no way of inheriting her father's estate. Her future so uncertain, and yet her resolve so firm.

Nick cleared his throat. "You saw Whelan at the Temple of Jupiter," he said. "You saw what he can do."

The *duumvir* didn't respond.

"Whelan doesn't just have the power to control lightning," Nick continued. "He can also control time."

Barbatus looked at him sceptically, and then rubbed

his chin. "I heard a man once say that time is a sort of river of passing events," he said. "I think its current is too strong for men like McMahon or Whelan to take a swim."

"But what if a man was swimming in the river," said Nick, "and he was scooped up and brought upstream?"

Barbatus didn't reply.

"That's what happened to my friend, Canus, at the bathhouse. He was taken into the future. He is safe."

Calpurnia edged into the room. Barbatus didn't seem to have noticed her. She looked like she wanted to say something.

"McMahon and Whelan won't be threatened," continued Nick, "because they have the ultimate escape route. They can be sucked into the future, and out of harm's way."

"No," said Calpurnia, quietly. "No, that won't happen."

Barbatus studied his daughter, then turned back to Nick. "I agree. Your friend Canus was a nobody; very different to your leaders."

"I think you're missing my point."

"No, you're missing my daughter's. Do you think that if Jupiter had granted Nero this power, Nero would have saved the Emperor Gaius?"

Nick hesitated. "No."

"No," repeated Barbatus. "Of course he wouldn't."

"Because what circumstance would create the greatest catastrophe among men?" asked Calpurnia. "'If the dead were to rise and demand back their property'?"

Nick recognised the Aesop quote. He was about to

respond, but the *duumvir* interrupted him. "And if your friends were going to use this power against me, they would have done so already. As soon as I revealed my hand."

Nick's mind blanked. Thirty years. If anyone in charge of NovusPart wanted to stop Barbatus thirty years from now, then they weren't showing it. But why?

And then it hit him.

He was about to clear their path to power.

Nick looked at the *duumvir*, knowing his expression must have been grim. The progressing coup also explained why he hadn't been transported from the British Museum, or the bathhouse. Which meant he'd been right: he was the key to it all. The man who'd moved the pieces into position. The man who'd allowed the current NovusPart regime to fall.

The man who'd deposed McMahon.

The man who'd killed Hitler.

He just needed to hold his nerve.

In his hands, the tablet started to buzz. Nick answered the call and Whelan's face appeared.

"It seems you have control of our villa," said the operations chief. His tone remained neutral, but the muscles in his face were strained. "I want a guarantee that you will not harm our people, especially the woman and her boy."

"You have it," said Barbatus. "Of course, some may have been injured during our arrival."

"Casualties of war?"

"We're not at war," replied the *duumvir*. "Indeed, I

hope we can turn this situation to our mutual benefit."

"How so?"

"You have a lot of resources, but don't understand how to wield them. I can provide you with the muscle to run this town effectively. Stop you becoming the victim of kidnappers and murderers."

Whelan looked amused. "You would give us your protection?"

"I would."

Whelan said nothing.

"What do you say?" said Barbatus.

Whelan's face was screwed up in silent frustration.

"We should meet," insisted the *duumvir*. "Cement our new alliance."

Nick looked down at the tablet. Whelan wasn't on his own. He could see a shadow thrown on the wall behind Whelan, probably Astridge's. He couldn't see McMahon. With Patrick gone, Nick was now the only channel of communication between Whelan and Barbatus.

"He's worked it out," said Nick, in Greek. Just in case there was someone listening he didn't know about. "He's worked out that he's in danger because you haven't been transported. And he doesn't know how to react."

"Then what do you suggest?"

Nick felt his cheeks burn. Barbatus hadn't been transported. And the *duumvir* had Maggie and Noah. There was only one logical answer. They needed to give Whelan some leverage of his own. Something to encourage him to come to a meeting.

Instinctively, he looked at Calpurnia.

"We will send you my daughter as collateral," said Barbatus, understanding all too well. Or maybe coming to the same conclusion. Either way, it didn't lessen Nick's guilt. But Calpurnia remained quite calm, her expression not betraying doubt or anger. Almost as if she knew how her father's style of politics would play out. As if she'd seen it before.

Nick cleared his throat, trying to focus on Whelan. "I don't believe he's tricking you," he said, in English.

Onscreen, Whelan growled. "Very well. Where do you want to meet?"

"The forum, tomorrow at midday," said Nick, repeating Barbatus' words. "Where better to make a public statement of our new alliance?"

"Fine. But I suggest we each allow the other only one armed guard. And limit the total numbers to no more than three."

"It's agreed. My daughter will go to your House of McMahon. As a gesture of good faith." Barbatus grunted and disconnected the call – using the device as instinctively as someone who'd been using it all their life.

"You will need to teach us how to use these properly."

Nick quickly checked the call had indeed been ended. He needed to be careful. He thought about what Calpurnia had told him about Carthage, and wondered who'd shown the Romans how to build their first ships.

"Whelan will want the villa back," he said.

"Your Whelan is a fool. He shouldn't have told me

anything about the villa. We were blind, and yet he told us everything we needed to know. He could have bluffed. Said our takeover had failed. Given me something to think about. Given himself some time."

But Whelan was used to instantaneous communication, thought Nick. And used to dealing with people who also knew all the facts. He was a man out of time, fighting people he didn't understand. "Still," he said, his mind whirring even as the penny dropped, "Whelan will be plotting his next move. He won't accept losing control of the villa."

"Of course he won't." Barbatus laughed, and slapped him hard on the shoulder. "You wouldn't make a good soldier, Nick. Or a politician. Don't mistake a cessation in hostilities for peace. Tell me, what happened after Octavian made a deal to rule with Mark Antony?"

65

CALPURNIA HAD BEEN gone for several hours — escorted to the House of McMahon by three of Barbatus' men — when the *duumvir* entered Nick's room and held out the tablet.

"It wasn't like the last time," said Barbatus. "It just buzzed once. And not for long."

Nick took it wordlessly. The screen was black but when he tapped it into life he saw there was a message from Whelan. He tried to explain the concept to the *duumvir*.

"Why do you think he no longer wishes to show his face?" asked Barbatus. Nick shrugged and kept quiet. He could tell that Barbatus already knew the answer. "He wants time to think through each response," continued the *duumvir*. "He probably regrets being put on the spot earlier. He doesn't want us to see him react. So what does he say?"

Nick didn't read the first part of the message out loud. *Your helicopter will arrive tomorrow.* He hesitated for a second, considering the implications but knowing it meant he was running out of time. Barbatus stirred, waiting for the translation. Whelan had been wise enough to add another unrelated section to the message. *Directly after we meet, we want to put on a show at the amphitheatre. Jointly hosted.*

Barbatus inhaled loudly as Nick read it out. "Your Whelan is a better tactician than I thought."

"I don't see what's changed."

"Games," replied Barbatus. "The people love games, and they love the people who put them on."

"They're not going to suddenly fall in love with Whelan and McMahon."

"No. But if they're jointly hosted, then they're jointly advertised. Possibly as a joint gift. Which would make your people's sudden demise... unfortunate."

Nick kept silent.

"Send a message back," continued the *duumvir*. "Tell him it's too late. My gladiators aren't ready."

Nick typed the message. Whelan would barely have been able to read it before the tablet signalled his response: *We'll supply some animals to act as grist to the mill. Let me know how many you need.*

Nick snapped his attention back to Barbatus. The old Roman was smiling to himself. "It may be that your man thinks I'll have to withdraw my men from his villa in order to allow them to compete in the arena. He would be mistaken." Barbatus paused again, as if checking his plan for errors. "Tell him it's a deal. I'll supply five pairs of gladiators if he can supply a lion or two. That'll test the cocksucker. In the meantime, I'll send out the news regarding the town's games."

66

KIRSTEN LOOKED AT the photograph but hardly recognised the face staring back at her. The caption told her it was Joe Arlen. But his cheeks – Octo's cheeks – had none of the youthful enthusiasm she remembered. Instead, he looked at the camera with resignation. Pain. Anger.

"What happened to him?"

Harris raised an eyebrow. "He didn't seem able to cope with the complexity of what he'd unleashed."

Kirsten pulled her attention away from the tablet. "Pardon?"

"How do you create something that could unravel the timeline and be comfortable with what you'd done?" Harris paused as Kirsten looked back to the newspaper article. "Very few people in history have had to cope with that sort of pressure. Oppenheimer, perhaps, is the closest example. Anyway, Arlen became obsessed with what he called 'intersections'. Where people were and at what time. Tracking and researching people who had influenced his own personal timeline with the same rigour and obsession with which some people trace their family tree."

Kirsten scrolled down the article. "It says here he

spends hours researching who he's been in contact with."

"Yes, but as I said: no one's seen him for quite some time. It seems he doesn't want to create any new intersections."

She looked up. "What if I told you I could kill Harold McMahon?"

"I doubt you'd have the stomach for it."

Kirsten shook her head. Once she'd got the hang of the tablet, she'd been using her time between interviews carefully, reading up on NovusPart, and absorbing everything she could about the potential threats to the timeline. How it was thought it could be manipulated. The dangers of splintering and fragmentation.

And it always came back to the same thing. Nothing would change, as long as they only took people who were already dead. Except she hadn't been dead. She'd been taking a bath. And because of what McMahon had done to her, she'd lost thirty years.

"NovusPart seem to be comfortable with creating paradoxes," she said.

"Yes."

"Why do you suppose that is?"

"Because despite what Arlen may have thought, it would appear the timeline is difficult to break."

"So why don't we give them a paradox big enough to make them choke?"

Harris didn't respond at first. But she could see the calculations running through his mind. A smile started to flicker across his lips as he came to the same conclusion as she had. "They would have to be tricked into removing you at birth. You would die."

"And so would McMahon. Which would be a hell of a paradox, don't you think? At the very least, I wouldn't have to spend a lifetime lost in that godforsaken college."

Harris stared at her. "It could be dangerous. I need to talk to Marcus first. There may be unexpected consequences."

67

THEY REACHED THE forum's northern triumphal arch well before Whelan. Nick hadn't been surprised to be asked to join the group, given his role as a translator. But Barbatus had brought Cato along, rather than one of his thugs. And despite Cato carrying a sword, Nick couldn't help but feel they were arriving a bit light.

With time to kill, it didn't take long before Barbatus started to greet passers-by as if they were old friends, the consummate politician. He probably barely knew them, but they returned the *duumvir*'s attention enthusiastically, and their sense of anticipation was already palpable. It certainly hadn't taken long for news of the games to circulate.

Nick looked up at the Temple of Fortuna Augusta. It seemed long ago that he'd spoken with Calpurnia there. Her concerns at the time now seemed inconsequential. Bare tremors against the coming eruption.

She'd better be okay.

"He's here," Barbatus said, his voice low. "And he's got more than two men."

Nick turned quickly to look up the *via*. Bizarrely, Barbatus didn't seem concerned. He was just noting the lack of basic arithmetic. But he was right. Whelan was striding towards them with Astridge, and one of the NovusPart security guards. Behind them a wagon was being driven by another guard. Nick squinted. He recognised neither of them, but both guards were clearly carrying handguns. And maybe because of it, Whelan had ventured out without his Taser-enhanced, leather wrist-guard.

"The man in the wagon won't be joining us," said the operations chief.

"Good," replied Barbatus. He glanced at Astridge. "Where's McMahon?"

"Mr McMahon is ill," said Whelan. "I speak for him." He nodded towards Astridge. "I am joined by another key member of our team, Robert Astridge."

Barbatus glanced at Nick. "No matter," said the *duumvir*.

"Now, the woman and the boy," said Whelan. "I trust they're safe?"

"Yes. They arrived back in town this morning, and remain under my protection."

Whelan didn't reply. His mind was clearly ticking over. Probably thinking that if he killed Barbatus now, then he wouldn't be able to get to Maggie before she was killed in turn. But he also looked slightly confused. "My information is that she's still at the villa."

"Her clothes are," replied the *duumvir*. "As are the boy's." He turned towards Nick. "I heard there's something special about your belts that allow you to track people. But she wasn't wearing one, and I didn't want to take the chance there was something sewn in her *stola*."

Whelan offered a bitter smile. "In turn, your daughter remains in good health," he said.

The *duumvir* didn't reply. Instead, he cast a cool stare behind Whelan towards the wagon. It held a wooden crate with thick steel bars built into it. "Wagons aren't allowed in the street during…"

He didn't finish his sentence. There was something alive in the crate. The sound of a body rubbing up against rough wood. A long, low growl. "You managed to find a lion," Barbatus said, clearly impressed.

Whelan grinned. He waved the wagon forward. Nick immediately moved back on to the pavement, but Barbatus stood in the street, only stepping away a moment or two before the wagon's mules reached his feet.

The wagon came to a stop at the threshold of the forum. Now everyone could see through the bars of the crate.

"What do you call it?" asked Barbatus. His features had lost some of their Mediterranean lustre. Nick felt dizzy. No, he wasn't seeing things. NovusPart had just topped the reconstruction of Pompeii. He could finally now see the huge money-spinning potential of the town.

"Smilodon," said Whelan. "We call her Smilodon. For this afternoon's games. We can provide a lot more like her. And a number of other special creatures you won't have seen before."

Barbatus turned to Whelan. The *duumvir* was smiling broadly, but couldn't hide his astonishment. "Let's talk," he said, heading into the forum. Cato followed his master.

Nick didn't move. He was still staring at the crate. "It's a fucking sabre-toothed tiger!"

68

NICK RAN TO catch up with Astridge.

"Where's McMahon?"

"He's ill," said Astridge. "Whelan wasn't bullshitting. We think he's got the flu."

"Is he leaving town?"

"No. He won't leave the house. And if that bastard hadn't got Maggie we'd just shoot him where he stands!"

"I'm sorry."

"Don't be," said Astridge, his voice turning grim. "He can't hold her for ever; and then we'll see if it really is impossible to crucify a Roman."

Nick looked ahead towards Whelan and Barbatus. The NovusPart guard and Cato hovered at a respectful distance – but close enough to intervene if needed. All around them, the citizens of Pompeii watched, and stared. Whelan appeared relaxed. Then again, any doubts about his personal safety were probably covered by the security guard he'd brought with him, and the fact he held Calpurnia. That much of the plan had certainly worked.

"Where the hell did they get the cat?"

"We have a few surprises ready for the launch events.

There's a zoo attached to the amphitheatre."

"Yes, I know. But I hadn't expected… Shit. That means they can reach back over ten thousand years…"

Astridge smiled. "I overheard Whelan saying that was pretty much the new limit. Though I guess they're looking for ways to punch back further. After all, a sabre-tooth is going to make a big splash – but they'll always need the next big thing. If only they could get better at near-past transports too…"

"Nick!"

Whelan was waving him forward. The COO took a firm hold of his arm. "Two things to think about before this starts. Firstly, the helicopter is inbound, and it's carrying the mole we found in our logistics chain. So when it arrives, we're finally going to be able to identify our spy."

Nick felt his stomach contract. "I told you…"

"The second thing," said Whelan, tightening his grip, "is that Patrick and your friends at the British Museum were transported into the future."

"I know that."

"Which means NovusPart continues to exist. And Harris loses. Just take a second to think about that when you're choosing sides."

Nick prickled, sensing the threat. But Whelan wasn't finished. "Barbatus will almost certainly make his move at the arena. My security team are already assembled there, and they're armed. So the outcome of this little *coup d'état* is inevitable. We win. They lose. And NovusPart continues."

Nick felt his lip begin to twist, but fortunately Barbatus

stepped forward before the emotion registered on his face. "We'll take a short stroll first," said the *duumvir*, pointing around the forum. He waited for Nick to translate. "Let them see us together. All we have to do is talk and smile."

"Fine," replied Whelan, but not before giving a final, angry glance in Nick's direction.

"So, you can provide more beasts like the one outside?"

"Yes."

Barbatus mulled this over. "I presume it's from the lands south of Egypt?"

"Something like that."

"So many strange creatures out there," the *duumvir* mused. "Last summer we imported a camelopardalis."

"Camelopardalis?" It wasn't a word Nick knew. A camel with leopard markings?

"Yes, you know – from across the sea. With long necks. It made a fine addition to my dinner table. So what else can you offer me?"

"We already supply the town with food and money," said Whelan. "And we know we can supply a lot more in return for your wine, pottery and textiles. So I think it's more like, what can you do for us?"

The *duumvir* waved at the watching crowd. "You think you would last two seconds here, if people didn't know we're now friends?"

"We have your daughter."

"Stability. Direction. Purpose," said the *duumvir*, ignoring the comment. "The story you told us when you brought us here was too... limited. True, they need a strong leader. But they also need to know where they're being led to."

"We just want a peaceful town. Somewhere where we can live, and conduct our business."

"And you'll have it."

Nick finished translating Barbatus' last sentence, trying to ignore the unease in his gut. They seemed to be getting along well. A deal was being brokered. But Nick couldn't help but wonder: was this how Octavian spoke to Mark Antony? Just before they went to war?

They took the direct route from the forum to the amphitheatre, down the long straight road linking the town's south-west quadrant to the Sarno Gate in the east. Barbatus continued to ostentatiously acknowledge his people. Nick watched him intently. The *duumvir* exuded great confidence even though he must have known Whelan still presented a problem.

As soon as they got to the amphitheatre, Barbatus steered them away from the steadily thickening crowd who were making their way towards the cheap seats.

"Impressive."

Nick couldn't help but agree with Whelan's understated sentiment. Because in front of him was the sight he'd really come here to see. The real Pompeii. From the outside, the arena looked like a low-slung salad bowl pushed tight up against the town's outer defences. Almost as if it had been forced into a space that was clearly far too small. But now packed with people, and with dozens more funnelling in up the ramps, the stone-tiered seating rippled with colour and noise.

"These are our seats."

Nick hesitated. Barbatus was waving them into a section guarded by men who looked like the city watch. Although the *duumvir's* men were simply separating an area of more exclusive seating from the rest of the crowd, it was clear they represented a threat. Whelan, however, walked straight into their midst and took a place on the front row. He was joined by the *duumvir*.

"We'll give the plebs time to settle before bringing out the first two fighters."

Whelan didn't reply, and Nick was left to find a seat near Astridge, one row behind Whelan and Barbatus. Just like at the theatre, cushions had been provided to make the stone seating more comfortable. After moving them into position, Nick glanced down at Whelan and Barbatus, ready for translation duties.

The *duumvir* continued to appear completely relaxed, unconcerned about the fate of his daughter. Whelan sat in complete silence. Nick glanced behind him at Cato and the NovusPart security guard settling into their seats, both alert and watchful.

It didn't take long before Astridge broke the silence. "You know, Dr Houghton, when we first arrived here, you told us all a Roman joke," he said. "I thought you might like to hear one I picked up from Patrick before he left."

"Go on," said Nick.

"Oh, how does it go? Ah, yes, that's right. An absent-minded professor approaches a eunuch and a pretty young woman. He says: 'Ah, what a beautiful wife.' But when the eunuch says he isn't allowed to marry, the professor replies: 'I'm sorry; this must be your daughter.'"

Nick didn't reply.

"You don't get it?"

"It must be the way you told it."

Astridge laughed and pushed back into his stone seat. Nick tried to ignore him. Which was easy, because a pair of gladiators had appeared and were now walking into the centre of the oval arena. The noise from the crowd grew.

One, a *retiarius*, held a trident and net, while his fish-helmeted opponent, a *murmillo*, carried a shield and *gladius*, a short sword. Both wore armour that provided protection to only one side of their bodies – metal plate covering their right shoulders, with pads wrapped around their right legs. The rest of their bodies were left exposed.

Different and yet balanced. Opposite and equal. And yet neither had what could be described as a six-pack. There was no sign of any flexing tendons or sinew. No, this was muscle overlain by fat. Giant hulks of men for whom weight was just as important as strength.

Whelan looked over his shoulder and beckoned Nick to lean forward. "Your attention should be on us, Nick," he said.

Nick nodded, but felt a flare of anger. It almost distracted him from a blur of white material and movement: Naso was hurriedly taking his place beside Barbatus. The *duumvir* gave a lazy nod in the direction of the aedile and then turned his attention back to Whelan.

"You are either very brave or very foolish to come

here with me." Barbatus cast a cool glance around the crowd – and the city watch now separating them from the rest of the spectators.

Whelan remained impassive. "My men don't need to be so close to provide protection."

It was only then that Nick saw them. Roman soldiers – NovusPart security men – all wearing the imperial eagle, lining the very back row of the arena. He couldn't quite see at the distance they were standing, but he guessed that each would be carrying a rifle instead of a sword.

The *duumvir* didn't seem to feel the need to pick them out from the crowd. He indicated down towards the gladiators, while keeping his eyes firmly on Whelan. "You'll notice that each fighting man has his strengths and weaknesses," he said. "The skill is to play to one's strengths, while neutralising those of your opponent."

"Indeed."

"Then let the games begin."

Nick smiled. Despite their prevalence in popular culture, actually very little was known about what went on in a Roman amphitheatre. Many academics had tried to piece it together – from the order of events, to what was said, to how the individual gladiators fought. And, of course, Hollywood had also had its say as to what had happened: *Those who are about to die salute you!*

He'd always guessed it was all so much bullshit. And, despite the current fight being nothing more than a hastily arranged foretaste of what could be delivered in New Pompeii, he got an immediate sense that what was unfolding on the sand in front of them would be a disappointment to a modern audience. Astridge put it into words first. He gave his usual snort of derision. "Well, this will have the TV networks salivating."

Sure enough, in the first few minutes of the fight, neither gladiator tried to land a blow. They simply circled each other, with only the occasional lunge forward. This was clearly a careful sport. And with so much flesh and weaponry on show, it shouldn't really have been a surprise.

The *murmillo* edged forward – padded and armoured side first. The *retiarius* shuffled away to the left. A small cloud of sand and dust kicked up around their feet. Each man was clearly trying to seek an opportunity to strike the other while not leaving themselves exposed. Nick smiled in spite of himself. He'd once heard someone compare gladiators to modern-day boxers. And in that moment he remembered there was a vast difference between the different types and weights of fighter – depending on whether the aim was simply to collect points or to gain a knockout. But, then again, there was always the chance of that one epic fight. The attraction that kept the punters coming. The chance to see a great champion fall, and a new one rise.

Nick leant forward in his seat and spoke quickly in English: "I take it your men are carrying guns?"

Whelan gave a shallow nod, but kept his attention on the fight below. "Any sign of movement from your friend, Barbatus, and his head will come clean off his shoulders."

"So what's the endgame? We seem to be at stalemate."

Whelan shook his head. "The helicopter heading our way isn't just carrying our spy," he said. "It's also filled with reinforcements. Men who will first take back the control villa before heading here."

Nick nodded, nervous of the *duumvir* – but Barbatus didn't ask him for a translation. "How does that help us?"

"Maggie and the child are still there. I'm certain of it. There's been little movement on the north road since this thing started. Your *duumvir* may say he's brought them here, but I think he's bluffing."

Astridge leant in to join the debate. "What are you suggesting?"

The architect's voice was taut and it had attracted Naso's attention. The aedile fidgeted in his seat – obviously desperate for Barbatus to ask for a translation even as the *duumvir* continued to watch the action below without comment.

"Gladiators may have been able to beat a handful of men who had no warning. But men coming in fast, with machine guns and tear gas, will be another matter entirely. Maggie and Noah won't even suffer a scratch."

"They'd better bloody not!"

From somewhere close came an electronic warble. Whelan took a phone from his tunic, and indicated for Nick to speak with Barbatus. "Tell him to release the Smilodon."

Nick relayed the instruction while Whelan spoke into his mobile. Below, the fight was picking up. The *retiarius* had thrown his net, but it hadn't quite snagged his opponent. And when Nick turned back to Whelan – he immediately knew something had gone wrong.

69

"ANOTHER INTERESTING TOY," said Barbatus, dryly. The *duumvir* waited for Whelan to put the phone back into his tunic, and then reached back and let Cato place a thin slice of plastic into his hands. The tablet from the House of Samson.

Barbatus didn't ask Nick to help him use it. Instead, the device lit up underneath the *duumvir*'s touch. He activated the GPS app. It showed a map of the town and a line of bright red dots. "The supposed location of your men," said the *duumvir*. "Or, at least, their belts." He waited for his words to be translated. His patient, almost disconnected delivery seemed to drive each word deeper into Whelan's gut. But it was the movement below them that slowly twisted the knife. The red dots weren't along the back row of the arena. Instead, they were moving as a single column out on to the sand.

A line of Roman men were walking into the centre of the arena. Their position matched exactly the location of the red dots on the map. Nick watched them, realising what was going on even if his brain wasn't quite ready to believe it.

Each Roman held their right arm out straight; letting belts hang away from their bodies as if marking out a procession route with a series of plumb lines.

And they all pointed straight to hell.

Nick's attention snapped to the back of the arena. The NovusPart security guards still appeared to be standing in their allotted positions. Their uniforms and rifles clear against the stone of the amphitheatre. Even if their faces weren't.

All anonymous men, he realised. Just like the slaves attending the *duumvir*'s household. Puppets rather than people.

"Your metal mosquito has arrived at your villa," said Barbatus.

"Yes," replied Whelan.

"But they couldn't find my men."

"Correct."

"By comparison, those belts made it easy to find yours."

"I still have your daughter," said Whelan, his voice cracking.

"My daughter knows the dangers of politics. And somehow, I suspect you care more for the old shrew who's in my possession than I do for the girl who's in yours."

Nick completed his translation and looked behind him. The exits were already being covered, and the faceless NovusPart security guard who'd accompanied them from the forum was suddenly nowhere to be seen. The trap set for Barbatus had been neatly inverted. Astridge was panicking. The architect was shaking in his seat, acrid yellow water already dribbling down on to the steps beneath him.

And despite it all, Nick felt some grim satisfaction. Because the Romans had run a continental empire without the benefit of telecommunications. And, in that context, gaining an advantage in a town the size of Pompeii would hardly have been a challenge. Was he the man who'd let NovusPart fail? Is that how history would remember him?

"You people," said Barbatus, getting to his feet. "Whenever we were summoned to your mansion, I saw the contempt on your faces. The same expression that must have been worn by the Greeks, the Egyptians, even the Carthaginians when they first met us. But where are they now, if not bending and scraping at our feet?"

Nick rose. He could already sense a watchman heading down the steps to stop him getting too close to the *duumvir*. But he had to say something. He spoke in Latin. "You're going to kill us?"

"Yes, Pullus. And your leader, McMahon."

"What did he say?" Astridge screamed.

"He's going to attack the House of McMahon."

"He'll not get in," said Whelan. "We left instructions to keep the door sealed." The operations chief's eyes searched Nick for a reaction. "Tell him. We need time to negotiate."

"He's already inside."

"What?"

"Calpurnia."

"A pregnant girl?"

"No," said Nick. "A Trojan horse."

70

"You know," said Whelan. "I think I've finally figured it out." He appraised the Romans encircling them: the two gladiators, Barbatus and Cato. With the trap sprung, it hadn't taken long for the city watch to drag them on to the sand.

They were the main attraction. Only Naso was absent – having been dispatched to the House of McMahon with another trio of men. The Smilodon, meanwhile, remained safely in its crate, Whelan's last instruction having not been acted upon. The power of NovusPart restrained, just moments before it could be unleashed. "We didn't transport you from the bathhouse, because this way I can kill you myself."

For the first time in a while, Nick felt a migraine building. "You don't get it, do you?" He glanced down at the sand and then back up to the colours of Pompeii as they swirled around them. The crowd remained largely silent. Waiting for the fun to start. "You don't run the future. Someone else does. And they didn't stop me because I opened up your job for them. And that means you won't be transported out of here. No matter how bad it gets for you."

"You think this is your purpose in life then, Nick? To put me at the mercy of thousands of baying Romans?"

In truth, he remained uncertain. But he hadn't been transported. And Barbatus still stood there, when he could have been snuffed out so easily by those running NovusPart in the future. So yes: all the pieces fitted.

This had to be why he'd been brought to New Pompeii.

But then he suddenly felt dizzy. His surroundings started to spin, and his gut contracted so hard he gagged. Because, if he was right, it meant he'd completed his mission. And he'd be killed just as surely as Whelan.

The operations chief, however, hadn't given up hope. "The offer to join us is still open," he shouted.

Barbatus laughed. "Join you? No. Dictatorship is always preferable to a triumvirate."

Somewhere, deep in Nick's brain, a moment of clarity emerged. The scenery around him stopped spinning. *Triumvirate*.

McMahon. Whelan.

And who?

The Temple of Jupiter, the statues of Jupiter, Juno and Minerva. He thought back to their first meal in New Pompeii, and the couch made for three, but only occupied by the two men running NovusPart. And he recalled the photo of Stalin, and the removal of the man who'd fallen out of favour in the Soviet regime.

But most of all Nick thought about Rome. And the reason NovusPart had suddenly found themselves needing advice from Samson in the first place. "Neither you nor

McMahon have any real interest in Rome," he whispered, turning to look directly at Whelan. "There must have been somebody else. Somebody who dreamt up this scheme in the first place. Someone who's no longer here…"

"This isn't the time, Nick."

"No – it's absolutely the right time. There's somebody missing!"

"This is a long established project—"

"You said it was a Roman bubble," said Nick. "I assumed you meant it was an escape from the criticisms and protests back home. But then there are the children and the reasons why they're being brought here. So it's more than that. More than just a factory for producing Roman wine and frescos."

"You don't build a chair using just one leg."

Nick glanced at Barbatus. The *murmillo* and *retiarius* continued to prowl, but they were being held back. The *duumvir* appeared to be in no hurry. After all, he must have wanted the crowd to fully understand the situation. For them to know he was about to plunge the dagger in. For Whelan to feel he was about to die.

"But there must be a reason. Why did you *really* build New Pompeii?"

"You're standing in it," replied Whelan, looking towards the sky.

"No, I don't buy it. There must be something else…"

Whelan didn't say anything further. He continued to look upwards, as did Astridge. And the architect was suddenly smiling. It took a few seconds for Nick to hear it.

THUMP – THUMP – THUMP.

The helicopter. Coming directly into town. And there was only one place big enough for it to land.

"Your missing person is a founder member of NovusPart," said Whelan. He glanced at the gladiators, checking that they weren't getting too close. "He wanted somewhere he could become a gladiator."

"Dangerous."

"You ever heard of a guy called Commodus?"

Nick nodded. Like Caligula, another mad emperor of Rome. And one of the few to fight in the Colosseum. Not that the fights were ever fair.

"And there are a lot of people who would pay for the same opportunity. A lot of powerful men, who contacted us to find out if we could arrange... special events. The chance to fight in the arena. To kill people. With the thrill rather than the danger."

Nick started to shake his head. "Men like Commodus and Caligula had an endless supply of men they could put to the sword," he said. "But here there's only a couple of dozen opponents..."

Flight 391. It crashed into Nick's mind as heavily as the plane had plunged into the sea. He'd seen the plans back in the control villa. An amphitheatre built with a zoo and a holding room. And NovusPart had a potentially unlimited supply of people it could suck from the past. A potentially unlimited supply of puppets. "No," he said. "People who died in disasters..."

"They're already dead, Nick. They're already dead.

So what does it matter if they die in a plane crash or are butchered in an amphitheatre?"

THUMP – THUMP – THUMP.

The noise from the helicopter was getting louder. The spectators were all looking upwards. Only Barbatus stared straight ahead, his grin growing wider. Nick wondered if it was because he knew it was going to be too late. The metal mosquito would take some time to land. Far longer than it would take for the *murmillo* or *retiarius* to strike.

"No," said Nick, shaking his head. "It just wouldn't work. No one would kill a person if they knew they'd just been saved from a plane crash." He stopped. Choked. Thought of his mother. "Or a terrorist attack."

For a second, Whelan looked him squarely in the eye. His voice shrank to a whisper. "You're right, Nick. But it came really close to happening. So we killed him. We stopped him. We watched him being sucked from history, and in that instant we knew we'd ended it."

"You couldn't have stopped him another way…?"

"Do you really think you can reason with a madman?"

Nick felt sick. A man who would make his horse a senator, and collect seashells as booty in his war with the sea. A man who would rape his sisters and kill on a whim. A man who would only rule for four years, but be famous for two thousand. The golden boy of Rome, who'd become the sick child. The Little Boot.

What if someone could have stopped him?

Why didn't they?

Nick shuddered. Because, of course, they *had* stopped

him. Deep in the tunnels of Rome, those closest to Caligula had ended his reign with a flurry of stab wounds. "And this is why you killed Professor Samson? Did he get close to the truth?"

Whelan looked to the sky, his face grim. The helicopter was getting closer but it was going to be too late. Just like the *duumvir* had already figured out.

Barbatus signalled for the *murmillo* to engage.

"I told you, Nick. I don't know what happened to him."

71

"SO THE TIME is right for you to die."

Barbatus grinned and waved to the crowd. It responded as if being whipped up by a conductor. The helicopter was now just a heavy bass line, playing in the background. Nothing but a fading hope.

"You want them to see us," said Nick. "It's not enough that we die, they have to see us dying."

"I think you're starting to get it, Pullus. How to be a good Roman politician. Just that little bit too late."

Nick closed his eyes, and started to count. Augustus, Tiberius, Caligula, Claudius, Nero. The Julio-Claudian dynasty. Poisoned. Suffocated. Stabbed. Poisoned. Suicide. All known deaths. And yet somehow his brain changed gear. The needle skipped the groove and he started thinking about Professor Samson. And the British Museum. And the bathhouse. And the missing person at the heart of Novus Particles.

If those in the future had wanted Barbatus to kill Whelan, then there was no real point in Nick's being involved. It could have been made to happen in any number of ways: the *duumvir* had sent men to the control villa without his interference. So whatever he was here to do, this wasn't it.

He looked upwards. Almost expecting to see the gods circling above the amphitheatre, rather than the helicopter. Waiting for them to dive in and intervene. And, as he searched for them, the words of another emperor of Rome rose from his subconscious. *Consider yourself to be dead, and to have completed your life only up to the present. And remember that man lives in the present, in this fleeting instant; all the rest of his life is either past and gone, or not yet revealed.*

He looked back at Barbatus. Stared squarely into the *duumvir's* eyes. "Kill me first," he said.

Whelan raised no objection. Astridge looked positively relieved. Nick opened his arms out wide. Let the crowd see him. Sensed a soft, white mist start to mingle around his feet, and waited for the *murmillo* to draw in.

The academic side of his brain ticked over. He knew the Roman sword was a thrusting weapon. It wasn't designed for slashing or cutting. His body tensed as the gladiator pulled his arm back. Expecting the weapon to slice into his stomach and rip out his intestines.

The gladiator disappeared.

Sucked from time. His eyes screwed up in confusion and terror as he disintegrated and was pulled into the air. His sword clattered to the sand in pin-drop silence.

Nick didn't wait. He scooped up the weapon. He raised the blade towards Barbatus, and listened for the crowd. They weren't shouting, or laughing, or screaming. They

were silent. Watching a man point a sword at their leader.
The blade glinted in the sun like the weapon was on fire.
Behind him, the Smilodon roared in its cage.

Smiling, Nick thought of the words that Tacitus had
claimed the mad emperor Caligula had spoken as he died
– as one of thirty or more knives rained down on his body.

"I live," he said, simply.

Nick looked up at the crowd. "I live!" he screamed.

72

Barbatus stared ahead, isolated but refusing to yield. Cato and the other gladiator were running fast across the sand. They reached the boundary of the arena and disappeared from view.

"This is my town, Pullus, and I'm not going to run." The *duumvir* didn't look at the sword. "And only a fool pays out while the dice are still rolling."

Nick didn't move, didn't say anything. He still had value to whoever was pulling the strings in the future. Like Whelan had told him: *There are various ways in which you can contribute to history. A random, off-hand remark that helps someone else find a solution to a problem.* He just needed to get back to the House of McMahon. Because he'd worked it out – and the thought was the only thing stopping him from being killed, the reason those in the future had kept him safe. So no, he wouldn't say anything. Because then someone else would know and someone else could act.

He pushed past Barbatus and started walking towards the exit, carrying the sword loosely by his side and knowing the *duumvir* wouldn't stop him. Whelan and Astridge stood frozen, perhaps not comprehending what had just happened. It was only the noise of the helicopter landing that seemed to bring Whelan back to his senses.

"Nick! Wait!"

He turned. Whelan and Astridge were both running towards the helicopter, the rotors whipping up the sand.

Nick thought of the fake NovusPart soldiers in the back of the arena and he squinted. The helicopter pilot was sitting at an odd angle. Even from this distance, he could see the fear in the man's eyes and the knife at his throat.

You couldn't find my men, Barbatus had said. *But it was easy to find yours.*

Nick turned away. He had to get back to the House of McMahon. In the wake of thousands of scared and angry Romans who were now scurrying for the exits – and who would soon be engaging in the mother of all riots.

And yet despite the people stampeding from the stands, he didn't feel any need to hurry. As long as he kept hold of the thought, there was no real rush. He could take his time. Move through the streets and take his final look at those two-thousand-year-old faces; all of whom were now rushing to their temples and shrines.

"Nick!" The final shout had been Whelan's. Nick didn't look back. He now knew who was pulling the strings in the future. And that could only mean that Harold McMahon was going to die.

73

ALTHOUGH THE RIOT was building around him, the walk back to the House of McMahon wasn't in the least frightening. He was too detached to feel fear. And he knew that he wasn't going to be stopped from reaching his destination.

A small crowd had gathered outside the House of McMahon. Nick watched them from a distance, but quickly realised this wasn't the core of the mob. No, these looked like the true believers. Those that still thought NovusPart had been sent by the god-emperor, Augustus.

Nick was unsurprised when they parted before him. The door to McMahon's mansion was another matter entirely. It was shut, and didn't swing open on his approach. He tapped in the code but the door remained closed. He hammered on the wood. Nothing.

Nick hammered on the door again, using the butt of the sword. On the last strike, it slowly swung open. The porter's angry face appeared. The dog-at-the-door was still alive. "Where's Whelan?"

"On his way," Nick replied. "I've been sent ahead. McMahon is here?"

"Upstairs."

The porter let him pass and quickly re-secured the door. "It's all gone to shit," he said. "And there are hundreds of people heading out of the town on foot. We might not be able to get them all back."

Nick ignored him. Maybe they wouldn't. Maybe the containment of New Pompeii was about to be broken. Not that it mattered any more. All that did matter was reaching McMahon and finding out the answer to one very important question. He looked up towards the atrium balcony, and headed up the stairs.

"Pullus?"

The voice stopped him a few steps from the top. Calpurnia stared up at him from the doorway to the *tablinum*. Her expression was sad. She'd clearly not put her father's plan into action yet. Maybe she'd been waiting to see how the pieces would fall.

"Are you all right?" he asked.

She didn't answer at first, but then slowly nodded. "My father?"

"Alive."

It wasn't clear if Calpurnia was relieved or not. Nick continued upwards, holding the sword loosely, and hoping he wouldn't have to use it.

He found the CEO of NovusPart in his private quarters. McMahon occupied a large sofa that looked like a fallen soufflé. He didn't look up as Nick entered, his attention focused on the screen. As Nick approached, he became aware of wheezing. The man was having difficulty breathing. And he looked pale. His dyed hair was saturated with grease and sweat.

"You brought me my grapes?"

"No," said Nick. He took a few steps forward, but kept the sword close to his side. McMahon glanced in his direction for no more than a second, and then returned his attention to the television.

"Oh, it's you," he said. "They're burning my town."

"You don't sound concerned."

McMahon just shrugged. Like he already realised it was too late.

"You're kidnapping children, aren't you? Taking them from history, and bringing them here."

McMahon looked at him, his eyes cold. "Huh. If only it was that simple. The truth is, it could be me *or* Whelan. But one of us is, that's for sure."

"And you killed Professor Samson."

"Now *that* I can answer with certainty."

"And?"

"You're wrong. We didn't."

The remaining colour had gone from McMahon's cheeks. He stood up, his legs seemingly too weak to hold his body. A hand reached down for his remaining few grapes. He flicked them into his mouth, one at a time.

Nick took another step forward. He sensed movement behind him. Mary, the chef, was standing in the doorway. She looked tense, which was understandable given what was going on outside. But her eyes kept flicking towards the empty bowl of grapes. Her mouth curling at the edges as if wanting to smile. Her brain seemed to be calculating something. *Had he eaten enough?* Because the odds were that the grapes were poisoned.

And now McMahon knew it too.

74

"YOU STUPID BITCH!"

McMahon was wrong. Mary wasn't stupid, *Nick* was. He'd been given all the pieces of the puzzle, but he'd still not seen it until it was too late.

"Wait," Nick said, lifting the sword but finding his voice weak.

McMahon grabbed a nearby tablet. "Let me show you, Dr Houghton, how we deal with these sorts of betrayals."

A face appeared on the tablet. Nick couldn't tell who it was.

"I want Mary Kramer transported. Wipe her out." McMahon jabbed a chubby finger at the chef, suddenly energised. "We're going to take you from birth. You'll be brought back here as a baby, and I'll take personal pleasure in leaving you outside the walls to die."

Nick shuddered. McMahon's weapon against his enemies. Which maybe explained why most resistance to NovusPart had all but disappeared. Just like Harris had told him. But there was also a problem.

"Paradox," said Nick. "You're about to create a paradox."

"It'll just be a bump in the road. A few odd details for

lunatics and conspiracy theorists to debate while they play video games. Instead of her, we'll just have appointed a different chef. Some other stupid cow to serve us dinner and change our sheets. Except her replacement won't be adding anything to the food. And she won't be working for Harris."

The tablet chirped. "We've checked with *Who's Where*," came a distant voice. "She's a green risk. There are no intersection points prior to her joining NovusPart. However, there is an issue with her birth information…"

"Good. Proceed."

Nick felt his brain whirr. The puzzle was once more being disassembled. And he suddenly found himself looking at a Rosetta Stone. But not of language; one of time. Imperial Rome with its bloodbath of imperial succession. The question of what would have happened if someone had killed Hitler before 1933. And Perkin Warbeck; the name finally clicked into place. Three chapters of history from different times.

But all telling the same story.

"How long do I have?" asked Mary.

"A few seconds," replied McMahon, turning and tossing the tablet on to the couch behind him. "Just until they get a good enough lock."

"Good," she said. "So tell me. Who do you think is going to give you that slap on the back?"

Nick didn't hear McMahon's answer. He was thinking about the flipside to the question of what would have been different if Hitler had died before 1933. *Because if Hitler had died, and you were already living in the alternative reality: how much would you give to ensure no one accidentally brought him back to life?*

Nick started to shake. There was someone missing. Someone terrible. And if McMahon was removed, did that mean he could continue to exist?

White mist had begun to seep into the room. Nick ignored it. He wasn't going to reach the tablet in time without a struggle. But he moved forward anyway, dropping the sword. McMahon made an instinctive swat at him, but Nick slipped past, reaching for the tablet.

He heard a slow scream behind him, like a warped cassette tape. He didn't hesitate. He grabbed the tablet. "Abort!" he shouted. "Abort! Abort! Abort!"

75

"WHO'S MARY KRAMER?"

"Nobody important."

Kirsten looked down at the papers. Her photograph sat uncomfortably next to someone else's details. She looked back at Harris. "You've kept my real birth date."

"It's fine," said Harris. He stared at her from across the desk.

The time, place and date of her birth. The names of her parents. The papers made her far older than she looked. It was a clear error.

"Who's Mary Kramer?" she asked again.

"She's dead," Harris said. "Last year. You don't have to worry about her cropping up. And you don't have to worry about her ever having come into contact with McMahon, Whelan or NovusPart. She's completely unknown to them. And that's all they'll care about."

Kirsten looked down at the papers again. Saw her photograph. Saw her new name, and her new profession. Personal Assistant. A secretary by any other name. She'd have to get used to deciphering shorthand. "So when do I meet Professor Samson?"

"Soon. And it turns out he's working on an interesting new project."

76

"SO YOU KILLED McMahon?"

Nick didn't answer.

"Did you need to?"

Again, Nick didn't answer. Whelan lay on the floor of the *tablinum*, staring up at him. He'd been beaten. The left side of his face had been battered purple, and he was breathing shallowly.

Barbatus and Calpurnia waited at a safe distance in the atrium. Nick had asked them for a few minutes alone with Whelan. Astridge hadn't been brought back from the arena, and Nick didn't know what had happened to the porter. Perhaps Calpurnia had acted when she realised her father remained *duumvir*. Or perhaps the porter had been slain while Nick had been dealing with McMahon. Either way, there was now nothing left of NovusPart. Other than Whelan. The discarded toy soldier.

"Are you going to say anything at all?"

Nick cleared his throat. In truth, he didn't want to reply. Before Barbatus had arrived, he'd managed to find a phone and call his father. The conversation had been short and painful, but they hadn't argued. Whether they'd ever see each other again was another matter. But he'd still needed to talk.

"I want to know about the missing man."

Whelan coughed. "His name was Joe Arlen, Octo, we called him."

"And his fixation was killing people who were already dead? Playing with them in the arena?"

"They say there's no genius without a touch of madness."

Nick grunted. Whelan's eyes suddenly filled with regret.

"You're right though," Whelan continued. He coughed again. A few spots of blood dribbled down his chin. "We knew there were risks when we first tried to transport people – that they might not make it. But Octo told us not to worry; that they weren't really people any more. That they were already dead. It wasn't long before he started to talk about murder."

"And New Pompeii was just a mask, wasn't it? A convenient cover story for you to play out your little schemes."

Whelan didn't say anything.

"Arlen had his obsession with the arena," continued Nick. "And the town allowed McMahon to take his enemies while they were children."

Whelan didn't say anything; one eye was swollen shut and the other concentrated on the floor.

"And what would *your* route to madness have looked like?" Nick paused. Thinking about the one piece of the town that still didn't fit. "The empty townhouses? Not for the children, who were to be given away, so…?"

Whelan flicked his one seeing eye up. Nick could still

sense some pride in him. "You've already seen my big idea," he said, his voice bitter. "If you were on a plane that was plunging towards the ground, how much would you be willing to pay for your salvation?"

Nick nodded, understanding. He thought back to the restaurant – his first meal with Whelan and McMahon – and the protestors. He remembered what Whelan had told him: *People only have one chance to live. The world doesn't have the resources for two.* He wondered what the protestors would say if they knew the rich might have access to the ultimate form of life insurance.

"You needed somewhere to keep them out of sight," he said. "The price of their rescue was to keep hidden. To stop you being overwhelmed by dissent, to stop the chaos of people turning up to claim their property years after their deaths."

Whelan didn't answer. In the silence, Nick heard footsteps approaching. He just had one last question for Whelan. "So what did the guy in the helicopter tell you?" he asked.

Whelan took a long, rattling breath. He sounded like he was drowning. "The spy was a woman in her fifties," he said. "Working somewhere in the town. Which doesn't fit the description of anyone we employ here. Though I suppose Maggie would be the closest."

Nick nodded. Calpurnia appeared at his side. "My father will grant you safe passage to wherever you decide to go," she said. "But we both very much hope you will decide to stay."

Nick gave a half-smile, glancing back at Barbatus. "We?"

"*I* hope you will stay," she corrected. "After all, your good judgement saved my life when they came for Felix. I can't help but feel I owe you a debt."

Nick thought of his father, and what waited for him at home. The world was about to change, and he needed to decide whether or not he wanted to be at the centre of it all. "And you?" he asked her, casting another quick glance towards the *duumvir*. "Will you stay with him?"

"Yes." Calpurnia's voice was tinged with resignation. She stopped to massage her stomach and the baby within. "I belong to him. But it won't be long before I'm joined by little Marcus."

"Named after your husband?"

Calpurnia nodded silently and then looked down at Whelan, her mood darkening but her voice soft. "He will tell us his secret to control time."

Nick tensed, but then remembered that it all revolved around this. Those in the future, protecting their path to power. From Arlen. From McMahon. From Whelan. He looked over at Barbatus, and wondered what sort of emperor he'd become. "Do you think he'd be able to cope with that much power?"

"It's a rare gift to wield the sword and be remembered as a great man and not a tyrant," she said. But then she lowered her voice, as if something amusing had suddenly struck her. "But perhaps, in the future, a woman might rule?"

Nick grunted.

"So if you'll translate for us one last time," said

Calpurnia, returning her attention to Whelan. "We need your friend here to tell us everything he knows."

"And if he refuses?"

"Then, first, we'll drill a hole in the top of his skull…"

77

"YOU DIDN'T TELL them."

Nick shook his head. The *taberna* was nearly empty. He sat at the back with Kirsten, and sipped a small cup of heavily watered wine. "No," he said. "They think I killed McMahon."

"Why?"

He shrugged. "Because Lee Harvey Oswald shot JFK, and Princess Di's driver was drunk."

"I don't understand."

Nick thought about Ronnie. "The simplest explanations are usually true," he said.

"Oh. I see. Then thank you."

Nick let his eyes close for the briefest of seconds. He'd only just dropped the tablet. Only just turned back to face McMahon when the scream erupted and the *murmillo*'s sword pushed its way out through McMahon's stomach. Behind him stood Kirsten. Who'd grabbed the weapon from the floor and taken her revenge. "I thought you were going to kill me too," he said.

Kirsten smiled. The tension broke. "It was already too late. There would have been no point."

"But you killed Samson." He tried to spot any emotion in her face. But perhaps she'd always been difficult to read. "I'm right, aren't I?"

"He'd started to panic about the plan. Thought it wouldn't work, even though he wouldn't explain why. Just kept on going on about Perkin Warbeck." She looked at him. "He wouldn't even tell me who that was."

Nick took a deep breath.

"You know, don't you?"

"Yes, but it's not really my era."

"Spit it out, will you?"

"Okay," Nick said, trying to recall his boyhood history. "So when Edward IV died, his two sons were locked in the Tower of London for their own protection. They soon went missing and Edward's brother became Richard III."

"I don't see the connection."

"Perkin Warbeck turned up, years later, claiming to be one of the missing princes. He was an imposter, of course, but if he'd attracted supporters it could have brought down Henry VII. Which means no Henry VIII, or Elizabeth I. It was obviously something that was niggling at Samson in his last days here. I think he'd noticed the missing part of the NovusPart triumvirate. And it mixed with another hobbyhorse of his: how would the world have turned out if Hitler had been killed before 1933? It's just that McMahon was never really Hitler. There were three of them at the start, and McMahon was the number-two guy. Goebbels, maybe. Not Hitler."

Nick cleared his throat. Having now heard Kirsten's

side, he hoped the final form of the puzzle was now correct. All those years she'd been skipping forward in time – and she'd been able to see two very different slants of history: one where the survivors of Flight 391 had been saved, and one where they'd been murdered. And all had been down to the presence or absence of just one man. "McMahon and Whelan removed Arlen from the timeline just after they removed you," he said. "And Samson was worried that, by killing McMahon, you would cause Arlen to re-emerge."

Kirsten nodded in silence. "I don't remember him as being any sort of threat."

Nick didn't say anything. He couldn't help wonder at what point the Romans knew Caligula had gone mad. At what point he'd stopped being the golden boy of Rome, and at what point they'd known they needed to act. "What do you remember?"

She looked at him sadly. "I just knew him as a kind, sweet-natured guy. And given that they took him and when, I suppose that's how I can still remember him, isn't it?"

ACKNOWLEDGEMENTS

M ANY PEOPLE WERE involved in getting this book published, and I would like to express my thanks to every one of them. My mum and dad (Maureen and Andrew Godfrey) provided the invaluable first wave of proofreading and encouragement. The team at Cornerstones (Helen Bryant, Kathryn Price, Ayisha Malik, Sophia McDougall and Will Mawhood) supplied advice on the story's first and second incarnations. Sophia's input in particular helped identify which parts of the story needed to be shown the axe and what could be further developed.

A big thank you to my agent, Ian Drury (Sheil Land Associates), for helping me nail the ending, and for the amazing speed with which he found my novel a home at Titan Books. And, of course, many thanks to my editor Miranda Jewess and everyone at Titan (Lydia Gittins, Philippa Ward, Chris Young, Natalie Laverick, Cath Trechman and Sam Matthews) for taking a chance, offering me a contract, and for their enthusiasm in turning my manuscript into a finished book. I was also delighted with the cover designed by Martin Stiff (Amazing15) which I think perfectly captures the concept of *New Pompeii*.

Finally, thank you to everyone who supported my self-published efforts over the last few years. The positive feedback really did help get this one finished and accepted. Cheers!

ABOUT THE AUTHOR

Daniel Godfrey lives and works in Derbyshire, but tries his best to hold on to his Yorkshire roots. He studied geography at Cambridge University, before gaining an MSc in transport planning at Leeds. He enjoys reading history, science and SFF.

EMPIRE OF TIME
Daniel Godfrey

New Pompeii has control of the time travel technology, which keeps western governments at bay. But the public call for the destruction of a place that allows slavery and gladiatorial combat. Meanwhile Calpurnia is fending off threats to her power, aided by Pullus, the man who was once Nick Houghton… Has Nick truly embraced the Roman way of life? Can the Romans harness the power of time travel or will the new world destroy them?

"Reads like a reincarnation of Michael Crichton at his best"
Barnes & Noble SFF Blog

THE RIG
Roger Levy

Humanity has spread across the depths of space but is connected by AfterLife – a vote made by every member of humanity on the worth of a life. Bale, a disillusioned policeman on the planet Bleak, is brutally attacked, leading writer Raisa on to a story spanning centuries of corruption. On Gehenna, the last religious planet, a hyperintelligent boy, Alef, meets psychopath Pellon Hoq, and so begins a rivalry and friendship to last an epoch.

"Levy's writing is well-measured and thoughtful, multi-faceted and often totally gripping."
Strange Horizons

AVAILABLE MAY 2018

TITANBOOKS.COM

For more fantastic fiction, author events,
competitions, limited editions and more

VISIT OUR WEBSITE
titanbooks.com

LIKE US ON FACEBOOK
facebook.com/titanbooks

FOLLOW US ON TWITTER
@TitanBooks

EMAIL US
readerfeedback@titanemail.com